AWOKEN

SARAH NOFFKE

One-Twenty-Six Press.
Awoken
Sarah Noffke

Copyright © 2014 by Sarah Noffke
All rights reserved
Copyeditor: Christine LePorte
Cover Design: Andrei Bat

This is a work of fiction. The characters, incidents, and dialogues are products of the author's imagination and are not to be construed as real. Any resemblance to actual events or persons, living or dead, is entirely coincidental.

Summary: Humans sleep at night unaware that an ancient evil man is preparing to steal their consciousness, but the person he needs to do it is the only one who can stop him.

Published in the United States by One-Twenty-Six Press
ISBN: 978-0986208003

Praise for Works:

"There are so many layers, so many twists and turns, betrayals and reveals. Loves and losses. And they are orchestrated beautifully, coming when you least expected and yet in just the right place. Leaving you a little breathless and a lot anxious. There were quite a few moments throughout where I found myself thinking that was not what I was expecting at all. And loving that."
-Mike, Amazon

"The writing in this story was some of the best I've read in a long time because the story was so well-crafted, all the little pieces fitting together perfectly."
-The Tale Temptress

"There are no words. Like literally. NO WORDS.
This book killed me and then revived me and then killed me some more. But in the end I was born anew, better."
-Catalina, Goodreads

"Love this series! Perfect ending to an incredible series! The author has done this series right."
-Kelly at Nerd Girl

"What has really made these books stand out is how much emotion they evoke from me as a reader, and I love how it comes from a combination of both characters and plot together. Everything is so intricately woven that I have to commend Sarah Noffke on her skills as a writer."
-Anna at Enchanted by YA

For Luke, because I wrote every one of these words
hoping you'd like them.

Prologue

The howling wind always marks his arrival. Tonight I'm not sleeping when it shakes the trees and sends debris flying around outside. The recurring nightmare woke me an hour ago. I wipe away the sweat beading my hairline and steal a glance out my window. The figure lurks in the shadows. He's never any closer than the old oak tree, but that's near enough. A chill shakes my core. I can't do this one single night more. Shaking fingers scroll through my phone contacts until I find the right one.

"Hello," a groggy voice says on the other end.

I speak in a whisper. "I'm not sure I believe what's happening, but I'm ready to let them protect me."

"Good," the voice says with relief. "You'll be glad you did."

"What do I do now?"

"They want you to meet someone. He'll explain what happens next."

Chapter One

I wouldn't believe any of this was real if it wasn't for the two-inch gash in my arm. Still, denial has rented a room in my head and frequently stomps around slamming doors. I have never considered myself normal, but only now do I fully realize how extremely abnormal I am. That's not the part I'm denying anymore. It's my potential fate.

Now I have to do the one thing that feels impossible: focus. It's difficult when my life has quickly turned into a mass of confusion. I force myself to shake off the distractions. The answers I seek reside in a place I can only get to if I let go.

With immense effort, I relax enough to concentrate. In my head, I see the dam. The concrete stretches out like a barrier, pushing the water away. I pay attention to the water, how it voyages down the spillway. Slow breaths intensify the meditation, giving it color and sound. I continue to visualize until I sense the change. It's polarizing, in a good way. My body remains planted in the comfy bed while my consciousness dream travels. Now I'm racing through the silver tunnel—my transport to the other dimension. Adrenaline tastes like salt water in my mouth. And too quickly the journey is over, leaving me panting as I'm tossed into a vast space.

The tunnel deposits me at the edge of the spillway on a concrete embankment. A cursory glance behind reveals a calm lake reservoir; ahead the spillway plummets for a hundred feet or more before cascading into the lake. The moon overhead is full. Beside me is a woman.

"I was beginning to think you were lost again," she says.

"It's nice to meet you too," I say.

"I assumed you already knew my name."

Apparently the Lucidites don't believe in greetings. "Well, some ID wouldn't hurt."

Shuman's black hair resembles strands of silk. She wears a leather vest and blue jeans. I straighten, feeling smaller than usual next to her.

"Did you decipher the riddle on your own?" Shuman says, ignoring my comment. The moon reflects off her high cheekbones, making her appear angular.

"No," I admit, "Bob and Steve helped."

I'm confused why Shuman gave me a riddle instead of just telling me where to dream travel to meet her. I guess as the Head Mentalist for the Lucidites she has to make everything as perplexing as possible. She must be great at her job.

"Yes, it was forecast that they would assist you," she says.

"Right, of course," I say, not masking the irritation in my voice. It isn't Bob's and Steve's help I resent, it's that the Lucidites are privy to my life through psychic means.

"And we are here because of a different prediction."

"Yes, I've heard about it."

"Have you also heard that it involves you?"

"Well, I know there's a *potential* I'll be involved."

"We have new information. Your name is the only one in the forecast now."

"What?" I breathe with quiet disbelief. "No, that's impossible."

"It is possible and I assure you it is true. The speculation of predictions solidifies as the approaching event draws closer. Now forecasters see you as the true challenger."

"No," I say too fast, denial evident in my tone. "And I'm not here because of the forecast; I'm here because they said you'd help me."

"They are correct. The first way I can help is by getting you to accept what has been predicted."

"Predictions are just guesses though. What if they're wrong?" I say.

Shuman raises her eyebrow in disapproval, shakes her head. "Roya, do you doubt it because it involves you?"

"Mostly I doubt it because it's absurd. None of it makes sense."

"Maybe not yet, but it will," Shuman says. "Unfortunately we are running out of time. The forecasters have determined the static moment to be twenty-one hundred hours on June thirteenth."

That's in a month. My throat closes and my chest shrinks in on itself. "What? I can't…There's no way…" I trail off, lost in morbid thoughts of my impending death. "Why not you or someone else more qualified?"

3

"If I was chosen I would be honored, but I was not. You were." Shuman gazes at the full moon, her silver earrings highlighted by its white light. "I have tracked Zhuang for decades without success. Many of us have." She turns and looks at me for the first time. Her dark eyes resemble amethysts. "This fixed point in time is the only chance anyone will have the opportunity to challenge him. And the forecast states you are the person with the best opportunity to end his brutal reign."

"That's ridiculous. I'm not a threat to anyone."

"A few days ago you saw yourself very differently than you do now, is that right?"

"Well, yes, but—"

"Then consider it possible that in a month you will be a deadly force."

After what I've learned, I'm almost willing to believe this might be true. I sigh. "So what do you really want from me?" I ask.

"Make a choice," Shuman says at once. "You must decide whether you accept this role. If you do, then I can give you the help you asked for."

"If everything you've said is true then I *don't* have a choice."

"It is all true," she says through clenched teeth. "And in waking life and dreams, you *always* have a choice. This is what makes Dream Travelers different from Middlings. We do not sleep and fall into dreams that happen to us. We create our dreams. We choose where we travel."

I rub my eyes, frustrated and strangely tired. "It's just facing Zhuang sounds like a death sentence. I don't want to go through all this just to die in June."

"If you make the choice to be the challenger then you will face many dangers. You may not even make it to June. You may die tonight." Shuman's face lacks any compassion.

"If you're trying to convince me to do this then you're not doing a very good job," I say.

Shuman stares at the moon for a minute as if she's calculating something. "I will need your answer."

"What? Now!?" My voice echoes over the spillway. "Just like that? I don't get a minute to think it over or go home and weigh out my options?"

"You do not have a home," she reminds.

4

My foot connects with the concrete curb in front of me. I want to throw an all-out tantrum. Running and hiding also sounds like a good idea. Shuman's oppressive demeanor, indifferent to my predicament, makes it tough to think. I wait for her to say something, but she just stands motionless watching the moon. She's starting to creep me out.

"What's going to happen to my family?" I ask, the last word sounding strange as it tumbles out of my mouth.

"I suspect Zhuang will maintain his hold on them, but who he really wants is you," Shuman says indifferently. "Your family is officially classified as hallucinators. He has the ability to keep them like this for a long time. Or he could finish them rather quickly."

Finish them? Does that mean what I think it does? This man, this parasite, is stealing my family's ability to dream, causing them to fall into hallucinatory states. And I'm powerless to stop Zhuang if he decides to drain them of their consciousness. Then they'd be shells, sleepwalkers. Dead in no time. A shiver runs down my spine.

Shuman continues, "Zhuang's plan was to make you panic and surrender to him. It is fortunate we found you first. My guess is your family will hang in limbo. Zhuang's attention will be on finding you. If you want to help your family then stay away, otherwise he will use them against you. And if you want to release them then you need to fight Zhuang."

"And win," I say, doubt oozing all over the words.

"Well, of course."

"This whole thing makes no sense." I rub my head with a shaky hand. "Why me? I'm barely old enough to drive. I've only known about this mess for a few days. How was I chosen? How am I the best person to face him?"

"I do not know the answers to these questions," she says, still fixated on the moon.

"Then why should I do this!? Why should I jeopardize my life without knowing why I've been chosen?"

Shuman takes one long blink as though contemplating or meditating. Her words are airy and quiet when she finally speaks. "The great Buddha once said, 'Three things cannot be long hidden: the sun, the moon, and the truth.'"

I bite down hard on my lip. So this is the way it is? Either I live my life alone on the streets and watch as Zhuang ransacks humanity's dreams. Or, option two, I volunteer to kill him and most likely die trying, but my consolation prize will be I'll know why I'd been chosen. I'll know who I was and where I could have belonged…if I hadn't died in Zhuang's hands. This seems like a scam, although an ingenious one.

A sincere part of me wants to return to my family and shake them until they're released from their hallucinations. Then we can go on living our lives where the most interesting things that happen are football, church, and barbeques. It's not a great life for an agnostic vegetarian, but is it better than death? I may be a product of the East Texas soil, but the winds here have never agreed with me. I've been looking for a way out of this town, but not like this.

"I cannot grant you any more time," Shuman says. "I need your answer."

I scan the surface of the water, looking for nothing in particular. She *can* wait for my answer. She will.

I push my fingers into my eyes and inhale deeply. This duel is inevitable. Zhuang and his challenger's futures are intertwined. Any attempt to evade the other person will only bring the two together. And somehow I was elected by people I don't know, for a danger I only recently knew existed. Still none of this makes sense, which is why I know I have to rely on instinct. It's all I have left. "Fine," I say a bit pathetically. "I'll do it."

A smile would be nice, or maybe a "good for you." Instead Shuman, who appears to be all business, all the time, begins spouting instructions. "Your next step is to find the Lucidite Institute. Since you are relatively new to dream traveling there are many risks you face."

No big surprises there.

Shuman continues, "You must dream travel to the Institute while fully submerged in water."

Um, what? "Are you serious? I'll drown."

"There is that risk, yes, but the only way to enter the Institute is through water. To travel there you must return to your body and then immerse yourself in water. I advise you to *know* you are one with it. It is through this knowledge that you overcome the fear of drowning and focus on the higher task of dream traveling. If you remain calm and focus properly then you will travel and arrive at the Institute. If you are unsuccessful, then yes, you will drown."

"Oh, is that all? Sounds like a piece of cake." I'm wondering now if I made the right decision.

Shuman narrows her eyes, but doesn't respond otherwise.

I rub my temples as an overwhelming pressure erupts behind my eyes. "This is all so strange, it sounds like a recurring dream I've been..." My words fall away as the inevitable truth dawns on me. "You put those dreams in my head, didn't you?" I accuse, staring at her rigid persona.

"The Lucidites are responsible, yes," she says, her tone matter-of-fact.

"What! That's insane! That's awful. Night after night I dreamed I was drowning myself. Do you know how horrifying that is?"

"You should be grateful. We have prepared you for the journey you are about to take. Your subconscious mind has already practiced much of what you are going to do."

"Grateful!?" I shake my head in disbelief. "I thought I was losing my mind. I didn't sleep well for weeks. No. I'm not the least bit grateful. You invaded my subconscious," I spew, more frustrated now than frightened.

Shuman takes a long inhale and says, "Everything that has been done was to protect you and the future."

How do I argue with that statement? How do I argue with any of this? I want to run, to abandon this farce which has become my life. However, my instinct is concrete around my legs, pinning me in place, assuring me this is where I belong.

"Roya, we are running out of time," Shuman says, breaking the silence. "Do you have any questions?"

"Why does it have to be so complicated to dream travel to the Institute? Isn't there an alternative?" *Like a spaceship or a drug?*

"No, there is not," Shuman says. "The Institute is heavily protected by water. The difficulty it takes to travel there is what makes it the safest place on earth."

The idea settles over me like a down comforter. Safety. What would that feel like? Every moment has been cloaked with a hidden threat for so long. When the recurring dreams weren't plaguing me, the paranoia lurked in the shadows and was all but incapacitating. It was almost enough to make me take the pills the therapist kept pushing. Almost.

"If I do all this"—the words drip out of my mouth— "if I don't drown, then I'll be at the Institute? I'll be safe? At least for a little while, right?"

Her eyes jerk away from their focal point. There's a twitch at her mouth. "Yes."

I sigh. It's the first one of relief in a while. "All right then, I'll do it," I say halfheartedly.

She turns and faces me, resting her arms across her chest. Around one of her forearms is a tattoo of a rattlesnake. The serpent's tail lies on her elbow and its head on the back of her hand.

"There is one last thing," she says, a warning in her voice. "Only Lucidites can enter the Institute. You must want to be one of us, or you will be forbidden from entering."

I blink in surprise. My mouth opens to voice hesitation, but she disappears, leaving me alone and feeling as though I'm standing on the edge of the earth.

Chapter Two

Hurling myself over the spillway is an intriguing idea. With my luck the fall wouldn't kill me. I'd only be maimed while still being hunted.

The energy bounding out of my chest is intense. My pacing does little to expend it. I throw my hands through my hair and notice that once again my arms and hands have a ghost-like appearance. I'm guessing my face probably does too.

Ten minutes pass where I do nothing but wallow in uncertainty. I said I would do this, but the actual "doing" part is difficult. There's one place I need to go before potentially drowning myself. I know they told me not to, but this is probably my last chance.

I stand firm, the cool wind drifting against my cheeks and the back of my hands. With my eyes closed, I experience in my mind the place I intend to dream travel to: Green leaves flicker in the wind, a hammock sways, vanilla wafts from the garden, and familiarity punctuates every single thought. I'm enveloped by innocence, so pure and real. Hands brush long sheaves of grass as the shoreline draws closer. The buoy bobs in the far-off waters. A mountain of books sits in neat stacks, both prized possessions and contraband.

The silver tunnel engulfs me again. I'm moving forward, like on a subway train. But it's more like I'm the subway train itself, speeding through a claustrophobic passageway. My heart pounds and just when I think I'll run into something I turn down a different silver tunnel.

My landing is punctuated with a flash and a jolt. I open my eyes to find an angry forest and a darkened house. Even though I stand at the end of the pier, I know it's risky being this close. I won't be long.

The tunnel has dumped me in the spot where Trey told me who I was, what I was capable of. I remember thinking then that the Associate Head Official for the Lucidites looked a bit like a young Harrison Ford with his silver hair and turquoise eyes. It's hard to believe that was only days ago. It feels like months. I guess that's what happens when you don't lose the nights to meaningless dreams.

My meeting with Trey was the first time I dream traveled. Bob and Steve had arranged it after giving me the dream travel protocol. They wouldn't tell me anymore. Said it wasn't their place. "Just close your eyes and have some faith," Bob told me. I didn't believe what happened next was real. Still, Trey knew about the nightmares, about the strange figure I kept seeing in the woods, and why my family was losing their minds.

"We can help you," Trey said as he dangled his feet over the side of the dock. Our casual sitting arrangement on the pier was absurdly contradictory to how tense the whole meeting was. There I sat with a stranger who was telling me this dream was real. That I was a part of a special race of people. That if the Lucidites didn't protect me, I'd be murdered. Conversations like that really should happen in a more formal environment.

"How do I know I should let you help me? What if *you're* the bad guy," I said to Trey, pinning my eyes on the button of his rolled up white shirtsleeve.

"We've been protecting you. Well, the best we could from the dreamscape. I'm sorry we weren't able to help your family. That all happened too fast."

"What has Zhuang done to them?" I asked.

"Zhuang has lived for entirely too long because he slips into dreamer's heads while they sleep. Takes over their consciousness by weakening them, usually by causing nightmares, creating anxiety and stress, or completely severing their ability to achieve REM."

"But why my family? I get that he's after me because of some ridiculous prophecy, but they're totally innocent. They're Middlings."

Trey shook his head. Sighed. "It's not just your family. Zhuang has done this on many levels to thousands for centuries. Sometimes he operates quickly as in the case of a heart attack or aneurism. Sometimes his attacks are slower. Like with a stroke. The ailment takes many forms. And these are some of the conditions Middlings have used to describe what Zhuang does, but you should know the truth."

"Zhuang's responsible for all these different diseases?!" I asked horrified by the news.

Trey nodded. "Mostly Zhuang. Unfortunately there are other Dream Travelers who abuse their powers in this way. We are a

10

powerful race of people, capable of destroying Middlings if we choose. For the Lucidites this is not an option. It's against our laws. We protect. That's why you should trust us. Allow us to guard you."

After I awoke from that meeting with Trey, I fully intended to forget his words, his persuasions, and his pleas to allow the Lucidites to protect me. Intentions are flimsy in the face of opposing danger. Determination, on the other hand, is resilient to challenge. It's the antidote.

Now from my place on the dock, I steal a glance at my home. Since I'm dream traveling, I anticipate that the house will appear different, but it doesn't. Everyone in there's asleep, locked in dreamless slumber. I expect to gaze at the house and be bombarded by sorrow. I'm not. It's like I'm looking at someone else's home. My family has been ripped away. I'm unable to go home. And all I feel is a hollow ache, but that's normal. I was born with that.

A snippet of my last conversation with my brother plays in my head. "I don't know why, but you're different. You don't belong in our family. Never have, never will," Shiloh said before attacking me. True he'd been suffering from hallucinations, but his words stuck with me. So did the bruises.

It was obvious from a young age that I was different from my family in many ways. My fair hair and subdued nature stuck out like a sore thumb among their black manes and toothy grins in all the holiday photos. Eventually my mother made us wear Santa hats, but still she couldn't force me to smile. And she couldn't dispel the rumors which had always circulated around town since the first tow hair sprouted from my head.

I was the outcast and I'd always known and accepted this. But when Shiloh used the words "don't belong," a darkened corner in my heart grew with illumination. His words should have made me feel rejected. Instead I felt hope.

Shuman's words from before feel heavier, even more meaningful. *Three things cannot be long hidden: the sun, the moon, and the truth.* My hands are steady now, no longer shaking. Inside me an emotion has risen to a new height. Longing. It has a sound, a color, a taste. It's sharp, red, pungent. My steady fingers push against my temples, pushing against the longing, but it doesn't relinquish its hold on my intestines.

One question remains in this confusing web that has become my life. The fire it fuels within me burns slowly, but has the ambition to scorch down an entire forest. *I want to know where I belong.* Sadly, this is the reason I accepted the role as challenger. I want to say it was to save my family, but that's secondary. Although I haven't lived long, I know to exist in a world feeling capable of moving mountains and only allowed to dig tiny holes is wrong. I'm determined to understand who I am, why I'm the only Dream Traveler in my family, and why I was chosen to fight Zhuang.

One last look, followed by a loose swallow in my throat. I see the imprint of the house inside my eyelids when they're closed. Its shape. Its light. Its darkness. I release this place and travel back to my body. Rising, I feel a million miles from where I was seconds ago. This will make the next few steps easier.

I walk through Bob and Steve's house, neatly lit by Tiffany lamps set on dim. No doubt they're gone, dream traveling. They said they had business in Taiwan and Iceland tonight. Right. Who doesn't?

I laugh as my feet find the Persian rug. I'm almost to the back door. I could retreat now, curl back up in the canopy bed and rise to Bob making pancakes. I could leave this whole challenge behind. Bob and Steve said they'd help. Did that mean they'd take me in while my family was pillaged of their dreaming capacity and the Lucidites battled Zhuang? Why should I care? Who were the Lucidites or Zhuang to me? But my family... I wish I *wanted* to protect them, rather than felt obligated. It's hard to be loyal to people who nicknamed me "Stake," short for "Mistake." But still they're my blood, and shouldn't that bond me to them regardless of their cruelty?

From the beginning I questioned why Bob and Steve would socialize with my mother. They were cultured and she was a soap opera addict. And she hadn't tolerated them well either, but still insisted on accepting their invitations to dinner parties.

"Why are you dragging me along to these people's house?" I asked her as we drove on the bumpy road.

"Because they invited you to join me," she said.

"But why are you even going to this dinner? You just got finished going on about how they're too pretty."

"Roya, you really understand very little about politics," she said, condescension laden in her tone. "And honestly, what man gets his nails professionally manicured? That's ridiculous."

"So you're just wasting my evening so you can get a fat check for your charity?"

"It isn't about the charity. You'd know that if you paid attention. A new position on the board is opening up. If I secure this donation then I'm a shoo-in for that spot."

"Seriously though, all these pretenses just to get money, that's—"

"Pretending to like someone is nothing," she cut me off. "I don't think you get it. A position on the board never opens up. I'll do whatever it takes."

I rolled my eyes. "Well then, let's hope Emily Dickinson was right and 'fortune befriends the bold.'"

Her lips hardened into a thin line. I almost flinched thinking she'd slap me again.

My mother didn't tolerate three types of people: career women, men who plucked their eyebrows, and anyone who quoted literature. She found this all too "pretentious."

Maybe it was my mother's intolerances that made me love Bob and Steve at first sight. They spoke with sophistication, but also a vivid touch of humbleness. It was almost like I could feel their sincerity in the shortest of words. No one had ever spoken to me like they had—with respect. When they showed me their library I loved them even more. And then they drugged me, gave me bizarre instructions, and I awoke to a strange new world where I wasn't certain what was real. Hell, I didn't even know who I was anymore.

I did know that my mother's pretenses didn't matter because she was the one being conned the whole time. And still I trusted Bob and Steve. These men had gone to great lengths to help me—they tolerated my mother. And they rescued me when my brother, Shiloh, was about to run me over. It was because of them that I was safe and knew I wasn't a freak. I was different, but in a powerful way. Bob and Steve's role was to guide me in my first dream travel so I would meet Trey, but they'd done more than that. Bob and Steve were the first people I could remember being sincerely kind. It truly hurts me to leave that now, but I have to.

My haste brings me to the pier within a minute. Much like Jay Gatsby, I stand on the dock and stare into the distance. Somewhere on the opposite bank is the home I've just left. Unlike Gatsby I'm not drawn to it, yearning for someone. My dark secret is I've always wished I was Gatsby. As heartbroken as he was and as horrible a fate as he endured, I admired that he loved. It's a difficult thing to do.

Feeling heartless makes it easier to swing my legs over the side of the dock and slip into the chilly lake. My clothes are instant anchors. Ignoring this, I slide through the water. After a few strokes I turn over and float on my back; my blonde hair glides beside me. I really should have thought to restrain my long tresses before the plunge. I close my eyes, but still see the bright light of the moon penetrating through my lids. My arms push through the water to keep me afloat and I force out all unwanted thoughts.

I take a long deep breath and hold it. Slowly I let it out and then draw in another. Without knowing a specific location I'll have to use cognitive tethering to draw me to the Institute. Information I've learned over the past few days will link my consciousness to the location. Or I might just drown. Only one way to find out.

I pull oxygen through my nose to the bottom of my lungs and float through my thoughts. *A secret race. Ancient people. With superior utilization of their dorsal lateral prefrontal cortex. A private society within this population. A society built to protect.*

On the next breath my thoughts gain color. They're dynamic, carrying the emotions I entrenched in them when they were stored. *A society of Dream Travelers. The Lucidites.* I feel rather than think about their presence around me the last few weeks. It was like a blot on the corner of my vision. And it always disappeared under closer inspection. They watched me while I was awake interacting with my Middling family. Later Trey would comment on how I didn't deserve the abuse my family heaped on me. His voice carried a strained weight when he said, "You don't deserve to be treated with such disdain. If there was something we could have done to intervene to protect you from their abuse then we would have. I hope you know that." I never replied. My throat caught at the idea that he was watching me from another plane of existence. And from there he and the other Head Officials of the Lucidites kept Zhuang at bay while he lurked in the forest, luring me towards him. *The Lucidites, like Zhuang, play tricks with the wind and the tides.*

I seize one last breath, stop paddling, and relax my muscles. The water rises over my cheeks, covering my closed eyes, and then entirely over my face. Like a stone skipping over water my mind flicks to every idea connected to the Lucidites. *News reporters. Protective charms. Summoning powers. Mugwort. Projections. ESP. Clairvoyance. Illusions. Trey. Ren. Shuman. Bob. Steve.* And finally the stone makes one last skip before plummeting. *Me.* They want *me* to join them.

I'm not struggling to breathe as my body sinks farther to the bottom of the lake. I've slowed my breathing enough that the last breath will sustain me for the next few minutes. To distract myself from the fear of drowning I think of the Lucidites. *They have an Institute. It's a safe place. This is where I'm headed. I'll be their challenger and face Zhuang.*

The tug inside my lungs voices its hunger for oxygen. I'm still sinking. The weight of the water on top of me is equal to a hundred quilts. They're suffocating me. *This is not the time to be overcome by fear,* I tell myself. By now I have used my reserved oxygen. I'm too far under the water; if I kick up now I'll never make it to the surface. I have to stay calm and focus.

The Lucidites are a tiny segment of the population who travel when they dream. I'm one of them. I'm a Lucidite. I'm a Lucidite. I'm a Lucidite. My body makes contact with the uneven, sandy bottom of the lake. *I'm a Lucidite. I'm a Lucidite. I'm a Lucidite.* The ground, cold like metal sits under my soaked skin. A motor boat roars overhead, its engine muted by what feels like leagues of water. Although my consciousness is bursting with excitement and anxiety I try to stay tranquil. Without thinking I part my lips and take a deep breath. *I'm a Lucidite. I'm a Lucidite. I'm a Lucidite.*

"And you're about to be a dead girl if you don't get up!" a guy yells.

Chapter Three

Effervescent light assaults my eyes. "Come on, you've got to get up! We're running out of time!" the stranger urges. I gaze at the halo hovering over his head. *Have I died? Is this heaven? Is he an angel?*

Worry surrounds his features as he edges away. With the light no longer directly behind him the effect is gone. The halo disappears.

He waves his hands, imploring me to get up, to follow him. If I'm fully awake it sure doesn't feel like it. Somehow I'm caught between a dreaming and waking state. Stuck. Everything seems blurred behind a sheet of plastic. Every action and voice sheathed. Muffled. Muted. There's a humming in my ears like gallons of water are pressed against my eardrums. Just over it I hear a voice. Half asleep, I try to make out the rhythmic chant.

"I get it!" the guy shouts again, breaking into my concentration. "You're a Lucidite. Now be quiet and get over here! Now!"

He's yelling at *me*. I'm the one chanting. He points at a raised table, eyes urgent. It looks like something from a doctor's office. Slowly, as if swimming up one layer through the haze engulfing me, I recognize myself lying on a metal floor. That's what I'd felt last before awakening. The metal grate.

I push up to a standing position, and slowly my current reality sinks in—I've done it. I'm finally safe. "Oh my God." I exhale. A quiet victory. "I'm here."

"Not quite," the guy argues, looking worried, irritated. His eyes flick to a screen in the corner. "You have about ten seconds to get your ass on this table and lie down."

"But I'm at the Institute, right?" I ask, confusion swimming in my head.

His eyes bulge. "NOW!" he demands, pointing at the table.

I usually don't follow orders, but the severity in his expression can't be ignored. I float to the exam table, hop onto it, and lie down. Around the outline of my body snakes a thin rope of blue lights. Above me, a series of lasers scan, making the roaring sound I've been hearing.

I don't feel anything for a second or two. Then I do. It's the vilest sensation ever. Moments prior I'd been light and airy. I could float and transcend all of space and time. With a sudden jerk a trillion cells gain mass at once. In a flash, I become vulnerable and raw. The scorching begins at my core and travels until it meets my skin, until my entire being is encased in fire. Just when I think I can't take another second of this torture, the pain turns freezing cold, shooting every single pore on my skin into a sharp goose pimple.

The blood that had just begun to circulate pulses deeper, steadier. I'm hyperaware of my heart. When it contracts, I hold my breath, thinking it has died. And then the beat comes and I breathe again wondering if this is my last. Dozens of times this happens until the burning spreads into the rest of my organs, even my brain. I cough and seize my chest from the sudden onslaught of convulsions. Confusion rakes my mind. The pain in my chest intensifies, a bomb ready to explode. It will surely split open on the next convulsion and I'll die. End of story.

I double over in pain and confusion, falling to my hands and knees on the floor. I cough, believing each one will end me. A hand claps me on my back, firm but not hard, and then again. On the third time water spurts out from a deep place in my lungs. Forever I hack up tiny bits of liquid. Forever I kneel hunched over on all fours on a stainless steel floor. Forever I feel the presence beside me, encouraging, gently rubbing my back. When the final heave passes I curl up in the tiniest ball, cradling my tortured body with its own limbs. His arms steady me. They rest on my shoulders, warm on my shivering skin, before pulling me from the cold ground and to a seated position. I sit back, resting tired arms on my knees. Exhausted.

I fade into nothingness until I can't ignore him beside me any longer. His long fingers reach over and tug my chin in his direction. He tilts my face upward. My eyes find his. They're blue. So blue, even behind his black-rimmed glasses. I sink into them, feeling an unfamiliar draw. He flashes a pen light in my eyes. I jump. Betrayed. The guy sighs loudly. "We almost lost you."

I hiccup, holding my soaked and freezing arms. "I don't understand," I say, rousing from my sleeping state. "I made it here." I point to where I was moments ago. "I was lying on the ground there."

He shakes his head, his spiky, dark brown hair unresponsive to the movement. "Yeah, your consciousness made it. That's just the first step. If we didn't get your body here then it would have drowned." He's standing now. Extending his hand, he reaches out for me. I hesitate before wrapping my fingers around his and letting him pull me into an upright position. Tentatively he peers at me sideways. "Didn't Shuman tell you that?"

"Nah," I say, shivering. "She didn't mention it. She was too busy telling me I was probably going to die trying."

"Well, you almost did," Mr. Blue Eyes says frankly. His gaze focuses on a computer screen in the corner again and relief spreads over him. His urgent manner has disappeared, replaced with an expression I can only describe as endearing.

"My name's Aiden." He extends his hand. I eye it cautiously and then bring my gaze up to his eyes. Dark blue outlines a softer sapphire. "I take it you're Roya."

My hands and arms aren't transparent anymore. I'm solid. "Wait, so this is my body?" I ask, confused, never shaking his hand.

"I sure hope so." Aiden laughs, looking down at my soaked jeans and bare feet. "Or otherwise I've got some explaining to do."

"Am I still dream traveling?"

"Nope, you're awake."

I scrunch up my face, more confused than ever.

Aiden looks at a printout on a tiny device he's picked up and then flashes me a grin. "Shuman should have really explained this. No wonder you were so confused when I was yelling at you. Sorry about that."

I want to say something, but my voice is caught in my throat. I manage a meek smile through my chattering teeth.

Aiden takes a plush blanket off a stack and wraps it around my shoulders. "Here."

I pull it around me like it's fuel and I'm fire. "Thank you," I manage between the waning shivers.

"When you dream travel you leave your body where you fell asleep, right?"

I nod.

"Well, that would be all good and well, except you left your body submerged in water while you dream traveled. If you left it there it would certainly die. And without your body your consciousness would survive like a ghost, but not for long. Anyway, the best way to get around this is with our handy dandy GAD-C." Aiden swipes his hand in a large movement, apparently to show that half the room is this device. "The *generateur automatique de corp*. It automatically generates your body." He shrugs, his bright blue eyes betraying his enthusiasm. "It's actually more complicated than that, but it worked and that's all you should be concerned with, since without it you would have died."

I'm still shivering, still exhausted, still confused.

"It's probably time I told someone you've arrived," he says, an edge of reluctance in his voice. Aiden picks up a telephone receiver and after a few seconds says, "Yeah, Roya's here." Inexplicably I like the way he says my name. It sounds soft in his mouth. After that single sentence he hangs up the receiver.

"Someone will be here momentarily to fetch you," he says, hurrying over to the computer in the corner. He begins typing, flicking his eyes to me every so often.

Nervousness sets into my chest as the aching slowly recedes. I have no idea what to expect next or what's happening with my family. For a second I consider questioning Aiden but he looks engrossed in his work. I wrap my fingers around the blanket and pull it tighter.

A minute later an automatic door slides back, disappearing into the wall. At the flash of red hair I reflexively straighten. *Oh no.* The last person I want to see.

"Well, look who has decided to join us." Ren smiles, but he doesn't look especially happy to see me either. His emerald green eyes almost appear dark in this room. The first time I met him I studied those eyes, searching them for honesty. His crow's feet made me think he was wise, could be trusted. I was wrong.

"You're late," he sneers, his British accent making the offense sound atrocious. "I should have guessed. Come on already, follow me."

I turn back to Aiden, searching for a way out. He shrugs, only half looking at me.

I slide off the table and push my toes forward, but my body is sluggish and doesn't readily respond to the commands from my brain. It takes an eternity to reach the door. Ren has already bolted down the outer corridor and is standing looking at me with

19

exaggerated contempt. Again I've pissed him off; maybe I've actually done something this time or it's just my very nature of breathing that's setting him off. Hard to tell.

I turn back at the threshold. Aiden is typing away at a computer station. He looks busy. Focused.

"Hey," I call to him, "thanks for saving my life and all."

He's still typing on his computer, engrossed in whatever he's working on. I turn and head toward Ren. A few steps down the corridor I hear Aiden sing, "Just doing my job."

Chapter Four

Ren shoots down a narrow silver hallway. Since I've just dislodged a gallon of water from my lungs it's difficult to keep up. I hardly have time to take in the corridor we're moving through. The walls and ceiling are brushed stainless steel. The floor is a strange aquamarine, with a shimmering effervescence.

"Where are we going?" I pant. "Can you slow down?"

"'Fraid not, missy. I'm trying to get you to orientation before it's over." He gives me a sideways glance. "You still mad at me for scratching you at our last meeting?"

"Scratching me? You stabbed me with a filthy pocket knife." I pull up my sleeve to show the fresh gash which is destined for infection. Who knows where that knife has been or how many other people he's cut with it.

"Blimey, stop being so dramatic. All I did was give you what you asked for."

"I asked for proof that I was dream traveling, not an injury," I seethe.

"But you knew it was real when you awoke, didn't you?" he leers.

We're still hurrying through the hallway when a stabbing pain splinters through my side. I stop and double over. "Look, I'm sorry if I'm going to be late to some orientation. I've got to rest for a second," I say between wheezing attempts to breathe. We've already walked a long distance. *How big is this place?*

"I don't think you'll want be tardy to orientation, that's all I'm saying," Ren says, checking his watch.

I wrap the blanket tighter around my shoulders. My frustration rises to the surface and erupts. "I'm the challenger," I argue, pointing at myself. "I've decided to risk my life for this whole mess. I think I can be a tad late to this stupid orientation."

Ren bites his lip, a look of mischief in his green eyes. "Yes, Challenger, you're right." He holds up his hands as if surrendering. "Your call. I'm just trying to help."

"Yeah, right." I sigh and start walking forward again, but this time at my own slower pace.

Ren lets me walk off a few steps before ambling up next to me. "Let me guess, you're probably also peeved that I did that whole projection business on you. Is that right?"

"You think?" I first met Ren while I was dream traveling. Trey had arranged the meeting. However, I got lost in a strange apartment building in London. Ren sent a projection of my cat to steer me in the right direction. He knew I'd follow that cat, not just because he was mine, but because he'd recently been murdered—by Zhuang.

The projection of my dead cat led me to a room where I found Ren, looking bored and irritated. "Finally," he said, when I tentatively made my way into the darkened room. "Oh stop being so cautious. I'm not going to bite you," he said flashing an evil grin at me. "Name's Ren. I'm the Head Strategist for the Lucidites. Trey sent me to fill in some of your missing gaps. Apparently, you're still in need of convincing." He slid his hand into his trouser pocket and retrieved a silver pocket knife. Without taking his eyes off me he opened the blade and began cleaning his nails. "Here's how it's going to go. You currently don't think the dream travel with Trey last night was real. You've probably spent most the day explaining the whole thing away. Now you're here with me and the doubt is starting to recede and give way to belief, but you're not there yet. I'm going to fill your consciousness with enough information and by the time we finish our little chat you're going to be convinced this whole thing is real." Ren looked down at his nails, admiring them. "'Cause it is."

"So this," I made a broad motion, "this is all real? It isn't a dream?"

"The furniture is real, this place is real, I'm real, and you're really, really here with me right now. So to answer your question, yes."

I nodded and chewed on my lip.

"Well, the cat," Ren said, "he actually wasn't real. He was a projection."

Letting the memory wash away I stomp beside Ren through the strange hallway of the Institute. "Did you really have to use my deceased cat like that when we first met?" I say.

Ren turns a corner and I have no choice but to follow him. "Using your dead pet was the easiest way to lead you to me," he says.

22

"Hmm," I muse. "Because finding me like a normal human being would be too difficult?" I lose my breath as our pace quickens gradually. "And my cat wasn't dead before all this mess."

"And thanks to us, you aren't resting with it." He stops abruptly and turns to me, swiping a finger over his lips. "Shame too, 'cause you'd fit so nicely in a shoe box or whatever you bury inconsequential pests in these days."

I bunch up my nose as though the air smells rancid.

"By the way." He yawns loudly and points his head to the door beside him. "You're in there." His hand hovers over a button to the right of the door. "Oh, and one quick, tiny thing Shuman forgot to mention."

I stop and stare into his cold eyes with sudden dread.

"You aren't exactly *the challenger*." He puts air quotes on the last two words. "You're more or less on the list of potential challengers. For some strange reason she omitted this part. Silly girl."

"What?!" Horror rips through me. "How many other people are on this list?"

Ren taps the button, shoving me into a crowded auditorium. "Only one way to find out, luv." He steps back and the door shuts.

I stand frozen. Row upon row of faces gape at me. The auditorium is silent except for a few drops of water that drip from my jeans. They sound like drum beats. I push a few pieces of wet hair that have clung to my face back behind my ear and feign a smile. My vision tunnels for several seconds as at least a hundred eyes gape at me with interest. Suddenly I'm burning hot. I let the blanket drape off my shoulders.

"Welcome, Ms. Stark," a deep voice says behind me. I jerk and find Trey standing on a stage, staring at me curiously. "I'm pleased that Ren has safely delivered you to us." He offers me a small smile. The rush of familiarity washes over me, just like the first time I met him. "We were just getting started. Maybe you can find a seat at the back," Trey says before turning his attention back to the crowd.

I hug the wall and carefully move up the steps. Finding an empty row, I slip into the first seat. People around me whisper, turning back to gawk. *Great, this is just like high school.*

Trey clears his throat. "Where was I?" He thinks for a second and then continues, "Right, welcome. I'm Trey Underwood, the

23

Associate Head Official for the Lucidite Institute. Flynn, the Head of the Institute, regrets that he's unable to be here, but he has other matters to attend to."

Who's Flynn?

"I know it's difficult to enter the Institute, but please know that now you're in a secure place." Trey's eyes flicker in my direction.

"Now, as you all know, you're here because you were forecast as the potential challenger to face Zhuang."

No, some of us didn't know that.

"Each of your names was recorded by a news reporter over two decades ago because one of you has a fate tied to Zhuang's. That person is the one we choose as our challenger. You see, time isn't linear, especially if you're a Dream Traveler, which I realize is a new idea to some of you." He stops, gauging the crowd. "Our next step is to determine which one of you will be the challenger. Additionally, six alternates will be chosen to assist or replace if necessary, should something occur."

The crowd rustles uncomfortably. I take this opportunity to look around and notice how analogous this group is. Everyone's between the ages of fourteen and eighteen. Most wear the same navy blue T-shirt. My partially wet white shirt and mane of knotted, blonde hair stand out in this room, pulling curious eyes to me repeatedly.

Trey continues, "We've set up a series of tasks which you'll all complete tomorrow. Your performance will be scored. The person with the highest score will be our challenger. The next six highest scores will be alternates. It's pretty simple. Those who aren't chosen can return home. The challenger and alternates will begin training immediately."

Trey picks up a remote and clicks it once. A row of words materializes in the air beside him. "First, find your name on this list under one of the different headings. They will indicate the room in which you'll be staying. In this room you'll find your group's schedule for tomorrow. Please locate your group and room number and go there now." Trey bows before walking off stage. From our first visit I appreciated how concise and delicate he was when he spoke. As I watch his retreating back I'm torn, because now I also know he employs a bunch of liars.

24

Half the group claps in a noncommittal fashion. The rest of us stare in a daze. I locate my name in the third group. There's four. I'm in room number 300. People file through an exit at the back of the room. As I descend the stairs a realization washes over me making my eyes narrow resentfully. Ren could have snuck me in through this back entrance. Instead he thought it would be funny to prance me soaking wet and confused in front of my competition. *That redheaded, British jerk.*

Back in the silver hallway, the smell of citrus and mint tingles my nose with the urge to sneeze. This combination of scents reeks of artificial cleanliness.

Some kids file in the opposite direction or drop off. I follow the rest of the group into an elevator. I don't make eye contact or even pay the least bit of attention to anyone. For the rest of my life I want to mind my own business and have everyone leave me alone. It's a big request, but I'm a heartless optimist. This combination could make me lethal, but mostly it has led to a successful hermit lifestyle.

When the elevator arrives I hang back to let everyone get off first. I march, forcing my breath to slow as anger burns in my veins. I've been waiting for it to erupt and it happens about the time my humiliation fades.

A guy with spiky blond hair stops to tie his shoe. When he stands back up and continues walking he's in stride with me.

"Hey there," he says light-heartedly.

"Hey," I manage.

He wears the navy blue T-shirt everyone else is wearing. On the front is an eye and around it a squiggly circle. Underneath that are the words "Focus=Life." I laugh to myself. Are the Lucidites branding us like we're their Olympians? I won't be caught dead in one of those shirts.

"You just got here?" the boy asks with a subtle southern drawl.

"Didn't realize I was late to the party," I say a bit more resentfully than I intend.

"Not sure if you've checked, but no one's really partying." A reluctant smile tugs at his mouth. "I just got here myself. I beat you by about ten or fifteen minutes. That was enough time for Shuman to throw me a T-shirt and get me to orientation. She's such a sweetheart, isn't she?"

Bile washes up my throat. It tastes bitter in my mouth. I swallow hard, pushing the tension I'm carrying to the bottom of my stomach. I decide it wise to keep my mouth shut about Shuman, Ren, and just about everything else *Lucidite*. Faking a smile, I sing, "Yeah, she's fabulous."

"My name's Joseph."

"Good for you," I say, keeping my eyes on my feet.

"Should I just call you Ms. Stark?" Joseph prods.

"Sure," I allow as we file into our living quarters.

Chapter Five

Bunks sit along the two main walls. Why didn't they just call these barracks? That's exactly what they are. I half expected I'd be given a room all to myself like what I had at Bob and Steve's. Instead I find my name neatly written on a sign attached to a bottom bunk. Joseph stops when I do and stares at the sign.

"You're Roya?" Joseph gives a triumphant smile and then nods. "I thought so."

"What's that supposed to mean, that you thought so?" I ask.

"Don't worry about it." He scans the room. "I think my bunk is down here." He strides away, looking smug.

Neatly folded on top of my bunk is the navy blue T-shirt, a pair of light green scrub-type pants, flip-flops, and a small foam stress ball with the logo neatly printed on it. I shove it all under my bed. This is where it will reside for the entirety of my stay—which will be short.

The smell of moss and dirt assaults my nostrils, making me cringe. It's me. I keep my head low while I search for the bathrooms. People chat all around me. As I expected there's a set of bathrooms at the back. I enter the door marked "Women" and head straight for the shower. Luckily it's stocked with shampoos and soaps. I'm guessing no one arrived with more than the clothes on their backs.

I wash my clothes and hang them on a towel rack to dry while I shower. When I'm done I wrap my towel around me and go to work drying my clothes under the automatic dryers. This takes forever. I stop when my jeans are almost dry and turn my attention to getting ready. I'm pushing the comb through my hair when a voice echoes over an intercom, "Dinner will be served on the first level in the main hall in ten minutes."

What time is it? Haven't I traveled overnight? Shouldn't it be late morning or at least early afternoon? The Institute must be in a different time zone. Begrudgingly I throw on my partially wet jeans and start for the door. If anything I can hope to be the first person to dinner. I'll eat and leave before anyone else has a chance.

Thankfully I manage to get into the elevator alone. Most of the others are socializing and changing into their green scrubs. *Losers.*

The elevator stops at level two and a few people file into the silver compartment. It proceeds to level one.

"I'm sure they'll have options for you," a guy says to a girl as we exit.

I stay within earshot, curious to know what they're talking about.

"They'll know, better than anyone, the strict diet one must have in order to dream travel properly."

"I know," the girl whines behind her scraggly brown hair. "It's just I'm used to having a certain type of goat cheese and that's not something that's readily available. It really gives me the best results."

I cringe at the sound of the girl's whiny voice. She's around my age, but dainty and prissy—a repulsive combination. Her vacant, light blue eyes keep looking up from the floor to her companion's as if searching for consolation from her dietary concerns.

Get a life.

We file into the dining area. With each step I take into the large room the odd sensation of déjà vu sinks in deeper. *I've been here before.* The fluorescent lights. Wall-to-wall blue carpet. I've dreamed of this room. It isn't from the recurring dream about reaching the Institute. It's a different one I'd never given much thought to. In it I stood in a line and once at the front I scribbled my name on a list. I've done this a dozen times in my dreams over the last few weeks. *Was this the list of challengers? Was this another message planted in my subconscious by the Lucidites?* It's hard to trust people who don't allow me to think for myself.

Feeling violated on a level I don't fully comprehend, I survey the room. Several buffet stations line the perimeter. Round tables with white covers fill the interior of the space. Each place setting holds a large goblet of ice water, a napkin, and utensils.

I pick up a plate at the first station. In front of me stand more than a few rows of berries. The mountains of berries are radiant in color as well as in design. I've never seen such a wonderful display of fruit. Around the berries sit brightly colored melons, ripe bananas, shiny apples, and the most pristine oranges I've ever laid eyes on. I take nothing from this table. Instead I charge off. Berries piled high and artfully arranged makes my head burn with anger for some reason. Everything makes me mad at the moment.

The next table consists of only breads: croissants, sourdough rolls, baguettes, hoagies, and a dozen other types. I pick up the least exciting one I can find.

I pass a carving station, reeking of flesh. Kids are lined up, eyeing chucks of meat with hungry eyes. Suppressing the powerful gag reflex which is churning up my esophagus, I charge as far away as possible from that area. The last thing I need right now is to vomit in front of these people.

At the next station, the aroma of milky cheeses is overwhelming. There are over a dozen varieties. Some are soft, others hard. Labels indicate the names of each of the varieties, over half of which I've never heard of and can't pronounce. Picking up a slice from the nearest two I charge off. My anger deepens now that I realize Goat Girl is probably going to get the kind of cheese she wants.

I find an empty table at the back of the room. I poke at my food, molding it with each prod of my fork. I'm not really hungry, but rather jetlagged. Maybe that's the reason for my sour mood. Then again it could be the false pretenses used to lure me here. Being humiliated in front of everyone in the auditorium for Ren's entertainment is just the icing on this awful cake. I crumble a piece of bread in my hand.

"Mind if I sit down?" someone says behind me.

The word "no" has all but escaped my lips when I realize I recognize the voice. Curious, I turn to find Aiden, the guy who saved my life, precariously balancing two plates on each arm. His lanky, pale arms provide enough surface area for all the porcelain white plates, but their contents make them teeter dangerously. Giving him a furtive glance, I shake my head. I'm in no mood for company. I'm just about to say so when I get a flash. It streaks across my vision quickly, the way it always does. It's a picture of one of the plates falling from his grasp.

"Watch out!" I exclaim. In one movement I stand, dart forward, and grab the plate just as it's falling. I set it down on the table with a sigh. Aiden clumsily lays down his other three plates, spilling rolls and pats of butter.

His bright blue eyes light up. He gapes at me. "You grabbed that plate before it started to fall."

I swallow, turning back towards the table. "No, I just got it as it was falling."

As he sits down next to me, the corners of his long mouth suppress a smile like he knows a secret. "No, I saw it happen. You knew." Aiden spreads a pat of butter on his roll and says, "Oh, and nice reflexes."

"Thanks." I look down at my plate. My reflexes had been quick, more so than normal.

"So that's your talent, is it? You see stuff in the future?"

"Just stupid stuff like plates falling," I say, sticking a piece of bread into my mouth.

"Saved me from looking like a fool," he says, taking a sip of water.

"Then we're even."

"Nope, I saved your life. You owe me *big*," Aiden teases, flashing a smile.

I tense and try to pull my gaze from his too-white teeth. My eyes roam over his dark brown hair, spiky in some places and limp in others, as though he ran out of hair gel or got distracted. The black rectangular glasses he wears frame blue eyes that are just as bright and astonishing as when I first saw them. On his tall, lanky frame hangs a white lab coat on top of a black Fall Out Boy T-shirt.

"So you work here?" I ask.

"I wouldn't call it work." He laughs playfully.

"'K," I say and pretend to ignore him.

Silence.

"I'm the Head Scientist for the Institute," Aiden finally says.

"Aren't you kind of young to be a scientist, let alone the Head Scientist?" I can't help but ask.

"It's all about how you define young."

I sigh, feeling the jetlag tunnel in my brain. "I define it by the number of years one has been a resident of earth. Where are you from?"

He laughs and takes a bite. "Earth, mostly," he says, giving me a sideways grin. "But those numbers of years are relative, depending on the person."

I push my plate away. "That doesn't make any sense."

Aiden nods, an understanding look in his eyes. "Don't worry, you'll catch up. I realize you're new to this whole thing."

"I guess all the other Lucidites in here were given a manual at birth. Mine must have been lost in the mail," I say, swallowing down my frustration.

"I didn't mean anything by it." He shifts in his seat and gives me an uneasy glance. "I apologize."

I remain silent.

"Some Lucidites choose to accelerate their careers, since we have the opportunity to utilize our dream time for learning and acquiring skills," he explains matter-of-factly. "I was raised by devoted Lucidites and began dream traveling fairly young. My parents required me to spend my nights reading, studying, and training. Their expectations in all aspects of my education were high. I had my masters by the time I was your age, and now that I'm about to turn eighteen, I've almost completed my doctorate."

"What?!" I almost choke on the water I'm drinking. "You have a PhD?"

"Actually, I'm ABD—all but dissertation. I expect it to be done soon though."

"Well, you must be kind of smart then."

"I have my moments," he says playfully. "Really most of my success is due to the excellent teachers I've had. For instance, I learned the theory of relativity from the *very* best." He grins.

"You're not implying…?"

"I am," he says.

"Einstein? That's who you learned the theory of relativity from?"

Aiden nods. "As well as other stuff." His blue eyes flash with confidence behind his glasses.

I gulp down the rest of my water feeling impressed, but not wanting to show it. "Is every Lucidite a super star genius then?" The knot rises in my throat as I realize how far behind the pack I'll be.

"Nah, same principles of motivation apply to Dream Travelers as well as normal folk. Some people spend their nights studying and applying themselves to a subject or talent. Some people spend their nights hanging out by the pool in the Bahamas. And still others spend their nights watching *Doctor Who* or sci-fi movies." He's already polished off an entire plate of food and places it to the side. "Everyone's different and therein lies the beauty."

31

Although I hate to admit it, I'm buzzing with more questions. Before I have a chance to ask anything else a loud ring emanates from his pants pocket. Aiden purses his lips, disappointment written on his face. He retrieves his phone and holds up one finger. "Pardon me." He puts the phone to his ear and says, "Aiden here." Someone on the other side speaks hurriedly, but I can't make out their words. He glances at me briefly with a smile. "Hmmm, that's very interesting indeed." His gaze falls to the table as the voice on the other end continues. "And you say this just started?" He pauses, looking disconcerted. "An hour or so ago?" His eyes flick to mine and he gives a sly expression. My heart races suddenly. "That's fascinating. I'll be right there." Aiden shuts off the phone and stands up from the table.

"Sorry, I enjoyed our chat, but I've got to run," he says. "I'm fairly certain I'll be seeing you around." He winks and then strolls away.

By the time I finish eating, my mood has softened. I'm intrigued with everything Aiden has told me. If what he said is true then I have some underdeveloped potential I should start exploring. Unfocused but motivated, I head back to my bunk.

A schedule for tomorrow's tasks has been posted. It reads:

8 a.m. – Task 1: Ganzfeld, Room 444
10 a.m. – Task 2: PK Party, Room 200
12 p.m. – Lunch
1 p.m. – Task 3: Calisthenics, Gymnasium
3 p.m. – Task 4: Kung Fu, Studio 3
6 p.m. – Dinner
9 p.m. – Task 5: Dream Travel

We're being tested on kung fu? That's just one more item on the long list of things that don't make sense in this place. I don't care to compete or be graded on these tasks. Honestly, I don't want to be the challenger. Still I'd rather not be known as an epic failure. I've already had enough embarrassment in the last twelve hours. I make up my mind to give the tasks my best effort. Besides, if even a few of the potential challengers are half as talented and prepared as Aiden then they'll outscore me without even trying.

A couple of kids sit on bunks playing cards in the corner. I ignore them and climb into my bed, pulling the covers over my head. The thing Aiden said about Einstein is still stirring in me. Hell, everything he said is racing around my brain, but one thing in particular has given me an idea. However, I'm not real confident in my dream travel abilities just yet, and where I want to take my consciousness fills me with nervous tension. I'm not sure of the risks, but I do know I don't have much to lose.

I clear my mind and the fear edges away. My breath slows, steadies. Everything I know about this person flips through my head like a picture book: his look, his voice, his talents, his influence. When I run out of ideas, I repeat the ones I already thought about. More than anything I concentrate. I don't let go and allow myself to be forced into a dream. Instead I force the dream. I create the perimeters. I instruct my consciousness where I intend to go. The neural pathways in my brain shift. I feel it as I focus and I know something's changing. I'm changing.

Minutes pass. Maybe hours. At some point during this focus I'm dumped out of a window and fall through a silver tunnel. I actually drop this time. I'm not driving the subway train like before. I'm descending. The wind sweeps by me gradually and then rushes as I gain speed. My stomach meets my throat and they both twist together, intertwined. Free falling isn't a freeing feeling. It assaults my senses. Rips my mind of any peace. Each second I know I'm getting closer to a hard surface, one where my body will plummet to its death. I need to wake up out of this illusion, or disillusion. Something's wrong.

The intention to pull out of this dream travel is halfcocked when I suddenly stop falling and turn through a tunnel. I'm moving like before, like I'm driving at lightning speed. The silver tunnel rushes by. I turn again and again. And then I really do fall. Fortunately it isn't far, but enough to make me scream. Two men stand in front of me in a courtyard.

I clap a hand to my mouth. "Sorry."

The men exchange words, bounce on their toes. Neither turns and acknowledges me. I lower the transparent hand covering my mouth. Fumbling backward I whisper, "I'll just be leaving."

No doubt they're wondering where I came from and formulating a plan to kill me. I take another step back, preparing to dream travel before they attack. Then one of the men bounces and shoots a punch at the other man, who deflects it easily. *What are they doing? Are they about to fight each other?*

The smaller of the two men says something I can't hear. He turns and faces me. I straighten, rigid. With a graceful elegance he strides toward me. I throw my hands over my face, ready to defend myself against his attack. It doesn't come. Instead he pivots and stands at my side. I remain paralyzed. All focus seeps out of my brain. The fear takes over. The dark-haired man beside me says, "Begin." The other man launches into a series of moves.

I figure out three important things all at once: 1) I've just time traveled. 2) These people, from the past, can't see me. 3) I'm about to learn kung fu from Bruce Lee.

Chapter Six

Mesmerized, I watch as Bruce Lee instructs this gentleman on what he calls Jeet Kun Do. I do my best to memorize the different moves. Even though I know they can't see me, I'm still too shy to try the moves myself. When their lesson is over I travel to a different time with Mr. Lee. As the confidence in me builds, I get up the nerve and begin to practice alongside him. Each time the lesson ends I travel again until hours later I'm jolted awake by an annoying bell. *Ding! Ding! Ding!*

I bolt upright in bed, ramming my head into the bunk above me. The bell, our wake-up call, rudely pulls me back to my present reality where kids groggily awaken from their own dream travels.

The deep eyes and focused expression of the mentor I spent my night with are fresh in my memory. My first hour with Mr. Lee had been awkward. The second overwhelming. The third intense. And by the fourth, I was enchanted, in awe, completely and utterly inspired by the presence of this man who moved with grace and power. Maybe it was because I was isolated in my own time dimension where no one could see or judge me, but last night, once I got used to the situation, I was more myself than I ever remembered. My mentor's humble demeanor stripped away my armor, leaving me a bundle of potential.

Throwing my legs over the side of the bed, I start for the bathroom. I half expect my body to be sore from the thousands of punches, blocks, and kicks I practiced. In my one night with Bruce Lee I learned speed and non-telegraphic punches, striking with efficiency, directness, and simplicity, stop kicks and hits, multiple ways to attack, the various ranges of combat, and a poetic philosophy which wove through the martial art.

"Empty your mind," Mr. Lee chanted with confidence. "Be formless, shapeless, like water. If you put water into a cup, it becomes the cup. You put water into a bottle and it becomes the bottle. You put it in a teapot it becomes the teapot. That water can flow, or it can crash. Be water, my friend."

My throat itched when Mr. Lee's words sunk into my consciousness. I'd always known we were pure energy. For how

35

long had I been a stagnant puddle, allowing sediments of dirt to settle within me? Wasn't it time I embraced my potential and became flexible and free flowing? A true force?

◆

An uneasy sensation settles in my stomach as I think about the tasks ahead of me. *What kinds of skills would the person to challenge Zhuang excel at?* It's odd that the Head Officials are putting us through an obstacle course. Apparently, I'm alone in this perspective. Everyone else appears excited and privileged to be at the Institute. This is what I gathered from eavesdropping on a group of girls in the bathroom.

The windowless room for the first task is full when I arrive. It resembles a waiting room in a doctor's office and no one who's waiting seems excited anymore. They all look like they're about to have a lobotomy. Tension drapes over shoulders, drips down long faces, creases foreheads.

I pluck a magazine from a coffee table and take the first available seat. From behind my *Psychology Today* I scan the room. Three doors are on one wall and three other doors sit opposite. At the far end of the room is a counter. Sitting behind it is a woman with short, curly red hair. She's far away in thought as she types at a computer.

"Good, I'm not late," Joseph says, taking the chair next to me.

"How do you know?" I mutter dryly. "Actually we're all done and waiting for our results."

He flashes a sideways smile. "You're a bad liar."

"I'll work on it." I pull the magazine up closer to my nose and pretend to read.

"So, Stark, what's your talent?" Joseph asks, ignoring my obvious nonverbal cues.

"Huh?"

"Maybe you call it a gift. What's yours?"

"What are you talking about?"

Joseph rolls his eyes, but smiles still, not looking too put off. "You're kind of thick, aren't ya?"

"You're kind of annoying, but you don't see me pointing it out."

"You just did," Joseph snorts, amused.

My eyes dart back to the article I've tried to read a half dozen times now.

Once again Joseph ignores my attempts at solitude. Rudely he points to a girl across the room; her long whitish blonde hair falls straight over her shoulders and shows no contrast against her pale skin. "That's Samara. She's apparently telepathic." Then he nods his head to a boy with black dreadlocks and a complexion the color of coffee grounds. "That's Trent. He's telekinetic, whatever that means. The girl next to him, I don't know her name, but she's super smart, and then the girl next to her reads auras." Joseph gives me a triumphant look. "I could go on, but you get the point."

"Are you sure everyone here has a gift or talent or whatever you want to call it?"

"I'm not certain, but I gather as much."

"How do you know?" I ask, despite the urge to ignore this guy.

"It's called conversation. You should try havin' one sometime."

"I prefer reading."

"Haven't you talked to anyone since you've arrived? How do you not know this yet?"

"Why would I want to speak to anyone? I'm not here to make friends. I just want this whole thing over with already."

"So I've gathered." He then lowers his voice. "Actually, to be quite honest, I'm a little worried because I don't have any powers. I've got no clue what I'm doin' here. What about you?"

"Yeah, I'm with you," I say, happy to have an out. "I'm as normal as they come."

Joseph laughs suddenly, making a few kids around us jump with surprise. "Yeah, whatever."

I grimace to no effect.

"Well, I only knew 'bout all this stuff a few days ago. All this is new to me." His southern drawl is more pronounced now.

"Me too," I admit.

"Well, that's a relief," he says.

I don't reply.

"Imagine my surprise when I'm mindin' my own business, sleeping like I normally do, and Trey happens into my dreams. At

37

first I was pretty skeptical, but he proved himself and now here I am. A Dream Traveler. Who would have thought it?"

His story sounds oddly like mine. Maybe I'm not the only one behind the pack. This whole gift business makes me uncomfortable though. These other competitors sound like they have real gifts, not just the ability to know when insignificant events are about to occur.

I have a brief moment to reflect on this while Joseph whistles quietly to himself. The sharp, nasally voice of the woman behind the counter cuts through the tension, bringing everyone out of their fog. "When I call your name please go to the room number that follows. You'll be given further instructions once inside. If I don't call your name then you'll be in the second test group." She calls six names, each followed by a room number. My name isn't called.

Joseph jumps up cheerfully. "That's me! See ya later."

Half an hour later, after I've read six different magazines, the participants begin exiting the rooms. They all look bleary-eyed and disoriented. I pretend I don't see Joseph give me a small wave on his way out.

The lady behind the counter reads another list of names. Five more strangers are listed. "Roya Stark, room four." I head to my assigned room. It's dark. Small. Also windowless. Oddly I don't think I've seen any windows in this place.

A tall, slender woman wearing a lab coat sits on a stool next to a computer. "Hi, Roya. My name is Amber. Please lie down and we'll get started." She indicates the bed next to where she's sitting. A soft red light is positioned overhead.

I continue standing and stare at her, trying to will my eyes to adjust to the lack of light. The woman's long brown hair is pulled back into a low ponytail. Silver loops hang from her ears, catching the light emitting from her computer screen.

"All right, you can stand while I explain the task," she says after I don't move. "This is called the Ganzfeld task and it will test your ability to receive information being sent to you. In a minute, when you're comfortable, I'm going to put you in a state of sensory deprivation. This is to ensure nothing around you interferes with the prescribed message we're going to mentally send you. I will also be hooking you up to this EMG machine. The reason for this is it's imperative you perform this task without going to sleep. You're forbidden from dream traveling. Instead you'll focus, stay completely conscious, and tell me the message, if any, you think you're being sent. Shuman will send you the message. Sometimes knowing who is sending the information will help, that's why I'm telling you this. When she's ready she will let us know and then you'll focus. How does all that sound?"

Shuman? Really? That's who's sending me this message? Good thing I'm indifferent to these results. After casting a skeptical glance at Amber I resign and lie down on the bed. I'll play the part of a lab rat just this once.

"Great," she says with a disingenuous smile. "Now first I'm going to stick a few of these sensors on you." She begins placing little round, plastic-covered sensors on my head, face, and chest. They're covered in tape and attached to wires. "Now if you do fall asleep then you'll be disqualified from this task," the lady warns. "Next I'm going to place these over your eyes to block out any visual stimulation." She shows me what appears to be a ping-pong ball sliced in half. I nod consent and close my eyes. Once in place the small circular objects rest precariously along the curvature of my eye sockets. "Lastly I'm about to put headphones over your ears. They will block out any auditory stimulation. When Shuman is ready to send you the message I will tap your wrist three times. Until then you should relax, focus, and stay awake. When you believe you've received the message in its entirety then click this." She places a cylinder object in my hand and positions my finger over a small button. "I'll record the message and you'll be free to go."

Apparently, there's no time for questions. The lady promptly clamps headphones over my ears and all I hear from that point forward is static. Unable to see or hear and locked in a closet with an uptight scientist is probably the strangest predicament I've been placed in thus far, which is saying a lot. This almost makes me laugh. I suppress it.

I need a strategy. Something that will help me to open up a channel to receive this message. I picture a telephone. I know the telephone is about to ring. Allowing my mind to remember the sound of Shuman's voice I imagine she's on the other end. My breaths lengthen. Deepen. I keep my mind's eye trained on the telephone. At least ten minutes pass. Sleep trots through my mind, tempting me to follow it many times. I stay alert. Focused. When

Amber's cold, bony fingers tap my wrist I'm alert and ready to proceed.

I focus on the telephone. Nothing happens. I steal a long breath and decide to pick up the receiver, even though it hasn't rung. It is light blue and done in the old rotary style. On the other end there's no dial tone. "Hello," I hear myself say. There's no reply. *What am I going to do if I don't get a message? Should I make something up?* I lay the receiver back down. The smoothness of the plastic in my hand is real. When the receiver meets the cradle it falls into place comfortably. I stare at the silent phone, willing it to ring. It sits soundlessly, mocking me with its stillness. Erupting with emotion I yank the receiver off the cradle again and hold it up to my ear.

Nothing. No dial tone. No voice. No message. I run my fingers along the seam of the front and back part of the receiver in a nervous fashion. Even in my visualizations my strange habits still shine through. I laugh in my mind and swear I hear it out loud, through the static.

This is stupid. A waste of time. Of resources. Why are we all doing this? It's absurd. I bring my attention to my physical reality. The remote in my hand. The button just under my finger, waiting to be pushed. That would end this whole experiment.

As I must do, even in my visualizations, I take the receiver once more and go to replace it on its cradle, where it belongs. When it's almost there a voice splinters through my consciousness. Low. Muffled. But still it erupts from the light blue phone, catching my attention. With a jerk I hold the receiver to my ear.

"Incoming. Incoming. Incoming," the voice on the other end of the line speaks. And then quite clearly it gives a message. Three times it sounds in my head. On the last time I click the button in my hand.

Amber gently removes the earphones and halved ping-pong balls. Then she turns to her computer and places her hands on the keyboard. "Please tell me the message, if any, you received."

I don't hesitate for a second. I've been repeating it in my mind so I don't forget it. "Shuman said, 'Hope deferred makes the heart sick, but when dreams come true, there is life and joy.'"

Amber records this with no reaction of confirmation. "Thank you," she says, tapping one last key. "You're all done."

"When will I know my results?" I ask as she removes the sensors.

"After dinner." Amber hastens opening the door, causing the startling bright light from the waiting room to slice into my eyeballs.

Chapter Seven

With half an hour to kill before the next task, I decide to explore the Institute. Oddly, everything's spread out in this place. The Institute must take up an entire city block. It also seems we're pretty free to go wherever we want. Even so, numerous doors don't open when I push the button beside them. Arrogant key card scanners stare back at me, snobbishly blocking my way. Still I explore multiple passageways, all with brushed stainless steel walls and blue carpet. Something about this place is strange, besides the fact I almost killed myself to get here. Each floor goes on for miles. And the numbering isn't always consistent.

I somehow end up on the fifth floor, which is colder than all the rest. A voice behind me calls out, "Umm, miss, are you lost?"

I wheel around. An older woman is poking her head through an open door. Her loose curls are pinched in barrettes. The lavender scrubs hang loosely off her bony frame.

"No, I'm just exploring."

"Hmm," she says, bristling with quiet disapproval. "Well, I'm not sure if this is the right place for that. Are you a contender?"

I hesitate, trying to figure out what she means. Then it dawns on me. "Yes."

"Well," she says, her withered hands fidgeting. The wrinkles in her face are deep, but her hair and eyes give the impression she's just a girl. "You see, the thing is, this level is really to be kept without disturbances."

She's trying to be polite. It seems to hurt her to even say what she's said so far. For this reason, I simply agree and retreat to the elevators.

The doors open and I walk forward without looking up, running straight into Trey.

"Excuse me," he says, stepping back. "I didn't expect anyone." Hesitation muddies his expression for a second before he recovers. "What are you doing here?"

"I was just leaving," I say, stepping into the elevator.

A worried look passes across his turquoise eyes. "Did you have business down here?"

"No." I bite my lip, embarrassed. *If we aren't supposed to be down here then why don't they block it off with the ample security devices they have?* Trey nods and walks down the hallway.

The button is under my fingertips when something registers. I step back out of the elevator and stride after Trey. He's halfway down the hall by the time I catch up with him.

"I'm sorry, but did you say 'down' here?" I ask when I'm a couple feet away.

He turns, looking startled. "Why yes, I did."

My eyes catch the yellow and blue medallion he wears around his neck. It looks like curly-yin-yang-type waves. "But we're on the fifth floor?"

"Level," he corrects.

The woman in the lavender scrubs returns to the door, looking at me with disapproval. A beeping sounds off behind her.

"Mr. Underwood," she calls urgently. "I think you should get in here."

He turns to me. "Roya, I believe your second task is about to begin. We'll talk later."

As I head for the second task, I mull over what has happened over the last few minutes. *What did Trey mean by level? How's that any different than floor? And what's that lady protecting? What was the beeping?* One thing I'm certain of is this place is full of secrets. Intrigued, I make a silent plan to explore more if given the opportunity. For now though, I have to focus on the upcoming tasks.

◆

I thought the second and third tasks were jokes. Apparently, they weren't. My performance was. The second task, PK Party, named for a fad created in the eighties, was administered by James, the tallest scientist I've ever met. His curly brown hair piled high atop his head overshadowed his prominent canine teeth. He thought it was fascinating that in the eighties people would have parties where they tried to "awaken" their abilities to manipulate metal. The people of this generation sounded dumb and lame, but no one asked me. Since bending metal was apparently quite advanced as far as telekinesis went, we were asked to move a nutshell. He called us into a room individually and placed a single peanut shell at the far end of a table. With all our mental strength we were expected to move the casing. My nutshell sat quite still for a good two minutes. I was then dismissed.

After eating a sack lunch in a remote hallway I head to the third task. The gymnasium is filled with multiple athletic stations. I should have turned around immediately. During P.E., I spent many solitary hours hanging out on bleachers. My gym coaches had given up on trying to force me to play volleyball or walk around the track. But now in this strange metal box of a compound, I'll be forced to perform endurance and strength tests in front of a bunch of strangers.

We're issued a pair of shorts and T-shirt. I'd decline, but I'm afraid I might sweat in my only set of clothes. Once I change, I line up in front of one of four stations. I'm to perform at each one of them in rotation.

The only thing that makes me feel any better is that most of the other kids are really quite wimpy too. Most everyone in my line can hardly do more than one pull-up. There are a couple of kids who perform fine, but the rest of us are beet red and exhausted by the end of it.

"Why is this even a task?" the girl named Samara says between gasps for breath.

I shrug, guessing she's probably talking to me.

"I can't even lift that bar by itself," she half laughs, "and the guy asked me how much weight I wanted to add to it."

I suppress a snicker. I'd been in the same predicament.

The next task is kung fu. I shockingly find myself excited. The room for this task is large, with a cushioned floor. Mirrors line one wall. We're asked to file into four lines. At the front of each line is a person wearing a long-sleeved white top and black pants. One by one we're called from our line and asked to block assaults.

I don't know what to expect when I step in front of the man in the white suit. He bows and then begins throwing punches at me. It all happens too fast. I find the man's attacks to be obtrusive. Invasive. They strike me, not hard, but in a manner that suggests they can. With every part of my being I try to deflect the assaults but each time one comes at me I miss it. My arms move aimlessly around as I just hope by luck I'll block something. Completely out of breath after only thirty seconds of this, I ask him to stop and give me a minute.

I take this time to gather myself. Everyone stares. I do my best to block them out and focus the way Bruce Lee suggested. After I catch my breath, I open my eyes with a renewed energy. It courses through me like blood in my veins, like the DNA in my being. I step back up and beckon the man forward.

This time things are different. I see the man's hands before they move. I sense them seconds before they push the air in front of me. Allowing my mind to follow this blueprint I throw block after block, always in perfect timing. Again my reflexes are heightened. The man raises an eyebrow at me after I block three rapid attempts. Then he straightens and dismisses me with a bow. I file to the end of the line.

Attacks are the next part of the task. The guys in white suits retrieve boards from the shelves. We're supposed to break the thin, yet solid pieces of wood. Short, unfulfilling breaths shoot through my chest as the panic takes over. My mind races through my training from the night before trying to find a strategy.

The first person in my line, a lanky boy, steps up and is instructed to strike the board in any way necessary to break it. With an uncertain jerk he throws a punch into the wood. It doesn't break, but one of his fingers does. Nervous tension constricts my chest as I watch him cradle his hand with his opposite arm.

My fists, like stones, hold tight as each person attempts and fails the task. I should be relieved each time another competitor slumps off defeated by a one-inch piece of pinewood. I'm not. This is a million times worse than any gym class. My humiliation is a tethered ball I'll be unable to retrieve. It wraps around and around the pole, too high above my head for me to send back the other way.

Samara, the girl with hair like sun-bleached straw, towers in front of me. She's up next. In a whisper she asks the guy in white to hold the board down low. He does. I'm confused by this request and watch with new interest. Slowly she backs up, seeming to count the paces between her and the board. I take note of her precision, her focus, her confidence. Then in a flash she steps, pulls her foot in, sending her hip back and then launches forward. This is all one movement and the ax kick that follows is a blur. It drives down sharply. The board splits evenly. I take a gulp of air.

My turn. I decide to try a hammer fist. The guy in white holds the board down low, a few feet off the ground. I position myself on top of it with my fist up high. I take a deep breath. I'm just about to give it everything I have when I hear it. Bruce Lee's words, like an ingrained track on the inside of my consciousness, echo, "Be water." I open my eyes, which I realize were tightly closed, and step back. Holding up one finger I indicate I need a minute.

Loosening up my fist takes the tension out of my arm and then it follows suit in my shoulder. I need to be water. Fluid, like a waterfall plummeting to earth, past the board, past the earth. Unstoppable. I need to be a force. Quickly I draw up this visual in my mind and feel it. When I'm ready I step back into position and give the man holding the board a nod. My arm floats into position. I tell the muscles to relax, to be fluid. Then, like a waterfall being let loose, I shoot my fist downward and only allow the muscles to tense when they're extended. This, to my surprise, is just past the point that I break through the board.

"Very good," the man booms as he tosses the boards to the side. He bows, dismissing me.

Chapter Eight

I've never needed to shower so desperately. The pungent smell of sweat assaults my senses as I stride through the stainless steel hallways. Once in the shower, the hot water soothes my muscles, which already ache from the strain of physical endurance. Afterwards I dress in my dirty clothes, which are stiff against my skin, but not bad enough to force me into the awful uniform.

Surprisingly, as I comb my hair, I have an odd sense of pride. My performance today hadn't been atrocious. It wasn't stellar, but I broke the board and that was more than I could have wished. At least I had done what I set out to do: maintain some dignity. Hopefully by tomorrow morning, I'd be scored as an average contender with some praise and then sent back to Bob and Steve's house. That's the arrangement I hoped the Lucidites would set up for me until my family drama was sorted out.

I'd fantasized about spending the rest of the summer curled up on their patio furniture, reading a book from their library and watching the sun rise over the lake. In this fantasy, we'd all go out to dinner on Friday nights. They'd ask me about my day, and listen with sincerity. They'd tell me about their day trading antiques and I would ask thoughtful and curious questions. We would laugh and decide to stay late to dance to mariachi music.

I make my way to the main hall for dinner, fantasizing about future conversations with Bob and Steve. The elevator stops at level two and a few people file into the compartment.

"So how'd you do it?" a girl asks her friend.

"Oh, it wasn't hard," another replies. "I just pictured I was a waterfall and my only purpose was to fall and fall. No board can stop a waterfall."

My attention is assaulted by these babbling girls. I want to ignore them, but I'm curious. I steal a glance and realize, to my horror, it's the girl obsessed with a specific type of cheese—Goat Girl. How can anyone be irritating on so many levels? Her long thin brown hair hangs in pieces around her face. She's skinny, devoid of curves, like a street sign. Fat, round freckles fleck her button nose. I have no idea where she came up with this technique for breaking the board, but it sounds eerily like the one I used. Suddenly I have the urge to break her pretty little nose.

"I just couldn't believe it," her friend gushes. "You were so amazing at all that stuff."

"Well, that's what a well-rounded education will do for you," Goat Girl admits as we step off the elevator. I can't stand to be anywhere next to that group. I hang back a little and wait until they move down the buffet line.

It's the same spread as the night before. I load up, my reserves depleted from all the exercise. Once I have my plate in hand, Joseph waves me over. He's sitting at a table with Samara and a few other people from our group. I pretend I don't notice him. I even pretend to drop my napkin and hope he'll forget about me when I stand up again. He doesn't. He waves so frantically that even a blind cat would notice him.

I sigh and walk over to their table, where I find a seat beside the guy who apparently moves stuff with his mind, Trent. Maybe he'll give me a demonstration of his abilities and pass me the salt. Aiden materializes on the far side of the hall at the end of the buffet line with his plates, searching for a place to sit. I'm hyperaware of his every move as he strides through the crowd and sits down at a table with a bunch of white coats. I wish I was at a table alone with him, staring at his brown spiky hair and listening to his prodigious stories.

"So, good job with the board today," Samara says.

"Thanks," I reply as I chew on a grape. "You too."

"How'd you guys do with the first task?" a boy asks anyone who's listening.

A few people chime in about different messages they received. I keep my head down and listen. Most people seemed to have understood something and everyone's message was apparently different.

"Yeah, I think I was better at the second task," Trent, the guy with dreadlocks, says. "I moved my peanut shell across the table before launching it into James's 'fro." He chuckles a bit. "Honestly, I didn't mean to, but that's just how it goes sometimes."

I let them all do the talking while I eat bread, cheese, and fruit. The group is nice enough, and no one makes any direct attempts to talk to me, which is a relief.

Everyone has finished their food when Trey steps onto a stage at the front. A light shines on him and he clears his throat. The room falls silent.

"I want to start by thanking each and every one of you." He pushes his hand through his silver hair and stares at the back wall. "I know this hasn't been easy for anyone. But what we're facing is no easy challenge. Some of you have known you were Lucidites for a long time. Some of you are just learning this. No matter, we're all part of the same team. We face a deadly force, and he will persist until he has squashed all the consciousness out of every Dream Traveler and Middling." Trey halts, seeming to push his fury down. This is the exact same demeanor he had when he first told me about Zhuang. When Trey speaks again his words are slow, calculated, carrying weight. "Zhuang wants power and doesn't care about the consequences. He has to be stopped."

Since I plunged into this new world everything has felt brand new and exciting. It's easy to get away from the purpose, the reason I'm here: to risk facing a merciless villain. A man who would crush his adversary to dust if they stood in his way. A man who sounds undefeatable. And in this room is the person who must challenge that man. They're a sacrifice. This all seems so strange and artificial. But still I'm here, staring at this world like it's my very own surreal *Alice in Wonderland*. I know better though. I don't believe in fantasies. But at times I find myself wanting to believe in this.

Trey clears his throat and I awake from my little world. "We're here because we must choose a contender. That's our goal. This is what has been forecast and the day is almost upon us. By tomorrow we'll know who will challenge Zhuang. I believe this person can bring him down. And I know by defeating Zhuang we'll stand to live a better life."

A waiter clearing a table in the back accidentally drops a dish, causing a momentary distraction. When the noise has settled Trey continues, "Flynn once again apologizes for being unable to attend. He knows the right challenger will be chosen and wishes to meet this person once they are."

There are some "aws" and "ohs" made at this.

"The results from today's tasks have been tallied. Your reports will be placed on your bunk tonight for your examination. Before then I want to review those tasks and go over what you can expect

49

tonight." A hush settles over the room. "The tasks weren't given in a consistent order, since we had four different groups. We'll start with the calisthenics task. This tested physical stamina because the right challenger will need to be physically as well as mentally prepared to battle Zhuang. It's expected that he will challenge his opponent both in a dreamscape and a physical reality. The results on this task were quite low, but we did have a few of you who performed well.

"The kung fu task was chosen because this is the martial art form which we believe Zhuang to know best. If there's to be a physical test then we believe it will take place in this form. There were some surprisingly strong candidates who displayed promising talents.

"The Ganzfeld task is about accessing information, which is an important quality for our contender. There were only two of you who received the message in its entirety." The crowd is audibly upset. Trey quickly holds up his hand to quiet everyone. "Many of you got the essence of the message, but not the exact message.

"Lastly, the PK Party was to demonstrate a quite amazing talent that could be harnessed against Zhuang. Those who control objects with their mind are quite revered and would be a great adversary to our enemy. I'm proud to say that a few of you excelled at this task."

Cheers echo around the room from a few different crowds. When everything dies down Trey continues, "Tonight is your final task. You're to dream travel to a room within this Institute labeled with your first and last initials as well as the number on your room."

That means I would travel to room RS 300.

"Once there, you'll find instructions. Follow them. Please note there will be an hourglass timer in the room. When it's done then your time to complete the task is over, Trey says. "The results of the tasks and your contender will be unveiled tomorrow in this room at eight a.m."

A loud eruption of noise from the tables hurts my ears. Trey tries his best to settle everyone back down. "Please try to get to bed at a decent hour. This really is for the best."

I excuse myself at once to go straight back to my room. A few pairs of eyes try to draw me in, but I hastily look away and continue my retreat. It isn't that I'm aimed at performing well on the last task as much as I can't shake an uneasy feeling in my stomach. It's a feeling I get every time I look at Trey. He's always holding something back, and it makes my insides twist uncomfortably.

When I return to my bunk, I find the card with my results from the day's tasks. It's in a dark brown envelope with a red seal. I open it at once and pull out the card. It reads:

Roya Stark:
Task 1: Ganzfeld – Pass – 100%
Task 2: PK Party – Fail – 0%
Task 3: Calisthenics – Fail – 45%
Task 4: Kung Fu – Pass – 88%

One hundred percent on the first task is absurd, but the next two are much more believable. With scores like these, I'll be given accolades and then sent home to live out my summer in the quiet calm of Bob and Steve's house.

Now all I need to do is finish the last task and then I'll snuggle up in that chair on their deck, just as I dreamed. I pull the covers over my head, as I did the night before, and work at slowing down my breathing. When the time comes I see a sign in my head that says RS 300. I know this is where I must go.

Chapter Nine

The tunnel is short this time. Within seconds it spits me out into a poorly lit room. It isn't really a room as much as a large closet. Junk is piled everywhere, on tables and shelves. Luckily a cramped walkway allows for navigation through the clutter.

What in the hell am I supposed to do in here?

The light overhead provides hardly any visibility. I squint through the darkness, and with relief find a floor lamp pushed in the corner. After one long pull on the brass chain, bright light fills the small space. I notice three things all at once: a chalkboard, a security camera, and an hourglass.

On the far wall hangs the chalkboard. It reads, *"Find object of most importance."*

The tiny room is literally filled to the brim with hundreds of objects—books, jewelry, clothes, electronics, and boxes. From the ceiling hang dried herbs. On a shelf sits a large plate of armor and a helmet. The floor is littered with shards of broken mirror and nutshells. *Was this a riddle or a joke?*

The security camera hangs down a few inches from the ceiling in the far corner. Its red light flashes at me disapprovingly. I try to ignore the camera, pretending it doesn't exist.

I steal a glance at the hourglass, which sits teetering high on a stack of books. *What!?* It's almost empty. I gape at it in disbelief. *Oh no, I've lost before I even had a chance to try.* This isn't the way I want to go down, especially with a camera blatantly recording my every move of failure. The sand filters through the narrow neck, piling up higher and higher.

Instantly struck by an idea, I press my eyelids together trying to clear my mind. It's hard to block out the bright light from the lamp or the sound of my pulse racing in my head. Taking a deep breath, I focus on only one thing. Suddenly I'm in the tunnel again. The wind surges past me. All around me. I'm falling, like I did the night before. Luckily this only lasts for a brief moment before it deposits me back into the cramped closet. Immediately I pull the chain on the lamp, sending light to every inch of the room. The hourglass is full. Sixty minutes remaining, or five million granules of sand. I'd once read that this was the approximate amount in an hourglass. I had a thing for knowing and seeing useless stuff.

The camera hovers overhead, spying—making me doubt every move. I guess there are forty-nine other rooms just like this, with forty-nine contenders hunting around just like I am. *My gosh, how big is this place? How does the world not know about it?* Now the camera watches as I shake my head. Maybe the person watching me somewhere in the Institute thinks it's because I'm baffled by the random contents of the box I'm exploring. Although true, I'm mostly baffled by the Lucidites and their Institute.

Inside the musty cardboard box are yellowing photographs of people I don't recognize, a penny bank with change locked inside it, a broken smoke detector, and an old mink stole. I push this box to the side and scavenge through the next. All crap. There isn't anything that sticks out as super important. This is like the contents of someone's forgotten storage room. They'd never be back to sort through this junk or claim it, because in the end we really don't need things. The belongings people accumulate throughout their lives will always own them. People seem to think if they had more they'd be happier or freer, but their possessions only chain them to the earth.

I open another box, taking a quick glance at the hour glass. Four million grains of sand remain. Forty-five minutes. Inside this box a rotary phone sits beside a doll, a pair of ballet slippers, and a trinket box. I pull off the lid of the velvet-wrapped trinket box, and with my fingertips push around the small objects inside. I gasp and the box hiccups between my fingers—its contents almost spill to the floor. Recovering myself, I probe at the tiny objects that startled me. Four pearl-and tan-colored teeth. Small ones. Baby teeth. *Still gross.* Mingled with some stranger's teeth are a couple of lone earrings which have apparently lost their match, and a tiny little piece that looks like a hearing aid.

Slamming the lid back on the box I throw it sharply against the wall, sending it sliding back behind a mountain of boxes and books. A growl escapes my clenched teeth. The camera flashes its judgmental eye on me, greedy to record my frustration.

Snaking through the tiny path, I make my way to the oak shelf at the far end. A piece of medieval armor looks out of place beside some type of animal horn and a hand mirror. Up high on the top shelf stands a vase, another stack of books with faded covers, and something shiny, too high for me to reach. I pull a box down from a nearby stack and step onto it, grabbing the object that stole my attention. It's a bracelet, a beautiful one. Two inches wide and made of alternating bands of silver and copper. It's tapered at one end, where it sits closest to the wrist. The silver bands have raised circles. The copper is smooth, like water. I love it instantly.

A small pin releases the bracelet, and it opens in half on a pair of hinges. I stick it on my wrist and snap it shut. *Clink.* It's cold and warm at the same time.

Like one of those plastic bracelets people adorn in a hospital, it makes me feel I've been admitted to a place. The coolness slowly starts to fade as my body heat presses against it. Maybe it's my imagination, but the metal seems to soften as it connects with my skin. We're one.

The bracelet isn't the answer to this stupid riddle, though. I love it, but I can't explain why it's important. Scanning the room, I search desperately for something that catches my eye as incredibly useful.

I pick up the hand mirror on the bottom shelf and look into it. The handle is gold and ornately decorated with flowers and vines. Spots from age fleck the surface. Looking into the mirror I see myself for the first time in a long while. I've been so overwhelmed with everything that I can't remember the last time I looked at my reflection. I'm older somehow, although for the most part nothing has changed about me. Maybe the green outline of my eyes is a little darker than I remember, but it could also be the lighting. A smile spreads softly along my pink mouth. This girl, the one looking back at me now, she's a Dream Traveler. An odd expression lingers in her eyes as the label sinks in. The smile subsides, but the neutral appearance doesn't disguise an emotion I've rarely witnessed on my own face. Pride.

Somewhere in the shadows behind me, something moves. I don't see it directly, but instead in the reflection. I drop the mirror, sending it to the ground, and spin around ready to attack. Silence. I pace to the corner where I saw the movement and check every available space. There's nothing and no place that someone could be hiding. I turn to check the opposite corner and feel the broken shards of mirror under my bare feet.

Two million granules of sand remain.

I bite my lip trying to think. My mind races over everything I've seen in the room. I kick a piece of mirror out of my path and feel the pain of a shard enter my toe. *Damn it, this isn't the time to retrieve a broken piece of glass from my foot.*

A minute ago, I thought I was beginning to figure myself out. Now I'm swearing and cutting myself. More than anything I want to know who I am. That's why I'm here. I know I'm a Dream Traveler. Trey said I belong with the Lucidites. Honestly I don't know where I belong. I don't want to go back and live with my disingenuous parents and emotionally abusive brother. I want something different. A life that fits me. I deserve that. When I saw my reflection in that mirror, I felt there was a life out there that belonged to me.

The room spins in my mind 360 degrees. I have an idea. It feels right, like the way good poetry falls off my tongue. A wave of satisfaction sweeps over me. If I looked into the mirror right now, I'd see a smile.

With a quick pivot, I swing around and address the camera directly. "I'm not playing your little game." I wave my finger accusingly at the camera. "I'm not another piece in your stupid chess match. None of this crap matters. Not the competition, not the objects, not even the people. I don't care if this means I forfeit. I can't give you a legitimate reason that any of this is important. I don't believe in anything, not objects, not technology, not even the Lucidites. I only believe in myself."

I pull the chain from the light for effect, close my eyes, and focus. I travel to the first place that comes to mind. Within seconds I stand on a deck, looking out at the darkness, the lake hardly visible through the waning moonlight. Taking a long breath I settle into the chair beside me. Bob and Steve will be off dream traveling.

I pull my knees to my chest and listen to the gentle crashing of waves on the retaining wall. The sound of my childhood. It was always in the background while I played in the yard, read in the hammock, or watched television with the screen door open. The only time I don't remember the sound of the lake was when I was in the woods, where Zhuang shut out everything. He had tried to keep me away from the Lucidites, away from discovering I was a Dream Traveler. The pride from earlier begins to swarm my chest like a brewing storm cloud. Nothing is going to stop me from discovering who I am and where I belong. This lake, my entry to another world, is a part of my entire life, in a way. It has always held a key. Now I'll have to find others.

A book sits on the chair next to me. One of them must have left it out. It's called *Awareness* and was written by a man named Anthony De Mello. I scoop the book into my hands and randomly flip to the middle and begin reading it with a sense of quiet satisfaction. Everything I said and thought back in the fifth task is right. I eye the bracelet still on my wrist. I am truly proud of myself.

Chapter Ten

My body isn't stiff or cold as I'd expect when sunlight kisses my closed lids a few hours later, much earlier than I anticipated. Still curled up in the chair, I recall there's a time difference between the Institute and this place. Orange and pink colors intensify as the sun surges to the surface of the horizon. Each second the sky grows brighter my chest warms. From shoulder to shoulder the expansion of heat spreads, generating an energy that matches the sunrise. Slowly, the warm sun peeks out from its hiding place and then rapidly stretches into the pale blue sky. I'm smiling again. I know this emotion is fleeting. I don't try to hold onto it. Instead I picture my happiness as an uncaged bird perched on my shoulder. Any moment it will take flight.

Behind me a shuffling noise. The blinds slide open. Steve stands in his bathrobe and slippers looking puffy-eyed. Strangely this isn't the first time I've seen him in such attire. It's the same robe he wore the day he rescued me, calling it inopportune timing on my part. He'd discovered I was in trouble through the online newsfeed. Later I learned this is the way the Lucidites receive their news. A team with various psychic powers, news reporters, picks up on worthy events prior to their occurrence, and these are published on a website. The feed that day reported:

A Middling, suffering hallucinations caused by Zhuang, is about to cause bodily harm to a notable Dream Traveler - a Ms. Roya Stark.

I didn't know about the news reporters at that time. I didn't even know I was Dream Traveler. And I didn't know I had "notable" status because I was on the list of potential challengers. All I knew was if I stayed in the car with Shiloh, my deranged brother, for one second longer he'd attack me again. What I didn't realize was that outside the car I was an easy target. I guess it never occurred to me that my brother would run me over; that's probably because it hadn't occurred to me that my brother would have his mind hijacked by a madman. If it hadn't been for Steve's brilliant timing I would have been roadkill.

I hop up from the patio chair and wave, excited to see Steve's honest face and tell him about the last two days. He stares out to the lake and yawns. After a brief moment he turns, heading off to the kitchen. *He can't see me.* I slump back in the seat, deflated.

Does this mean only those dream traveling can see me? Like when I met Trey? Ren? Shuman? They had all been dream traveling too.

Even if Steve can't see me and I'm unable to tell him and Bob all about my current drama, I'm still glad to be here by the lake. This is my home, whether my family is lucid and wants me or not. I pick the book back up and resume, this time from the beginning. The first chapter in this book's entitled "Wake Up." The author, in a somewhat abrasive fashion, explains that most of us don't want to wake up; we don't want solutions to our problems. Most everyone on this earth is sleepwalking in their nightmares and they only want a bit of relief. We're all conditioned into a brainwashing that tells us our happiness is dependent on certain people and ideas being in place. But the brainwashing has contradictory points and therefore we constantly live a life of struggle and sacrifice, with really no authentic happiness.

A deep part in me begins to ache as I read page after page. The printed words taste bitter in my mouth, like burnt coffee. My rush of happiness—was it because I was starting to learn who I was? I was growing attached to the idea of being a Dream Traveler. A Lucidite. Now some stupid book states my happiness isn't real because it's based on an idea; one that could dissolve at any moment. My current happiness, grounded in my perception, is as fragile as a watercolor left out in the rain. What happens when I fail as a Dream Traveler? When the Lucidites reject me? Will I be back where I started, lost and unhappy? I close the book and throw it across the yard.

My brain feels tight with confusion as I look out at the blue sky and lake. Fortunately, I don't have much time to wallow in this newfound state. The sliding glass door opens and Steve steps out onto the porch. He holds a cup of coffee in one hand and wears a funny expression on his face.

"You should know," he says out loud, "that I'm aware you're here, Roya."

I jump out of my chair and stand completely frozen in front of him. Baffled, I wave my hand in front of his face. His eyes don't register that they've seen anything.

"I can't see or hear you," Steve explains, "but I know you must be here."

Is he mad at me? I can't tell from the tone of his voice. It makes me upset to think I've invaded his privacy, that I've trespassed.

"We honestly don't mind you coming here." He smiles sincerely. "I'm honored, actually."

I relax a bit.

"However," Steve continues, "this gives us an important area to address." He walks out to the yard and picks up the book. "When dream traveling, it's best to summon an object to you, rather than take it and use it in its physical state. You see, we live in a multiverse." Steve shrugs, like that explains anything. "When you dream travel you're in a different dimension, but it's still parallel to your waking reality. The two dimensions, your waking and dreaming, blend together while you're traveling, allowing you to pull objects between the two.

"As we discussed before, you can't summon an object that doesn't belong to you. For now that doesn't give you much to work with, but in the future you'll have possessions. I promise."

He lays the book on the table and takes a gulp of his coffee. "You see, this is a law among the Lucidites. It was established to protect us, as well as everyone else. Things would get out of hand quickly if people started witnessing objects levitating all over the place, don't you think?" He laughs easily. "When you summon an object it's on your dimension and therefore can't be seen by Middlings."

He takes a long glance at the book before saying, "This is a good read. How about I buy you your own copy to read on another night?"

Without a way to say "thank you" I'm helpless, but also touched. Steve merely smiles and then strides back into the house. I sit down in the chair, in no real hurry to go anywhere. This whole dream traveling thing is complicated. Inside the group of Dream Travelers is an individual society known as the Lucidites. They have their own laws. But what about other Dream Travelers who aren't Lucidites? Do they follow these laws?

With a few spare hours of idle time on my hands, what I really want to do is explore Bob and Steve's library some more. My mind flashes back to the first time Bob gently slid back the thick oak door, revealing the incredible room and all its treasures. I remember nearly passing out. Later I found out that was probably more from the drugs than my elation. Bob and Steve had drugged the tea they'd given me in order to draw me into a lucid state of dreaming that night, ensuring that I'd dream travel once the seed had been planted.

I remember their library smelled of leather and smoke, laced with strange herbs—which I later learned was mugwort, another herb used to lure me into a more conscious state of dreaming. Steve later explained that they knew they only had one opportunity to do what they needed and that everything was riding on that one night.

I remember the fireplace in the corner was lit, which seemed bizarre since it was almost summer. From floor to ceiling, and all along the walls, books lined every square inch of the room. I was in my very own personal heaven. I remember smiling, the aroma of herbs wrapping around me. Suddenly I was so relaxed that I pictured my skin, blood, and body parts melting off my bones. Strangely, this didn't bother me.

That's when something magnificent caught my eye. Perched beside a large, sleek leather couch was a Native American headdress on a stand. Its bright turquoise and white feathers pulled me in immediately.

"Pretty neat, huh?" Bob asked, noticing my fascination. "We acquired this piece a few days ago. We're currently trying to track down its provenance, or history if you will."

"It's beautiful. I can't believe someone would actually wear that though."

An intricate pattern of mostly red beads lined the front of the headdress. Attached to the band were dozens of long, silky feathers in an unnatural shade of turquoise. More large feathers and beads hung like tassels in the front. It was no doubt heavy.

"Wear it and wear it proudly they did. These types of headdresses were a sign of bravery and those who wore them were highly respected by the tribe. However, you had to earn the right to wear something this incredible."

"Hmmm," I mused without anything to add or ask.

Bob continued, "Something else of interest. The Native Americans believed by carrying various items within the headdress, the wearer could gain the powers of the animal it belonged to."

"So could the guy who wore this fly?" I knew this question sounded dumb, but I asked it anyway.

Bob's kind eyes smiled before he said, "Maybe he couldn't fly, but quite possibly he was gifted with a special wisdom or gift when in battle. These types of gifts tended to be of a personal nature, kept in secret between the animal and the warrior."

"Hmmm." Speechless again.

My eyes traveled over the various objects in the room, fascinated by each one's uniqueness. Above the fireplace hung an old paddle from a large rowboat. In the center of the room, a gigantic globe stood in an ornate wooden base. And on the wall where we entered, a large tablet sat inside a glass case. It was made of stone, and carved into it was a short man with a flat nose, long curly black hair, and his tongue sticking out of his mouth. He was hardly dressed besides a small piece of cloth over his privates. I laughed.

"That's Bes," Bob said, pointing at the tablet.

I blushed. I thought I appeared as ignorant and uncultured as all the East Texas Bubbas who lived in this town, giggling at this ancient artifact.

"That's most people's reaction," Bob explained, putting my fears quickly to rest. "If you can believe it, he's an Egyptian god."

I couldn't. Most Egyptian gods I'd seen were tall and slender and, well, looked like gods. This guy resembled a troll.

I'm unsure if it was from the herbs in the air or the heat rising from the fire, but I started to feel intoxicated. For a moment my head seemed to swim a few inches higher off my neck. I drew my hand up to touch my cheek just to check. My head sat in the same place I usually kept it, but my skin was hot.

"Bob?" I asked, looking at my host's round face.

"Yes, Roya?"

"Earlier when you were talking about dreams being real, that was just a joke, right?"

Something danced across his eyes as he stared at a far-off wall. Then his attention focused on me. "Maybe it's a joke." Bob wasn't done speaking. I could tell by the way he held his mouth, like he was processing a thought and about to churn it out. "But what if it isn't? What if something in you just has to be unlocked for your dreams to be real?"

He still wasn't done speaking. This pause was for my benefit, so I could process. This was like a philosophical lecture, or how I dreamed they would be when I got to college.

"Roya." Bob woke me from the heat washing over my brain making everything foggy. "What if it has been unlocked in you? What if your dreams are real now…"

I awake from this memory feeling bathed in a delicious warmth. I think about that conversation daily. It's what changed everything. It's what preceded my first dream travel experience.

Instead of trespassing on Bob and Steve's library, I spend the next few hours trolling the beach. Lucky for me and my fair skin, it appears I can't get sunburned while dream traveling. Hunger is also nonexistent, which is good because I don't own any food I can summon and I'm a lousy fisherman.

At one point, as I sit in the sand enjoying its softness on my toes, a little cat settles down next to me. I swear he knows I'm here. His gray and white stripes contrast nicely against the blue of the lake behind him. I don't dare reach out and scratch his head. I've learned my lesson. He's in the physical realm. I'm not.

Chapter Eleven

I soar through the silver tunnels and take three consecutive turns. When I stop I see blackness. My eyes are open but everything's dark. I close and open them repeatedly, wondering where I've landed. A minute later, light streams in from different places and I recognize the coils of the bed over my head. I'm in my bunk. The bracelet is gone.

With a sigh I roll out of bed and stumble off to the bathrooms to shower and wash my clothes. I realize I could throw on the scrubs they issued me and be done with it. But I've made it this long and soon I'll be headed home and I'll want my clothes with me.

Home? Where is that?

By the time my jeans are dry, most of the other kids are rousing from their travels. I wonder what other people chose as their most important object. Something tells me that most people didn't forfeit at the last moment.

I'm combing my hair when the first set of girls comes into the bathroom jabbering about their night.

"I ran out of time, and picked up the first thing I could find," one girl says, embarrassed. "It was this really pretty violin."

"Oh, well, I know what you mean," another girl chimes in. "I felt really rushed too. I pointed to the painting in the corner." She laughs nervously.

"At least you two had time enough to do that," one girl gripes, running a curling iron through her hair. "I had no time at all. By the time I got to my room the hourglass was empty. A bit unfair if you ask me."

The last girl slumps into a mound of desolation. Then she finally admits, "I traveled and traveled, but never found the room."

Everyone sighs with empathy, but their emotions are hollow.

My room didn't have a violin or a painting. What did that mean?

I shrug this off and head down to the main hall. The buffet tables are piled high with an assortment of breakfast foods. I stop at the first table and load up on pineapple, oranges, berries, and melon. I then grab a couple pieces of toast from the next table and head to the back of the room. As I'm sipping a glass of orange juice, a girl from my group approaches my table eyeing the available seats.

"Can I sit with you?" she says, brushing some hair out of her face.

I don't have the heart to tell her no. When I nod, she smiles and then waves to some of her buddies still up at the buffet. Before too long, every seat at my table is taken by someone from the third group. They exchange accounts from the various tasks the day before.

"What message did you receive for the first task?" Trent asks the boy next to him.

The boy shrugs. "I dunno. I made something up."

Trent laughs. "Well, what did you make up?"

The boy turns red. "I said that I heard 'Love thy neighbor.'"

Everyone at the table burst out laughing.

"That's from the Bible," Joseph says.

"Yeah, I knew that," the boy says with a scowl. "It was the only thing I could think of."

"Mine was awfully weird," Joseph says in a consoling type way. "I'm sure I didn't hear it right. It was something about 'Things that build our dreams will in the end slip away.'"

"You definitely didn't get that one right." Samara laughs. "That's a line from a Queen song. Close enough though."

"Yeah," Joseph says honestly. "I passed, but with only a seventy-six percent."

"How'd you know that?" Trent turns to Samara accusingly.

She shrugs. "My mom. She's a music fanatic. She says it's the only thing that transports her." The girl trails off on her last word, looking far away, like trying to remember something long forgotten.

"I wonder who those two were who got a hundred percent," someone says to no one in particular.

I take a couple of bites of my toast and pretend to be engrossed in my fruit.

"It wasn't me," Samara admits. "My message was about how lies travel around the world before the truth can get dressed. I only squeaked by with sixty-five percent."

"How about you, Roya?" Trent asks me.

I spit a piece of my pineapple out with a small cough. "Oh, I didn't do so well."

"Well, did you get a message? What was it?" Trent asks.

I stare at the middle of the table for a second trying to come up with a lie. When nothing comes to mind I say, "I heard something about hope being deferred will make you sick, but when dreams come true, there is happiness." I hope I've screwed up the quote enough to sound believable.

"Yeah, I think that one's from the Bible too," Joseph says.

"What's with you and the Bible, man?" Trent teases.

"Aw, man, I'm sorry. It's just that's how I was raised. I can't help it. I understand it can become kinda annoying though." He smiles and winks in my direction. "I apologize."

Trent throws his napkin at Joseph. "I was raised on rap and Rasta music, but you don't hear me apologizing for it."

Joseph pretends to look offended and then breaks into a sideways smile. "Yeah, well, there's time for that."

We're all laughing when Trey taps the microphone to get our attention.

"I hope I've given everyone the opportunity to eat. I'm about to announce the results." There's a look in Trey's eyes I've never seen there before. He looks worried. "I know you've all come here willingly and offered your time and efforts to determine the right person to face Zhuang. I can't begin to express the pride it gives me to be a part of a society like this. If we didn't, if you weren't here, then I'm afraid of where we'd be headed. Inside the walls of this Institute it's easy to forget what Zhuang is doing to people. It's easy for us to forget why we're here."

He looks across the room, making eye contact with several people before continuing. "I know this feels like a competition, but it isn't a game. These tasks were designed to choose the best person to challenge Zhuang. The forecast states one person in this room, and only one, will be able to defeat this man." He coughs. "He's hardly a man, but that's what I'll call him, although parasite would be a better term."

He pauses, staring into the crowd, lost. "I'm excited and nervous for us to progress to the next stage. The Day of the Duel is almost upon us and now that a challenger has been chosen this all feels surreal."

Trey clears his throat. "Before I announce the results, I'd like to thank everyone. The Institute is forever in your debt. You're welcome here any time, but as a Lucidite you already knew that, or at least you do now."

Trey rubs his hands together and looks out past the crowd. "Now let's get on with this. The person we've chosen to challenge Zhuang on the Day of the Duel is…" Trey takes a long inhale and says, "Misty Templeton."

There's a scream from two tables over. Then an eruption of clapping. The room is torn between talking and applauding as more stirring and movement occurs two tables over. My own table is ambivalent. We clap, but many of the people exchange worried looks. I pretend to smile. I don't know who Misty Templeton is. I don't really care. I want to be done with this whole thing and back in the cozy library at Bob and Steve's. I promised myself that when I got back there I'd wake up early a few times a week and watch the sun rise over the lake. Also, I'd track down that cat and give him some proper attention. *They'll take me in, just the way I'd take in that cat. They have to.*

I'm off in my sunrise and cat fantasies and therefore really confused when Goat Girl jumps on stage shrieking like a hyena going into heat. *What's she doing standing up there? Why is she hugging Trey? What have I missed?* Trey holds up her hand and says, "May I introduce you all to our challenger, Misty Templeton." The girl with the sheet of thin brown hair smiles between fits of tears. She waves to her table as she jumps up and down hysterically. All I think about is the annoying comments I heard her make, the ones that made me want to barf. On the plus side, maybe she'll make Zhuang barf too.

"As you all know," Trey continues when the crowd has regained composure, "we have also chosen six alternates. These people will step in as challenger in case something happens to Misty."

Goat Girl shakes her head in a deliberate manner.

"This group will also assist Misty and the Head Officials as we prepare to take Zhuang down," Trey yells above the crowd's hollers.

At this Misty pumps her fist in the air. I push my plate away instantly queasy. *Just a few more minutes of this and it will all be over*, I console myself.

"I'm about to read the names of the alternates. I'd like them to join Misty here on stage."

Silence falls over the crowd.

"The very first alternate is…" Trey pauses, causing the entire room to go even more still. Then he shoots his turquoise eyes at me and says, "Roya Stark!"

"No!" I hear myself scream hoarsely. My reaction is immediate. I'm in shock and appalled and completely depressed all at once. My table of peers gawk at me, astonished. Their faces are ones of disbelief too. I manage a pained smile.

"I know, Roya," Trey says with a smile. "It's hard to believe, but you're the first alternate. Please come up here when you're ready."

How about never?

I stare at the faces of the people around me for a lifetime. They stare back urging me to get up, to accept the challenge I've been elected for. I wince. I realize I was willing to be the challenger in the beginning, but that was before the lies. And now Goat Girl has been elected and is obviously excited about the challenge. Why waste my time when I'd rather be anywhere else. I stare around at the faces, searching for a way out. When I can't find anyone to offer the consolation I'm looking for, I push the chair out behind me and sluggishly make my way to the stage.

"I know this is quite the shock, but welcome to the stage and thank you for accepting," Trey says, taking my hand in both of his. His grasp is tight, his eyes earnest. I look away as politely as I can, but before I know it he's pulled me in for an unexpected hug.

I've heard people remark about being "beside themselves." Well, I'm in the next room. I never in a million years expected this and now I'm trying to figure out how to get out of it.

"I'll go ahead and read the remaining alternates," Trey says directly to the crowd. "Please join me up on stage when you hear your name. George Anders." There's a round of applause and then a guy about my age emerges from the crowd. He has wavy, blond hair and wide shoulders. He isn't smiling when he walks on the stage. His expression is a mix of pain and frustration, about how I thought I appeared at that exact moment. As he takes the place next to me I can almost feel him vibrating. From the corner of my vision I notice he flinches slightly every so often, as if fighting something internally.

Trey pulls the microphone back to his mouth and reads the next four names much faster. Each of the alternates makes a startled noise when called and then rushes to the stage as everyone claps. When it's all done I'm joined by, in addition to George, the Bible-loving Joseph, a girl from the first group named Whitney, and Samara and Trent. We stand on the stage for what seems like forever while everyone claps, hugs, takes pictures, and then files away. I'm almost free to go when Trey announces that we will be having our first meeting in just a few minutes. "Go and collect your items from your bunks and then you'll meet me in room 222."

I don't have any items and therefore I'm ready for the meeting. I'm ready to be done with this whole thing.

Chapter Twelve

Completely appalled, I start for room 222. I'm seated in a leather chair ten minutes before anyone arrives. Sadly, the first person who shows up isn't someone I want to share my punctuality with. Ren. He sits opposite me, tapping a pen on a pad of paper.

"Terribly troublesome about you not making the top spot and all, right?" he says with an edge of indifference.

I shrug my shoulders, dispelling his indignation. "Honestly, I wish I hadn't been picked at all."

"Oh, is that the way it is?" he retorts with relief. "Good, 'cause I was wondering how long we were keeping up these pretenses."

I give him that look. The one I give people when I wish they'd stop existing. I suddenly wish I had new superpowers, ones that made my looks work.

"I knew from the beginning you weren't going to really be into this whole thing." He smiles with satisfaction. "I told Trey you wouldn't really comply, but he seemed to think you'd give it a go."

If only glares could kill.

"I'm glad to see I was right," he says, toying with his gold ring. "'Cause I was, wasn't I?" Ren's red hair catches the light overhead as he leans forward. "You're here 'cause you've been chosen and all, but you don't want to be. Your heart isn't in it. Now that we're being honest with each other I can say that's what I always thought about you. You don't have the gumption."

He stares at me, smiling wickedly.

"Wow," I say, devoid of emotion. "What gave it away? Oh, how about when I yelled 'no' in front of everyone when my name was called. You don't have to be great at telepathy to know I don't want to be here, so quit pretending you know something secret about me."

Ren's eyes scan mine momentarily. I suddenly feel naked. "You're right, I'm not telepathic. But I'd venture to say I know more about you than you know about yourself."

The urge to jump across the table and scratch Ren's eyes out races through my head. *What's this guy's deal? Why's he always antagonizing me?*

Reeling myself back, I take a deep breath. "Why don't you keep what you *think* you know to yourself, since I don't give a damn."

"Very well." He doesn't look the least bit disturbed by the conversation. "But just to correct you on a tiny, little thing." He pinches his thumb and pointer finger together to indicate he's holding some imaginary small item. "I'm not just speculating. These aren't things I think. I *know* who you are."

We're glaring at each other when Trey walks in the room. "Well, I'm glad to see that you've had a change of heart," Trey says matter-of-factly as he thumps a stack of folders onto the table in front of me. "I was worried about you during the announcements."

I look down at the table and try to pretend Ren isn't present.

"I know this is all unexpected and a lot to digest," Trey continues as he sorts through the folders. "But I think, with time, you'll be committed to this mission, and to the Institute." He throws a folder down in front of me. It's loaded with papers.

"Yeah, maybe." I pull the thick folder toward me.

Ren's eyes bore directly into me. I feel them like a wall pressing against my skin. I fix on the table in front of me and refuse to look up even though an intense pulsing is starting to erupt in my chest. Trey's talking to an alternate who has just arrived. Ren taps his pencil on the table and snickers. I maintain eye contact with the table. My instinct tells me to avoid him and pretend he hasn't flustered me.

Ren's doing something now but I can't tell what it is. My curiosity gets the better of me and I flick my eyes up and immediately know my instinct was right. My attention, my focus, my consciousness is sucked into him like a vacuum. Ren's covering a page on his notepad with cubes. I'm mesmerized by his drawing and can't pull my eyes away as he makes one line, then another, and connects them. For some reason, watching him doodle cubes on paper is the most relaxing thing I've seen in a long time. I hate him, but I don't mind watching him and he doesn't seem to notice or care. Now his paper is completely covered with cubes and I'm even more engrossed as he starts drawing cubes overlapping each other.

"Ren!" a voice snaps beside me. "Why don't you lay off?" Aiden takes the seat next to me, narrowing his eyes at Ren.

"Okay, Doc, just this once." Ren flashes an evil smile. He looks at me and I'm locked on his every move without wanting to be. I watch every chad as it's ripped from the notebook. Ren crushes the paper between his palms into a wad of broken cubes. I can't pull my attention away from the compressed paper as he tosses it into the air and it soars briefly before missing the trashcan.

I shake my head, feeling dazed. The room is almost full by now, but I don't remember the other people showing up, just cubes.

"It's a pleasure seeing you again, Roya," Aiden says, offering his hand to me. I avoid his eyes, feeling sedated, and instead maintain eye contact with the table. He gently wrings my hand. It's warm pressed into mine. Steady, but soft. My heart gives an unexpected shudder.

I attempt to withdraw my hand from his when he clasps my fingers tighter and pulls me in closer. His eyes peer into mine, willing me to look up and into his. "Are you all right?" he asks.

I force my eyes to meet his and feign a smile. "Yeah," I lie. "Just tired." Pulling my hand from his warm grip, I stare off at the ceiling while my head swims in a marsh of penciled cubes.

Aiden gives me a slow nod, concern written on his face. Then he turns to Ren and they exchange rude glares. I avert my eyes from both of them, for different reasons. Determined to get my bearings back, I open my folder and busy myself by leafing through its contents. Inside: a training schedule for the month, FAQs for the Institute, packets of reference materials on a ton of different subjects, and a blank notebook and pencil.

Everyone's gathered for almost ten minutes before Goat Girl decides to grace us with her presence. She breaks into the room holding a phone to her head and looking quite frustrated. When she sees we're all sitting around the table looking directly at her, she lowers the phone and addresses Trey. "There must be something wrong with my phone." She sounds annoyed as she jabs the screen. "I've been trying to make calls and it won't work."

Trey hands her a folder. "No, I'd expect it wouldn't work since you're underground."

The alternates and Goat Girl look around in confusion. A dozen observations click into place in my brain all at once. *Of course we're underground. That makes sense now.* I kept thinking something was missing from the Institute, but I couldn't quite place it. Sunlight. Trey's comment about level five now also makes sense. And the sheer size of this place is much easier to believe if it's underground where it can spread out for miles.

"But I need to let people know I'm the challenger," Goat Girl whines. "How am I supposed to do that?"

Trey points to the only open chair. "You're not. Your friends and family will find out the same as everyone else, through the Lucidite news feed. Now have a seat."

She rolls her eyes, slamming the heavy folder down as she takes her seat.

"Well, now that we're all here," Trey says flatly, "let's go ahead and get started. First of all, I want to congratulate our challenger, Misty. Her performance on most all the tasks was exemplary. We were actually quite impressed that you were able to do so well on such a variety of tasks. Usually people have one or two areas in which they excel, but you appear to be a multifaceted individual."

I itch to wipe Goat Girl's smug look right off her face.

"I'd also like to recognize the extraordinary talent of our alternates," Trey says quickly, glancing at the six of us. "Misty's role in this is quite clear. She will face Zhuang and the fate of…well, the world rests on her performance."

Goat Girl isn't looking so smug anymore. A bit of fear and anxiety has crept into her eyes.

"However, she won't be alone in these efforts. Much of her success will depend on the talents you'll provide. You see, although she'll face Zhuang alone, there are certain things I think you'll be able to do to assist her. Each of you has a special gift or two, and we can use those to level the playing field Zhuang will no doubt have booby-trapped. Specifically, you'll protect and possibly create the dreamscapes where Zhuang and Misty will face off.

"The Day of the Duel, as we're calling it, is in a little over a month. Everyone in this room is critical to that day being victorious for the Lucidites, for the world. You all are a team. From this moment forward you'll train to hone your skills. Misty"—Trey looks directly at her—"you'll mostly train on your own with each of the coaches. Alternates," Trey addresses the rest of us, "you'll mostly train together as a team. The training schedule can be found in your packet."

I open my folder and reference the first page.

"You'll work with Ren for strategy." Trey points at Ren, who smiles on cue. "Shuman for abilities." He holds out his hand presenting her. "And Aiden for weapons and devices." Aiden waves when his name is called. Trey clears his throat and continues, "Today you'll move into your new rooms. You're no longer in shared housing. You've each been assigned a room in the administrative lodging area. After this meeting you'll have a chance to get set up and have lunch. Once you're done with that then you should go directly to Aiden's lab on the fifth level. You'll be choosing your protective charms this afternoon."

Excitement and approval explode around the room, neither coming from me. Trey waits until the enthusiasm dissipates before continuing, "Note on your schedule, training begins tomorrow morning. Please attend all assigned trainings and always be on time." He stops, glaring at Misty who's chewing on her nails and looking bored.

"One last thing before I dismiss you. Dream travel for four of the seven nights each week is your free time. Tonight is one of those nights. I encourage you to use this time to continue to hone this skill, traveling to new and different places. Many of you probably want to return to a familiar locations, but know they may now hold dangers. Zhuang may already know you're on this team, and he could very well set up traps for you in places he knows you like to frequent."

Hmm. I don't like the sound of that.

Trey goes on, "Besides, traveling to new places and times will give you an opportunity to explore and this might prove advantageous for you in the future. And since I mentioned it, for those of you new to the Lucidites and our laws please know that traveling into the future is forbidden, unless approved by the Institute." Trey looks around briefly, scanning each of our faces. "Well, that's all for now. If you'll please follow Shuman, she'll show you to your rooms."

Shuman strolls to the exit and turns, commanding us all to line up in front of her. Misty cuts around Joseph and Trent, taking the first spot. I file into the line, dazed and disoriented. Ren, Trey, and Aiden stay behind looking cautious, like they're waiting for us to leave.

The shock is wearing off and now my mind is buzzing with questions. Does Zhuang still have control of my family? Maybe they've been released now that I'm not the challenger. What will they think of my absence? I don't want to be on this team, but I also don't think I have much of a choice. And I have to admit, I'm curious to learn more about the Lucidites and their Institute.

I'm halfway down the first hallway, following the group, when I realize I left my folder behind.

"Umm, Shuman," I stutter to the ponytail leading the group.

She glances over her shoulder. "What is it?"

"I forgot my folder in the room," I explain.

After a sigh of annoyance she says, "Go on then, go back and get it. You are in room Z, on this level. It is at the far end of this hallway and then through the double doors."

I turn at once and head back to room 222. I'm glad to get away from the group. That guy named George has been stalking right beside me, giving angry sideway glances in my direction. Every time my gaze met his he'd part his lips like he was about to say something. I had the distinct impression I didn't want to hear whatever was about to spill out of his mouth.

The button for 222 is under my fingertips when I hear someone shout from inside the room. Instinctively I hold my breath for a second and listen. It's Ren. No big surprises there. Something tells me he has a bad temper, and it isn't just the stereotype about redheads.

"You bloody well know she's a prat. Why ever did you pick her?! She's going to bodge this whole thing up!" he yells. I picture his face a bright shade of red, like his hair.

"Things like this have a way of working themselves out," Trey says in a calm voice.

"Blimey!" Ren hollers again. "This isn't the time for your Zen bullshit!"

They're talking about me. Ren is trying to turn Trey and Aiden against me. Angry tears jerk in my eyes. I suppress them.

"I know we're all shocked she made it as far as she did." Aiden speaks in a soft voice that surprisingly cuts through me sharply. "Something definitely isn't right about the situation."

My fingers press closely against the button. One more ounce of pressure and the button will release the door. I prepare myself for what I'll say when I charge in and tell the three of them off.

"We all know who should be the real challenger," Ren says.

Silence swallows everything around me—the space, my thoughts, my tenacity.

Chapter Thirteen

I forget about my folder and retrace the path I'd taken with the group minutes before. My mind races over the conversation I just overheard. *Were they talking about me?* If so, then that last statement Ren made doesn't make any sense. They must be talking about Misty. I know I have a distaste for her, but is it possible that everyone else feels the same way? Trey said she'd performed well on almost every task. He said he was surprised by how well she did. Ren asked Trey why he picked her if she wasn't right. Trey had to pick the person who performed the best, even if they weren't likable, right? However, who did they all think should be the real challenger? My mind continues to dissect these questions as I arrive in the lodging corridor.

The door to my room makes a sucking sound when it disappears into the wall and a shush when it closes. It's good to have a private place to think. The room has charcoal carpet and blue fabric rippling across the walls. This softens the space, especially since I'm guessing the walls are the same brushed steel as everywhere else. It's set up like a hotel room with a queen bed in the middle, bedside tables, dresser, and desk. I pull open the closet to find it empty except for some wooden hangers. An abstract painting hangs over the bed. Splatters of blue, gray, black, and white paint cascade together on a canvas, creating an out of control composition.

I throw myself onto the bed and stare at the ceiling, completely exhausted and wishing I could just fall into a blissful state of sleep. My brain is full of questions and curiosities, and I can't figure out where to start to unravel the whole mess. I press my fingers into my eyes.

The silver tunnel closes around me, tighter and tighter, until I'm wearing it as a dress. It's strapless, fits tight, and flares out at the bottom. I turn around to find myself standing in the main hall in the buffet line. Behind me I overhear a girl make a remark that sounds like, "I only eat things that don't make sense."

I whip around, my dress flowing with my movements, and realize the voice belongs to Goat Girl. She has horns and looks embarrassed. "You didn't hear me right. You misunderstood."

"I didn't say anything," I say to her.

"You didn't have to." She looks down at the floor. "I see the way you're judging me."

Samara's by my side now. She's wearing a pink box. "Don't believe everything you hear," she says. Then she looks directly at me and I hear her voice in my mind. "I said you shouldn't believe everything you think."

Trent and Joseph argue at the next table. I hear Joseph yell, "But he died so you could listen to rap music." He then throws down his plate and storms out of the room.

I'm about to run after him when a snake slithers in front of me. I jump back, knocking into someone. He wraps his hand around my shoulder. It's warm and soft. "I'll protect you." I turn and look into Aiden's eyes. For a brief moment they paralyze me. I sink into their blue, like I'm suspended in water.

"None of this matters. None of this matters. None of this matters," I hear someone say over and over again.

Aiden gazes at me, hurt evident at the corners of his eyes. "Why do you keep saying that?"

I thrust a postcard at him. "Because of this."

On the front of the card is a picture of my parents and Shiloh posing on a beach. He flips it over. It reads:

"We're having a great time in paradise. Glad you aren't here."

Someone taps me on the shoulder. I turn and catch Ren in my peripheral right before he punches me in the face. I fall toward the ground, but never find it. I just fall and fall. Then there's knocking. I'm twisted in my dress, getting more and more tangled as I fall. The knocking continues and I scream out of frustration.

I wake up tangled in my bed sheets. Someone's knocking loudly at my door. I fumble with shaking hands to release myself from the covers.

"I'm coming." My voice constricts in my throat as the incessant knocking increases. "Yes?!" I exclaim as the door slides back.

A short gentleman with white sideburns, a hat, and a mustache stands grinning at me. He wears shorts, a T-shirt, and sneakers.

"Courier delivery for a Ms. Stark," he sings, handing me a large box.

Confused, I let him shove it into my arms. "Thanks," I manage, stepping back from the sudden weight of the box.

He tips his hat at me as he trots off. "Anytime."

Why am I getting a package? I heave it into my room and put it on the bed. Confusion tunnels through my thoughts as the dream images bounce around in my head. Then I see the covers in a heap on the floor and instant panic races through me. *Oh, no! I went to sleep. What if I've allowed Zhuang into my dreams?* Bob and Steve had warned me never to fall into an unfocused dreaming state. They'd said this was how to fall prey to Zhuang's hallucination.

I race to the mirror to check my face, wondering if the blow Ren sent me had caused a real mark to appear on my face. Nothing. I scan my arms and legs for any signs of damage, but everything seems fine. The dream, although bizarre, appears to be just a dream. Somehow I'd been able to fall asleep without allowing Zhuang to get into my head.

When my heart stops racing, I edge over to the box and examine it. My name is printed on the top and it's sealed with three pieces of shiny tape. I grab a pen from the desk and use it like a knife to cut along the seam. Once I pull back the large flaps of the box I find an envelope lying on top of a layer of white tissue paper. I slip a thick card out of the envelope. On the front are two birds singing on a tree branch. I open and read:

Dear Roya,

We're proud of you. This has been a crazy last few days, but you've handled them well. Keep doing what you're doing and know you have our support. If things get tough try and remember that your perception is the only thing you control, so change it.

Love,
Bob & Steve

I read through the note three times. Then after a minute I realize I'm holding the card to my chest, like it provides comfort. I set it on the bed and peel the tissue paper off the top of the box. Inside are clothes. Ones intended for me. Clothes with tags still on them. New clothes. A quick burst of laughter escapes my mouth as my hands run over the soft fabrics and my eyes take in the beautiful colors. I imagine this is what Christmas morning feels like when your parents actually buy you something, instead of regifting whatever generic present your father got from the office holiday party.

A small squeal actually escapes my mouth as I unveil seven perfectly folded soft knit T-shirts encased in tissue paper. One for each day of the week. Under them I find three fleece pull-overs and six blouses in beautiful patterns with quarter-length sleeves. The excitement is intoxicating as I turn my attention back to the box. I don't know why these people have lavished me with these gifts, but at the moment I couldn't care less. If they're trying to buy my love and affection then they have it. If they want me to slay a dragon to keep the Lucidites from becoming extinct then I'll do it.

Three pairs of designer jeans are neatly folded under the shirts. Under those, my excited fingers find shorts, pajamas, underwear, sandals and sneakers. Only one thing remains in the box. I reach out and find a soft velvet bag. Christmas morning is almost over, and although I'm grateful and excited for all my presents, I know when the contents of this bag are unveiled it will be over. I pull the draw strings that tightly clench the bag shut. I decide against looking inside, and instead plunge my hand in. It meets a silky fabric, soft like flour. It's light. I can't control my curiosity any longer. I wrench my hand from the bag to find a mound of black and white striped fabric. It's a dress. The stripes are of varying horizontal widths. It's gorgeous and absolutely not my style. I push the dress aside and peer down into the not-yet-empty bag. There's more. A shiny pair of black, open-toed heels.

I put the dress and shoes back in the bag. Then I take my time picking up each of the other garments, holding them up, placing them to my body, before carefully folding them back into neat squares. I've never had my own clothes. The things I wore all my life had been my mother's hand-me-downs. These clothes are brand new, with the tags still on them. I've never worn anything brand new.

I pull off my stiff clothes and tug on a pair of shorts and a striped shirt. I slip on the pair of new sandals. It feels good to finally have shoes.

Smoothing my hair back down I steal a glance at the clock beside the bed. *Shit!* It's after one. I'm late for my first training.

Chapter Fourteen

Without a second thought I bolt down the hallway toward the elevators. Once I arrive on level five I stand frozen. The last time I was down here I'd gotten in trouble. I don't know what room number indicates Aiden's lab. My folder is still upstairs in the meeting room. Tentatively I walk in the opposite direction as last time, thinking it best to avoid the lady in the purple scrubs.

The rooms on this level aren't marked with numbers. They say things like, "Panther room," "Scape's Escapes," "Equipment storage," and "Shhhh." Confusion mounts in my mind as I travel deeper into the passageways of level five. When I'm just about to give up I hear music drumming from the end of the hallway. Curious, I pick up my pace and jog until I find an open door. Beside it a sign reads, "Aiden's lab." I smile.

I poke my head through the door to find Misty, the alternates, and Aiden standing in a circle.

"Come on in," Aiden says, offering me a smile and waving me into the room.

The dream is still fresh in my mind and reverberates through my body, making me instantly look away from him. He has a weird effect on me, one that leaves me breathless.

"Did you get lost?" he asks, handing me my folder. "You left this behind."

"Yeah," I say, my voice winded. "Thanks."

The other alternates give me strange expressions. They're still wearing the green scrubs and T-shirts. I must look a bit out of place in my fresh, clean clothes.

"You missed lunch," Joseph says like he's convicting me of a crime.

"Oh, well, I couldn't make it." I chew on my lip. "I was busy."

Everyone follows Aiden to the back of his lab. Joseph narrows his eyes at me and turns to follow the group.

Aiden's lab is the size of a furniture store. Around the perimeter countertops line the workspace. Computers and pieces of odd-looking equipment are stacked in piles on their surfaces. Black cabinets streak the silver walls above and below the workspace. In one corner is a large mounted TV. It displays geometric shapes which morph in unison with the music pouring out of the speakers. Below it sits an iPod. The center of the lab is mostly open with a table here and there covered in random objects, wires, and food wrappers. In one area a tarp sits on the ground covering up what appears to be a mound of dirt. I lean down to get a closer look when Aiden interrupts me. "We're back here."

He points to a long table maybe fifteen feet in length, covered in a white sheet. Once we're all gathered around the table Aiden begins, "You're about to choose your protective charm. For those of you who don't know, these objects should be worn at all times from this point forward. There's a special force fixed into these items and once it attaches to you it won't work for anyone else. For this reason, don't touch a charm unless that's the one you choose."

Aiden pauses, scanning the group for understanding. "All right, now here's the skinny on protective charms for those of you who didn't receive the Lucidite manual at birth." He winks at me. Without my consent my face blushes. Aiden continues, "There's a special technology we've harnessed and installed into these objects. It protects you from most outside thoughts being embedded into your conscious and subconscious. This is the most important use of these items, although there can be other benefits."

I think back to when I learned about protective charms from Bob and Steve. It seemed like so long ago, but it had only been days. My family was already suffering from hallucinations. They'd been brainwashed and were harsher than normal because of it. Zhuang had tampered with their thoughts, making them believe I was to be feared. Whatever he did was powerful enough that my mother told me she never wanted to see me again. Bob and Steve had explained this much.

"Then how do I know anything is real? How do *you* even know I'm real, or each other for that matter?" I had asked them skeptically.

"You don't," Bob answered at once. "You'll need your very own protective charm. Until you have something that's specifically yours then you must question everything. We"—he motioned to himself and Steve—"are wearing protective shields that currently Zhuang can't penetrate."

Steve stepped forward and pointed to the tiny silver loop in his right earlobe. Behind him, Bob pointed to a thin gold bracelet on his wrist.

"These pieces of jewelry were specifically created for us and they protect us from foreign thoughts being embedded in our memory," Bob said. "You've met some of the others. You probably will remember that they too wear a distinct piece of jewelry. This is their protective charm."

My mind now flashes to Trey's amulet. Then to the gold ring Ren wears.

Aiden claps his hands together, rousing me from my reverie. "All right, without further ado let the protective charm hunt begin. Take as long as you need to explore," Aiden says. "I'll be up front if you have any questions." He pulls the sheet from one end of the table and wads it up in his arms.

Along the table are roughly four dozen objects all calling our attention. Most of the group makes a quick rush for the table. I hang back a minute, and observe the others search for their own charm.

Tentatively I step up to the table. Once I'm closer, the choices are overwhelming. No doubt each of the objects has a luster and draw to it, but there's nothing I see that pulls me in, compelling me to wear it forever.

A gold and black watch with Roman numerals sits on the table eyeing me. Next to it, a small flawless diamond stud. There's a large looped chain with a box locket at the end, a gold beaded necklace, large silver rings, earrings of all types, sizes, and shapes, and so many other choices and options.

Misty is the first person to choose her charm. She grabs it hastily, like she's afraid someone is going to steal it first. "Oh! Look at what I've got," she says, holding up a small ring with a gold band and a row of three pearls. "This will be perfect on me!" Goat Girl exclaims, slipping it on her finger. It hesitates at the knuckle and she pushes a bit before it slides the rest of the way.

I watch as one by one each of the others discovers an object that calls to them. Trent chooses the gold watch. Whitney selects a silver necklace with a heart-shaped charm. Samara picks a pair of silver earrings in the shape of angel wings and Joseph a bracelet made of gold and silver links. George, the guy with the angry eyes, slips a platinum ring with multiple symbols adorning it on his thumb. As each of them makes their choice, everyone else admires their piece. Then they leave the lab looking lighter.

After a few minutes, on my third time around the table, worry edges into my thoughts. I'm alone now and nothing has appealed to me. Scanning the contents I search for something, anything I can picture wearing. I don't have my ears pierced so that takes care of a lot of the women's jewelry. The necklaces are either too long or too short. I keep picturing them getting tangled in my long hair as I sleep. After a long time lost with indecision the music in the room grows louder. It has a compelling beat and an eerie tone.

"Oh," Aiden squeaks. "I didn't realize anyone was still in here." He's carrying a stack of binders, which are dangerously close to slipping from his arms.

"Here, let me help." I take two binders off the top.

He reshuffles the other five in his arms. "Thanks. Mind setting those down over here for me?"

I do and he turns to me, looking curious. The expression in his eyes reminds me again of my dream. My insides squirm with apprehension. "So," Aiden says, "everyone else left ages ago. Not that I mind, but why are you camping out in my lab?"

"I can't find anything." I scrunch up my nose in frustration. "None of the jewelry is my style. I don't want something flashy or dainty or unpractical, you know?"

He nods, an easy grin on his face. "I do."

The beat of the music ramps up and I find myself moving my head to its rhythm. "Who's this?" I point overhead to where the speakers are.

"Black Gold. It's called *Plans and Reverie*," Aiden says. "You like it, huh?"

I nod. "And I don't usually like music."

He arches an eyebrow at me. "Sounds like you do, you just haven't been exposed to the good stuff yet."

"Well, the cave I live in only gets AM radio, so that's a real possibility."

His laughter makes the room feel instantly bigger. "Another good reason to stay here at the Institute."

"Another? Are we making a list now?" I say.

"Yes, it's something I'm putting together in all my spare time. Top ten reasons Roya should remain at the Institute."

I hadn't really thought about what would happen after this whole thing was over. *I'd go home, right?* "I'd love to see the list."

"And you will, when I'm done." His tone hints at something more.

Nervously I press my lips together and turn my attention back to the table riddled with shiny, protective charms.

"Have you considered," Aiden says, "that you shouldn't be trying so hard to find your protective charm? Maybe it's already found you?"

I furrow my brow in confusion.

"Try walking around the table, and instead of thinking about what you don't want in a charm, imagine how the perfect charm will fit and feel." He shrugs. "This may help, because I *know* the right one for you is on that table." Aiden turns on his toes and walks away. Something about him draws me in. His rhythm, his tone, his music. It all calls to me in a way I'm unaccustomed to feeling. I shake this off. *Focus, Roya.*

The music is slower now. I take a step and then close my eyes, trying to imagine a protective charm I'm proud of. Something that fits like a glove. This is a piece I don't mind wearing forever. It's part of me.

My eyes open. I walk roughly five steps and turn toward the table. My mind appears to make the ground falter and then steady under my feet. The table shifts slightly and then unfolds in a perfect order. I know this has to be my imagination.

I think again how my charm will make me feel. I look without focusing, seeing all the objects at once. Slowly my vision narrows until I'm locked on only one item. As I look down my heart quickens when my eyes rest upon *the* bracelet. It isn't like the one in the storage closet in the fifth task. It's the exact same one. How had I not noticed it here? Without a moment of hesitation I pluck it from its spot, feeling the cold metals in my fingers. Where the copper and silver join is seamless. The raised circles on the silver strips are like Braille under my fingertips. The smooth copper, water. Instinctively I know where to find the pin. I push and it opens on a hinge. Just like in the dream I place it on my right wrist and clasp it shut. The cold oozes relief against my skin like ointment on a burn. A pulse of electricity shoots through my arm and radiates down the rest of my body. I shiver. This is my charm and it *has* chosen me.

Aiden is pretending to work at a computer station. His foot taps lightly to the music, a stifled smile edging from his eyes.

"How?" I ask him.

"Hmmm, 'how' indeed." He turns, allowing the grin he's been hiding to unfurl. "How did I know? How was it in the closet in your fifth task? How did it choose you? So many questions to answer." He picks up the folder I've abandoned yet again. "Good thing we'll have time to get to them later." He hands me the folder. "Try holding onto this, would you?"

I purse my lips, but smile despite myself.

When I'm almost to the door he says, "Oh, and Roya."

I turn and look at him. "Yeah?"

"I do hope you won't be too *busy* to join us for dinner."

"Yeah, I'll be there. I'm starving."

Chapter Fifteen

With the music still drumming in my head I cruise back to my room. My protective charm catches the overhead light and shines, showing off its brilliant details.

I return to my room and immediately begin unpacking the box. It's more fun than I imagined pulling out each garment and designating it a spot in my closet. Once I reach the bottom of the box, I realized I missed something the first time around. It's the book Steve assured he'd buy for me. I should have known he'd make good on his promise.

My eyes roam over the clothes filling the closet and suddenly I feel cared about. It's a strange sensation that lifts my chest and creates a gentle pressure in my abdomen. I'm undeserving of such emotion, which brings a tickle to my throat.

It isn't that my parents didn't care about me, though part of me can't refute that at the current moment. Zhuang has taken control of their thoughts and memories and I refuse to blame them for this. The truth is I've never been close to anyone in my family. They subscribed to the lyrics of Randy Travis, and I the prose of Walt Whitman. They spent their weekends racing through the forest on four-wheelers. I usually sped to the opposite end of the woods, away from the squeal of their engines. There I wrote poetry and contemplated espionage on a spirit world I hoped existed between the ether and the moon.

Unsurprisingly we forgot each other existed half the time. Usually I'd return home in the evening to find they thought I'd already gone to bed. Now that I was at the Institute I was relieved of any of the obligatory family ties I put upon myself. I had dream travel to explore the world as I wanted and that was better than any family dinner. However, it would be nice to have someone to enjoy the Eiffel Tower with on occasion. Maybe Bob, Steve, and I could meet there one night?

Now that all the other contenders had gone home I expected the main hall to be mostly empty for dinner. I was wrong. Loads of people in white coats and varying shades of scrubs fork pork chops, pile mashed potatoes, and spoon green beans onto plates. I notice

Amber, the girl who administered my first task. Again she wears a pinched expression, like the air smells bad to her. Over at the bread table, the old lady in the lavender scrubs is having an animate conversation with a small man with wiry, gray hair and glasses. The delivery guy who woke me this afternoon is ladling salad onto his plate. I walk over to him and pick up a tray.

"Hi," I say, staring at a bowl of red cherry tomatoes.

"Not yet, but hopefully later," he laughs as he trots in the opposite direction.

I fill my plate with romaine lettuce, cucumbers, tomatoes, and olives. Another table has assorted pickled foods. I throw some beets, cauliflower, asparagus, chickpeas, and carrots on my plate. Then I stop by the beverage station and make a cup of lemon green tea.

My team sits at a table up front. They see me and wave. I consider pretending I haven't seen them and sitting in the back. Instead I pull up the only available chair next to George.

"Hey," I say to him when he glances at me.

He doesn't say anything, just looks away.

"That is a nice bracelet you chose for your protective charm," Shuman says to me from the other side of the table.

I look at her for a minute to determine if she is being sincere. Something tells me she is or at least faking it well.

"Thanks," I say, taking a sip of my too hot tea.

Fortunately, that's the last word I say during dinner. The rest of the meal everyone else takes turns asking Joseph questions about his experiences growing up on a hog farm. He has a southern charm that even the guys find endearing. I have to admit hearing him describe running outside in his underwear and wrestling a pig that had gotten loose in the middle of the night even makes me laugh. It doesn't even appear that he wants to monopolize the conversation. Yet somehow he senses no one else wants to speak and so he's just trying to be nice.

He tells us that their farm is called Hog Heaven because his mother said they'd own one when pigs flew. Apparently his father had bought the farm the day before as a surprise.

His parents are God-fearing folk who sent him to school once a week with a pound of bacon. He was to "give this to any lost sheep that might be down on their luck and need a bit of goodness to get them through until the good Lord could lift their heart." He didn't know how to tell his parents that sheep didn't much care for pork, but the homeless people by the river thought it was delicious.

Joseph wears an animated expression as he recounts spending his weekends with his siblings. "As the oldest of five, I've pretty much been in charge of their upbringin'," he explains. "We spend most our time catching toads in the river or picking blackberries by the road."

◆

Half an hour later I'm back in my room curled up on my bed in my new fuzzy pajamas. They're periwinkle blue with ruffles on the sleeves. I grab my twice abandoned folder and begin leafing through its contents. The schedule leaves me confused. It says endurance and strength training will start every single day except for Sundays. My brain has a hard time understanding how doing push-ups at seven a.m. is going to help us defeat Zhuang. I sigh in desperation. They'll probably make me run. People always try to make me run.

After the workout we're to train with Shuman in the morning and Ren in the afternoon. I bite my lip in dread. Fortunately, the next day, Friday, I only have to work with Shuman and then spend the rest of the day reviewing weapons and devices with Aiden.

The page after my schedule is a brief history of the Lucidite Institute. Apparently the Institute was originally created by the US government. The CIA initiated research on extrasensory perception, ESP, during WWII. Their scientists soon found a connection to dreaming. The Lucidites were invited to participate. Previously, the Lucidites had been an informal group with no real organization. With US funding and a research mission the group became official. In the 1970s the government grew bored with the research results and pulled out. The Lucidites, now well established, were able to fully take over the Institute. Since that time the group has operated the Institute free of any government control or awareness.

How would the government forget about something they created?

I flip the page over and find no answers to this, but many answers to other questions. It's an FAQs list for the Institute. As I skim the list a question immediately grabs my attention. It reads:

Q: Is it safe to dream freely at the Institute?

A: Yes. The Institute has a powerful protective field that encases all lodging rooms. This shield guards dreamer's consciousness from being invaded by other entities.

That makes sense. The dream I had earlier was just my own stupid subconscious, playing out the day's events and people.

A follow-up question asks:

Q: Is it all right for me to dream freely like this, since it's safe?

A: Yes. Dream traveling, although satisfying, can become taxing. To maintain a balance the consciousness should be allowed to let go for a time period in order to fully rest and recuperate. Furthermore, dreaming gives the subconscious a chance to express itself, which is beneficial if seeking guidance.

I admit it was nice to just fall asleep earlier. I worried I'd been careless and was going to get in trouble. It's a relief to know I actually did something right for a change. I toss the folder on the desk and get ready for bed. I don't really know where I should dream travel tonight. This is the first real free night I've had since I learned I was a Dream Traveler. It's a relief not to have to learn kung fu or meet a psychopath in London. I brush my teeth in the common bathroom and try to think of a place that sounds appealing.

"Nice pajamas, Stark," Joseph says as he rinses his toothbrush and picks up a tube of paste. "So what were you doin' during lunch today?"

"Toldja." Foam rushes out of my mouth.

"And I told you that you're a bad liar."

I hesitate for a minute, feeling weird. Somehow I sense that more lies aren't going to free me from this questioning. "Fell asleep," I mutter and rinse my mouth.

"Oh, well, I guess that's understandable," he says.

I clean the counter where I splashed and gather my toiletries.

"Yeah, this dream travel thing is crazy. I'm not used to it at all," Joseph says, still holding his unused toothbrush. "I can't figure out where I'm goin' tonight."

"Me too," I admit.

"Hey." Joseph sticks his toothbrush in his mouth and starts brushing. "You figure out what your gift is yet?"

I turn and walk out as I say, "Still working on it." Maybe his ability to detect when I lie isn't as good if he isn't looking at me.

Chapter Sixteen

I throw myself with an overabundant force into bed. Pulling up my legs, I push down the covers and get in properly. I already know where I'll dream travel tonight. The idea came to me after talking to Joseph.

I settle my limbs into a comfortable resting position. Then I focus on my breath, the steady filling and emptying of air within me. My consciousness starts to edge away into dreamland. I catch it, like a firefly in a net, and quickly I fill my consciousness with images, ideas, sounds, smells, and everything I've ever heard or known about this type of place. The most recent accounts are the strongest.

The silver tunnel engulfs me. My chest beats with anticipation as adrenaline courses through my veins. I wonder if I'll ever get used to this. Shooting around turns every so often I lose track of time until I'm haphazardly dumped onto a meadow of grass specked with little white flowers. The moon isn't bright now, but provides enough light for me to make out the curvature of a hill and buildings in the distance. I push forward and start in the direction of a big red barn.

A loud animalistic groan catches me. I freeze. Whatever made the noise is close. Angry. Something rakes across the soft earth. An impatient noise echoes from the beast again. It's directly behind me. Straightening my spine, I revolve my chin until it's even with my shoulder and flick my eyes just enough. Sincere dread fills the cavity within me that used to be occupied by oxygen. The largest animal I've ever happened upon stands a few feet away.

Shuffling angrily, the bull greets me with menacing eyes and a revolting odor. With a deliberate force he throws a single hoof to the ground. Immediately the beast lurches forward. Charging. At me. This is a bad dream. The worst dream. Without a single thought for bravery or perseverance I shut my eyes tightly and wish this all away. When I was a kid and having a nightmare this always worked. Usually I'd be transported to another less threatening dream, or I'd awake in my bed sweaty, exhausted. Now I see darkness, although I still smell the mossy earth below me and feel the cool air on my face.

Panicked, I open my eyes to find the bull standing on the opposite side of me, backing up and getting ready to charge again. The huff rips through the night. His hooves tear the ground to pieces. *Did he run right through me? Maybe he missed the first time?* Turning my attention away from the beast, I dash for the fence, afraid to find out if I'm indeed invisible. I clear it in one swift movement as though possessed by a foreign agile force.

My breath hitches in my throat as I hurry in the direction of the barn. Loud noises echo from inside it. Pulling my weight up tight onto my tiptoes I clear the next fifteen feet. Then the thought occurs to me that no one can see me except maybe Zhuang, and if he has then I'm already dead. I walk normally, driven by the curious sounds and movements of shadows cascading from the structure up ahead.

In my fantasy, I'll stroll into this idyllic barn to find farm animals asleep on the hay, looking sweet and happy. I've always romanticized the idea of living on a farm, but never truly been on one. I want to know how it feels, the way it smells, the way the people interact, the way it makes you wholesome.

Stealthily I pull up to the crack along the door and peer through. I don't spy one single animal, but I do see a man. He's large, sitting on a hay bale, and without a doubt completely drunk. The double chins and patches of gray hair on the man's head make him look old, but his overalls contradict this impression. There's also a childish expression on his face.

The man's talking adamantly to a lumpy burlap sack. His slurred words throw spit all around him as he grips the bag and pulls it close to him. "Don't die, Meg, please." Visible tears run down his eyes. "Don't leave me alone, all alone with dat boy. Please! I beg ya! Please just hold on 'nother year, 'nother few!" He pulls his hands off the bag, seemingly swimming up to consciousness for a second, and immediately grabs the bottle beside his leg. "Oh God, why'd you have to take her? Why?!" The man throws back his head and drinks for several seconds. He scans the barn with a disoriented disdain. "Joe." He chops on the word. "Where'd chu run off ta now? I'm gonna find ya and when I do…" The threat hangs angrily in the air. The man stands and staggers for the door where I'm peering. I stand back just as he and his smell flood through the doorway. He's headed toward a tiny house on the main hill, beside an overgrown driveway.

The pathetic farmer heaves beside a tree for a minute. I search for any animals besides the bull that almost ran me over. There doesn't seem to be any. Once the man is upright again he starts for the house. After tripping over the first step he pulls himself up and makes his way inside, leaving the door wide open behind him. I follow.

"Joe! Ya in here, ya good for nothin' piece of lard?!" The man squints around in the dark. He kicks the coffee table and curses angrily. The way this man swears he doesn't fear God, as much as despise him. With a thud he throws himself on the sofa and says, "Joe, ya know dis all your fault. Your momma's dead and it's always been your fault, boy." The man moans loudly like in pain. "You're a curse," he whispers then grows quiet and soon begins snoring.

Once the drunk is out I inspect photos lining the wall. The first is of Joseph and his parents when he was a baby. They're in a church, looking excited with wide smiles and twinkling eyes. The next is of them in front of the church when Joseph was a toddler; his mother wears a forced smile and his father has put on a bit of weight. In the last, they're standing by the river, and Joseph is maybe around six, his mother is skinny and his father sullen as he stares in the distance. Joseph smiles broadly in all the photos.

There aren't any other pictures. No pictures of siblings or prized pigs. The house is unkempt, disgusting. This isn't what I had in mind when I wished to visit a farm. I close my eyes and try to shut out the loud snores of the drunken man. My focus remains tight on the Eiffel Tower. That's where I want to go now. I'll go back there with Bob and Steve later, but for now I need some place great to take me away from this horrible mess.

Chapter Seventeen

My morning alarm rips me from my Parisian exploits. I spent the night exploring L'Avenue des Champs Elysées. I'd wandered until I stood at the top of the Eiffel Tower staring down at Paris. I wished to be one of its simple citizens, unaffected by dream traveling and crazy villains. Now my reality is telling me I have twenty minutes until I need to start endurance and strength training and the whole night seems like a sad joke.

My muscles don't respond properly as the training commences. I fear they never will. The trainer, Mario, explains that being in excellent physical shape is critical to maintaining balance among the three parts: mind, body, and spirit. He graces us with this information after we've run three miles and have two left. I never made it to the goal so I'm a bit out of balance the rest of the day. The only redeeming part is Goat Girl passed out after only two miles.

I take a long shower and grab a protein bar and a bottle of juice from the main hall before ducking into my room. I can't stomach one of Joseph's stories about his fake family. I have no idea why he's a compulsive liar bent on pointing the finger at me, but I don't really feel like figuring it out right now either.

♦

Shuman takes three large strides into the lecture hall, pivots, and stands in the middle of the platform. Commanding. Her black hair glistens under the bright lights. "Most of you miss a lot," she says, aiming an accusing finger at us. Cracking her knuckles she turns to Whitney. "Be really quiet and listen. Can you hear anything?"

Whitney, the girl with brown, curly pigtails, shakes her head. "No."

Shuman looks disappointed. "That is because you are not listening." She walks to the next desk where Trent sits. "How about you, can you hear anything?"

He stares for a second then shakes his head.

Shuman points out into the distance. "Out there, a ton of information is trying to get in here." She points to her head. "You have to be open to it, or otherwise it will hit the walls of your brain and land on the floor, completely useless. You cannot do anything with it there. In order for the information you receive to make sense to you, the mind must retrieve it and deliver it to spirit. This is where the magic happens."

She taps the top of Goat Girl's desk, startling her from a daze. Unfortunately, she's supposed to train all day with us. "You scored a hundred percent on the first task. How?"

Misty looks surprised. "I-I-I guess I allowed my spirit to retrieve the m-m-message," she stutters.

Shuman narrows her eyes skeptically. "I will consider that."

Her dark amethyst eyes find mine. "And you, Roya, also scored a hundred on the first task. How?"

There are startled noises at my back. All eyes hone in on me. I sense them. Trying to block them out, I recall the first task. "Well, I concentrated. Specifically, I focused and tried to relax. I pictured a telephone in my mind. I knew you were able to call on it and I waited until I received the message." I maintain eye contact with Shuman, although it's uncomfortable. Finally I shrug. "That's all."

She holds out her hand flat at me and turns to the group. "You must remain open and focused." Shuman steps back onto the middle of the platform, her commanding presence once again reinstated. "Today we will practice this openness and focus. Come and lie down here on the ground."

No one moves. We just stare.

"Now!" she orders. Everyone clambers to find a place on the platform. The floor is cold and hard on my sore body. I readjust several times to find a comfortable position.

"Why don't you watch it," George fires at me. "You just kicked me in the head."

"Sorry," I apologize, embarrassed. *Did everyone in this Institute lose their meds? Why are people so crabby?*

"Can we get a pillow or something?" Goat Girl whimpers from across the room. "This floor really hurts my head."

"Consider it good practice." Annoyance is evident in Shuman's tone. "You will rarely meditate in a comfortable location."

Goat Girl grumbles something under her breath.

"Let us take a page out of Roya's book," Shuman begins. "Visualization is an important way to receive information if you know what you're looking for. Later we will discuss methods for obtaining information from the unknown. Everyone close your eyes and concentrate on your breath."

For the next hour we're guided through a meditation. First we work our way from our toes all the way to the crown of our head, releasing tension from every single muscle and organ until we're completely relaxed. Shuman has us visualize several locations, always paying special attention to details. She explains that the more we focus on specific details the more in tune we become to the message being delivered. "If you only see the sunrise or a landscape in your visualization, then you will only receive broad pieces of information. If instead, you see the blades of grass and the grains of sand in that landscape, then you will receive a volume of information equally accurate to your level of detail."

I've always been drawn to meditation and visualization. It's something I did naturally as a kid. However, when Shuman speaks of it, or anything for that matter, my head becomes fuzzy and I find myself somewhat disinterested. I think it's her airy tone that lulls me into a confusing comatose state.

"Tomorrow, same place and time," she says as I stand stiffly. "We will go over abilities."

♦

The hostile vibes assault me as soon as I settle at the lunch table with my usual assortment of rabbit food. Samara, who's been friendly to me since the beginning, looks down in disapproval. Trent follows suit by shaking his head with irritation before returning to his mashed potatoes. Joseph stares, watching me; I shrug in confusion. He continues to stare and then looks down blankly at his food. George sits with the white coats. Aiden also sits with them, animatedly telling stories. I ram my fork into a cherry tomato causing juice to squirt all over my clothes. Glad to have an excuse, I get up and dismiss myself from the table.

I can't begin to understand why everyone's mad at me. True, I haven't really formed any relationships with these people, but I also haven't spent enough time with them to give anyone a cause to hate me. It seems like there's an epidemic of "hate Roya disease" spreading quickly. Maybe this is overdue. I spent my life distancing myself from people. It was only a matter of time before they started treating *me* poorly. However, being treated with indifference is one thing; disdain is quite another.

I throw my stained shirt into the laundry basket and pull on a new one. The clothes I'd taken off yesterday are already clean and hung in my closet. My bed is made and someone has tidied my room while I was gone. I could get used to this.

♦

I consider pretending to be sick so I don't have to train with Ren. Alas I decide against it and find myself the first one seated in the lecture hall. *Damn my rigid nature.* I have this affliction for being overly punctual. Considering that most everyone on the team hates me, I probably should consider showing up a little later from now on. At least that would prevent me from sitting in an uncomfortable silence while people shoot me dirty looks. I keep my head down and my attention locked on my desk while everyone trickles into the room.

From my peripheral I spy Ren, who suddenly appears in the middle of the room. He stands nonchalantly in a blue shirt with a shiny black blazer draped over it. His look of superiority ingests the room as he calls every eye to him.

He smirks, pointing at George. "Tell me, how did I enter this room?"

Looking startled but determined George says, "From the back, sir."

"Wrong," Ren rings out like a buzzer. Then he points at Goat Girl. "Next."

She shrugs, looking around the room with uncertainty. "I dunno, you came in through that door." She points to the front of the room.

"Wrong," Ren yells again. "You." He points at me.

"I don't know," I say flatly. "I wasn't paying attention."

"Typical," Ren says before turning to Joseph. "Next."

Joseph gives a sideways smile. "You and I walked in together just now."

"Nice try," Ren says and then smiles wickedly. "Wrong!"

Taking center stage Ren says, "Seven seemingly intelligent people and no one can tell me exactly how I entered this room. Why?! Is it because you really are a bunch of gits? Or is it because I tricked you? Before you decide the answer is the latter, please know both options could be correct." His smugness is tangible as he pulls up a stool and sits on it.

"Everything, and I do mean everything, can be an illusion." Suddenly there's no stool. Ren's standing like before. I close my eyes and reopen them trying to focus. There isn't even a stool on the stage or anywhere in the classroom. I shake my head. *Why did I just think Ren had sat down?* Looking around I realize everyone else is disoriented as well.

"Don't trust what you see! Question everything!" Then he's gone. Literally he vanishes right before our eyes. The door at the back slides open and Ren strides into the room wearing black slacks and a white shirt. "The answer to the question is I never entered the room—not until just now." We all look at each other, confused. Ren cackles

"Everything can be an illusion. We're all choosing a reality. Each reality can be different depending on the observer. For my little trick, you all were the observers. Some of you were worse than others." Ren scowls at me.

"Most of you do just that, you observe, which gives illusionists the opportunity to implant projections into this 'said' reality. This type of trickery, which you've just observed, is extremely difficult to manipulate in physical form. That means don't try what you just witnessed at home, boys and girls, 'cause you'll fail. Leave manipulating physical realities to the experts." He smiles, placing his hand on his chest. "That would be me."

"My job, and it will be arduous, is to teach you buggers how to use and spot these projections in a dreamscape. It's much easier in that reality because nothing is fixed." Ren looks annoyed. "What, Samara?"

Her hand is raised. "But I'm wearing my charm, wasn't that supposed to protect me from this kind of thing?"

Ren mocks her in a high-pitched squeal. "I'm wearing my charm, wasn't that supposed to protect me?" He pauses, probably for effect because I sense he likes the drama. "NO! Your little charm prevents thoughts and memories from being placed in your brain or, as is usually the case, erased. However, currently there's no technology that prevents you from witnessing an illusion. Herein lies the difference. When a thought is placed into your brain you have no choice but to accept it. When you witness a projection, if you're a keen observer and question it, then you have the option of rejecting it as a false reality.

"You see, even being a fantastic illusionist, as I happen to be, there's always a flaw. No one can create a projection without one. It's a built-in failsafe. God thinks of everything. If you had really been observing, and questioning, then you would have noticed that the first Ren was shorter than me, not wearing his protective charm, and his eyes aren't quite the same shade of green as mine. No projection is a hundred percent! That's the only way you have in physical form or a dreamscape to determine what's real. If you aren't paying attention then you'll be deceived by an evil projection and that will be right before Zhuang kills you!"

Joseph holds up his hand. "Real quick," he says nonchalantly. "How'd you do that?"

Ren isn't smiling. "If ever I think one of you is capable of doing anything remotely close, then I'll share some pointers. As it appears, though, I'll be taking that to my grave."

We spend the rest of the lesson learning ways to spot common flaws in projections. Ren explains how we tear down a projection when either in physical or dream form. This is the first time I've taken notes. I don't want to admit it, but everything Ren says seems incredibly valuable. I'm glad I decided not to blow off the session.

When we're dismissed I gather my stuff and leave before anyone else. Most people are chatting when I charge past. Trent and Samara roll their eyes as I exit. I head straight for the main hall, intent on grabbing dinner and leaving before anyone arrives.

◆

Two hours later, I'm leafing through the book Steve sent when a knock sounds at the door. I hit the button and the door slides open.

I halfway expect to see the delivery guy bringing another package. Instead Joseph strides uninvited into my room, tosses himself onto my neatly made bed, and makes himself comfortable.

"Excuse me?!" I gawk slapping the button to close my door.

"So, what's your reason for skippin' a meal this time?" He has the stress ball they gave us the first day. He throws it high above his head, watching it spin, and then catches it in his outstretched hand.

"I didn't feel like it." I breathe between clenched teeth. "Do you mind?" I pull my book out from underneath his back. Some of the pages are now bent.

"Would your not feeling like it have anything to do with the cold shoulder Trent and Samara have been giving you all day?" He catches the ball just as it falls toward his face.

"Maybe." I throw my book onto the desk.

"Well, you understand their distrust, I'm sure."

I stare at him, bewildered.

The ball pauses in his hand as he stares at me. "Oh, you are thick." Joseph laughs. "They don't know when you lie, like I do. They were pretty peeved to find out you'd lied about doing poorly on the first task. Imagine their shock when Shuman tells us you scored a hundred percent." He rolls over on his stomach and sits up on his elbows. "Why did you lie 'bout that?"

I sit at the desk, looking off at nothing in particular. I shrug. "I don't know."

"K," is all he says before rolling back over, throwing the ball high into the air again.

"Did *you* know I lied about the first task?" I ask.

"Oh yeah." Joseph waves a dismissive hand at me. "But I didn't know you had a perfect score. If that was me I'd have announced it to the whole table."

"I bet you would have."

He smirks and nods.

"So what about George? What's his deal?" I ask, resting my head on the desk in front of me.

"Beats me. Is he mad at you too?" He whistles through his teeth. "Man, Stark, you really rub people wrong, don't cha?"

"Yeah, it's kind of my thing." I raise my head and ask, "Can you tell when everyone lies? Is that your talent?"

"Nah, not everyone." He throws the ball at me.

I reach out for it before it's even left his hand. Joseph stares for a few seconds in surprise and then stands. "You need that stress ball, so use it," he says and then lets out an exaggerated sigh. I ignore him as I crush the ball between my fingers. He taps the button, sending the door sliding back into the wall. "See if you can be a bit more sociable tomorrow. It'd do you good."

I hurl the ball at the door just after it closes. A part of me wishes I told Joseph I knew he was lying about his family to make him feel exposed and lousy. I didn't, though, because I knew it wouldn't make me feel better.

Shrugging off my frustration I pull out a piece of paper. I address a letter to Bob and Steve. First I thank them for sending me the package. I roughly tell them what's happened so far: being chosen as first alternate, the bracelet, how much Ren makes my life miserable, and how I just want the whole thing to be over. I'm uncertain why I'm writing this letter, or giving them so much information, but it makes me feel lighter. I fold it up, put their name and address on the outside, and stick it in my notebook. There has to be a way to get it to them, I reason. If they can send me something why couldn't I send them something back?

Picking up the card they sent me I, reread it for the tenth time or more. The questions that plagued me all along rise to the surface, wanting to be stoked like a burgeoning fire. The night I'd come to the Institute, one reason above the rest propelled me here: I wanted to know where I belonged. This uncertainty is a constant dull ache in my chest. And to add insult to injury I have agonizing guilt. I want to care about my mother, father, and brother. But I don't. That's pathetic. What kind of person doesn't care about their family, at least enough to let it monopolize a small fraction of their thoughts? They could be dead right now, and for some reason that doesn't affect me. It's like they're someone else's family, like I heard about it on the news. It's sad, but I'm removed.

Maybe it's because I've always been different. But then the questions remain: Why? Why am I different? Why do I feel that difference coursing through my veins? Why don't I feel I belong in that house with my family? Opening up the letter from Bob and Steve, I reread it, feeling sad and far away from the possibility of a home.

Before I wallow around in any more of this pity, I shake it off and crawl into bed. I'm a loner. I've always been one. Now isn't the time to be weakened by questions and uncertainties. The sooner I accept this, the sooner I move forward and embrace my potential.

Chapter Eighteen

The workout the next morning is harder than before due to the soreness of my fatigued muscles. I grit my teeth through every exercise and pray it will be over soon. After an hour my prayers are answered and I shower and head off to breakfast.

I sit down at the table with my oatmeal and fruit, ignoring Trent and Samara. Luckily, they're both talking to Shuman about that day's lesson plan. Whitney smiles at me, her kind eyes glittering. Thankfully she isn't angry at me. She doesn't look like anything could make her angry. Her face is one of peace and her eyes sympathetic and gentle. I've liked her from the start.

My mind reels with a sudden flash and I push back from the table. It's quick, but shows a distinct image of me handing a note to someone. Instinctively, I stand and scan the room. Seconds later I stride over to the person who matches the image I saw in my mind. I pull out the note I wrote last night.

"Excuse me," I say to the courier guy in the hat and sneakers.

The delivery guy turns, holding a plate of eggs and bacon.

"Name's Patrick, sweetheart," he says, his white mustache covering his expression.

"You can take letters, can't you," I say in more of a confirmation, rather than a question.

"Yep," he confirms.

"And deliver them?" I ask to be sure.

"Of course." He holds out his free hand.

I lay the note in Patrick's outstretched hand, just as I'd seen moment's ago in my mind's eye. He tucks it in his pocket and then turns back to the buffet.

◆

"Each of you," Shuman begins in her airy tone, "is here because you performed well on the tasks. You are also here because you have a unique ability. However, these abilities have not been honed. You do not know how to control them. Maybe sometimes you do, but mostly you are surprised when they occur, as if by chance. I will be working to help you enhance these abilities. If you are going to contribute these skills to creating a dreamscape that will help Misty defeat Zhuang, then you must gain control over them first."

This isn't the first time I have absolutely no clue what Shuman is talking about. *Is she referring to the gifts that Joseph mentioned?*

"Most of you have trouble channeling these abilities because not only are you hiding them from yourself," she says, crossing her arms across her leather vest, "but also from everyone else." The snake tattoo on her arm catches my eye as she speaks, seemingly coming alive for an instant, flicking its tongue in my direction. "You must embrace these abilities. Be proud of them." She spreads her arms like wings. "This is your tribe. You are safe to explore these abilities here. From this moment forward, be honest with yourself. Do not run from it. And be honest with your tribe." She pauses. "Agreed?" she says with finality.

We all nod our heads in unison.

"Good. When I point to you, name or describe your ability." She points first to Whitney on the far side of the room. Whitney flushes red. "I can, um, heal. If I touch something I can repair it." She looks down doubtful. "Sometimes."

Without a word, Shuman points at Trent. Pride oozes from his voice as he says, "I'm telekinetic. I move objects without touching them."

Shuman revolves her finger on George. His shoulders slump an inch further as he brings his eyes up. Struggle coats his expression like tattered leather gloves on a hand. "I'm empathic. I feel people's emotions, without them telling me. At least, I used to…" Something simmers under the surface of his words, making them sound hot. Angry.

Shuman points at Joseph. "I talk to spirits," he says with a slight snigger.

Lowering her hand, Shuman gives him a piercing stare.

Finally Joseph waves his hands as if surrendering. "All right, that's not quite true." There's a pause and then looking at no one he says, "I see the future."

Taking a step, Shuman moves in front of Samara and points. Without needing to be prompted the girl with whitish blonde hair and gray eyes says, "I read thoughts. I'm telepathic."

A second later the finger is aimed at me. Everyone's eyes are fixed in my direction.

I rack my brain, searching through the layers. *What had Ren called it?* Didn't he have a name? My mind trails back and hooks into that moment in the past. A second later I look into Shuman's dark eyes and say, "I'm clairvoyant."

"Good." Shuman withdraws to the center of the platform. "Now let us open up this council so we can better understand each other. Whitney, go to the back right corner of the room. Samara, stay where you are. George, you to the back left corner. Now Trent, Roya, and Joseph pair up with one of these three. You each have two minutes to ask each other questions regarding your ability. Answer the other person's questions honestly. More importantly, as you speak, own your ability. Be proud of it. After four minutes we will rotate until everyone has been paired up. Go now."

Trent heads straight back to Whitney. Joseph is already turned around talking to Samara. This leaves me staring nervously at George and his defeated attitude. I walk back to where he sits and notice he's shredding a piece of paper in his hand, first in half, then again, then again. For a moment I just watch, feeling his tension.

"So," I say, taking the seat next to him. "You want to go first?"

"No," he answers without looking up.

"Fine." I look at the ground for a few seconds. "Have you, uh…" I search for a question. "Have you always been able to read emotions?"

"Yes." His hostility is palpable, like an angry stallion thundering across the ground, threatening to charge.

We sit in silence for the rest of the time. He doesn't say another word. When Shuman says, "Rotate," I find immense relief. Those were the longest four minutes of my life.

♦

Whitney reminds me of a doll, with her tiny frame, curly brown pigtails, and enormous eyes. After sitting with George she's like cool, spring water for a parched throat. Openly, she explains that she's mostly used her powers of healing on animals, bugs, and sometimes herself. There was one time her little sister had a high fever and wouldn't awake from a comatose state. She used it then, but wasn't sure if that's why her sister recovered. I'm immediately fascinated by her gift. The idea that this seemingly innocent girl holds one of the most important powers to all of mankind is exhilarating. Curiosity, a trait I'm not prone to, fills me with question upon question until Shuman tells us it's time to rotate. Whitney frowns, sincerely remorseful. "I'm sorry, I didn't ask you any questions."

"I'm not," I say.

◆

I'm worried Trent will be hostile much like George, but he isn't. He opens up right away, talking eagerly about his ability. In comparison to Whitney, he's confident.

Although complete concentration is necessary for his telekinesis to work, he's had dozens of successes moving objects as large as a shoebox.

When we have less than a minute left he asks how often I "know" things.

"More frequently lately," I answer honestly.

"I wonder why," Trent muses, pushing a dreadlock behind his ear.

"I don't."

"Why?" he asks, looking at me curiously.

I shrug. "Just doesn't seem important."

◆

As soon as I sit with Samara I bombard her with questions. "Can you read people's thoughts without them knowing? Do you? Do they know?"

She laughs. "Why is everyone so paranoid? What all do you have to hide?"

I stare at her and she stares back. Finally she says, "I can read thoughts without the other person's consent, but I'm also traceable. People usually know when I'm there. Can feel me somehow."

"Well, that's kind of a relief," I say.

"What about you?" she asks, braiding a piece of her hair. "What kind of stuff do you see?"

"Mostly stupid stuff," I say without enthusiasm. I tell her about that morning with the letter.

"That seems pretty helpful," she says.

"Back to you," I urge. "Have you read my mind at all?"

"No," she states at once.

I'm relieved and offended at the same time. Thank God she hasn't read my thoughts. And why the hell not? What's so wrong with me that she doesn't want to know my internal dialogue?

"It's draining to read thoughts," she says finally. "I have to be choosy."

I watch her cautious gray eyes scan the room before they return to mine. "Besides, I make it a habit to stay out of the heads of my friends."

◆

"It seems Trent and Samara have forgiven me for my injustices," I say.

"That's good, but I don't think that's what we're meant to discuss here," Joseph states.

"Just thought I'd pass it along."

"I'm sure you did. So I guess you figured out your gift," Joseph says, an edge to his voice.

"Yeah, and I guess you did too," I remark dully. "Were you lying about it the whole time?"

He shrugs in a noncommittal fashion. "Were you?" Joseph asks.

I don't respond. We're even. Best we start fresh. "How does it work for you?" I ask.

"I see things in the distant future. Nothing immediate. I'll see a flash of somethin' and know it'll happen in one, two, or five years. And it does."

"Wow," I say, meaning it.

"You?" He looks nervous. It isn't an expression he wears often.

"I usually see things that are about to happen, like within the next few seconds. It's always something stupid like a leaf falling off a tree right before it does."

"I'm gonna need you to repeat that and this time show more pride."

108

I glare at him.

"Shuman said."

Thankfully Shuman interrupts just then to tell us time is up.

"See ya." I flash a mischievous smile at Joseph as I stand.

"From here on out," Shuman says, "we will be honing these abilities, making them stronger, more reliable. We are going to make them what they should be: super powers."

Silence settles in the room, and I think everyone else is doing the same thing I'm doing: trying on this newfound pride and enjoying the way it fits.

"You are dismissed for today." Shuman stands, stoically staring at us. After a few more quiet seconds we all shuffle our belongings and move toward the exit.

"George." Shuman's voice interrupts the chatter that has begun to build among the group as we leave. "Stay behind. I need to speak with you."

Chapter Nineteen

Thankfully, after that we don't see George for the rest of the day. He's been a real drag and I'm glad to be rid of him. Without his presence the mood at lunch is light and fun. It's like a window has been opened, although that would have literally been impossible. While Joseph tries to get Trent to telekinetically throw a salt shaker at one of the white coats, Samara and I probe Whitney for more information about her ability. At first she's shy, but after a while she eats up the attention, like a baby with her first birthday cake.

Goat Girl isn't at lunch, and that's probably another reason it's so pleasant. We're told we won't see her that much from this point forward outside of morning workouts. Now if I could just get rid of Ren my world will improve drastically.

♦

A ton of equipment clutters up a large corner of Aiden's lab, making the space feel cramped.

"Welcome everyone," Aiden says, walking over carrying a small handheld device. "You all will remember the GAD-C, from your first few moments at the Institute." He holds out his hand, presenting all the large equipment jumbled around a bunch of wires and computers. "This is the second one we have here at the Institute and it's brand spanking new. I just built it." He slaps the side of a metal box and something sounds like it falls and breaks inside. With a guilty smile he waves it off. "No worries, that thing isn't really an important part of the GAD-C. Anyway, you'll remember this is how we generate your body from a dream layer. This large device is super helpful. For instance, let's say you decide to dream travel to France. Like so many, you fall in love with the French culture and decide you want to live there and eat croissants for the rest of your days. Airfare is costly and your consciousness is already there, you just need your body. Believe me, you're going to need your body to enjoy all those pastries. So what do you do? You go and find one of these handy dandy GAD-Cs in order to bring your body all the way to France. *Comprende?*"

Samara and Whitney giggle. Aiden looks pleased. Apparently his goal is to entertain, as well as educate.

"Okay, and on a serious note, while trying to fight Zhuang you might need to generate your body at some point. We aren't sure what the dreamscapes are going to look like, or the strategy for that matter. The point of today's lesson is to orient you with the idea of autogenerating your body, which takes some getting used to. We're going to practice this until you're comfortable with it and the shock wears off, which will probably take several turns. Also, I won't be there to operate the machine for you so you're going to need to know the proper procedure."

Samara holds up her hand. "The other GAD-Cs, how will we find them?"

"It all depends on the dreamscapes," Aiden explains. "If we know where you'll need them then we'll make arrangements. Otherwise, there are roughly half a dozen located throughout the world. You'll be given these locations and can travel to them to generate."

A spark shoots from a cluster of wires next to the GAD-C. Aiden eyes it nervously. When it dies out he says, "It's supposed to do that." Then he rubs his hands together eagerly. "So who's first?"

I don't volunteer. Neither does anyone else. It doesn't matter because when everyone's silent for too long Aiden points at me. "Oh, Roya, that's so nice of you. You're so brave."

I shoot him an angry grin.

"All right, here's what you're going to do: Dream travel to the room you arrived in the first night. You remember, the one where you almost died." There are several chuckles from my peers, which ignite a brilliant smile on Aiden's face. "There will be a GAD-C in that room. You'll then meet my lovely assistant, Amber. She will help you operate the GAD-C. Once you've obtained your body, I want you to dream travel back to this room and we'll test this ol' boy." Aiden points his fingers like a gun at the contraption. "Got it?" he asks with a smile.

I don't have the heart to say no, so I nod. With an arm around my shoulder, he steers me to the back of his lab.

"Do you usually *have* to volunteer people to get them to test your new equipment?" I ask him.

He gives me a look of mock offense. "I gave you the *honor* of going first."

"Well, I really don't want to take that privilege away from someone more deserving. Maybe we should go back and draw straws," I say, feeling rather giddy.

Aiden shakes his head. "We can if you want to, but you'll lose the opportunity at bragging rights."

"Oh, is that what's at stake?" I say with a laugh.

We exchange looks. The breathlessness that accompanies all of my interactions with Aiden intensifies. I quickly glance away.

"In all seriousness, are you ready to do this?" Aiden ask, tethering his excitement under his sensibility.

"Of course," I lie, caught up in his enthusiasm.

His excitement takes center stage again. "Fantastic! You'll be stellar!" We stop by a cot. "You don't have to lie down to dream travel, but until you've done it for a while, it's the safest way."

Lying down on a soft mat on the cot, I stare at Aiden nervously. He's grinning. *Is he always grinning? Is he one of those naturally happy people?*

When I'm comfortable, his grin fades from his lips and resurfaces in his eyes where it shines brighter. "You'll do great! I'll be waiting when you return." He turns and I watch him walk away, missing the expression in his eyes immediately. Closing my lids I refocus and within seconds I whirl through a tunnel, hopefully headed for the room four levels up.

When I arrive I expect a rush to generate my body. Amber, Aiden's "lovely assistant," explains that isn't necessary this time because my body isn't hanging out at the bottom of a lake, but rather resting comfortably on the cot in Aiden's lab. Then something odd occurs to me.

"How can you see me? How can you hear me? I'm dream traveling and you aren't, right?" I ask, confused.

Amber gives a knowing look. She's tall and willowy, making me feel like a child as I stand beside her. "You're correct, I'm not dream traveling. An exceptional technology allows us to interact. It's a screen on the GAD-Cs Aiden has built. Most GAD-Cs can't do this, but he invented a device that enables it on the ones in the

Institute. This is crucial because otherwise how would we know when to operate the machine to generate people's bodies? It really is amazing technology and on its own could be quite an incredible device." Remorse or maybe envy dances in her eyes briefly. She refocuses on me. "Well, you ready to do this?"

"Yes," I say.

She instructs me on the procedure for operating the machine to generate my body from its current position to where my consciousness is located. It consists of pushing a series of buttons, checking a few readings, and aligning some dials. Although it's scientific, it seems easy.

"If you misread something and make any misalignments then the results could be disastrous." Her pinched nose draws up a bit into the air cautiously.

This gets my attention and I have her run me through the process three more times. When I'm confident I take the measurements, align the dials, lie down on the table inside the blue lights, and tug the button attached to the long wire beside me. I press the button and the magic happens. Since I'm not drowning, the experience is way less intense. It still burns and there's definitely a jolt and a shock that occurs when consciousness rejoins with my body. The weirdest part is when I take the first breath. I hadn't noticed it the first time, because my lungs had been aching. This time I observe my breath move in reverse. Just as I breathe in I forget how and expect the air to breathe me. I inhale and my lungs are somehow outside myself. This has to be more of a mind game than anything and now I understand why Aiden wants us to practice this.

Once I'm stable, Amber tells me to relax and dream travel back to Aiden's lab. This is the part that makes me nervous. After I dream travel to Aiden's lab then I'll have to generate my body using the brand new, untested GAD-C, which seemingly has some bugs. What if it doesn't work? What if it deforms my body in the process?

Since I know I don't have a choice, I try to push these thoughts out of my mind and think of something to bolster my confidence. Before closing my eyes I tell myself I can trust Aiden and his device. That doesn't work. I tell myself, *if you can't trust the Head Scientist for the Institute, who can you trust?* That doesn't work either. I remind myself that this man built a machine that sees pure consciousness. This also has no real effect.

Truth be told, in the end it all comes down to odds. Aiden saved my life once. I don't think he'd make me a guinea pig for this experiment just to kill me off. He has a reputation to protect and from everything I've discerned he's gained this super scientist reputation by being incredibly competent. Logic is what tells me to trust him, and so I do. I close my eyes, feeling the fear subside, and focus on his lab. I hear the music, see the messy piles of gadgets, the posters covering the walls, and then I see him. Seconds later I push through the tunnel and then quite suddenly I stand in the lab next to the GAD-C.

Aiden's leaning against a nearby wall eyeing me with a clever smile. "Glad you could join us, Ms. Stark. I must say that was awful fast."

My body is hot and cold at the same time, although I know I don't really have a body at this point. Still I look down, wondering if I'm wearing clothes or if they've stayed behind waiting to be generated. Thankfully it isn't like one of those strange dreams.

"Now," Aiden continues, "if you wouldn't mind, please demonstrate to the spectators exactly how to generate your body."

I hit exactly six buttons. Take readings on thirteen different instruments. Align three dials. Lie down. Hit one button. And then there's a stall, like a car engine gives before it decides to turn over. It ambles on until I gasp and realize it's oxygen I'm pulling into my lungs. It's worked. I'm here, in body form—sweating, excited, and relieved.

"And that's how it's done," Aiden chirps with excitement. "Roya, since you seem to have mastered that after only one turn, I dare say you're officially done for the day and can go. Who's next?" the Head Scientist asks like a game show host.

I scoot off the platform and take a few breaths. They feel like kindling in my throat at first, jagged and sharp. The voices around me are distant, indistinct. All I hear is the music and my own thoughts as they pour through my consciousness. I float off in the direction of the exit.

"Oh, and Roya," Aiden calls to me.

I turn, feeling victorious.

"Nice job," he says with eyes full of meaning, no grin present.

"Thanks." I smile, lingering one second too long on his expression before leaving.

◆

For the first time in my life I finally understand the expression "puffed up with pride." My chest leads the way with an exuberant force as I march through the halls. Jitters run from my fingertips all the way to my belly, which feels full and like it will never be hungry again. Adrenaline pulses through my veins and I like it, but it also makes me nervous, like at any moment it will overpower me.

I round the corner toward the elevators and meet a familiar face. "Hello, Roya," Trey says, throwing his hand through his silver hair. I imagine in another life he was a surfer, but I'm guessing in the Institute he has little opportunity to catch waves.

"Hey." I immediately reel in the energy that has me skipping on my toes.

Trey smiles slightly, seeming to be infected by my good mood. "So how have the last few days treated you? Everything been all right?"

I nod, unsure exactly how to elaborate on this.

"Look," he says, taking up the conversation, "I know there are a lot of unanswered questions for you. I don't want you to be in the dark or confused. Believe me." Sincerity etches at the corner of his eyes and I do, I believe him.

"I've been overwhelmed with a particular task," he explains. "But soon I'd like the opportunity to sit down and explain a few things to you."

I don't have the faintest clue as to what he's referring, but I'm immediately curious.

Trey continues, "You should know that if you have a question, then I'd like you to feel free to ask it. And I will answer the questions I can."

For a second I concentrate on his protective charm—the talisman around his neck. I'm mesmerized by how the blue and yellow seem to swirl for miles into each other, but always stay separate.

Behind me I hear a noise and turn. The lady in the purple scrubs, the one with the waves of soft brown hair, wrinkles, and young eyes, exits her room. She sees us and retreats in the opposite direction.

115

My mouth asks the question before I can stop it. "What's in there?"

Trey draws in a breath. He seems to wrestle internally for a few seconds. His eyes focus intently on me and then on the ground. This happens several times. Then he gently grabs my arm and pulls me around a corner, away from the elevators.

"It's Flynn," he says his face suddenly grave, like a wilted plant on a blistering day. "He was…He *is* the Head of the Institute. He always has been. This is his place. A little less than a week ago he decided to hunt down Zhuang. He thought he could end this whole thing. It was never Flynn's intention to send a young person into a dreamscape to battle Zhuang. He refused to believe the news reporters. Anyway, he thought he could at least weaken Zhuang. At this point he might be a hundred layers deep."

I'm not sure I understand half of what's he's said. "Layers? What do you mean by those?"

Trey nods, seeming to understand my gap in dream travel knowledge. "Each location you dream travel to represents a layer. As a person moves from location to location, the layers stack on top of each other, like that of cake—hence the reason for the term."

"Oh," I say, still overwhelmed by the conversation.

"I think Flynn is trapped in one of the layers," Trey says, his voice distant. He appears lost, like a shadow of himself. "Flynn hasn't returned to his body in a while. We have him hooked up to life support. He's very close to being away from his body for too long. The consciousness can't live without the body and vice versa. We must report back or we'll die. Zhuang can sustain dream travel the longest, for sure, but even he must return at some point. Consciousness will only last for a short period without the body. I believe Zhuang is killing Flynn. It's all been a trick to lure him in, confuse him, and most likely finish him off. I can't find him to stop this. Honestly, I'm worried about trying because I don't know what I'm facing. News reporters offer little on the subject, but that's typical for Zhuang. Besides from the Day of the Duel, there are no real forecasts, that's always been the way. He's impossible to get a read on."

A shiver shoots down my back. Cold. Painful. I'm speechless. This is more than I asked for. More than I expected to hear. *Why did he share this much with me? Me? Roya? What obligation does he*

116

have to share anything with me? A part of me feels a charge from knowing this information and then the rest wants to run and hide.

We walk back to the elevator in silence. Trey finally says, "I tell you this because you need to know two vital things." He taps the buttons for the second and third level and then the elevator moves. "The first is, I will always tell you the truth and give you the information you seek when I can." He stops, eyeing me, and then adds, "I want you to trust me." Suddenly it's difficult to maintain eye contact with him, but I force myself. "The second is we're up against something very real and dangerous. Zhuang wants to win this, but it isn't a game. There are real lives at stake. It's understandable that you've struggled with your commitment to the Lucidites and this mission, but I hope that this puts the task in front of you into perspective."

I nod, although I'm hesitant. I want Trey to think I understand, but it's a lie. More than ever I'm confused and scared.

"I hope to talk with you again soon," Trey says intently as the elevator doors open on his level.

I nod again, feeling heavy as he exits.

Chapter Twenty

The next several days pass in a blur. I awake from traveling the globe, put on my sneakers, and sweat like hell. Mario, our sensei, has us do yoga, weightlifting, core exercises, and way too much running.

Meal times are actually enjoyable, especially since the team and I are finally finding a rhythm. George spends most of his time with the white coats and Goat Girl is always delayed or absent. This gives the rest of us ample opportunity to share stories. We soon realize each of us grew up feeling like or labeled as outcasts. Well, all of us except Joseph. He admits to being different, but hid it better than the rest of us. He has a certain knack with people, a gift with which the rest of us aren't blessed. It's good to hear others tell stories of feeling different from everyone at school, of hiding their abilities to prevent being ostracized.

Some of the group, like Trent and Whitney, were born into Dream Traveler families, ones who supported the Lucidites. I found the idea of living in a family who fostered my unique abilities and traveled with me around space and time appealing. Joseph shared my sentiment and confessed his parents had no special abilities. Samara, on the other hand, admitted that although she knew her mother was a Dream Traveler, her mother refused to speak about it or allow Samara to. This had been the case ever since Samara was five and her mother married a Middling.

From everything we gathered, there wasn't a logical order or reason for how Dream Travelers came to be. Were we born this way? Was it a syndrome we came down with late in childhood? The only thing the group decided upon was the ability to dream travel rarely came to an individual until they were over the age of fifteen. There were rare cases where children could dream travel as young as five, but the Lucidite laws forbade anyone under the age of eight from doing so. My mind flashed to Aiden. He'd spent more of his life traveling the globe and through history than he had being normal. This thought sparked something in a hidden passageway within me, but I quickly buried the feeling, the curiosity.

Within no time the team of alternates and I began to interact seamlessly. I had never been a part of a team. The camaraderie, the friendship, was all new for me. Even if Samara could read my thoughts, at times I was certain she hadn't and still knew what I was thinking. It only took one look from Trent for me to double over with laughter, knowing he was about to tease Joseph in his demonstrative way. And there was nothing I enjoyed more than to see Whitney's eyes light up when Joseph tickled her and called her our little fairy. "You're the only one who can save us for sure," he'd always say. Her look, the one where she was on the brink of laughter and tears at the same time, brought a subtle tenderness to my throat. Nothing felt so good as to see that expression on her angelic face. She's the youngest of the group, but I suspect she'll always look sweet, innocent.

At the end of every day, in the last quiet hour before dream travel, I found myself confiding in Joseph. His natural style with people was like the interpreter I'd been lacking my whole life. And maybe there was a part of me that offered him an introspective perspective, one that explained to him why the world didn't open on a hinge.

All in all we were proving to be a cohesive team and it was definitely to our benefit.

"Very good," Shuman remarked one day during training. She was referring to Trent's ability to pull a spear from a hundred feet, through an obstacle course to her outstretched hand. And Samara was now proficient enough with her telepathy she could just about breach Shuman's thoughts without a trace. "I felt you," Shuman remarked bluntly, "but only at the end. I knew you were there because you lingered too long. You already had what you were seeking. Go when you have retrieved it."

Ren, on the other hand, didn't really think it's so cute that we've formed such a healthy "tribe."

"Don't get distracted," he remarked one day. "That's what familiarity will do for you. It will distract you. Make you comfortable. Once you're comfortable then you might as well light the fire and spear yourself, because you're about to get roasted."

We all looked sideways at each other trying to suppress our laughter.

"Crikey!" Ren yelled. "This isn't a joke!"

He then spent every other lesson throwing projections at us and when we didn't recognize them for what they were they'd attack us. Luckily they couldn't do any real harm, except make us pee in our pants.

This is when group dream travels started. I'm hardboiled. That's how I'm made. I'm a hard-cased being, covering a softness I hope never to reveal. Still these travels opened me up, like a yolk, soft and runny on buttered toast.

We were told at night to all travel to the same location. The point was to learn to travel together. We'd meet, then move through the dreamscape, learning how to stay together. When cued, we'd travel to a new layer. Together. If someone got lost then we had to find them before moving forward. This would go on for three or four dozen layers. Never before had I felt that fluid movement of traveling beside someone. We'd travel and move, exploring real buildings, real waters, and a real moon. Then in unison we'd shut our eyes, like a fleet of ships and spiral to a new location, with new buildings, new waters, and the same moon. If there was one moment, aside from all the rest, this was the one where I came alive.

This is when I learned the rules governing dream traveling interactions. Apparently, I'd been right that only Dream Travelers can see one another. People in the physical realm can't see Dream Travelers, although the reverse isn't true. Those who have a consciousness like a person, dog, or bull will pass through a Dream Traveler like a ghost. This is in contrast to objects without a consciousness. As a Dream Traveler we can pick up objects, hold onto solid forms, or feel materials under our seemingly transparent skin. However, the law dictates that we're never to interact with an object, just as Steve had explained. This means we can walk on the bridges or wrap our fingers around monkey bars, but we're never to pick up or move an object in the physical plane.

The only downside to this life is trainings with Aiden have been suspended for an unknown amount of time. He's working on something important and can't take any time away from the project. This meant we've picked up extra lessons with Shuman. She spent this time explaining to us how dream interpretation could be used.

"My people have long known the importance of interpreting one's dreams," she explained. "This is a tool you can use to gain insight from your subconscious. By exploring the symbols and stories your dreams offer, you can discover special information. If you are stuck, need direction, or want to be made aware of something then turn to your dreams. The Institute offers a safe place to do this. You can dream freely here, allowing your subconscious mind to take you on a journey. It is not safe to do this anywhere else in the world, under the current circumstances."

Two nights a week we are required to record our dreams in a journal. In class we work in pairs to interpret what we've recorded. I spend most of this time working with Joseph. Shuman thinks he shows a special ability for dream interpretation.

"You see the fabric of a dream," she told him in her airy tone.

He smiled proudly. "It must be from all my time spent with Freud. That guy is cool!"

I laughed knowing Joseph had spent some of his free nights following the famous psychiatrist around.

♦

Just when the trainings had become enjoyable we're ordered to attend kung fu practices with Misty. Upon arriving Mario explains that Misty needs extra sparring partners. She's sitting in the corner looking pale and exhausted. We only see her in the morning during the workouts. I kind of feel sorry for her now, seeing how spent she looks from all the demands of training. My empathy doesn't last long.

"He means I need people I can beat up." She sticks out her tongue. "You all will do just fine."

Mario ignores her. "Besides, if you're familiar with her fighting style then you'll know how to assist her. This is especially important for the telekinesis expert, as you should become efficient at sending her weapons."

Trent has a guilty smile on his face. I don't know what he's thinking, but I suppose it has to do with "accidentally" sending an object into Goat Girl's head instead of placing it in her hands. I suppress a laugh.

Clapping his hands, the instructor commands our attention. "Now, let's start with breaking today. This practice is important because it forces you to focus your thoughts and thereby your energy. Fortunately, many of you were successful with this task during the competition."

He briefly explains the technique and then asks us to share our experiences. Suddenly I remember Goat Girl saying something in the elevator the day of the competition, right after I completed the kung fu challenge. At the time it really pissed me off because it seemed she had blatantly gotten into my head and stolen my thoughts on how I'd broken my board. I don't know that she isn't telepathic, but my instinct tells me that isn't her gift. I reason the whole thing must be a coincidence, although an infuriating one.

I give Goat Girl a dirty look and then mock her words in the elevator from the day of the competition. "I just pictured that I was a waterfall and my only purpose was to fall and fall. No board can stop a waterfall."

The instructor nods with a big smile. "Excellent! Roya, that's a perfect approach! Yes! Let's all use that idea as we practice breaking boards."

Taken aback by his endorsement, I stand rigid. I meant my comment to be a jab at Goat Girl. She gives me an evil expression and then stands up and forces her way to the front of the line. The instructor holds the board. I don't notice her stop to focus or practice. The strange thing is, she walks straight up to the board and as her hand is about to come down on it, but before it makes contact, the board breaks in two.

If the instructor sees this he hides it well. "Fantastic! Next," he says getting another board ready. The next person lines up.

My mind is all over the place, trying to figure out what's out of place. There's something wrong. When it's my turn I'm completely lost in thought. Just as my fist is about to come down I hear Ren's voice in my head. It's from our first conversation. It rings out in my mind like a bell: *There are no coincidences. If you see one, stop and pay attention.* Instantly the pain ripples through my hand and shoots up my arm. The board remains unbroken.

"You'll need to focus better next time," Mario says.

No shit.

"Go put ice on that before it swells," he says, sending me away.

Chapter Twenty-One

I slump off to the main hall where I know there will be ice cooling the drinks before lunch. My brain hurts worse than my hand as I try to figure out what's out of place. *What am I missing?* I grab a few pieces of ice, wrap them in a towel, and press it to my hand. Since I'm not planning on going back to training I head for my room.

As I round a corner I hear his voice behind me. "Just the person I was looking for."

I turn and my eyes meet Aiden's as he approaches.

"I need you…uhhh…" He hesitates midsentence. His teeth bite down on his lower lip softly. He opens his mouth. No words come out. My hand is numb, no longer throbbing. Aiden's mouth clenches shut, opens again. "In my lab." He motions with his head. "I need you for something."

Whatever awkwardness just transpired is whisked away with a slight smile and a playful look through his glasses. His eyes trail down to my hand encased in ice. "Will you follow me back to my lab? I need to run some tests on you."

"Sure," I agree.

On the walk to the elevator I take two strides to equal one of his. His long legs move swiftly as he speaks in his usual, excited manner. I stare down at his frayed jeans and black Converses and smile. I still can't believe this guy is a scientist. The funny thing is I consider him two separate people. There's Aiden, the guy who saved my life, makes me laugh, listens to good music. He's relatable. Touchable. A book in the public library. Then there's the Head Scientist, the one who speaks during meetings and trainings, and like a ghost surfaces during my talks with Aiden. He's indistinct. Untouchable. Inaccessible.

"So did you finally unload on Ren?" Aiden gestures at my hand.

I laugh. "I wish. No, I failed to break a board."

He scrunches his face in a look of pain. "Owwee, that sucks. We're over here." He points to a workstation.

Aiden pulls a few instruments out of a drawer and looks at me. He's all business now. Head Scientist. There isn't a sly smile present at the corners of his eyes or that antsy movement in his fingertips as he lays instruments out on the surface of the table. "I just need to get some measurements on you for the project I'm working on. It should only take a second and won't hurt a bit."

He holds a small box in his hand that contains a screen and a dial. "This is a TriField meter. It measures frequencies." Aiden flips a switch and a needle toggles back and forth. "I've upgraded this device to measure human frequencies, which isn't something the factory model originally did." There's a smile in his voice. "Actually, it was pretty sensitive to begin with, measuring down to 0.2 milligauss. I just tweaked it a little." Aiden puts the device an inch away from my face and stares at the screen with earnest concentration. "Anyway, I'll stop boring you with my technical talk."

"You're not boring me. I like to hear you talk about this stuff." *Shit! Did those words just come out of my mouth?*

A slow grin spreads across his face. "Well, most people don't."

My insides fidget with nervousness. At any moment the movement's going to penetrate my skin and Aiden will witness me twitch uncontrollably.

"I'm not like most people," I say.

He stares directly at me, raising his eyebrow slightly, and then records something on a piece of paper. "So I've gathered."

I hold my breath without regard for the awful shade of burgundy my face is about to turn. That would be better than having a fit of wild tics in front of Dr. Suave. I have no idea why he's making me this nervous.

He pulls out an object that resembles a screwdriver. Taking a long wire, he hooks it into the TriField meter.

"So what's this project all about?"

The Head Scientist holds the wand-looking-screwdriver-thing up and points it at me horizontally. I flinch. Instantly feeling stupid. He doesn't appear to notice. His eyes are fixated on the device. Then he swivels his gaze up to meet mine, a look of surprise on his face. Again he glances at the device incredulously. Aiden records another number on a piece of paper.

"Roya, your frequency is different," he says with a pause and then adds, "than most."

I frown.

"Curious, really," he says, holding the wand at a forty-five-degree angle next to my face. Another measurement is recorded.

"Different how?" I ask.

"I took a few base readings for this project. That included roughly fifty samples. They all were pretty close to each other on the scale." He holds the wand vertically next to my head, then records the number. "Yours isn't even near anyone's in the sample."

"What does that mean?"

"Scientifically speaking, I'm undecided, but entertaining numerous theories." Aiden turns, putting the devices back in the drawer. He steals a quick glance at me over his shoulder as he organizes the equipment. "Personally speaking, I think it means you're extraordinary." His eyes don't connect with mine again; instead, he holds up one finger. "Stay here for me, for just one more minute, would you?"

"Sure," I tell his retreating back.

His long strides take him to his main workstation, the one with the TV hanging overhead. Gingerly he picks up the iPod and taps it a couple of times, grinning. The TV screen comes alive with graphics of geometric shapes in bright greens and purples. They're dancing to the music that's just begun pouring through the speakers.

The song starts with a constant drum. It hints at a melody that's about to take shape, like the images dancing across the monitor. One key of a piano and then a nasally male vocalist begins telling his story. Within half a verse I know he's heartbroken without knowing love. He's half in love without knowing the girl he's after. Then just as the guitar joins the mix I'm certain I love this song without knowing where it goes or how it ends. I'm just as easily smitten as the singer. My logical side, which usually guides my way, must be on holiday. I settle into this newfound demeanor just in time for Aiden to stroll back in my direction. The geometric shapes dance wildly across the screen.

"I thought you'd like this song," he says, pulling up a stool next to me. His knees are less than two inches from mine.

Over and over I run my teeth softly against the curve of my nail, not biting it but pushing it back slightly, threatening to nip it from its place.

"So, tell me, why'd you lose to the board? I thought you could break one," Aiden says.

I'd forgotten. I forgot about my sore hand, the board, and the reason I hadn't broken it. My teeth sink deeper into the edge of my nail, still not altering it. "I let Goat Girl get to me?" My eyes widen and I flush as soon as I realize what I've said.

A sudden laugh escapes Aiden's mouth. "Who's Goat Girl?"

My face is hot as I explain why I call Misty by this nickname. "I know I should have more respect for her, since she's our challenger. She just gets under my skin."

He gives me a conspiratorial nod and leans down. "I know what you mean. Between you and me something isn't adding up about her. She isn't performing like she did on the competitive tasks."

"Really?" I ask.

He nods.

I chew on my cheek, debating if I should tell him. His blue eyes compel me to open up. "When I didn't break the board, it was because something weird had just happened." I tell Aiden about what Goat Girl said in the elevator during the competition, and then the kung fu training this morning: me mocking her, the instructor endorsing it, and her breaking the board prior to touching it. "I know it sounds crazy. Could it really be some strange coincidence? Ren said there's no such thing."

The Head Scientist jerks to an upright position, looking past me as if lost in thought. "No, it can't be a coincidence, but that's impossible," he says in a hush. "She couldn't have…"

"Couldn't have what? What are you talking about?" I ask.

Aiden stays focused on the floor, not seeing it. "Hold on," he says, off in thought. He's mumbling to himself, counting something on his fingers.

I will his eyes to return to mine, like when he started the song that's now over. Instead he stays dislodged in some mode of thought, unrelated to him or me or us. His gaze remains distant for a few seconds and when it returns I know the scientist is in control and "Aiden" is gone. The look on his face is cautious as he starts for the door. I'm baffled how he manages to be both professional and teeming with passion at the same time. It drives me absolutely mad. But none of that matters right now.

"I'm sorry," he stammers, "but there's something urgent I have to check out. I'll see you later. Promise."

Then he's gone and I'm left completely confused for a multitude of reasons.

Chapter Twenty-Two

"Think you're losing your mighty kung fu touch, Stark," Joseph says, throwing a punch into my arm.

Goat Girl sits with George at the white coat table, as usual. Trent points at her and says, "Yeah, we think you should ask Misty to give you some pointers on board breaking."

Everyone laughs except me. I obviously take myself too seriously to find this at all funny. I doubt that will change anytime soon.

"Oh!" Joseph says, suddenly thinking of another joke. "You could be her special sparring partner. I bet she'd take it easy on you, not beat you up too bad." He roars with laughter and everyone at the table follows suit. I put his hysterics to a halt with a sharp kick under the table.

"Ouch!" Joseph yelps, tears from laughter present in the corner of his eyes. "That hurt!"

"Good." I roll my eyes and pick at my beet salad.

Aiden materializes at the main doorway, ripping my attention from the current humiliation. He scans the room, obviously looking for someone. I wish it was me, but his eyes never find my eager gaze. He takes a few long strides, whispers something in Trey's ear, and they both leave at once.

After lunch we train with Shuman in the gymnasium. The lessons have been relocated there to give Trent enough room to move objects. Everyone's making progress with their abilities, except for me. I don't understand what I'm supposed to do to improve my skills.

"Everything I see is random," I tell Shuman when she presses me to concentrate. "I don't see what the point in trying to do this is. How it's supposed to help in the dreamscape?"

"You do not think getting glimpses of the future will help us fight Zhuang?" Shuman counters.

It won't help Goat Girl. The events I see are only seconds before they actually occur and that wouldn't be enough time to tell her, much less give her time to counter.

"If you put more value in this skill, then it will occur more frequently," Shuman continues. "It will be reliable. More importantly, it will most likely occur when you need it. As long as you keep dismissing the importance of your ability it will always be erratic. You have the choice."

She turns and marches off. I sigh and kick the wall. I don't understand why she's always on my case about honing my skill. She never makes Joseph work on his. His good looks and charm afford him the pleasure of sitting on the bleachers and reviewing dream interpretation books.

◆

The next day I'm told to go to meeting room 222 after breakfast. This is a welcome surprise since training with Ren is this morning. My entire team is gathered in the stuffy meeting room when I arrive. *Is the Institute trying to save on electricity? Someone turn on the A/C.*

Trey is doing a poor job of hiding his anxiety as he shuffles papers. The crease between his eyebrows is more prominent today. Aiden sits next to him looking intently at the table, drumming his pen. He's in Head Scientist mode. Ren, however, is about as happy as I've seen him. Leaning back in his chair he whistles, with his feet resting casually on the table.

Trey stands, pushing his hands through his silver hair, and begins pacing the room. "Thanks to Aiden, we've learned Zhuang has been much closer than we ever suspected." A soft silence settles throughout the space. "We now have proof he was inside Misty's thoughts, and thus controlling some of her actions." My gaze revolves around the room. Misty is absent. The team collectively wears nervous expressions.

Aiden's eyes briefly meet mine from across the room. He wears an expression I haven't witnessed on him yet. Not triumph, like I'd suspect, but rather a quality of anguish mixed with ambivalence.

"Zhuang forced Misty to travel to the future to learn about the tasks, rig them in her favor, or get the correct solution. This is how she was able to do so well and become the challenger. We believe Zhuang was controlling her up until she put on her protective charm for the first time. Also we're fairly certain she was completely

129

unaware of his presence in her mind. She is currently undergoing psychiatric treatment. We're uncertain of the amount of damage caused to her by traveling into the future. Just this alone can cause irreversible brain damage. There were at least three occasions where she traveled into the future at the same place and time as her past self. One of these times was yesterday during the kung fu practice. We've been able to determine that a past version of Misty was in dream travel form yesterday. It's she who broke the board and not the physical form of Misty. My guess is that she probably visited multiple points in her future timeline to secure her place as challenger. The Lucidites forbid this type of travel because it breaks a law of the universe, one that even Zhuang isn't brave enough to violate, past self-interaction. Unfortunately for Misty, breaking this law causes a schism in a person's conscious and subconscious." Trey's voice is matter-of-fact, even cold, based on what he's reporting.

I, however, am overcome with concern. It's immediate and unlike me. "Will she be okay by the Day of the Duel?" I ask.

Joseph's laugh is abrupt. Rude. "Wow, Stark, you're so thick."

I scowl at him across the table. "She's still the challenger," I argue. "She was chosen. Isn't she bound to compete by some Lucidite code?"

Joseph rolls his eyes and chuckles.

Trey centers on me, and one of his eyes twitches. "Roya, Zhuang did this." His voice is deliberate. "He did this so we would choose Misty as the challenger and put the odds in his favor. She would be a competitor he could easily defeat. I see that clearly now. He did this so the real challenger, the one who has a true chance of defeating him, wouldn't be chosen." Trey leans forward and everyone in the room seems to follow suit.

Why are they all looking at me?

Trey presses his finger through the air in my direction. "That person is you. You're the true challenger to Zhuang."

What? I stare at Trey. *How didn't I see this coming? I'd forgotten about being first alternate. How was that possible?* My head almost explodes under the pressure. The air in the room is thick and difficult to breathe. The harder I try to pull oxygen into my lungs the more constriction. The tightening starts in the middle of my chest, branching out, growing, spreading uniformly until it covers my heart, my lungs, and my throat. Someone in the room speaks, but I can't hear them. *Has Zhuang taken me over now too?* I look down and see my bracelet shimmer under the overhead lights. *No, I'm just having a panic attack.*

"And that's the reason I know you can do this," Trey says, his turquoise eyes encouraging.

Man, I really wish I'd been listening.

"And you have your team," Shuman says from the back of the room. She's leaning against the wall. As she straightens up onto her long legs, her voice casts authority. "You all work well together now. Zhuang is not counting on this. You working together as the alternate team provides a secret advantage."

My eyes flash on George. He's staring at me. We lock eyes and he doesn't look angry as much as pained. For sure he's the weak link in our team, but the others are strong and Shuman's right, we work well together.

"Let's give Roya a chance to digest this," Trey says in a brisk tone. He taps the button for the door and ushers people out of the room.

I lay my head on the table and close my eyes, wishing I'd wake up from this nightmare. Everything was going well for the first time in my life. *Why did this have to ruin it?*

Unconcerned for the time or space around me I wallow around in my pity, lapping it up, and feeling deserving of the way it burns my wounds like acid. I realize now I've lived an easy life, albeit lonely. As I look down the barrel of my own fate, and certain death, I long for the quietness of the woods in which I used to idle away my time. How simple things were back then. Back then when I wrote my poetry I had no real clue how grief actually felt. I thought I did. I thought it was a hollow ache that etches your features, marks your words, and punctuates your every moment with lack. But I was wrong. Grief isn't a hollow ache. It's raw, all-encompassing. It tears your insides in half, bit by bit, until all you want to do is curl up into the tiniest ball and become something so small you can't feel the pain inside you. That's grief. And it sucks.

Ten minutes? An hour? I'm uncertain how long I wallow. I lift my head to find Aiden sitting on my right staring at me with that same expression as before. I understand it now. It's remorse.

"It's because of you I figured out how she did it," Aiden says.

I must look confused or disoriented. I'm both.

"Goat Girl," he explains with a slight laugh. "I couldn't figure out before how she'd outscored everyone. I knew she wasn't the right challenger. You gave me the clues I was missing. You told me where to look."

"I wish I would have kept my mouth shut," I say, staring at the table.

Aiden reaches out across the foot and a half of space that separates us. A huge distance seconds prior. His hand grips mine. One squeeze. One small tug. My eyes jerk up and find his. This gesture startles me, but more surprising is the way his warmth fills my hand with more than I'm accustomed to holding.

He smiles. "I knew it had to be you."

My head falls back to its former position. "I've been given a death sentence."

"No. You can do this."

With his fingers still pressed around mine, he pulls my hand an inch closer to him. A small movement, but it says so much. "I know you can do this," he continues with enough enthusiasm I'm certain he's trying to convince more than just me. Locked on his sapphire eyes, I feel my breathe hitch. My pulse quickens. I squeeze his hand, enjoying the warmth it radiates around mine. His pirate smile surfaces at the gesture. Aiden leans forward and whispers, "I'll help you." I feel his breath against my chin. He freezes, taking in my expression.

A sharp cough rocks my attention. Aiden straightens, his hand recoiling from mine. He rolls his eyes, looking at the entrance. "Yes, yes, Ren, I get it. My time is up." The Head Scientist stands.

"No, it's just I was about to gag," Ren says, lurking in the doorway.

How long has he been there?

The Head Scientist doesn't look back over his shoulder as he leaves. He just leaves. And then Ren takes his place. I push back from the table.

"The kind of help he can give you"—Ren motions his head in the direction of the exit—"isn't what you need to defeat Zhuang. Sure, he can help you survive, but I can help you defeat him."

"Look, I'm in no mood for one of your dramatic and abusive monologues right now."

132

Ren's eyes narrow, lacking any sympathy or emotion. "Right, you're trying to come to terms with this news. Everyone's going to tell you that you can do this, that you aren't alone, that there's hope. It's bollocks. When you lie down to meet Zhuang you'll be more alone than you've ever been. No one will be able to save you from the torture he'll do to you. The odds aren't in your favor and frankly, he's probably going to kill you."

"Well, I feel much better now. Thanks for stopping by," I say. "The vote of confidence really helps."

Ren smiles.

Figures.

"Here's the deal, darling," he begins in his usual snarky tone. "I won't dress this up for you. You'll thank me for that later. I'm telling you straight how bleak this looks. I'm doing this so you'll understand it, get over it, and then focus on the fight. Fear makes you weak. Attachments make you even weaker. Face the facts and Zhuang will have one less power over you."

"Why does it even matter? I don't stand a chance against Zhuang."

"True," Ren chirps. "However, the Day of the Duel is our first legitimate opportunity to challenge him. Even if you don't stand a chance it's the first one anyone's had in over two hundred years. Lord knows I can spend the next fifty years happily chasing Zhuang through dream layers, trying to catch him. But to have what you'll have, the opportunity to face off with him in a set place and time…" He slams his fist onto the table. His green eyes bulge. "Bloody hell! Do you know what I would give for that? Zhuang is the most elusive wanker I've ever known. I've tracked him my entire life and I can't confirm I've ever been closer than fifty yards away. He can't run from you. The forecast is correct this time. He knows it or otherwise he wouldn't have gone to all the trouble of having Misty rig the whole thing. If you accept this role then your fates will be intertwined. He must face you on the Day of the Duel."

I crack my knuckles. "Why can't someone else go? One of the other alternates?"

"I'm not here to stroke your ego so don't even try," Ren says. "Of the names on the list, you're the best. I've known it since the beginning. Hell, Trey did too but he still made everyone compete, probably because like me he doubts your commitment to the

Lucidites." His nostrils flare as he draws in a long inhale. "Well, and also Trey likes to pretend he doesn't fancy you."

I huff at his insinuation. It's absurd, like everything else Ren says. I'm so tired of him. I wish he'd just die. "Why don't you go in my place?" I say, not as an offer, but as a threat.

"That isn't the way it works. The forecast says Zhuang will meet one person from the list the news reporters constructed. It says this is our only chance at defeating him. It doesn't say pretend to send an inexperienced, snotty prat and then put Ren in her stead. Okay? Got it?!"

"And what if I won't do it?"

Ren stands and looks down at me from hooded eyes. "Then you'll die a coward. I'll see to it."

Chapter Twenty-Three

Everyone treats you extra nice when they think you're about to die. I've seen it a zillion times on Lifetime movies. I really don't want to be handled like a frail little gerbil right now. More than anything I want to be left alone. Without a care for the schedule or even ever eating again I retreat to my room and lock myself in there for the remainder of the day. Numerous knocks rapped at my door during my self-imposed solitary confinement. To everyone's credit, I know they can just hit the button and march into my room, but they respect my privacy. It's well into the evening when a final knock rattles my door, followed by a voice.

"Hey, sweetheart, you've got a package. I'm leaving it by the door," Patrick says, followed by a thud.

I wait a minute before hitting the button. The door slides back to reveal a large box tied in a pastel pink bow. *What in the world?*

I push the package into my room, hit the button, and pry it open.

Inside is a letter from Bob and Steve. They must have learned my fate from the Lucidite news feed. It reads:

Dear Roya,

We know this must come as a shock. As much as we would like to be there for you during this difficult time, we can't. This is a journey you'll face alone, but you have much support. Please don't forget that. We loved getting the letter from you. Please write as often as you'd like.

Love,
Bob and Steve

I fold the letter and pull the tissue paper off the top of the box. Underneath the fine layer of paper are books, books, and more books! All classics! All my favorites! Lord Byron. Charles Dickens. Ernest Hemingway. William Faulkner. Neatly arranged under this library is a camera, a bar of dark chocolate, and an assortment of lotions, body scrubs, perfumes, and facial type stuff. For a good ten minutes I sit surrounded by all the stuff, feeling loved and lonely.

When I'm less fragile I put my books and other gifts away. Then I climb into bed and pull the covers over my head. Tonight I'm allowed to do as I please. I'm glad for that, because at the moment I want to be a million miles from here.

The first image I see when I close my eyes is of Ren. Just as I'm about to heave with disgust from the sound of his snarky British voice in my head, something occurs to me. Although the sound of his voice makes me cringe, his accent is still a favorable one. Maybe I've spent too many days watching BBC, but still I'm in love with Great Britain and even Ren can't completely tarnish that.

I painstakingly focus my thoughts. Within seconds I whirl through the tunnel, on my way to Buckingham Palace. A loud piercing sound hits my ears upon arriving in the damp square. Screaming. Stealing a glance around, I try to determine if the environment is safe. When I have my bearings I realize I'm standing next to a statue. Queen Victoria. Peering around the statue I connect the screaming to a nearby man.

"Help! Help us!" A woman calls from beside the man. She's holding his arms down, which are trying to flay around. The man is frenzied, out of control.

A crowd has begun to gather around the couple. The man's screams turn into painful moans. And then he suddenly falls silent. Still.

"Arthur! Arthur!" the woman cries, shaking him.

"Is he breathing?" someone asks.

"Barely. He's been seeing things that aren't real all day. And he hasn't slept in days." The woman mops the man's sweaty forehead with a handkerchief. "Oh, Arthur. What's happening to you?"

The balding man lies in a heap on the pavement. With a jerk his eyes roll back in his head, face pale, hands shaking.

Before I witness anymore I dream travel to a new layer, a place I've never been. I'm hoping to find something new to take my mind off my troubles. Turns out my troubles are following me.

Before I feel the pavement under my feet I know something's askew. The cold marble under my fingers steadies me as the noises meet my ears. More screaming. I crouch behind a light pole, my mind stiffening with dread. From my vantage point the line of etched stars stretches along the sidewalk. There's hardly anyone out at this hour, although a few cars pass every so often. The scream again.

The deep breath I suck in has little effect on the dread building deep within me. Tentatively I stand to a normal position. Another scream, this one guttural. My eyes search until they find the source—a man. He lurks in an upper floor window, yanking at curtains. Possessed. I recognize the wild expression in the man's eyes. He looks exactly how Shiloh, my brother, looked the last time I saw him. The look, the paranoia, the manic behavior are all the result of not being able to dream. Hallucinations have taken over. I jerk my attention away from the man who's now beating against the window, as if he's trying to escape his own personal prison.

Hollywood is supposed to be glamorous. Full of entertainment and opportunity. I'd always pictured the place as having an inescapable energy, one that hums through my chest with an energetic beat. This is not the Hollywood I envisioned. Its deserted streets are cloaked in grayness. Trash rustles down the sidewalk as a fierce wind barrels through the alleyway. A piece of debris entangles itself around my leg. I fetch it and am just about to let it slip through my fingers and be carried off by the wind when something catches my eyes. It's a newspaper. Today's. The front page of the *LA Times* reads:

Unclassified Epidemic Sweeps the Nation

Thousands across the nation are suffering from what scientists are calling Sleep-X virus. The origin and cause of the infectious disease are currently unknown. It doesn't appear to be contagious, but quarantine of infected individuals is required until more is determined. The Sleep-X virus is called such because a person's inability to reach REM state is the precursor to the other symptoms, which include hallucinations, malnutrition, paranoia, high blood pressure, heart palpitations, depression, stroke, dementia, heart attack, and heart failure. Most concerning to doctors is the abrupt onset of symptoms in some patients, whereas others suffer for long periods of time with the disease. Even more disconcerting is no medical intervention has been successful in treating the disease or relieving its symptoms. Dr. Randal Smith, the Chair of Neurobiology at UCLA states, "The disease intermittently paralyzes the cerebral cortex and the thalamus, especially during states of rest. As the disease progresses, the frequency of paralysis increases until one of the associated symptoms kills the patient." Researchers worldwide have come together to research the epidemic, which has also spread amongst parts of Europe and China. In some areas it's referred to as the Enigmatic virus since no real cause or treatment has been found. "There have been cases in history similar to the ones we're seeing today," Smith states, "but the frequency of cases is notable and it's imperative we employ all our efforts to ending this epidemic before…

I don't need to read anymore. People aren't suffering from a disease and there's no amount of research that will stop it. Zhuang is to blame for this. And it looks as though—as Trey predicted—his greed is building. I thought I could run from my current problems. I thought I could avoid this fight, but the only solution to the world's problems is to end Zhuang.

Chapter Twenty-Four

I awake the next morning and arrive early to workout. If anyone is surprised to see me, they hide it well. We all eat breakfast without a word. It isn't until we're seated in the classroom, waiting for Shuman, that anyone says anything that resembles normal speech.

Whitney's childlike voice echoes against the ceiling of my mind. "I always knew it couldn't be Misty. She was never right as the challenger." Whitney bites her lip looking uncomfortable, but determined. "I always knew it had to be you, Roya."

"Honestly," Trent says, tying his dreadlocks back in a ponytail, "even though Misty is probably off in a padded cell going crazy, I still believe she's intolerable. You know why?" he asks arching one eyebrow. "Trey said Zhuang's curse ended when she put on that ring, the protective charm. Well, she was still a big bitch to us after that, wasn't she? I think that's her true nature and that's the reason Zhuang chose her. It's probably easier to infiltrate evil witches with your thoughts than other people."

Joseph sits looking off. He hasn't said a word. I want him, of all people, to say something but he just sulks. He's my closest friend here. My first friend ever. As sad as that is to admit, it means I'm reliant on his consolation at this point. I've become dependent on it. And right now I need it more than ever. He crosses his arms and stares, transfixed, at a far-off object on the other side of the room.

Finally it's Samara who contributes to the conversation. "Roya, there's a place in Zhuang I know I can get to. I've seen it in my dreams. I can find his thoughts at some point and share them with you. I'll be able to help...but..."

Her words make me feel as good as I've felt in the last twelve hours. "Thanks," I say to cut off her doubt.

Then Shuman enters the room and I know it's time to stop looking for sympathy.

"Today we are going to begin to understand spirit animals. These are animals that visit you in your dreams and offer their powers to you in your dream travels. You must learn to trust their wisdom, or pay the price for ignoring it. To better understand this concept I want to demonstrate it. Everyone come and lie down on the ground here beside me."

Once we're settled around her, as we have become accustomed to during our meditation practices, she gives us one last set of orders. "Close your eyes and meet me right here, right now in the dreamscape."

I do as she requests and within seconds I'm back to exactly the same place, but in my subconscious form. Surprisingly I arrive even before Shuman. I watch as one by one the others spring up around me, pulling their consciousness from the body lying on the floor.

When we're gathered, Shuman gives a look of contentment. "When I was a young girl a snake regularly haunted my dreams. At first I was frightened and I would awake screaming. After some time the shaman of my tribe told me to approach the snake and to ask him what he wanted. On one occasion I did this. When I lifted the serpent into my arms for the first time he turned to me and spoke. He said, 'guide us as you will.' I knew from that moment on that the snakes in my dreams were not to be feared. They were offering themselves to do my beckoning. They were my servants."

From nowhere Shuman pulls a snake out of the air and holds it in her arms. Its rattle flickers and my chest flutters.

"My friends," she continues, "have aided me all my life and continue to be my guide." She throws the snake into the air and it lands safely on the ground and slithers through a maze of chairs. "My reason for showing you this is that if you have a spirit animal then do not run from it. Grab it. Ask it what it wants from you. And maybe it will offer its protection when you are in need. My guess is at least one of you is protected by the animals." She points at each one of us individually. "The question is which one?"

Shuman stares at us for a long second and then disappears. We all follow suit, returning to our bodies. I stare at the tattoo on her arm with a new interest. Suddenly it isn't as creepy. The rattlesnake's features are kind of beautiful as I spy the details of each of the scales along the serpent's body. Shuman waits until we're all back in our bodies and standing once more. Her words are quiet and raspy and I sometimes wonder if, like Ren, this is all part of an act.

"Pay special attention to your dreams," she says hoarsely as she strides out of the room.

♦

A few days later I receive a message from Aiden asking me to meet him in his lab. Mixed feelings tether my insides. I'm ecstatic to get out of training with Ren this afternoon, but I'm dreading facing Aiden. I grip the letter written in the Head Scientist's handwriting and my mind reels back to when he called me "extraordinary." *Did he mean it like I'm a special lab rat? Or is it how he thinks of me as a girl?* Honestly, I'm unsure which I prefer.

I've been avoiding Aiden since our last meeting. Ever since he held my hand, his touch has haunted me, painting my unconscious dreams with images of him. Many nights I've awoken with sweaty palms and a nervous hiccup in my throat, and it isn't because I'll soon face Zhuang. I'm the challenger, though, and therefore this emotion, my attraction, has to be ignored. *Focus, Roya. Don't get distracted.*

Before I'm even close to Aiden's lab I hear the music drumming its way down the corridor, beckoning me forward. The echo of the singer's voice courses through my veins. Unable to resist it, a smile unfolds on my face as her words hum passionately in my chest.

"You're a hard girl to get time with," Aiden says as he plays with a small, flat box hanging at the end of a necklace.

"I know. I've been busy," I say.

"Rightly so." That look of remorse falls on his face again. "Roya, this is all going to—"

"Don't," I stop him. "I've been getting this pep talk from everyone. Spare me." My words sound coarser than I intended, but still, there they hang in the air between us.

Silence. It's uncomfortable, like I put my shoes on the wrong feet.

"So why'd you call me down here?" I finally ask.

Aiden gives me a sideways look, lips pursed. "For a few reasons." His eyes fixate on me. Hungry. His look is infectious. My stomach clenches with an uncomfortable desire. His proximity, the music, that look. It's too much. I jerk my eyes to the object pressed between his fingers. It resembles a camera's memory card.

"Is that your protective charm?" I ask.

141

"Actually, my charm *is* a necklace, but this isn't it. I wear mine *under* my shirt."

"Oh." I swallow, staring at the necklace and not his piercing eyes. Suddenly something rises to the surface, like a weird déjà vu moment.

"Wait, I think I've seen that before." I point to the flat box on the silver chain. "Wasn't that in my closet in the fifth task?"

Aiden nods. "Indeed."

"But why?"

"It's complicated. The short answer is, it was in your closet because I'm about to give it to you." He gives a crooked smile as he plays with the device between his fingers like a poker chip.

"What was the right answer to the question for the fifth task?" I ask to avoid more silence and hungry stares. "What was the object of most importance? Was that it?"

Aiden snickers. "There wasn't a right or wrong answer. The purpose of the task was to test dream travel ability."

"Oh," I say, surprised.

"You know, dream traveling is a skill most have to hone to do properly, at least for the first few years."

"So?" I shrug in confusion.

"So, that doesn't seem to apply to you," Aiden says, gnawing on a smile. "Most contenders never even found their closets, since I kind of made them hidden."

I scowl at him to cover up my satisfaction. *I found my closet.*

"The ones who did find their closets successfully," Aiden continues, "had difficulty traveling back to when the hourglass was full."

"Then why the riddle?"

"Well, we had to have something for the few who actually made it and needed an extra challenge."

"But that's confusing, to give a riddle that there's no answer for." I huff with mock frustration, trying to conceal the pride his comments have unleashed.

"Oh, I don't know, I thought you had a pretty good answer," he says, his eyes dancing over mine like sunlight on the ocean.

"Well," I stir away from him. "You said you'd explain why my bracelet was in the closet."

142

"It's true, I did. Regrettably we don't have time to discuss that at the moment." A flirtatious smile spreads across his face before he adds, "Perhaps another time."

He's so devastatingly distracting. *Does he know he's complicating my ability to concentrate at the time I need it most?* The urge to reach across the space and wrap my arms around him traverses through my mind. I shake my consciousness, willing it to focus and abandon primitive desires.

"The real reason I asked you down here is, I need you to test a new piece of technology." Lowering his head he pulls off the necklace and holds it out with both hands offering it to me. Hesitation prickles my throat. I ignore it. Taking a few cautious steps forward I allow only inches to separate us. Aiden smiles, seemingly enjoying the budding tension. He drapes the necklace over my head. His fingers linger on my skin and I flick my eyes up to meet his. I'm frozen, staring into his sapphire eyes. Intoxicated. He's close. Closer than ever before. His breath is warm on my cheeks. All I want is to reach out and pull him closer. The hunger burns now, like a bonfire out of control. His eyes stoke this growing fire and I have all but abandoned any attempts to be practical in this situation.

"Excuse me." A voice splinters the air.

"Hey there." The Head Scientist breaks away from me. "Come in."

It's George. With drooped shoulders he stands awkwardly in the doorway. His eyes don't meet mine or Aiden's; instead, he stares somewhere to the right of us. "You requested my participation with something?" he asks dully.

I'm completely baffled. How has such a perfect moment, albeit unnerving, gone to one so lame? This is the opposite of satisfying. I turn and watch Aiden, who has straightened up and looks serious, yet excited.

The Head Scientist pulls two stools out onto the floor. "George," he says, indicating a stool. "Please have a seat." He points to the other. "Roya." I comply.

Pacing a circle around us the scientist begins, "Roya, you've no doubt noticed George is quite distant, right?"

He pauses, but I decide against answering.

"One might say George appears to be distracted, frustrated, and even angry at times. This is because he's always had the ability to read people's emotions." With his head down and hands clasped behind his back the scientist has made one complete loop around us.

"However, there's one hindrance to his ability and it showed up when you arrived. Mr. George Anders can't read emotions when you're around." Aiden stops in front of me and points. "You disarm him."

Me? How? Why? There must be a mistake. Stunned, I turn to George. Sad eyes stare at the ground and broad shoulders slump in defeat. He's hardly present.

The Head Scientist continues, "It's your frequency, Roya. The level that your frequency vibrates blocks George's ability to pick up on emotions. Actually, you block everything for poor Mr. Anders. Interesting, huh?"

More like bewildering.

He spins his gaze to George. "This hasn't been very easy on Mr. Anders. How do you think you'd be acting if you met someone who turned your world upside down?" A spark radiates in Aiden's eyes as we connect. He winks, making my insides grow warmer. I turn to George, relieved to find he didn't witness this gesture. He doesn't look as though he'd witness a missile if it struck the ground next to him. My mother would say he's in la-la land.

As if to make up for George's lack of life, Aiden ramps up his enthusiasm. "Naturally, you'd be completely and utterly distraught, which is why George appears to be a bit odd in demeanor. You see, your frequency isn't only creating a disturbance in his ability to pick up on emotions, it's creating interference with his senses. I hypothesize that your high vibrational frequency is overwhelming George. You're all he feels and it's actually too much, too strong for his intuitive ability to interpret—the way he has been able to with all other people his whole life. Pretty extraordinary, don't you think?" Aiden cocks his head to the side and looks earnestly interested in my reply.

I remain silent.

The scientist continues, "However, I've determined the level at which your frequency vibrates. With the device you're currently wearing I can change your frequency by just a fraction of a hertz.

This isn't much, but I think it will be enough to make the difference."

Aiden rubs his hands together eagerly. "Please pay attention, lady and gentleman, because I'm about to make history."

I eye the small box around my neck. George stares nervously at it too, his brown eyes wide. We both turn our attention to the eager scientist. With a large grin he says, "It's show time!" He leans forward, his smile widening as he nears my face. I freeze. In one movement he picks up the device, pushes a tiny switch on the bottom of the black box, and stands back. Eyes narrowed, the Head Scientist turns to George gauging his reaction. I follow suit.

George's face keeps the same pained expression it has worn for weeks. As I take in his dispirited stance all of his behavior begins to make sense. This is why he'd been hostile toward me and absent the rest of the time. He must have thought I was a demon of Zhuang's, sent to steal his powers.

With my eyes intently on George I see the transformation happen at the most gradual level. His firm chin softens. Fixed jaw relaxes. Tight lips part. Intense stare calms and revolves around the room, moving from object to object until his expressionless face becomes animated and meets mine. I swallow and it feels like a wad of fabric. A different person has taken the place of the dejected guy who sat opposite of me moments ago. Now I see George Anders properly for the first time. Soft. Sincere. Understated. Strong. Present.

Transfixed on me, he stands. A smile spreads across George's face. I've never seen one there. It shifts his brown eyes into something distinct and different, making his irises shine. It's as though Frankenstein's monster has just awoken, but he isn't horrid at all. He's the opposite. Suddenly I'm taking in every single ounce of this person who hardly existed moments ago.

George revolves his dark eyes until they find the Head Scientist standing triumphantly a few feet away. He starts forward, pulling Aiden's dangling hand into his, wringing it earnestly. "Thank you," George says in a low rush. "You did it."

Aiden beams. "That's fantastic! And the static, is it gone?"

George runs his fingers through his wavy blond hair. "Yes. Completely."

"Your empathesis? Has it returned?" the scientist asks, sounding very clinical.

"I think so," George says, looking pleasant but guarded.

"And your senses? How are they?"

He pauses, taking in a deep breath. The exhale is one of relief. "Normal. I feel like I can breathe after a long time of being suffocated."

My heart folds up on itself and then free falls down to my stomach.

George turns at once pointing at me with his eyes. He's the size of a linebacker but moves with agile grace. "Roya, you should know that what happened to me, what I went through, wasn't your fault."

Can he feel the ache erupting in my belly? Is that why he's feeding me this line?

"What your frequency does to me, it's random. Anyone could affect me this way. Don't you think so?" George pivots and glances at Aiden for confirmation.

"It's quite possible," the Head Scientist offers but doesn't look convinced.

"You see there." George turns back and consoles me. "If anyone should feel sorry it's me. I haven't been kind to you. I was confused and disoriented, which is a poor excuse, but the only one I have." An adorable dimple surfaces on his left cheek as he smiles at me coyly.

I nod, uncertain how to react. The guy in front of me is a complete stranger, and apparently has the ability to rummage through my emotions as frequently as I experience them. But I have the ability to disarm him. None of this is fair. However, I remind myself that those who speak of fairness are always on the losing side. Life is what I make of it. There are no odds on my side or luck to corral in my favor. I'm uncertain how this mentality is going to serve me in this predicament or my new life. Time will tell.

"Well, I dare say this has been a successful afternoon," the Head Scientist says as he escorts us to the exit. "I have work to do and you two probably have some catching up."

I hang back momentarily, waiting for one last hungry stare from Aiden. With his arms folded across his chest he gives a polite smile, the same one a neighbor casually offers when you see them on the street. I don't return it, but instead turn and leave.

"Oh, and Roya," Aiden calls behind me.

I whip around to face him.

"Please don't take off the frequency adjuster."

I nod curtly.

♦

"But why didn't you say anything?" Samara questions at once, her whitish blonde hair lining her shoulders like a veil.

"What was I supposed to say?" George pokes at his green beans. "'Roya's making me delusional.' It didn't seem right. I wasn't even certain it was Roya at first, but then every time she'd get near me the intensity in my head would become overwhelming, like it was about to explode. Fortunately Shuman figured it out and Aiden found a solution."

"So as long as Stark wears that little box thingy then you're fine? What happens if she takes it off?" Joseph asks, looking skeptical.

George sighs. "It's unbearable. I hear loud vibrating noises, my senses go into overdrive, and I can't pick up on the slightest emotional tone. All I feel is her and it's overpowering."

I stare at my brussels sprouts, knowing George and everyone at the table are focused on me. I'm the "her" who overpowers him, who puts him into a state of torment. Guilt scratches my skin like a Brillo pad.

George continues, "As soon as that necklace fired up the noise went away. I could feel emotions again."

"But it's only when Stark is around, right? So when she's absent, can you sense and feel again?" Joseph questions.

"Yes and no," George says, toggling his head back and forth. "This started a few minutes before Roya arrived in the auditorium on that first day. The closer she was to me the worse it got. I did get a bit of relief if she was farther away." He turns to me, his expression composed, although the pain he's harbored all this time still edges below the surface. "However, even if you're on the first level and I'm on the fifth I still get interference."

I catch Joseph eyeing George intently. He, like me, seems stunned by how George has transformed in the last hour. Joseph's eyes probe George, looking for an answer to this impossible riddle.

147

"It was luck Roya and I weren't in the same group in the beginning. I was able to perform well enough to make the alternate team."

Luck? Like he was fortunate? He's first alternate now. If something happens to me then he'll take my place and die. Is that luck?

George rubs his temples and then continues. "Although I felt the interference all along, it hadn't been as excruciating until Trey called me up during the ceremony and I stood next to you on that stage." George stares at me, looking apologetic and contrite. "From that point forward I thought I was going insane. Every meeting, training, practice, I was lost in this engulfing clashing of metal. It was awful." His head sags. We all stare at each other around the table, lost for words. None of us know how to relate. Any words I offer are only to console my own discomfort. We all remain silent until George pulls his head back up. He focuses on me with solemn eyes. "I didn't know how to react or overcome the torture in my head. I apologize for treating you poorly."

Goose bumps rise to the surface of my skin. I try to suppress them, but they won't allow it. *How's it possible that I have this effect on someone?*

"Don't guilt yourself," George says with a deep expression.

That's unfair. He can read me now. I bite my lip. "It's…." I hesitate, the audience around me hanging on my words, wondering how I'll respond. "It's just a lot to absorb."

He leans forward and says, "Let's put the past behind us now. We're a team. And I want to help." He looks directly at me, awaiting my answer.

I steal a glance at the others, who are looking at us with interest. It's like they're sitting front row, center stage at the best show in town, their mouths gaping open and brows furrowed. I turn back to George and offer him a gentle nod. I know he doesn't need any more.

Chapter Twenty-Five

"Hey, George," I say in a higher pitch than I intended. I reason my nervous tone is a result of awaiting a torturous lecture with Ren.

"Hey." He sits tall and turns in my direction.

The expression in his dark brown eyes stirs me to fill the silence immediately.

"So how are you?" I ask.

He doesn't answer but instead stares at me, seeming to take measurements with his eyes.

Of course my nervousness might also be from George. It's been there since he "awoke." Since his penetrating gaze fixed in my direction I've felt outside myself, saying and doing stuff that isn't like me. He makes me uneasy, and I'm uncertain if it's because he can read my emotions or because of the intensity that seems to accompany our every interaction.

I avert his stare and mumble, "I'm dreading training with Ren."

"I understand," he says. I can't help but catch the force in his eyes out of my peripheral.

"I wonder…" I say mostly to myself.

"What?" he clips sharply.

His tone cuts me and I look around for a way to be rescued from my attempts to make conversation. "Never mind," I say.

"You wonder…" He leans across the table daring to separate us by only inches. "What do you wonder?"

I take in the details of the table in front of me, speculating now if they'll rescue me from this awkward moment. Finally I decide on honesty. "I was just wondering what you feel from Ren. He appears to be such an unhappy person. I was wondering if it's as awful as I imagine, feeling his emotions."

He grabs a pencil from behind his ear and lays it next to his notepad, looking serious. "I can't tell you that."

"It must be dreadful." I sigh.

"No." He turns in my direction. "I can't tell you that or anything else about what other people feel. How would you like it if I broadcast every emotional detail about you to anyone who asked? It would be an invasion of your privacy. It would be an abuse of my skill."

"All right, forget I asked." I turn and face the front. Guilt and embarrassment shoot through me.

He takes the pencil back in his hand and twirls it through his fingers. "Honestly, sometimes I wish I could tell someone everything I feel. It's a lot at times, but it's my burden."

"Yeah, I can't even imagine." I agree as Ren blazes into the room.

With a flick of a remote the projector comes alive. "Today, my little lambs, we're discussing the most important subject yet."

A picture flashes on to the screen and stares back at us. It's a drawing of a man. He's Asian, has a receding hairline, and a braided ponytail that trails down his back. His long black mustache and goatee only partly hide an expression of power and arrogance. The man's dressed in flowing black and white kimono and holds a long curved sword. His eyes are black, hollow.

"Please meet Zhuang." Ren's voice echoes around the room. "You can rest assured he's already met you. If you're in this room, then when you've rested, traveled, frolicked with your friends, Zhuang has been there eyeing you, trying to understand how you could be a part of the team eligible to take him down. He's probably as baffled about this as I am."

Ren sits on the edge of the desk, pulls out his pocketknife, and begins picking at his fingernails. "Legend has it Zhuang dreamed he was a tiny serpent. He traveled to a village where he slithered into a person's ear while they slept. Lustful for command, he wrapped his body around their brain, absorbing its power. When he'd taken their life force he slinked out the other side of their head, leaving them dead. Each time he did this he became faster and stronger, but always remained the same size, for this was to his favor. Zhuang awoke and wondered how he'd dreamed he was a serpent able to steal consciousness. At the same time an incorporeal voice offered to Zhuang that he was dreaming he was a man, but actually someone capable of much more."

Ren interrupts his own speech with a loud yawn. "Legends are daft and full of a lot of bogus drivel, but this parable probably holds some truth. Our villain here is from the fourth century. He's been pinching people's ability to dream ever since he realized he could and using this energy to extend his life. Recently, Mr. Villain realized the more consciousness he stole the more power he could harness. Somehow he has been able to convert this power to abilities. These abilities are unprecedented.

"For instance, you will all remember that here at the Institute we have the GAD-C which generates your body from anywhere on the globe. Zhuang can do this on his own. We also have the modifier, which embeds and recedes thoughts in a person's consciousness. Zhuang can do this on his own. We have a screen attached to the GAD-C that allows us to see pure consciousness in the waking state. Are you getting the hang of this yet? Zhuang can do everything we can, but he doesn't need one of Aiden's little gadgets to do it. Actually, I think Aiden gets his best ideas from Zhuang. If that bloke can do it, then that scientist wants to figure out a way to copy it using a device."

I jerk, sudden anger flares up in me at this accusation. Ren doesn't notice, but a flicker from George's eyes tells me he's picked up on my eruption.

"Not only can he do all this fun stuff, but he's also an expert in kung fu, telepathy, and telekinesis. He's fast." Ren suddenly stands beside Whitney's desk. He leans down, his face inches from hers. "He's faster than a shark in the ocean, a cheetah on land, or an eagle in the air. Whatever the terrain, he's quick." Whitney looks like she's on the verge of crying as she tries to look away from Ren. I hate when he bullies people, especially her. He thinks it's so much fun to use his dramatic lectures to scare all of us, like we aren't all on the same team.

Standing suddenly, Ren holds up one finger. "There's only one area where Zhuang has a weakness. It's our only real strength against him. It's hardly enough and we'll probably all die, but at least we have this and he doesn't.

"The one area Zhuang lacks is clairvoyance. He can't see the future, can't remotely feel the right direction the wind will blow. He's forever and ever stuck in the present moment, because his own hunger for power caused his third eye to go blind. For this reason, we're hopeful a surprise attack could sneak up on him. You'll excuse me if I'm doubtful. Because even if I could sneak up on a cheetah, when I did they'd still be fast and strong enough to kill me."

Ren now stands over me, his eyes beading with disdain. I fake a yawn and then rest my hands in my lap nonchalantly.

Ren narrows his eyes briefly before charging to the front of the room. "Today, you'll have homework. As you go about your day doing all the repugnant things you do, visualize a metal door in your mind. Close and lock it." Looking up from the lint he's picking off his suit he focuses on us. "Work on shutting Zhuang out from your thoughts. Push his presence out behind the metal door. If you're successful with this then maybe, just maybe, he won't be able to spy on you and learn about the attack, however lousy, we have planned."

◆

"We need to work on weapon retrieval," Mario says shortly after we're all gathered in the kung fu studio. "Trent, you will telekinetically send Roya weapons while she spars with Joseph and Samara." He turns his focus on me. "Roya, you will not know when a weapon will be sent or what weapon it will be so remain aware while also fending off attacks. Take your places and let's begin."

Samara and Joseph take turns throwing punches and kicks at me. I do my best to block them. It's challenging to defend myself against two people. Too often I'm blocking Samara's kicks when Joseph's fist drill into my sides, not hard, but enough to let me know I'm losing this fight. I whip around to block him and miss an attack from Samara. It sends me to my knees, but I'm back on my toes in half a breath.

And then all at once everything slows down in my mind. Their attacks take a back stage and my hands automatically deflect them. There's a flash: Two sticks connected by a short chain soar through the air. If I reach my right arm across my back and down this is the ideal position for obtaining the weapon.

When I return from the momentary flash, my hands are still deflecting attacks. A countdown goes off in my head. At first I'm unsure why. I just listen and witness the quickness of my movements. *One.* I move forward, pushing off their assaults. *Two.* I step to the side, causing Joseph and Samara to rethink their formation. *Three.* A cord tugs at me and I copy the visualization, reaching my arm behind my back, outstretching my hand until the rounded wood connects with my palm. I close my grasp and pull the nunchakus around my body with a jerk and a flick. This is enough to break Samara's nose.

There's an explosion of blood. My brief moment of pride and accomplishment is immediately overwhelmed by people rushing onto the scene.

If I didn't know how horrible I felt, at least George is there to remind me. "It's okay," he says. "We all know you didn't mean to do it."

Samara cries as Mario holds a wad of towels to her nose. The nunchakus hit the ground with a loud thud. From under Samara's sobs I hear a small voice and I realize then I have my face covered. I pull my hands away to see Whitney standing over Samara, requesting she keep her hands down away from her face.

We stand silently in a circle around the two of them and watch. Samara's beautiful, thick hair falls around her on the ground. The blood covering her face makes her pale skin look whiter than ever before. But it's Whitney who looks out of place. She's confident. One movement from her and Samara tenses. We all instinctively back away. She rests her hands over Samara's face and gradually, as if sucking the pain out of the room, the whimpers begin to fade.

One uninterrupted minute passes as we stand motionless, staring. Samara lies on the ground, eyes closed. Whitney hovers above her in a trance, whispering. Samara is so still that a part of me wonders if I've killed her. Maybe the blow was worse than I thought. The nervous hush of the room makes my ears ring. I close my eyes and listen to the soft whispers coming from Whitney. They remind me of spring for some reason. Rebirth. Growth. Awakening.

A chortling erupts through the room, causing me to snap open my eyes. I hear it again and move forward. My eyes are open wide when I arrive at Whitney's shoulder and witness the expression of relief plastered over Samara's face. Her long pointy fingers trace across her blood-encrusted nose.

"You did it! Oh my God! Whitney, you did it!" Samara says, rising to her feet and wiping the blood off her face with her sleeves. "You freaking fixed my nose!"

A roar of relieved laughter echoes around me. Whitney's usually meek smile spreads wider until tears swell in her eyes and then rush down freckled cheeks. I don't even realize I've been holding my breath until Trent slaps me playfully across the back and

153

I cough out a nervous laugh. The guilt that had been building in my stomach shrinks with each new batch of oxygen I invite into my lungs.

I step forward and place a hand on Whitney's shoulder. She's of course taller than me, but only by an inch or two. Her eyes shine brilliantly through the red of her tear-streaked face.

"Thank you." My voice is raspy, restrained. "What you did was incredible."

Something flickers across her eyes. Disbelief maybe. She looks almost pained as she works her face into a smile. I want to say more to her, convince her she should be proud of herself, but Joseph rushes in right then, picking her up and hoisting her onto his shoulders. Everyone cheers loudly, like they're at a football game, as he parades the healer around the room.

Chapter Twenty-Six

The next morning I train with George. We're supposed to learn to work together seamlessly so he can relate Zhuang's emotions to me. There's a hope this will offer me insights and direction when the time arises.

Shuman hands me a small pin the size of my fingertip. "On this is a camera," she says, pointing to my shirt, where she expects me to pin it. "George is going to be watching what you see and working to communicate emotions to you through this medium. It is no ordinary camera though. Aiden has equipped it with sensors and if they work as intended then George should be able to remotely read the emotions of the people you come in contact with."

She hands him a portable television the size of the palm of his hand. "This may be difficult for you, George," she says, directing her attention to him. "You are used to being present to read people. That is the reason you need to practice. You will not be with Roya when she is tracking Zhuang and the expertise you can use to guide her will have to come through the screen, the earpiece, and more importantly, this." She holds up a small disk. "This is a receiver and if it works correctly, it will deliver the emotions Roya transmits from other people to you. Wear it on your chest over your heart," she orders, handing him all of the equipment.

George places the earpiece in his ear, angling the microphone in front of his mouth. Then he hesitates, giving me a speculative glance before pulling up his shirt and ducking underneath to place the disk on his skin. I get a glimpse of the tight skin stretched over his hip bones when his shirt comes up, but I dart my eyes to the side before I see anything more.

Shuman gives us one last set of instructions. "Roya, walk around the Institute. George, practice trying to determine the emotions around her. Communicate with each other. You two are the only ones on the radio right now."

I give George a determined look after positioning the earpiece. Then I head down the hallway, moving farther away from him. I put my hand over my ear and say, "Can you hear me?"

"Yes," he replies in a low chime in my ear.

"Great." I feign enthusiasm. "So where should I go?"

"Go find someone to read," he says dryly.

"Really?" I ask doubtfully. Didn't he tell me emotions were private and he couldn't share them?

There's a long pause. "It's unfair, but I don't see any other way to test this." His response feels too much like a retort to the question I'd asked myself.

"But—"

"What you learn, keep in confidence," he interrupts. It's obvious he isn't pleased with this arrangement.

"Of course," I say.

"All right, then let's get started," George commands.

"I do have another concern though," I say, trying to inject power into my voice. "If you see the person on the screen, how do we know you're actually feeling them, rather than remembering what you've already read of them in the past?"

"That's a valid concern." His deep voice is honest. "Maybe we should test this in a foreign place, one in which I don't know anyone."

I consider this for a moment. "No, it's too risky right now. They've already limited my dream travel outside the Institute. There's no way Trey will let us do that."

I hear his exasperated breath reverberate over the microphone. "Well, I don't know then."

"What if I turn off the video feed?" I ask and then pause, working out the details in my head. "If this remote sensor really works then you won't need the camera in the first place, right?"

"All right," he gives after an obvious hesitation.

I set off down the corridor and stop at the first door I come to. It's nondescript, about like everything in the Institute. There's no placard beside the door. Most of the offices are like this on the fourth level. I freeze; a nervous bubble rises up my throat. I knock and wait.

After thirty seconds without an answer I sigh and move on.

"If it makes you feel any better," George says as I stride to the next door, "I think the sensor works."

"Oh, yeah. Why's that?" I ask.

"Because I feel you," he states vacantly.

My first attempts to swallow the tension in my throat are met with defeat. Finally I force out a whispered voice. "It doesn't."

"Doesn't what?" George asks.

"Make me feel any better," I answer, staring at the door in front of me.

"I feel your nervousness." He breathes and then pauses. "But what I don't know is why."

I wince from the acuteness of his remark. "Can you only read emotions? You don't know the reasons," I state, rather than ask.

"It depends on the person," George says. "You're more guarded with the details. And you're in training so you're accustomed to shielding yourself. Most people aren't as vigilant."

His explanation makes me feel somewhat relieved knowing I've succeeded in shielding myself, to an extent.

"You're going to have to take down the guard though," he says on the tails of my thoughts. "If this is going to work, I need to be able to discern your emotions from those you encounter."

"That seems counterintuitive," I say, stalking off from the door I'd been staring at through most of the conversation. I pace aimlessly. "Maybe I should wall myself up instead and that way you'll know the emotions you feel are someone else's."

"You could try," George says coolly. "But you're burning useless energy, especially in battle."

I stop and lean against the stainless steel wall. *Why does it feel like I can't ever gain anything without giving something up?*

"Of course," he continues, "if you do succeed in walling yourself up completely then you'll be the first person I've met to do so. Emotions aren't easy to seal off, unlike thoughts. Most can put walls up around their mind, but the heart has trouble being contained."

"So you can always read someone?" I ask, astounded.

"I always get remnants. Most of the time I get more. Details."

His words echo in my head long after he's spoken. I begin strolling through the corridor, finally making the loop and arriving at the door I abandoned moments earlier. I give it a quick rap and wait. No one answers.

"So *if* I considered taking down the wall, how would I go about that?"

I hear a bristling over the headset and then George clears his throat. "It's pretty easy. Once you take down the shield Ren taught you to put up, then you just have to allow your feelings. If you know them, then I will. If you don't, then I won't."

"Is that all." I bite on the words.

"I'm only trying to help," he lashes back.

"Thanks," I say. I knock at the third door and am unsurprised when it goes unanswered.

The idea of working with George has been intimidating. I'm uncertain if he still resents me for the torture he experienced before I wore the frequency adjuster. I know he means to help me now and there's times I see tenderness under the hard exterior he projects. But I've also rubbed too close against his armor before and been reproached for it. I'm simultaneously attracted and repelled by him, which creates knots in my stomach every time we're alone. When he looks at me, I feel his probe pushing underneath the surface of my skin, searching for the part of me I hold most dear. It's taken many meditative sessions to be able to face him without flinching. Now I'm supposed to unshield my feelings while running around the Institute and allowing him to decode other people's emotions for me? None of this is natural or real. It's a strange dream.

I stride forward, eyes fixed on the next door. The fluorescent lights cast it in a plain glow.

I knock and in no time the door slides back. Before the figure says a word I jerk my finger to my mouth and say, "Shhhh...I'm conducting an experiment."

Narrow eyes slice me in half. A part of me immediately regrets this, but as the brooding eyes stare at me with half contempt and half amusement I lack the motivation to abandon my plan.

"Okay, all right," George says on the other end of the radio. "I've got something new. It's dark. Scared. Mad." There's a pause while I hang out, staring at the terrifying figure in front of me. He's growing impatient.

"Hold on a second." George's usual cool voice sounds flustered in my ear. "I'm getting more. There's guilt in this person, a shame, but they don't feel they deserve to bear this wound. They didn't do it." His words come slow at first like he's reading them from a blurry screen. "They're tired of blaming themselves for what went wrong. Remorse. He's sorry she's dead. Such suffering. He's always suffering. It isn't fair."

George falls silent. I stand petrified. The emerald eyes in front of me seem to sense my treachery.

"Whatever does this experiment have to do with me?" Ren barks, half past the verge of angry.

I've willingly walked into the belly of the whale and now I'm unable to evict myself from it. Terror threads around my spine making me stand up tall. It's only when I hear breath move into my nostrils that I realize I haven't inhaled in a while.

Chapter Twenty-Seven

"Roya!" George's voice makes me jump. "You're standing in front of Ren, aren't you?"

I take two steps back, looking lost, as Ren shoots darts at me. I'm uncertain if he knows what I've just done, but he looks all too displeased with me, more so than usual. He slams his fist on the button beside his door and it slides shut.

"Roya!?" George's voice is accusatory. I know I've already been tried and convicted at this point. "Roya?"

"Yes," I finally reply.

"Are you standing in front of Ren?"

I continue to step backwards through the hall, not daring to turn my back on the door in front of me. I'm terrified by what I've just learned, less so by the wrath which is about to come down on me.

George's voice echoes loudly over the radio again. "Roya? Was that Ren?"

I charge off in a new direction. "Well, at least we know this whole thing works."

George looks different when I approach him minutes later. His soft eyes have turned cold and narrow. His mouth is pinched, and I don't like the way he wears this contorted expression of anger. "That's a pretty rotten way to force me to disclose Ren's emotions, don't you think?" George throws his earpiece on the floor.

"I'm sorry," I say. "That truly wasn't my intention. I didn't know that was his office."

"You tricked me! Did you pretend to knock at doors? Biding your time and playing games with me until you set the stage?" Flames drip from his accusations.

"How dare you?" I revolt quietly.

"Did you do this all because you wanted to know something I refused to tell you?!" It's the first time I've heard George yell. The words sound unnatural and ugly as they spew out of his mouth.

My fingernails pierce into my hands as I grip my fists. "Honestly, I forgot I'd asked you to tell me about him. I really wasn't trying to get the information out of you."

160

He stands staring at me, trying to read me. Trying to assess my emotions. His attempts are like tiny needles piercing my skin. I fight the urge to resist and for the first time truly allow it, stripping off the many protective layers I wear. Exposing myself.

There's a long pause as George's eyes rake over me. He draws in a long breath through his thin lips and says, "Roya, I only mean to help you."

I blink with surprise. *What had he read? What did he know? I didn't mean for him to divulge Ren's secrets. Did he know that?*

"You're scared of me?" he asks in disbelief. With a fugitive step forward he says, "If you could only read my emotions you'd know the same is true of me."

I suck in a short breath and stare at him, bewildered. "What?"

"I can't explain it," he says. "You aren't like most people I've read. Nothing about you is straightforward or easy." His tone is gentler now.

"Why should that scare you?" I ask, tucking my chin into my chest.

"I'm used to understanding people," he says. "It gives me security to know what I can expect. But you..." He trails off, a trace of a smile coiling across his face. "You, Roya, are an enigma."

I avert my eyes. "I didn't know that was Ren's office," I say, trying to steer the conversation another direction. "I wasn't trying to betray you."

"I know," he states definitively. "But at the time, when I threw my own emotions into it, I wasn't sure. And you had part of your wall up too. I couldn't read you, not like right now."

Goose bumps spread across my skin like I've stepped into a freezer. I grip my arms across my chest. The smile he wore a moment ago has vanished, replaced now with a persuasive expression. "Now, can't you see the confusion we'd avoid if you'd trust me?"

I mean to nod, but remain frozen. He stares at me and for a moment I consider putting the bricks into place one at a time, until I've resurrected the barrier again. My heart hurts and the hesitation in this moment makes everything worse.

"I could try," I finally say.

"That's enough." He gives an encouraging smile.

"Can we start over?" I ask, skirting his gaze.

"Yes." George picks up the earpiece securing it in place. "And, Roya," he says, begging for my full attention.

I waver, but comply, finally turning to stare into his quiet eyes. "What?"

"Thanks for taking down the wall. I know it wasn't easy," he says.

◆

Later that afternoon when Ren strides into the lecture hall, I sense he knows I've trespassed on his privacy. This is probably my guilt welling up to the surface because he never says anything to give me this indication. He's just his usual offensive self.

"For the life of me, I can't figure out why Trey wants all of you to be here for this lesson. It could just be Roya since she's the one who has to die at the hands of Zhuang. She's the one who needs to know this information. You all could be off playing rugby on the beaches of Malibu right now, but no, someone has decided that wherever Roya is, that's where all of you will be. Whatever Roya needs, all of you will get." Ren pretends to gag.

"I despise team sports," he says finally. Then he strides around the room until he's lurking over my shoulder. The impulse to send my fist flying backward courses through me, but I resist.

"Dream layers," he says in an exaggerated hush. "You've heard the term, right? But what does it really mean?"

Maybe he senses I'm having trouble restraining myself. Ren hops down the steps and stands center stage. "You all know by now that when you travel from one dream to the next each one represents a layer. Inevitably you've traveled dozens of layers in a dream going from one sweets shop to the next, right? Well, this is all fine and dandy when you're playing with your friends in dreamland. However, when you're tracking it's more complicated.

"You see, if your friend decides to move into a new layer and you forget where he's going then you have only one way to find him. What I'm speaking of is called dream tracking. We've used it for decades to find Zhuang with dodgy results. I don't know why I'm even telling you about it now except for the repercussions. You should be aware of them because they can have assorted effects."

Ren leers at me and then begins pacing back and forth. "When your dear friend, let's call him Bobby, leaves on his travels, for a few brief seconds he will leave behind a ripple. This ripple looks exactly as its name implies, blurry like someone smudged the space. Stand in Bobby's ripple before it dissolves and you might catch wind of his tracers—the small bits of consciousness he left behind right before traveling."

Ren throws one finger into the air. "*If* you absorb the tracers in time then you can track someone, but it does take a certain bit of faith and a whole lot of talent. Your consciousness has to blindly jump into a rabbit hole and follow someone to an unknown location. When you don't know where you're going there are several dangers and usually they're waiting for you.

"Furthermore, returning to your body is quite straightforward while dream traveling. However, when dream tracking it's exponentially more difficult. You can't pull out of it the same way you do when you dream travel on your own. A part of your consciousness can snag on a layer because you're falling through them blindly. The deeper you follow a person through layers, the more potential for snags. When you pull yourself back to your body the unraveling can cause knots, tying your consciousness up, keeping it from rejoining your body. If you get stuck, there's only one ending." Silence. No doubt it greets Ren's ears with satisfaction. He gives a sideways smile and then sharply hisses, "Death."

I sit tense and unblinking for several seconds before Ren continues. Sadly my rescue is in the form of a lengthy lecture filled with technicalities on how to spot ripples and absorb tracers.

"One last thing before I let you all out for recess." Ren's usual sharp voice sounds hoarse from talking. "Only a damn good Dream Traveler can follow tracers, much the same way only experienced trackers can follow an animal's path through an overgrown forest." With an unsympathetic smirk Ren jerks his head in my direction. "Sorry, missy, I'd advise on getting good at hiding, since my guess is you'll make a poor seeker."

◆

Later that evening, feeling distracted, I flip through one of the books Bob and Steve sent. Joseph lies across my bed reading through my dream journal as Shuman ordered. Although I keep trying to focus on the book, a part of me wants to ask Joseph why he lied about his family. We're friends now and this could go one of two ways: he'd hate me forever or he'd be real with me. Twirling a piece of my straw-colored hair around my finger I sort through the pros and cons of airing this whole topic out. I'm unsure why I haven't said anything yet, except for any time I try I see his father's drunken eyes, full of disgust for Joseph. Maybe I'd lie about my family too if I were him.

"You know what's weird?" Joseph says, pulling my attention back to the present moment.

"Yeah, your face." I suppress a laugh.

"Look in the mirror, Stark." Joseph aims a pillow at my head. "Good thing you're kinda smart, 'cause you can't rely on your looks."

It doesn't even faze Joseph when I reach out to deflect the pillow before it's hardly left his hands.

"And you throw like a T. Rex." I take a bookmark and flick it at him like a Chinese star. It bounces off his forehead and then falls into his lap.

He grins. "But seriously this time, you wanna know what's weird about your dream journal?"

I shrug.

"Peacock-related images keep showin' up in almost all of your dreams."

I scrunch up my face trying to recall this from any recent dreams. There is only one that comes to mind. In it I'd been walking through a house trying to decide if I should live there. Suddenly I heard a child making a noise behind me. When I turned there wasn't a child, but instead a radiant and brilliantly decorated peacock. He tilted his head to the side, and with a whoosh his feathers spread out around his body, taking over the entire open space of the living room. I remember being overwhelmed by his beauty, the silkiness of his feathers, how they formed such an intricate pattern as they rose up around his neck like a wall. His neck was the richest shade of blue I'd ever seen.

"There was just the one dream with the peacock in the house," I say, shaking my head at him.

He rolls his eyes. "Stop being so literal all the time. Dream interpretation's about seein' patterns and analyzing images. Gosh, have you learned nothin' from Shuman?"

"No, she's always too busy telling me how I'm doing something wrong. Maybe if I batted my eyes at her like you then she'd be a bit nicer to me."

Joseph ignores this and flips to a page in my journal. "Here you say 'plastered across the side of a barn was a green circle with a brown middle and inside that, a blue circle with a black center.' I'm no scientist, but that seems to resemble the design of a peacock feather, doesn't it?"

"You're right," I say seriously, "you're definitely no scientist."

Joseph flips to another page in my journal. "Then in the next dream you say that 'a man with a long blue neck' kept following you around." He reads from the journal in a high-pitched voice, "'I didn't feel threatened by him. Actually I forgot he was following me for the longest time, but each time I turned around he was always there.'"

I laugh. "All right, so what's your point?"

Joseph shuts my journal. "My point is, I think the peacock is your spirit animal."

"Oh, you have to be joking," I laugh again. "Shuman gets rattlesnakes. Trent is pretty convinced his spirit animal is the almighty tiger. Even Whitney has that white dog she keeps seeing in her dreams. And you're telling me my spirit animal is some flamboyant bird that's about as useful in battle as a mink stole?"

Joseph shrugs his shoulders as he stands and stretches. "Take it or leave it, Stark. No one said you got to pick your spirit animal." Then impersonating Shuman's airy tone he says, "They choose you."

Chapter Twenty-Eight

I work the nervous knot down my throat as I nod. Securing the tiny pin to my shoulder I give George one last look before heading off. We've been practicing a little every day, but only by ourselves. Now he's suggested I seek out the kitchen and maid staff. This was Trey's advice to our dilemma. Neither one of us will have had too much contact with these individuals.

Working with George has gone more smoothly than I expected. Up until now we've just sat in a room alone together. This involved me failing time and time again to shed the defense I longed to hide behind. Each time I tried to pull it down, as I'd done during that first session with him, it felt like I was sticking my toe in icy water, readying to submerge my entire body. It took many sessions for me to pull off all the layers like I'd done before. It was an unnatural process for me to expose my emotions.

And almost as strange was the process of sitting opposite George while he quietly probed my emotions. Talk about an uncomfortable silence. I found myself rambling just to fill it. This is when I learned of his lack of a sense of humor. No matter how hard I tried he rarely laughed at my jokes.

"Distraction isn't your friend," he warned the last time I tried to make light of something. "Those who fear intimacy laugh in order to suppress their tears." His words were soft and deliberate, meticulously chosen.

I smirked with indignation but chewed on his words long after he'd spoken.

And so we went on like this for quite a while. I actually found my flippant nature to be the perfect accompaniment to George's overly formal one. He'd trap me every now and again with something personal, something he'd drawn out of me, but I was quick to shelter my ego behind a snide remark. He'd pause and silently scold me with a glare for not taking the training more seriously.

"Oh, come on now, George," I'd complain in retaliation. "You're cutting through chunks of my childhood. How should I respond? We both know I'm unsuited for tears."

"You know I'll only peruse the emotions you make available," he replied. "If something's too personal then put it in the confidential file."

"The confidential file." He'd advised me early on to put the emotions I wanted to continue to shield in there. He didn't need to know every emotion I harbored, just enough so he could ascertain mine from others in the dreamscape.

The only other advice George gave me was to come to training with all emotions I didn't want investigated wiped off my chest, so to speak. If something's fresh, full of energy, then even if it's in the confidential file it can still be accessed.

I trot away from the center of his prying attention and an unsettling emotion takes seed in my chest. It didn't seem natural to examine people unknowingly the way George had done to me, even if Trey had signed off on it. These people wouldn't know to put their emotions in a secure place. "They have no time to prepare for the invasion you're about to wage," I say.

"No one ever does," George replies. "Most everyone walks around an open book. You aren't doing them a disservice. I'd read it on them anyway, if I walked past them or even stood in the same room and cared enough to read. Few are bound shut like you, so stop punishing yourself over what you're about to learn."

"Fine," I huff as I disembark from the elevator and make my way to the main hall. I've never ventured past that area, but know workers often carry food in from a set of doors in the back of the large room. I head there now.

"Miss?" a lady says, startling me as soon as I pass through the doors and into a food waiting station. "Can I help you with something?" She's busy sweeping the floors in gray scrubs. *What's up with the bland uniforms in this place?*

"I was just looking for some water." The words spill out of my mouth too quickly, rehearsed.

A wrinkle marking the space between her eyes creases. "Wasn't there some in your room? I'm certain your room has already been stocked, Ms. Stark."

She knows who I am? How is that? I'd never seen the people who clean my room, but I'm hardly ever there.

"It was. Thank you." I smile. "But I was down this way and just hoping to get some while here."

She pauses and straightens, her annoyance forgotten. "Of course," she says. "I'll just go and retrieve some water from the kitchen staff. I'll be back in a few." The woman pivots and strides around the waiting station to the kitchen prep area from where sounds emanate.

"Well?" I whisper.

"Interesting," George says in a quiet tone.

"Like how?" I urge, searching the space for others who could be listening to me talk to myself.

"You caught her off guard when you arrived, making her annoyed," he says.

"I already knew that." I almost laugh.

"Well, maybe you don't know that all her emotions are overwhelmed by a single one that runs deep inside her. If I'm reading this right then it's coloring all her feelings, like a pair of tinted sunglasses."

"That sounds major," I whisper.

"In this case it is," George says, just as the woman rounds the corner.

"Here you are," she says, handing me a glass of water complete with ice cubes and a slice of lemon and cucumber. "Just the way you like, according to the kitchen staff."

I blush as I take the glass. "What do you mean?"

"Which part?" the lady asks swiftly.

"How do they know how I like my water?"

A stray piece of brown hair falls into the woman's eyes. She blows to try and corral it back, but it doesn't work. With an irritated expression she tucks it behind her ear. "They know everything about your dietary preferences, just like I know what clothes you wear most often and how tidy you keep your room. It's our job to know you and how to assist your needs."

I suck in a surprised breath. "Oh."

"Is there anything else I can bring you?" the maid asks, looking curt.

"No, and thank you."

It's only once I've exited and ducked into a small abandoned room that I say anything to George. "So...?"

"Hmmm...." George muses.

I remain quiet, taking in my dull surroundings.

168

"This maid you encountered, she wasn't an easy read, but I'm confident I did it successfully."

"Was your initial reading correct? About the major emotion that affects her perceptions?"

"Yes," George breathes. "I think so."

"Well, are you going to tell me?" I question, hoping I'm keeping my voice down low enough not to attract attention from anyone in the hallway.

"It's pain. This woman is suffering very much."

"Oh." I'm not sure what I was expecting, but this answer seems rather simple.

"It masks all her emotions, to the extent that it perpetuates itself." I listen to George's breath over the radio and await his next words. I sense he's processing. A few seconds later he says, "She's in a vicious victim cycle. And in her case, this overwhelming emotion is so significant that it's created a blockage. This pain has blocked her sixth sense."

"You got all that from that brief encounter? Are you sure you're reading her right?"

"Yes and yes," he says with conviction.

"Then that's awful," I say.

"I agree," he says.

"George?"

"Yes," he replies.

"Do you ever wish you could do something for someone, like this woman? Do you ever wish you could help them with their problems? Their pain?"

There's a long pause, but I urge myself not to be the one to interrupt it.

"No, not usually," George finally says, a graveness to his voice. "There's been a time or two, but it's never really been my place."

"I kind of thought you might say that."

"Still, at times, other people's emotions do weigh on me. That's when I have to remind myself that 'the great art of life is sensation, to feel that we exist, even in pain.'"

I sink into a more intimate space all at once. Those words were written by someone with whom I'm not just familiar, but rather obsessed. "Lord Byron," I whisper.

"Yes," George says, a delicate smile in his voice. "His words always pick me up when I lose my own."

A switch flips in my head and I want him to keep talking. I want to hear more of his words which weave together perfectly creating symmetry in my asymmetrical world. However, George remains quiet.

"So now we know the sensor works," I say.

"Yes," George says. "It works."

"That's good news." I try to inject enthusiasm in my voice.

"Yes."

Another silence follows.

"Okay," I say as I make my way to the elevator. "I'm ringing off. I'll meet back up with you to debrief in just a few."

"I look forward to it," George says in a low voice.

♦

The stainless steel walls, which used to feel cold and sterile when I first arrived at the Institute, now have a comforting warmth. Even the clinical smell of the hallways somehow is soothing. It must be the cleaning chemicals they use, masked by a citrus perfume. Whatever it is it's slowly taking over the mossy lake water I used to associate with home.

The shiny walls and blue carpeted halls are becoming a part of me, although I'd never admit this to anyone. I don't want to say I belong here with the Lucidites, mostly because I don't think I'll be staying much longer. Actually, I'm pretty certain I won't be a resident of earth much longer. The constant uneasiness in my stomach rumbles slowly, as if the lion has managed to chew through another bar. I draw in a long deep breath and with its contents I hum to myself thinking that this will make me lighter. That's what happy people in movies do, right? They hum. Destitute people don't hum. Those headed to the guillotine don't hum. That would be absurd.

After my long walk through the corridor accompanied by the nervous rambling in my head, I step into the elevator. Another place I've strangely grown attached to. I used to travel to school in a van. Now my travels are all in this silver compartment. Bouncing between the levels of the Institute is almost like moving between worlds. Each time the silver doors slide open I find myself stirring uncomfortably under a new experience.

Nervous excitement stirs in my chest as I recap my afternoon with George in my mind. I tap the button for the second level, thinking of how his reassuring presence has given the team a new confidence. We worked well together before, but when George fully joined us a missing chain in our armor forged into place. His input into the emotional fabric of each of our missions is the piece we needed. Now when we move through the streets of Amsterdam, Tokyo, or Manhattan we're fully prepared on all levels. Before, we could access the thoughts around us, control the objects, know the future, and protect ourselves. But we never knew the emotional landscape. George's narrations at each destination bring color. They make those cities come alive. Where before they were two-dimensional obstacle courses, now they're three-dimensional terrains, alive with people and expectations and desires. Never before had I realized how the world is dictated by our desires rather than our thoughts. The prior puts the latter in motion.

The doors of the elevator start to close just as a voice pleads, "Hey, would you hold that please?"

I tap the button and Aiden clumsily rushes in, trying to balance a keyboard, speakers, a bundle of wires, and a stack of books. I reach out and grab the speakers before they tumble over the side of his arm.

"Thanks." Aiden grins. He pulls up a knee to add an extra support to the load.

"Why is it every time I see you, you've got your hands full?" I say.

"'Cause I know that's the best way to get your attention." He pouts with a sly expression.

I laugh. "That's one way, for sure."

"Though I wish I didn't have my hands full right now."

Blood rushes to my face. "Why's that?"

He gives me one long look and then lowers his voice. "I'm looking forward to picking up where we left off the last time I saw you."

The image of Aiden's hands on my shoulders and his eyes holding mine zips into my mind. I've thought about that moment dozens of times. Constantly I punish myself for wondering what

171

would have happened if we hadn't been interrupted. I've been trying to avoid it, but my affection for him is undeniable...unfortunately, the timing is all wrong.

"Do you always flirt with girls who are about to die? 'Cause you should know right now, if you're trying to get in my will, I don't have one."

He laughs. The keyboard slips a bit from his grip. "Actually, I never flirt with girls. Just you."

My heart hammers in my chest.

"Oh, and you're not going to die," he adds.

I turn the speakers over in my hand, pretending to inspect them. "So, what do you use this for? Is it to increase the gamma rays on some device thingy you're working on?"

"I use it to listen to music." He gives me a wolfish grin. "And please note that in all instances, it's better to decrease gamma rays. They're kind of deadly."

"I see. Well, that's why *you're* the Head Scientist."

The elevator teeters at my level before the doors bounce open.

"I need you to stop by my lab tomorrow. I've got to go over some devices with you. They could prove helpful. *And* I have a present for you." He winks.

Blood rushes to my face, and my eyes seize the floor in front of me. "Okay, I'll come by between sessions," I say.

Feeling rushed I wedge the speakers between the books and Aiden's chin. "You got this?" I ask, allowing myself to connect momentarily with his blue eyes. Instantly, I'm trapped by their allure. *Step back, Roya. Get off this elevator now.*

"For sure," he says confidently.

Without another look I walk away, wishing for the heat in my chest to dissipate as quickly as it arrived. Just as the elevator doors close I hear a loud crash from inside. I laugh easily.

I'm whistling and half giggling when a voice breaks into my head. "Hey, Roya."

Oh shit.

"Yeah," I say tentatively.

There's a pause, but I still hear George breathing.

"Never mind," he states sharply. "I'll tell you when you get here."

"Uhhh…all right." I squeeze my eyes shut. Embarrassment unravels in my stomach. How could I forget to turn off the monitor? George has obviously sensed my emotions for Aiden. But why does that matter? There's nothing between George and me, and who knows what's going on with the Head Scientist. I have no right to get swept up in any of this right now.

♦

George is different when we meet up a few minutes later. It's infuriating. He hardly makes eye contact with me as he puts the equipment away.

"So what did you want to tell me?" I ask.

He turns and looks at me, dissecting me, his eyes hot and sharp. Opening his mouth, he goes to say something but then shakes his head.

"I forget," he lies. "I'm sure it's nothing."

"George." I step toward him, trying to decipher the odd expression he's wearing. I want to see him soft and thoughtful again, the way I know him when we're training. The way he is most of the time lately. Every now and then, though, this demon crawls into him making him angry with a passive aggression I can't battle.

He takes one deliberate step back, putting what feels like a mile between us. "I've got to go and catch up on some other work," George says matter-of-factly.

I turn in the direction of the wall and pretend to put away equipment. I clench my eyelids shut. "Sure," I say. "See you later." I listen to him rustle behind me, standing in place. And then all I hear are his slowly retreating steps.

Chapter Twenty-Nine

Since my conversation with Joseph, I've been trying to wrap my brain around the peacock in my dreams. I'm getting nowhere with it. There isn't a single part of me that wants to endorse the idea that my spirit animal is some flashy bird. However, I've combed through my dream journal and found that Joseph might be correct: peacock imagery shows up in most of my recent dreams. I go back to my room and grab my dream journal. I also grab the chocolate Bob and Steve sent.

Shuman's office is supposedly next to Ren's. I knock and stand there awkwardly. The door slides open. Shuman's amethyst eyes stare at me, puzzled. "Can I help you?" she asks.

"Yes, I have some questions," I say, feigning confidence.

She turns at once and strides back into the darkened office. "Come in then."

A floor lamp with a round paper shade in the corner gives off a dim light. From that I make out a painting of a wolf hanging over a large desk in the corner. Shuman takes a seat in a brown leather armchair and points for me to sit in an adjacent one. There's a large dream catcher on the main wall. It's purple and has five fluffy white feathers dangling from it.

I sit tensely on the edge of the seat, holding my journal in my hand. Remembering the chocolate, I set it down on the wooden coffee table beside the chairs. "Here, I don't know if you like chocolate, but I brought this for you." I stop, trying to find the right words. "It's to show my appreciation for your help."

"Thank you," Shuman says with her fingertips steepled.

"Look, I'm here because Joseph seems to think my spirit animal is a peacock. He's right that it shows up multiple times in my dreams, but…" I stare down at my dream journal, a wave of insecurity sweeps over me.

"But you do not approve of it," she says.

"Well," I begin, "peacocks are beautiful and all, but I don't understand their usefulness."

"Everything is about perspective, Roya," Shuman says thickly. Bob and Steve put something similar in their first letter.

She stares at me impassively.

"Okay. Thanks for your time." I stand, irritated, wishing I hadn't come.

"In Greek mythology a goddess by the name of Hera placed eyes on the feathers of the peacock to symbolize that they could see all," Shuman says as if she's reading out of a book.

I freeze, staring at her flat expression.

She continues, "The Buddhists believe the bird represents openness. The Hindus associate this bird with good fortune. It may also interest you to know that the peacock can eat poison without becoming ill or dying. For this reason the bird represents incorruptibility."

Gradually I push back until the chair is pressed against my calves. Then I sit. "Yes, that does shift my perspective a bit."

"I thought it might," Shuman says.

"So how will my spirit animal help me?" I ask.

"These things are not for me to know. You won't even know until the animal comes to assist you."

I should have known this would be Shuman's answer. Why had I brought her a gift? She hadn't *really* helped me. Mostly she'd thrown riddles and lies at me.

"Why don't you like me?" The question tumbles out of my mouth.

Shuman doesn't budge, she just holds my gaze and takes her time before responding. "Why would you think I do not like you?"

I hold up a finger and begin counting off the reasons. "You've been cold since we met. You bold-faced lied about me being the 'chosen one.' And you conveniently forgot to tell me my body was going to die if I didn't act fast once I arrived at the Institute." I will myself to stay focused on her intense gaze.

"I do not prove myself to appease others. That is for the lavish and wasteful. For this reason you view me as cold. It is not the first time I have heard it." She pauses. "I will admit I had my doubts about you. However, when you chose the bracelet as your protective charm I knew you were the person to face Zhuang. My people have their own forecast on this situation. The shaman of my tribe told me the Lucidites would be saved by the girl who wore the bracelet. I believe this might be you."

175

She laces her fingers together and sits with a peculiar expression, like that of a cat's, seeming to know more about me than I'd like, but less than they pretended.

"To answer your other question," she says, "I believe you would not have come if you thought you had to contend. You were hesitant when you thought you were the chosen one. What if I told you that you were one of fifty chosen possibilities?"

"That's still deceitful," I say. The room remains silent. I finally ask, "Why didn't you tell me my body would die if I didn't autogenerate? Why leave out this important detail?"

Something flickers across her eyes. It's tiny, like a spark. "I had my reasons for leaving this out."

So she did do it on purpose. My insides flare with disgust. "And they were?"

"Roya, asking questions has consequences. Maybe you should not ask them so freely."

I squint at her. Like speaking to someone hard of hearing I say, "Why did you leave out those details?! And why does it sound like you're meddling in my life?!"

She gives me an unhurried glare and then seems to resign slightly. "You were not told about your body needing autogeneration because this was a part of the fabric which created your future. A necessary part of *the* future."

"So you are meddling in my life." I sigh. "I should have guessed."

"Everything that happens to you is not about you," she says.

"What? Who else did my almost dying, because you left out an important detail, affect?" I ask, pushing back the frustration threatening to erupt.

"It is hard to say, but I approximate millions."

I gasp, wondering if I've misheard her. "That's impossible," I say. "Something so insignificant can't affect so many."

She shakes her head. "Your history books want you to think so. They teach you great victories are the results of exaggerated efforts. If one actually studied the fabric of these events they would find wars are won from a wink, a gesture, an event that transpired a millennium before the battle. Humanity has always been saved by small acts; the ones where someone gained a piece of their own puzzle, not the ones where a hero stood prodigious on a battlefield."

I shake my head, mimicking her earlier movement. "I didn't gain anything from almost dying. I was drained by that experience."

"You still want to believe this is all about you," Shuman says, leveling her gaze to mine. "A person who saves someone is much more altered by that event than the one who almost dies, wouldn't you think?"

Aiden. She's referring to him. But why? "What?" I ask. "What does *that* person have to do with any of this? You said this was about me and my future."

Shuman doesn't answer, but instead tilts her head as if saying *figure it out for yourself.*

"You're obviously privy to my life in ways I'm not," I say, failing to soften my tone. "You seem to be orchestrating something. Wouldn't it be easier to tell me what you're up to, so I act in the prescribed manner and then the 'fabric' of my life will go as you've seen it?" I say, condescension crawling over every word.

"It is true. I know a part of the future. I know if I do one thing it could cause a certain reality to take place. There are no certainties though. Too many variables. But I would never tell you what to do or even what to expect. I admit I have built the setting in some of your choices, but you have always had a choice in the end. And that is the way it should be," she says.

"Choice!?" I argue. "I don't feel I've had many choices. I've always got you or someone else messing with the details. I don't feel in charge of anything anymore now that I realize the intervening Lucidites are always on call."

"Do you wish you would have been left in Texas to live in oblivion?" she asks plainly.

I stare at her with quiet contempt instead of answering.

"You were born a Dream Traveler," she continues. "But to be a Lucidite is a choice. If you choose to not associate with us anymore, then will you be happier? All tribes affect a member's life, as they should. If you see this as meddling, then you must ask yourself if this is the place for you. Maybe you belong elsewhere."

In four short words I feel abandoned all over again. *Maybe you belong elsewhere.* I'd never belonged anywhere until I entered this place. But I didn't know that until just now…

Shuman pauses, and her look holds a challenge in it, as if she's tempting me to stop her from saying any more. "Roya, when you stop viewing your life as something done to you and rather a reality of your choosing then you will find peace. I am not certain of much, but of this I am." After this statement she smiles. She actually smiles. It looks strange on her face, like the moon wearing googly eyes. In an instant the small expression is gone and her stone face returns.

"Whatever." I shake my head at her as I stand. "It's easy for you to say that from your vantage point of knowing the future. It's so easy for you to talk about accepting realities when you're not the one who has to face Zhuang."

The insinuation hangs in the air like gasoline, chemical and pungent.

Her eyes narrow, only slightly, but I spy it. "I believe we are done here," she says with authority.

I blink at her, clench my teeth, pluck my journal off the table, and turn to leave. "Coming here was a mistake," I say to the air as I leave.

Once I'm in the privacy of the elevator I let out a sigh that sounds more like a yell, all my frustration finally rising to the surface. It feels good to push all the air out of my lungs. When the elevator stops at my level the lady in the lavender scrubs stares at me strangely and I promptly know the elevators aren't well insulated.

Long, angry strides carry me to my room. It will take time and space to process my conversation with Shuman. She knew something which inspired her to orchestrate my first meeting with Aiden. But what? And why?

I immediately write a letter to Bob and Steve. It helped the last time and I could really use the relief. I tell them about the peacock, breaking Samara's nose, my sessions working with George, and how Ren is strangely the most repulsive and helpful person I've met so far. When I'm done I've written several pages. My stomach is lighter and I realize suddenly that I'm hungry and haven't eaten all day. I fold up the letter, address it, and head toward the main hall to find Patrick.

Chapter Thirty

The next morning after breakfast, I head to Aiden's lab as he requested. Voices echo from the space as I approach. I peek around the corner and spy the Head Scientist with his hands in the air, irritation coating his expression. "Well, that's my solution. If you don't like it then find someone else to help you."

I knock on the door frame. "Hey, you told me to come by. Do you want me to come back later?"

Aiden's tousled hair looks even wilder than usual. He smiles and waves me into the room. "No, come on in. I was just reviewing some of the equipment with Ren."

"Yes, Mr. Mad Scientist was just over here being a Negative Nancy," Ren says, standing beside a table in his usual dark green suit.

I ignore Ren, which is becoming easier with practice. "You said you had some stuff to show me," I say to Aiden.

"Yes." He pulls a small box out of his pocket and withdraws a tiny earpiece.

I freeze. Petrified. It's another object from my closet. From the fifth task. *Why?* It was one of the things in the box with the baby teeth. The one I threw.

"This is a VDR Shield," the scientist sings, oblivious to my nervousness. "It sends out an electromagnetic shield which encases the cortex, also known as dream central. If a person wears this then they're protected from Zhuang infiltrating their thoughts. This is the same technology that works at the Institute, keeping us all safe while dreaming. I've been able to isolate it into a tiny personal unit. Pretty, cool, huh?" he says, his eyes dazzling with delight.

"Yes, that's very cool!" I say. "So now that we have this type of technology then can we just give these to everyone in the world and call it a day?"

After I ask this it seems like a stupid question. If Aiden thought it was stupid then he doesn't show it. "They're expensive, hard to reproduce, and the technology is unreliable," he says. "I just wanted you and Ren to see it because it marks a new era of development. In the future, it would be great to offer these to Lucidites not housed at

179

the Institute, the same way we give them protective charms. Unfortunately, we're still a little way off from that."

Ren flashes an arrogant grin at me. His pointy canines make him look menacing, although I sense he's all talk. "We have enough food to feed everyone, sweetheart, but still people go hungry. Be realistic, would you?"

I shoot him a dirty look before focusing my attention back to Aiden. "What does VDR stand for?"

"Ah, yes," he says with enthusiasm. "It's a term that in French means 'dream stealer.' *Voleur de reve.*"

"What does French have to do with any of this?" I ask confused.

"That"—Aiden holds up his hand—"is a story for another time."

"Honestly," Ren says, folding his arms across his chest, "I'm unimpressed. That's what you're looking for, right, Dr. Hotshot? You want me to say this is the future that will save us all. Right?" Ren laughs and then continues, "It's not. If you ask me I think we're better off with less technology. Flynn should have gotten rid of the entire science department when we took over this place. I'll never understand his stupid love for science."

Ren turns and looks at me. "You know Flynn thinks that if the spirit of dreams and the logic of science married then the world would be a happier place. Next time you see him, why don't you ask how that's working out for him?"

With a turn he makes for the door. "This, as I suspected, was a huge waste of time. Glad to know you're throwing millions of dollars into this rubbish, Aiden. Keep it up, you daft scientist."

Once Ren is gone the room gets bigger, brighter. I blink rapidly for a second. "What in the world was that all about?"

Aiden laughs, obviously letting off some steam. "That was Ren acting exactly like Ren."

"Yes, I know, we've met. But what's he going on about? What was that whole thing about getting rid of the science department?"

"Oh, right." He scratches his chin and says, "Well when the US government pulled out of the Institute forty years ago, many of the Lucidites wanted to abolish the science part of it. As you heard Ren say, Flynn loves science and against many people's wishes he kept the department alive and funded. It's because of this that I have a job. Ren personally believes my work complicates the Lucidites' mission. You would understand how we're natural enemies, although personally I think he'd make an excellent party guest."

We laugh and I automatically loosen up. Then I'm reminded of something I read in the folder recently. "The US government abandoned the Institute because they weren't able to prove there were any results to lucid dreaming and ESP, right? Well, how's that possible, since we know it's real?"

Aiden sits in his chair and leans back. His jawline looks more defined as he gnaws at the inside of his cheek. "Yeah, this is a good part of the history. When the Dream Travelers were invited to take part in the research the first person they brought in was Flynn, the founder of the Lucidites. He assessed the situation pretty quickly. Apparently, he'd been trying to secure a location for the Lucidites for a while, but was finding it difficult. This was exactly what he'd been looking for. However, he knew the US government wouldn't go away unless the whole project proved useless. Flynn also knew the government would abuse these powers if they discovered them to be real. It didn't take long for Flynn to infiltrate the research with his own findings, which showed ESP and all related fields to have inconclusive results. Almost everyone working for the government packed up their suitcases and took the long submarine ride home. Since then this place has been mostly free of any Middlings."

"W-w-wait," I stammer confused. "They took a submarine?"

"Well, naturally, that's how people originally got to the Institute. This mode of transportation is only used now for shipping goods in and out."

I'm uncertain why this new bit of knowledge instantly cramps my stomach, making me feel uneasy. Although I knew the Institute was underground, I hadn't considered it was submerged in water. Now the crazy way that it takes to enter the Institute makes more sense. At least it makes more sense for people who are becoming accustomed to accepting strange alternate realities.

"Wow," I finally say, hopping up on one of the stools next to the work bench. "That's fascinating."

"I thought so too." Aiden stands and walks to the table where I'm seated, only six inches away. "So, naturally, people want to know how the US government would just forget they funded an

181

Institute. Why wouldn't they come back and take it over with some new research mission, right?"

I'd thought the same thing when I first read the history of the Institute. I nod, staring into Aiden's excited blue eyes. His passion for his work isn't just attractive, it's inspiring. I hope one day to do something that touches people, either because of its significance or because of my enthusiasm for it. Aiden does both.

"Thanks to a remarkable technology we never have to worry about the US government again," Aiden says, almost jumping up and down. His mood has infected me and I'm ready to jump on the balls of my feet with him before even knowing what he's going to say. "With the modifier we're able to implant ideas or, more importantly, in the case of the government, remove histories from people's minds."

Even as Aiden speaks, these words have a hard time registering. They catch in my brain like slippery stones in a net. If I tried to pick them up they'd slip through my fingers, their mossy surface defying my ability to grasp.

"I don't understand," I finally admit.

Aiden gives a sensitive smile and nods, like my inability to understand my native language and this string of familiar words isn't ridiculous. "The Lucidites used this device to extract all memories of the Institute and the project from the government employees. Like pencil marks on paper, all their experiences here were erased. They'll never remember those years working here. It's a blank gap, but not to the point that they want to ask questions. It's just like they had one long night of dreamless sleep."

I swallow and stare at Aiden, lost for words.

"Well, and of course all paper records mysteriously disappeared as well. There are no traces this place ever existed." Aiden laughs abruptly like this is a funny practical joke.

"This device, it erases memories? Realities? I thought you said it implants ideas."

"It does both."

Aiden flashes a cunning smile, but for some reason it's easier to resist than the last one I'd seen him adorn.

He carries on, "What we did to the US government is known as receding. With the modifier we also can implant. Now you're seeing how fantastic this piece of technology is," he coerces in his passionate manner. "It both removes memories *and* puts them in someone's mind."

"The Lucidites used this back in the 1970s when they took this place over, right? So this type of technology has been around for a while?" I ask.

"Oh yeah! However," he hesitates, "the earlier versions had kinks. I've worked them out now, but…" He looks at me for a few seconds and then says, "There were issues with the implanter part of the device. With time people forgot the embedded reality."

"That must have made things pretty complicated," I say.

"It was, but not in the way you'd think. The people being embedded ignored the reality we were trying to get them to accept. This just created extra work for us."

"So the modifier is still used?" I ask.

"Oh yes," he says triumphantly.

A knot rises automatically in my throat. I no longer feel like bouncing on my toes. "Why does the Institute use the modifier?"

"Only to protect good," Aiden says, leaning down on the table, closing a few more inches between us. "We never manipulate lives for anything else." His breath coasts against my cheeks.

I ease back a few inches. "Manipulate lives?"

Aiden counters with a look of confusion.

Something in me is on fire. This conversation has ignited a fast-burning fuse. "Seems like you're playing God," I say, an undercurrent of bitterness in my voice.

Aiden recoils. There's a flash in his eyes. He's offended. In one small whispered statement I've created distance. "Why would we be given these talents if we weren't supposed to use them?" he says in a quieter voice than usual.

"I'm sure that's exactly what Zhuang's telling himself."

"No, this is different," Aiden says. The anger in him engulfs the passion, like a hot blanket. I've struck something, a place in him he's used to defending.

"Maybe I see what Ren was talking about." I slide off the stool. "Manipulating lives," I repeat, shaking my head. "That's an abuse of power. You can't do that, Aiden. It's wrong."

He stares at me for a long time. His expression is one of hurt laced with disappointment. I feel exactly the same way. But I can't condone this. How can Aiden or Flynn or anyone think it's their right to tell people what to think? Or erase their memories? Erase their lives? Everyone always uses the "greatest good" argument. That's how wars happen and people die. They always die to protect the greater good. But we shouldn't have to lie, cheat, and kill to protect good. That's counterintuitive.

I'm torn as I stand looking at Aiden. I don't want to argue with him. The last thing I want to do is argue with *him*. But now that I know the truth I can't look at Aiden the same way. In a matter of minutes everything has become tarnished and ruined.

"I've got to go." I turn to leave. I focus on each step that carries me to the exit. I try to distract myself from the heartfelt music resonating overhead and the disappointed eyes on my back.

"But…" Aiden says.

I halt gently in that large space and stand motionless. One second passes, then two, then ten more. I'd been hoping and waiting for that little "but," so when I heard it I stopped. It took a great deal more effort to turn and face him. His expression is pleading and also hard like stone, unchanging. I need him to say something to repair the last few minutes. I need him to fix things. I need him to make me want him again.

He takes a long breath, closes his eyes for a second, and opens them again. "I'm only doing my job. Don't be mad at me, please."

I tilt my head sideways, baffled. "It isn't about *me*, Aiden. It's about abusing some power *you* think you own." I shake my head at him, at this whole preposterous conversation. "I don't want Zhuang to hurt people, but I won't allow that threat to excuse this. It's immoral to erase or plant ideas in the minds of innocent Middlings. If that's what the Lucidites do, then maybe I don't belong here."

Aiden closes the space between us in two strides, his eyes dark and narrow. "Maybe you don't, because this is what the Lucidites do. They save lives."

I'm assaulted by his accusation, but I hide it. "At the stake of others' lives? Is that fair?"

"We're trying to help, to ensure there's a future, for us, for anyone."

"Who gave you or anyone the right though? And where's this arbitrary line? When do the Lucidites stop? What else will they take over if they think it could benefit them? Homes? Businesses?

Countries? My God, this is a slippery slope and even you, with all your genius, have to realize that."

His hostile eyes rake over me. He doesn't see it. I know for certain he's just concocting an excuse in his own brilliant head and it infuriates me.

"Roya, you're wrong. The Lucidites wouldn't do anything to abuse this power. You haven't been with us long enough to know that. It's not as cut and dry as you're making it. Don't you see that?"

"I don't. All I know is that if someone put or erased ideas in my mind then I'd feel invaded."

"You wouldn't if you knew they were saving your life!" he shouts at me.

I slip my hands into my pockets to hide my shaking. "You can't know that. You can't know you're saving them. That's just something you're telling yourself so you can excuse what you're doing, so you sleep well at night."

"You're more like Ren than you realize. Obtuse! Self-righteous!"

Repulsed by his audacity, I trip backwards. The distance separating us is no longer charged with desire, but rather disdain. He isn't who I thought he was. How could I have been so stupid? Betrayed by my own emotions, I retreat to the exit, to the hallway and away from Aiden's fuming eyes.

Chapter Thirty-One

It's a good thing I have a stack of books to keep me entertained since I have no immediate plans to leave my room. I skip lunch and dinner, dreading seeing Aiden. I also skip training with Shuman. After yesterday's argument I can't do it. I don't want to let anyone down, but I also need to strip myself of obligations. I hang in my room until I hear the knock. I've been expecting it.

It comes half an hour after dinner started. I hit the button, hoping he's brought me something to eat.

"All right, Stark, you've got some explainin' to do." Joseph strides into my room, setting a small box on the desk before flopping on my bed. "Where ya been?"

I snatch the box and open it, pushing the utensils through the plastic bag that encases them. "I've been in hell," I say between bites.

"Mmm…I'm not sure the eternally damned would agree with the comparison," Joseph says in his usual blunt style.

Remembering Joseph is religious and fears places like hell, I restate myself. "I've been having a tough day."

"Understandable," Joseph says, resting his face on his hands. "DD is approaching."

"Yeah, whatever, that can't get here soon enough."

A shadow falls on Joseph's face. How can I be so heartless? The Day of the Duel isn't just my last possible day on earth. Remorse courses through my hot skin. I swallow a rough bit of pride and apologize for my careless statement. Then I fill Joseph in about my arguments with Shuman and Aiden.

"You know, Stark, you might save us all still," he says when I've finished. "You've got heart. That's what's obvious to me right now. You stand up for what you believe. And you sure throw a rotten tantrum. If I was Zhuang, I wouldn't want to be on the receiving end of that."

I smile, folding up the box that used to contain a scrumptious salad. "Thanks for bringing me food," I say.

"I have to admit," Joseph yawns, "I did it for selfish reasons. You'll be an easy target for Zhuang if you're malnutritioned."

I laugh, ushering Joseph to the door. I'm scheduled for dream travel training and I need to get ready.

He pokes me in the ribs and says, "Hey, will ya do me a favor? Tell George that when he's around, I make a point of pretending to be in love with him. I've seen the confusing looks he's been giving me and I think my trick has worked."

♦

Tonight George and I are supposed to meet in the dreamscape to work on tracking. Trent has agreed to be the target. We'll meet in the usual place and then Trent will move to a new location, or layer. I'll have a chance to absorb the ripple, move into it and follow his tracers. If I can't track him, then George will be hooked up through the camera and microphone to sense where I should go. This is a brand new part of our training and we'll all be in dream travel mode, which adds a new intensity.

George is leaning against the wall when I arrive.

"Hey, there," I say.

"Hey," he says, emotionless.

"Trent showed up yet?"

"Nope." He stares off in the distance.

"How's everything going?" I ask casually.

"Fine."

We stand silently. Trent's late.

George opens his mouth to say something and apparently changes his mind. He's doing a lousy job of hiding his frustration. I stare at him, wishing just this once I could read his emotions.

Finally he says, "So you didn't show up to lunch or dinner."

"Yeah, I wasn't hungry."

"Seems like someone else felt the same way," he says with an edge to his voice.

"What are you talking about?" I feign innocence.

George knows better though. He flashes me an irritated expression. "I shouldn't have said anything, I can't divulge other's emotional states. Never mind." *He's talking about Aiden. Is he jealous?*

Internally he looks to be wrestling with something. He bites his bottom lip and locks eyes with me. "We have a really important

187

mission to attend to right now, Roya. It's unfair for you to get distracted, skipping meals and practices. It's….careless." He drops his chin and stares at the ground like it holds some great points of interest.

There's that word again, *unfair*. I'm starting to hate it. Every time it comes up it always draws a line creating winners and losers. Those with the upper hand and those holding the short straw. I thought we were all in this together, but it appears I was wrong.

I barrel forward until only inches separate George and me. When he lets his eyes meet mine I say, "You know what's unfair?"

His eyes narrow slightly.

"You know how I feel and where it stems from," I say. "You know my family made me feel insecure from a young age. You know they ignored me and pretended my clairvoyance was a joke. You know I hide from everything as a result of being an outcast my entire life. You've had access to my fleeting and long-seeded emotions." I jerk my chin in the air with a new confidence. "What's unfair is you know so much about my emotions and think that entitles you to judge me. Why don't you level the playing field and tell me something, anything, about you. Because honestly, all I know is your name is George, you read emotions, and you're passive aggressive."

His eyes remain fixed on me, cold and strained. I've hit something, but who knows if it's the part I intended.

"Here!" Trent's voice rings behind me.

I turn and see his white smile glow across his dark skin.

"Are we gonna start this chase party or what?" he says with gusto.

"After you." I wave my hand and pretend to be completely present.

"All righty then," Trent says before disappearing.

Exactly where Trent stood is an almost unnoticeable wave. It's so slight that without knowing what I'm looking for I'd miss it completely. The pigments of colors blur in a wave. It's transparent, but makes the area behind it blurry, like an old piece of glass. I draw in a deep breath, striding toward it.

The ripple of Trent's consciousness hits me like a wave. The current is mild, but still carries momentum. I clear my mind and remain pliant to allow my consciousness to be sucked into the vacuum his recent travel momentarily created. My mind goes dark, like all lights have been stamped out. It's followed by an eerie quiet, one that makes my skin shiver and my chest vibrate. I don't think words, but rather feel the idea of *letting go*. A blinding light explodes across my vision and I fall terrifyingly over an arc and then speed blindly through blurry tunnels. It's the most petrifying roller coaster I could ever imagine. My mouth opens to scream, but nothing comes out. Over and over I open my eyes to see, my mouth to scream, and there's nothing.

The tunnel heaves me out next to a large round fountain. Inside the middle of it stand two statues of women—caryatids, their hands over their heads hold up a large bowl. The water cascades from the center of the bowl and trickles in droplets over the rim, into the larger pool. Moist air smells of both moss and concrete. Soft and hard. The location is a city, but it has the aura of a small town.

I scan the area around the fountain, searching for Trent or another ripple. His devilish cackle pulls my attention immediately in his direction. Like a villain in a comic he stands, feet shoulder-width apart, arms crossed, and his chin tucked into his chest. The smirk across his playful face completes the look.

"Well, that was fast! I thought tracking was supposed to be tough." Trent laughs. "So, do you want me to keep going now, or let you catch up?" he says.

"Don't take it easy on me, keep going as fast as you'd like," I tell him, sounding more confident than I am.

"All right, I'm moving," Trent says with a smile and then he's off.

I have seconds to move into his ripple. I sprint for the tiny wave encoded with the DNA of his last thought. It's so slight that my body only barely registers the difference in the space, like a small segment of thick air. But my body reacts at once, my stomach lurching as I'm whirled off my feet and sucked into another void. This time the process is immediate. The tunnel blankets me with an angry wind, which shoots through my ears and makes me feel hollow. I know I have to remain focused and yet pliable in order to stay on course. Wherever that is.

The busy street beside me is claustrophobic compared to my last location. Cars pass behind me. In front, a white arbor-like structure stands among green grass. This time I recognize the place.

The knoll. The place Kennedy was shot. Somehow I always pictured it starker. Gray. Even sad. This place isn't any of those. It's…touristy. People jostle by, carrying cups of coffee and talking excitedly. A guy stands on a nearby step selling postcards and T-shirts.

Out of the corner of my eye I see Trent running down the sidewalk. He's trying to make it difficult by getting some distance between ripples. I push forward on my toes, ready to spring after him, when my reflexes catch a new presence materialize behind me.

I tense and turn, praying the dark outline in my periphery isn't Zhuang. The streetlights cast an eerie glow around his broad shoulders. It's George.

Chapter Thirty-Two

"Don't follow him. I'll tell you where he's going. I feel it strongly. This will give us at least a minute," George says, looking more frustrated than before, but also more determined. It's a cute combination on his otherwise innocent face.

I shake my head, completely baffled. "George, you're supposed to stay at the Institute. What are you doing here?" I say motioning to the busy street. "I need to follow Trent. That's the goal."

"And you will. I know where he's going and I'll tell you. First I want to tell you three things, out of fairness."

His words hang in the humid air between us. I try to read his flat expression and simultaneously realize he's reading me. My efforts are futile against him.

"Fine, what are they?" I acquiesce.

The traffic speeds by us, but we remain locked on each other. George opens his mouth to speak and then closes it again. Time's running out. I need to chase Trent. George has something up his sleeve here, but I have my own mission. He senses my anxiety immediately.

Tension stretches across his forehead as he opens his mouth again. "Three things: The first is my mother raised me alone. The second is I'm always quiet because I'm listening to the emotions, they're quite distracting at times. Lastly, I've spent much of my time alone too. It's hard to make friends when you know people better than they know themselves."

His pain in this intimate confession slices through me cleanly, like a knife through dry, three-day-old cake. I swallow down the emotion. "Our minute has to be up. Where'd he go?"

"New York City. Empire State Building. Eight a.m. EST, today."

"Thanks," I say. "Go back. We'll talk later."

I shut my eyes and within seconds I spiral into a gigantic lobby. A bank of elevators sits at the back. The far wall bores a large depiction of the building. The walls are shiny and slick. I scan the crowded area for a ripple just as George's voice echoes in my ear. "Baton Rouge. Tiger Stadium. Present."

Instantly I close my eyes and shoot to this location. This time I'm alone in the middle of the field. Darkness stretches around me. No sign of a ripple. The streets outside the stadium hum as the traffic passes. With the lights off, the stadium is eerie in its vastness. Beautiful. My reflexes pick up Trent a half second before he materializes. I grin.

"Man," he grunts. "How'd you do that? I wasn't even here yet!"

George laughs in my ear. I love that sound. It's so rare. "I got a hold on him," he says. "Roya, go ahead and tell him I know his next location too. This guy is too predictable. He wears his emotions around his neck like a medal. I'll always be a step ahead of him."

I hold up a finger at Trent, asking him to wait while I converse with George over the radio. "But I still need practice tracking," I argue, staring off in the distance where I know George is.

"You seem to have it down pretty well already," he counters.

"Beginner's luck."

"Or Trent is as easy to track as he is to read. Maybe we should practice with someone else to test that theory." George's tone is cool and confident. "But for the rest of our free night we could just catch up…the two of us."

"Maybe," I breathe into the headset.

Trent stares at me with wide eyes when I turn my focus to him. "Let's go back to the classroom and regroup. George has something to tell you."

◆

"Well, sorry for being *predictable*," Trent seethes. Disappointment is plastered across his face as George explains how he knew all his locations prior to him traveling.

"Am I really that easy to read?" Trent looks at George with a worried expression.

George seems to assess something internally for a few seconds and then says, "I wouldn't worry about it."

"But if you know, then…" Trent says, taking in the pattern of the floor under his feet.

"Doesn't mean anyone else can read you as easily," George replies.

Trent looks dejected as George's words wash over him.

"Your secret is safe with me," George continues, looking straight at Trent.

The firmness in George's voice makes me believe him.

Relief spreads over Trent's face, giving him back his usual casual essence. He turns to me and says, "Maybe you'll have better luck tracking someone less readable. Try Joseph." Trent laughs before disappearing.

George and I stand alone in the room. "Nice work back there," I say.

"Thanks, I'm pretty surprised it was so easy to read locations from his emotions." He sighs. "I'm doubtful Zhuang will be that straightforward."

"Well, even still, I had practice with tracking ripples. That's progress."

George takes a seat on the step of the platform in the middle of the lecture hall. His broad shoulders are emphasized by the overhead lights. "You were right." His tone is heavy. I stiffen, worried where this is going. My sensitivity registers instantly in George. His expression softens. "I'd pretty much robbed you of any emotional privacy and you didn't even know the first thing about me." He stares at his hands for a long while. "I'm sorry. It gets easy to know everyone, to feel them. I forget it isn't an automatic two-way street."

I take the seat next to him. His posture straightens at once.

"So how'd you spend those lonely hours growing up?" I ask.

"Reading mostly."

I wait for him to elaborate and when he doesn't I say, "And where did you grow up?"

"Chicago."

Another long silence.

"Seriously, George, you're going to have to help me out here."

He chews on his lip, staring at a distant wall, and then his eyes connect with mine. "Sorry. I'm new to this."

"Well, you don't *have* to tell me anything."

"No, I want to." George fidgets with his protective charm—a silver thumb ring. "I spent a lot of time at the aquarium growing up." He pauses and looks at me, seemingly gauging my interests. "I had

193

a season pass and I think after a while the employees just assumed I was obsessed with fish. On the weekends I was there from the time they opened until they closed." He stops and I nod my head, encouraging him to continue. "Usually I sat next to the dolphin tank. I read books and listened to the emotions broadcast by the visitors. They were typically good emotions, which is why it was where I spent most of my time."

"Why didn't you go someplace remote, like a forest or a lake? Why go to a place where you were bombarded by emotions?"

"I feel better when I'm around people. If it's too quiet then I go insane. I know it doesn't make sense, but it's how I'm used to living my life."

I shrug. "I'm not judging you."

"Yeah," George says with a nod, "I know."

"Can I ask you something?"

"Of course," he says.

"Is it difficult to be alone because then you'd feel your own emotions?" I know this is a bold question. But I don't really have time for pretenses anymore, and besides I'm curious. George appears to be sensitive and attuned to the emotions around him, but is he really? There are times I steal a glance at him and see something. A wall. A barrier somehow created between George and his own emotions. Could it be possible that this magician of empathy is clueless when it comes to his own emotional state? And if he's that out of touch with himself, then can I really trust him? *Trust*—it feels like copper in my mouth.

"Who wants to really feel their own emotions?" he says, leaving my question unanswered. "Sure, the good emotions are wonderful. However, those are the rarity for people like you and me." He gives me a commiserate expression over brooding eyes. "We live as outcasts and with that comes a lot of negative emotions."

"Mmmm." I ruminate on his words. "Maybe. I guess it *would* be nice to distract myself from my emotions with someone else's," I say, thinking of my dismal fate.

Slowly, almost clumsily, he stretches his arm around my shoulder. A few seconds pass as he assesses my reaction from the inside. I don't mind his touch. It's nice actually. Warm. Accepting. Comforting. He hugs me into him softly. "Everything's going to be all right, Roya. I know it feels really complicated right now, but a lot of people really care about you."

I lay my hand on his. It isn't hot. Or cold. It's inviting, begging me to hold it a minute longer. His words are exactly what I need to hear. And this closeness is essential to my well-being, although I have a hard time admitting it, and not just because I know George is riffling through the contents of my emotions.

Simultaneously, the urge to both run and stay courses through me. I witness these emotions wrestle, watching as they take turns pinning the other to the mat. The longer I stay sitting beside George, holding his hand in mine, the more it begins to feel right. My emotion to stay is winning. For a minute I settle into the embrace, enjoying it. I feel George's breath in my hair as he pulls me in closer to him. Then unexpectedly my anxiety shoots back from near defeat, pushing up into a fighting stance. Fierce, ready to go another round or ten. George withdraws. He's the one to unfold his fingers from mine, the one to stand abruptly and put distance between us. Right when I've had enough and can't overcome my unease, George pulls himself away.

His face is unreadable. "Roya, I know you're more scared than you let anyone else see. But I also know, in all areas, you're braver than you think."

George doesn't speak like this often, but when he does I lose it. I may look restrained on the outside, but inside I'm melting. His words always feel like they have a double meaning. He must be intelligent to speak with such complexity.

I stare at him, not knowing how to respond. He nods his head, like I have said something and he completely agrees. "Thanks for wearing the frequency adjuster," he says. "And also, for keeping down the wall."

I don't respond or even nod. I don't have to with him.

Chapter Thirty-Three

I'm brushing my hair into the usual ponytail for the morning workout when I hear a familiar rap on my door. "Pretty early for a delivery, wouldn't you say?"

Patrick smiles. "No rest for the wicked and the righteous don't need any." He hands me two small packages.

"Thanks," I say as he trots off.

Both packages are the size of a shoe box. Excitedly I pull open the lid to the first box expecting to see the familiar note from Bob and Steve lying on top of a piece of tissue paper. Instead I find a sheet of yellow, lined paper with small, compact handwriting. It says:

Roya,

I'm sorry. I'm sorry we fought. I'm sorry I said you were like Ren. I'm sorry we disagree about the modifier. I fear this will become more confusing before it gets easier. When you're ready, I'll be here.
This is the gift I meant to give you yesterday. I've loaded it with music you'll love. I think you have to agree life is better when you have a soundtrack.

Aiden

Inside the box I find a silver iPod. I take it out, place the buds in my ears, and fire up the device. The first song that fills my head is the one I heard in Aiden's lab and asked about, *Plans and Reverie*. Realizing I'm running late I head out the door with a sideways glance at the other package. It will have to wait.

I listen to music as I run and sweat. The five miles flashes by quicker than ever. Each song registers something in me. There are certain ones that make me run faster and harder. When I'm finally done I push sweat out of my face, feeling alive. Aiden's right, my life is better with music. How had I gone so long without it? Charged and ready for the long day of training I head for the shower.

The trainings have intensified since the Day of the Duel is less than a week away. Directly after breakfast I report to the gymnasium to train with Shuman and the group. If she's mad at me after our heart-to-heart she doesn't show it.

However, when the training is wrapping up she dismisses everyone but me. This is it, I know I'm about to get it for disrespecting her. What will she do to me? What will I do if she throws a rattlesnake at me? Suddenly my kung fu training seems useless against a venomous and angry serpent. This makes me feel hopeless for my upcoming battle with Zhuang. Maybe it's better if Shuman just kills me now.

When everyone has left the gymnasium, Shuman centers on me. "Roya—"

"I can't say I agree with what you said to me in your office," I cut her off. "However, I do apologize for yelling."

Shuman raises an eyebrow and says, "Fine. I just needed to tell you to report to room 222 immediately."

"Oh!" I say, blinking back my surprise.

♦

I stride into the meeting room, shocked to find Trey sitting alone, his hands crossed and resting on the table.

"Thanks for joining me, Roya," Trey says gravely when I enter. "Mind shutting the door for us?"

I hit the button. *It's just going to be the two of us? Why?*

Trey points to the chair opposite of him and smiles at me. I edge into the seat and gauge his nervous expression.

"A few weeks ago, when I sat on that dock and spoke with you for the first time, did you ever expect your life would change so drastically?"

I shake my head.

"First I want to congratulate you. I'm proud of you for many things, but I want to congratulate you for only one. I'm proud of you for putting so much of yourself into becoming the challenger and for how well you've dealt with all the stress." Trey runs his fingers through his silver hair, betraying his confidence. "I want to congratulate you for who you're becoming in the midst of all of these obstacles. You've demonstrated amazing character over the last couple of weeks. I believe you could benefit from someone pointing this out, since you don't give yourself credit in this area."

Although I sense he's working hard to hide it, there's something in his tone which makes me think he's working up to deliver bad news. "You've had to cope with a great deal of pressure. I know this hasn't been easy for you." A long pause punctuates his statement. When he continues his strained voice carries a hint of strength. "Just when I think you can't possibly impress me more you do something astonishing. We're fortunate to have someone with your ability and strength. The Lucidite administration is forever in your debt for the sacrifices you've made to be our challenger."

Where's this going?

"Secondly, I need to apologize. You've been kept in the dark a great deal. With all the pressures around you I think you've ignored certain questions, but there's a history I must now share with you. The implications of what I'm about to tell you has far-reaching effects."

I tense. My heart suddenly hammers in my chest and then seizes as I await his next words. Trey's eyes scurry between his hands and my eyes.

"You've always felt like an outsider in your family." It's a statement.

I swallow and stare at him.

"That's what brought you here, right?" He pauses again.

How could he know that?

I grip the side of my chair but give no response.

"The day you were born your mother, your *real* mother, was in an accident in the Baltic Sea. You were born on a ship right before she died. There's no information on your father."

I freeze. The air around me freezes too. I don't allow it or me to move. I just wait.

Trey's eyes dart about the room, searching. When they obviously don't find what they're looking for he reaches across the table with his turquoise eyes and fixes on me. "The forecast had already been released with the names of the potential challengers against Zhuang. This fight has been coming for a long time. We knew we had to protect you. We placed you in a home deemed safe and your family, the one you grew up with, was embedded to accept you as theirs."

My recent conversation with Aiden barrels to the forefront of my mind. I remember his hesitation when describing the earlier versions of the modifier. *Did he know this? Was Aiden involved in this conspiracy?* Fury bursts forth in me as I put it all together. *The modifier was used on my family. I was the lie they were forced to accept.*

Trey must sense I'm off in thought trying to connect the pieces of this strange and abstract picture. His voice is slightly deeper when he says, "It's too late for you to ever go back to this family. But you're a Lucidite anyway, and you've always belonged with us."

"I'm a Dream Traveler," I argue. "That doesn't automatically make me a Lucidite, right? Why do you keep saying I belong with the Lucidites?"

"Your mother." Trey's voice chokes on the last syllable. He recovers, sounding stronger with his next breath. "She was a powerful Lucidite. And she was important to this Institute. You're a Lucidite by blood."

My mother? My mother? Another mother. Not the one I know who speaks to me from sideways, disapproving glares. The one who forgets I'm there half the time. Forgets to pick me up from school. The one who wears a look of embarrassment when forced to take me out in public. Not this woman, but a different one. I had a mother. *Had.* And she was a Lucidite. *Was.*

This is far too easy for me to digest, although still it takes a great deal of chewing. Trey is right, I knew this was coming. Although I didn't know how or why, hearing what he says doesn't feel wrong. It's like a part of me has finally been revealed, like arms I'd always used but had entrenched in thick fabric are uncovered, ready to meet the sunlight for the first time. I clear my throat, my mind, and speak steadily. "If my mother had been a Lucidite, then why wasn't I here from the beginning?"

"This is no place to raise a child. We wanted you to have a chance at a normal life."

"What was normal about my childhood?" I say.

Trey's eyes soften and his remorse reaches across the table, trying to wrap around me.

"So, I have no one? I'm an orphan?" I ask, trying to block the pity.

Trey remains silent.

"Didn't my mother have family? Couldn't I have stayed with them? Couldn't I be with them now?"

"No. Her family wasn't accepting of Lucidites," Trey says flatly.

This brings up more questions, but my head is already swimming and I don't know where to begin. "Who was she? My mother? You said she was powerful. Important, right? How?" I ask, the words oddly tickle my throat.

"Roya, I really want to answer that for you," Trey says, looking earnest. "Unfortunately, I can't."

His last three words deflate me in an instant. I'm still so far from the truth.

"Fine," I say and manage a fake smile. "If I survive. If we beat Zhuang, then I'll live with Bob and Steve."

I'm lighter all of a sudden, but Trey still looks heavy. Strangely, I hoped my words would take the pressure off him, although why should I care about him at the moment...

"You could, but it isn't as safe." There's a catch to his voice.

"But if we defeat Zhuang then there won't be any threats, right?"

"There's always a threat," Trey says coldly. "There's so much you could contribute if you stayed here."

I don't understand why we're discussing my future housing at the moment. Honestly, I think we should be picking out caskets. I suppress a morbid laugh.

"Besides, you aren't as alone as you think." Trey threads his fingers together. He looks at his hands intently like they hold the answers to this complex equation called "my life." "The day your mother died, she gave birth to two children." His turquoise eyes flicker up at me. The expression he wears is a mix of elation and stress. He wears it well. "Roya, you have a twin."

I jerk to a standing position, toppling over the chair behind me. "What?! Where?!"

The questions run through my head at a rate much faster than I can process. This explains Trey's anxiety. The first bit I digested easily. He was bracing himself all along for this point in the conversation.

Trey shakes his head, looking remorseful. "We had to separate the two of you," he says.

I stand motionless for several seconds. The air in my chest is ragged, like pieces of cotton running over ripped cardboard. I fail to compose myself, though, and when I manage to pull a full inhalation into my lungs I explode. "How dare you!? You did this?!" I accuse him. "You, Flynn, and your team of scientists! You manipulated my life." I shake all over with disbelief. "I can get over sticking me in some strangers' home, thereby ruining their family vacations, but how dare you separate me from..." I stop finding it difficult to say that word, "...m-m-my twin."

Trey throws his fingers through his now overworked hair. "We did what we had to do to protect you. The forecast—"

"Enough with the stupid forecast. I'm just a pawn, aren't I? This forecast has ruined my life." My arms have taken on a life of their own, waving wildly over my head. "Have you ruined this twin's life too with your manipulation?"

"No," he says softly. "He's taken this all quite well."

My eyes bulge. "*Him?* Did you say *him*? Did you bring *him* here too?"

"Roya, if you'll sit down for a second I'll answer your questions."

I stare at Trey, trying to judge his expression. He's stoic as he locks eyes on me. Finally I pull out another chair and sit leaning in the opposite direction as Trey.

After several seconds he says, "We separated you for your protection. Zhuang would have found you two early on and killed you."

"Why?" I question immediately. "Why would he come after us instead of the other people on the list?"

"You and your brother have something special. You're twins and as such you share consciousness, which equates to energy. This type of energy is hard to hide; believe me, we've been struggling with it since you arrived. When you two are together, you set off all sorts of energy fields. Scientifically it's quite amazing, but it wouldn't have gone unnoticed by Zhuang. He'd have found you both long ago and killed you before you became a problem. That's why we *had* to separate you."

"Who is he? You said you'd already told him this. Why? Why am I the last one to find out?"

"Roya, I didn't have to tell him," Trey says. He pauses and when he continues his words are gentle and deliberate. "I only had to fill in the details. He already knew. He sees far into the future."

"No!" I say, shaking my head. "That's impossible!"

Trey's voice is still steady and soft. "He saw a future where you two are close, like family."

My mind sorts through what I know and all of this starts to piece together. Anger and betrayal cloud my head at once. "How long has he known?"

"Probably for a long time. It's kind of hard to say with Joseph. He's tough to read."

Joseph is my twin.

My hands cradle my head as the emotions boil to the surface, about to spill over. I pull my head up and meet Trey's eyes. "And who else knows? Aiden, right? Ren? Shuman?"

Trey's face doesn't give anything away.

"Why in the hell does everyone know my life but me?! I'm about to die for you people and you can't even tell me the truth!" I slam my fist on the table. Trey doesn't flinch.

"I didn't feel it was right to tell you this until now." He swallows. "You have to understand, I've had to make a lot of decisions and they can't all be right."

"Oh my God!" I yell. "I can't believe you're going to make this about you now! The manipulation just never ends around here, does it?"

Trey's expression is pained as he says, "I'm truly sorry to have hurt you. We've only meant to keep you safe."

"Is that why you put us in unfit homes?"

His eyes close for a half beat. When he opens them they're rimmed with guilt. "We didn't know the homes weren't conducive for your growth when we picked them. By the time it came to light, it was too late. You would have been very confused if we placed you in another home. You must know I only meant to protect you and your brother."

I can't take one more minute. The sound of the words "your brother" incites me. I have to get out of this room, away from Trey and his lies.

With urgency I charge down the hallway. Suddenly I wish I was in a huge field, where I could feel the sun on my back and face.

It's been too long since I felt the sun. Every time I dream travel it's usually dark or dusk. I miss the sun so much. I miss the lake and my home and how uncomplicated my life used to be.

Chapter Thirty-Four

The training studio is crowded with people when I arrive, tired and sweaty. My team is gathered around, waiting for our kung fu lesson to begin. They turn and acknowledge me as I charge into the room, straight over to Joseph. Everything moves fast. George's eyes widen. He reaches for me, but I'm fast, much faster than him or anyone else in the room.

Confusion and then fear race through Joseph's eyes. I sprint forward, pull my fist back and punch him in the face. "You knew!" I scream, and George catches up with me. He and Trent restrain my arms as I shout, "You knew all along and you never thought you should tell me!?" I push forward, wanting to tackle Joseph to the floor.

Samara and Whitney surround him, but he waves them off, clutching his bleeding nose. "I couldn't tell you. Trey wouldn't let me." His eyes are full of regret. He pushes the blood away with the back of his arm. "And you had so much to deal with, it didn't feel right to tell you yet."

"Why does everyone get to decide what I can deal with? Shouldn't that be my choice!?"

"Roya." His voice is almost a hush compared to my volume. "There hasn't been a single day I haven't been with you. Please believe me when I say I've tried to give you what I could. I tried to be your friend since I couldn't tell you the truth."

Rage erupts in me like white fire. "So that's even a facade? Our friendship's just another act? It was you taking pity on me?!"

"No, that isn't what I meant. All I was saying—"

"Shut up!" I cut him off. "You're a liar. I've known that since the beginning." I jerk out of Trent's weak restraints.

George steps forward. "Roya." His voice is cautious. His eyes say *stop*.

I know he feels what I'm about to say, but I don't care. I'm only bent on destruction. "George, mind your own damn business for once! You know as well as I do Joseph's a liar. Every word out of his mouth is a lie. He isn't who he says he is."

Hurt flashes on Joseph's face, but I don't stop. I don't know how. I'm officially out of control.

"And who else knew?" I round on my team. "Did any of you know Joseph and I are twins?"

Tension cuts through the room as my uncharacteristically authoritative presence takes over. I'm overwhelmed with power, justified in attacking anyone at this point. This is how people go down the path of evil; they let hurt tear them in two.

From the corner of my eye, Samara raises her hand like she does when she has a stupid question in class. I turn on her. Of course she knew. I should have guessed. No shame traces her opaque blue eyes.

You should have told me. I had a right to know. Something makes her mouth twitch slightly, but she doesn't say a word.

Beside her, George's face catches my attention. Strain creases his forehead and painful guilt streaks his eyes. He wears his emotions on his face like a neon sign. It must be that he's overwhelmed by everyone else's and has no room internally to store his own.

"George?" My voice is low now.

His tone is flat, his eyes burdened. "I knew."

"How?" My head twists with confusion.

"It's Joseph's connection to you. I've felt that type of emotional connection thousands of times between people. It's unmistakable." George clears his throat. "Only families feel that way about each other."

Of course. George knew how Joseph felt about me. Relationships are built on emotional foundations. George doesn't just know how everyone feels at any given time, he also knows how we feel about each other, our past, things, events.

"And you didn't think it was important to tell me this?" I say, narrowing my eyes at him.

"I can't reveal someone's emotions." George gives a sympathetic look. Recently I'd seen his guardianship of other's emotions as noble. Not anymore. Now I see it as betrayal. With all my heart I focus on feeling betrayed, letting it envelop me in a powerful storm.

"I'm sorry you feel that way," George says, obviously picking up on my inward emotional outburst.

"What else do you people know that you're keeping from me?!" I yell, my face flushing hot.

A crowd of speechless, sullen faces stares back at me.

"Please, Stark." Joseph's eyes beg along with his words. It's a look he's perfected no doubt to manipulate people. I knew all along he was a liar, a cheat. *Why did I let myself get close to him?* "You have to listen to me. I can explain." Joseph steps forward.

I shake my head. "I don't *have* to do anything. I don't have to listen to you. I don't have to fight Zhuang. I don't have to pretend any of this or you matter, because to me, right now…it doesn't." I whip around and stomp away, feeling all their eyes on my back.

Chapter Thirty-Five

If I knew where one of the other GAD-Cs was located somewhere on the globe I'd travel there, autogenerate my body, and forget I'd ever been a Lucidite. Even though I already ran five miles this morning, I know the only thing left for me is to run. To hide in my room all day is lame. And going to trainings isn't an option after I've just punched my brother in the nose.

I grab my iPod and set off for the workout facility. Luckily no one's in there. I jump on a treadmill, crank it up, and run. The music now holds new meaning than it did this morning. Every song is about lies, confusion, betrayal, loneliness. When I finally slow the treadmill it's only because my body is past the point of depletion. I haven't eaten or drank anything in several hours. Now my fear is I'll pass out here. I drag myself to the showers before this happens. The water is frigid and I drink it in as it pours over my head. It stings my hand as it runs over my knuckles, which are red and cut where I punched Joseph. It's nothing compared to the searing pain in my heart.

I return to my room, still warm from the run, exhausted and emotionally burnt out. *Why did I have to give that stupid chocolate to Shuman?* It would be really great to have at this point.

The other package I didn't have time to open this morning sits on my bed. I grab it, hoping Bob and Steve packed me some more food. I yank open the box. On top of a piece of tissue paper is a card with a sailboat navigating choppy ocean waters. My heart aches at the sight of the image, knowing somewhere out there is the boat Joseph and I were born on. Our mother died on this boat. And then we were separated.

I rip open the card, trying to get the ship's image out of my head. It reads:

Dear Roya,

Forget who they say you're supposed to be. Become who you are. Deep down there's a place in you and this is where you'll find the strength to defeat Zhuang. We're proud of you. We believe in you.

If all else fails then maybe this will help. You're a warrior and we felt you should look like one.

Love,
Bob & Steve

Did they know about Joseph and me? Maybe they've known all along? Fury flares at the thought. Could it be possible that every Lucidite knows more about who I am than I do? Am I their fool? Their puppet? Protected for the purposes of fighting their battles? Angry tears constrict my throat and I try to breathe them away.

I yank back the tissue paper and find an object which fills me with confusion. In the box lies a braided leather headband fashioned with two iridescent peacock feathers. Magic seems to glimmer around them as I take in their richness. Vibrant blue encircles sturdy brown and encases soft green, like a lake with a shore bordered by grassy knolls. Enchanted by its beauty I sweep the headband into my shaking hands and wrap it around my head with the eye of the peacock feathers horizontally above my ear. The fanned ends trail behind my shoulder.

I steal a glance in the mirror, inspecting myself like I've just put on a pair of earrings. The image isn't what I expected. The girl who stares back from the mirror is a stranger. Somehow I've been transformed. The peacock feathers contrast boldly against my blonde hair, casting a powerful glow across my face. My cold, red eyes give away my forlorn heart, which actually completes the effect. All fighters are scorned in some way, that's part of their motivation. With my headdress and a broken heart I look the part. I am a warrior.

Guilt prickles my throat. The letter wasn't about Joseph and me. Bob and Steve don't know he's my brother. They were just being supportive. How in the world did I ever land them as guardian angels? Once again I feel I don't deserve them. Nothing that's a part of my current life feels like it should belong to me. I have a twin brother, a dead mother, and a host family who was programmed to accept me. My entire life is an assortment of lies and there's still much I don't know. But I don't want to know anymore. The pain is a knife pressing into my chest, sharp and threatening.

Those people who raised me aren't my family. They're strangers who were forced to adopt me. No wonder I never truly connected with them. Understanding and pain take turns sifting through my chest as I force myself to revolve on the implications of everything I've learned. I was never truly theirs. I was a person placed into their home who they were forced to accept. But they never really did. *My entire life...a lie. My entire life...manipulated. My entire life...wrong.* All so I could become this warrior for the Lucidites.

Furious, I rip the headband off and send it to the far corner of my room. The wall is cold when I slam against it and slide down until I'm seated. Clawing at my throat are a thousand hurts and scars and words I've never expressed, all protesting to be released. This is it. I won't allow myself another moment like this. Not in battle and never in front of anyone. Silently I agree to these terms. The dull ache in my throat races forward, enjoying its first moment of freedom. The pain I've held onto for so long, the pain unearthed by this new discovery, emerges in hot tears which sting my eyes and sop my cheeks. My chest convulses with each eruption. I'm on fire and my tears are lava as they pour and flow. Just when I think I'm done and regain control there's another explosion. This goes on until the tears dry up, and only because I'm dehydrated. I can't cry another drop even if I want to. My well is empty.

I sit staring off into the abyss for an hour. The dark space of a corner has never been so intriguing. My stomach awakens my attention. It's imperative that I eat.

I creep down the hallway, hyperaware of every noise. My reserves are so low at this point I'm like a threatened coyote, ready to attack at the slightest offense. Each step is torture. *How have I allowed myself to get to this point?*

The main hall is mostly empty when I poke my head around the corner. There are only a few staff members prepping food stations. I sigh, grateful I don't have to face anyone. With my head down I race for the drink table. The ice water freezes my throat as I gulp it down, but it instantly makes my body feel human again. I consider drinking straight out of the pitcher as I shakily refill my glass. The frigid water is once again racing down my mouth when I see a figure press into my periphery. I lower my glass and stare forward, afraid to turn and face him.

"I knew you'd have to eat sooner or later, especially after all that running." Joseph's voice has an uncharacteristic shyness to it.

Through clenched teeth I say, "You've been watching me?"

"No, that would be creepy." A sliver of his familiar tone returns.

I swallow the last of the water and wipe my damp lips with the back of my arm. "Then how do you know I've been running?"

I'm still standing with my back mostly toward him, afraid to look at his face, afraid of what it will make me feel. From the fringes of my vision I see him lean against a table and cross his ankles as casually as if he's waiting to get his hair cut.

"Well, for starters you're still beet red like after the a.m. workouts. You don't have to be Sherlock Holmes to know you've been beating the treadmill to death with your feet."

The dryness in my throat hasn't vanished and I need more water. However, I'd rather Joseph not spy my shaking hands as I refill my glass.

He pushes up from the table and strides until he's in front of me. I focus on the bottle of water he shoves into my hand. "Of course, if I wasn't a detective I would still know what you've been up to." His nose is red and swollen and he wears a masked expression.

I twist the cap off the water and take pleasure in the way it pinches my dry fingertips. Sometimes physical irritation is a welcome distraction from emotional pain.

"What is that supposed to mean?" I ask before downing half the bottle.

"Drink up. I've got another couple bottles as well as your dinner here." He gestures to a small white sack in his other hand.

I flick my eyes back up to meet his. His casual attitude is making me want to punch him even harder than before. "Answer my question," I seethe.

"Why don't you eat somethin' first and then we'll talk?"

I almost lunge forward at him, but instead take the momentum and turn on my heels. Adrenaline races through my limbs as I stalk off toward the exit.

"Wait!" Joseph yells, sounding half amused. I hear him jog up behind me, the plastic of the bag in his hands crinkling as he moves.

"Look, don't run off. I just meant that you'd feel better if you ate somethin' and then we could discuss stuff."

"I don't need you to tell me what to do," I say, staring wildly into his eyes.

A laugh escapes his mouth. "Lord knows you wouldn't do it anyway. Just tryin' to be helpful."

"Helpful would be answering my questions." I down the rest of the bottle and toss it in the trash bin. With my arms now free I automatically cross them over my chest. "How do you know what I've been up to? How do you seem to know so much about me?"

Joseph's casual expression disappears as he takes a long breath. He's dreadful at being serious. It melts away his fake exterior. "At times I know you as well as I know myself. I get these ideas and I know they're about you. It's usually somethin' you're doin' or thinkin', and rarely what you're feelin'. Sometimes I predict what you're gonna do before you do it. It's been like this since the moment we met. Somethin' tells me when you're more composed you sense these things too."

Although I wouldn't admit it, I know he's right. When I was younger, before I built a fortress of armor around myself, I used to think I had an imaginary friend. I didn't talk to him or play with him or set a place at the table. I just knew he existed. I knew when he was happy or sad or excited. There were rarer times where I'd get a flash and know he'd just done something like spent his allowance on a gadget or done poorly on a math exam. Since I've always believed I was straddling the borders of insanity I just thought this was another indicator of my craziness. *Was this actually Joseph? Was he my imaginary friend growing up?*

By the way Joseph is chewing on the inside of his cheek I'm guessing my silence is making him nervous. He isn't one to embrace quiet. "You feel it, right? A connection between the two of us, even if just a tiny bit?"

I roll my eyes to suppress the rawness of the situation. "Maybe, but I'm not about to go pick out matching sweaters."

"Did you know that my name wasn't even on the list?" he says.

"What? Then why are you here?"

"Because your name was. Trey knew you'd need me in order to fully perform at your best."

"I don't understand. Did you know this from the beginning?"

"No, but when I figured out that we were twins I confronted Trey and he told me."

"But you were picked as an alternate," I say, shaking my head.

"No, you were, but we're a package," Joseph says. "Trey knows this. Haven't you noticed your clairvoyance is stronger since you've been at the Institute? Well, for that matter, everything about you is stronger and faster. Please tell me you aren't so thick that you've missed this."

I grimace. A crowd of white coats files into the hall.

Joseph grabs my arm, dragging me to the exit. "Come on, let's get outta here. We've got some catching up to do."

Normally I'd push him off, but I'm tired. He's right too, I need answers and this is the only way I'm going to get them.

Once we're back to the main lobby he lets go of my arm. It's quiet and open here. I plop on the ground and take the bag from Joseph. The container he's packed is full of pasta salad. *Perfect.*

"Stark, we're two parts of a whole," Joseph begins. "You see the immediate future and I see what's gonna happen way in the distance. You're naturally quiet and introverted. I'm loud and extroverted. Your ability to dream travel is amazing, which usually takes practice. This makes you great at tracking and strategizing. On the other hand, I see the unseen easily. I'm an interpreter." Joseph has a deep sincerity in his eyes. "We're the perfect team."

"So that's why you're here? To bring out my abilities? That's bizarre."

"Well, and I'm a Lucidite. I belong here. Trey had to bring me in because otherwise Zhuang would have found me and then I'd be dead. It was just a matter of time. Anyway, Trey always brings new Dream Travelers here when they're young to help guide and train them. Then they're released back out into the wild." Joseph says this last part with a laugh.

"What? What are you talking about?" I'm starting to worry he's making all this up.

He rolls his eyes. "Dream Travelers are a type of people, like a race. Most Dream Travelers have adopted an association with a society like the Lucidites. That's how things stay organized. There are probably rogue Dream Travelers out there livin' off the grid, but I'm sure it's easier to stay connected for mutual reasons. Anyway, they have ways of discerning Dream Travelers who are about to come of age. I guess if they think they're within their jurisdiction then Trey or Flynn or whoever runs this place pulls them in. It takes place usually around age sixteen, but in some cases families elect to send children to orientation earlier."

My head isn't swimming at this point, it's drowning in a sea of questions and confusions. "How do you know all this?"

"Unlike you, I talk to people. I'm curious by nature. You, on the other hand, wouldn't care how a bridge that materialized out of thin air in front of you came to be. That's because you're stubborn," Joseph says with a smirk.

"So there are other societies?"

"I guess so. I don't know the names of any, but I sense there are others. Maybe being Lucidite is a regional thing, like being an American. We don't have to worry about it though. We're Lucidites, just like our mother."

The mention of our mother sends a sudden ache to my back. An odd sensation. Then I realize it's my heart aching so badly I feel it in my chest, my back, all over, like the worst case of indigestion ever. "Our mother," is all I say after a minute.

"Yeah." Joseph's voice drops a beat. "Odd story, huh? Makes you wonder 'bout all sorts of stuff."

"Yeah," I say. "So how long did you know we were twins?" I ask and take a bite of a cold marinated mushroom.

"It was after we were picked as alternates. I knew something since the moment I saw you. For years I'd seen flashes where you and I were together and older. At first I thought you were my future wife. Seems kind of gross to think about now. Anyway, when we got to the Institute and started spendin' time together the flashes got stronger, more frequent. I decided to approach Trey if I was picked to stay. Since I was, then I did, and he told me everything you now know."

A sudden ray of hope opens up my chest, like the first day of summer. "Wait! If you see us together in the future then that means we survive. That means I survive. That we defeat Zhuang!"

Joseph shakes his head. "I'm sorry to tell you this, but that isn't how it works. You and I see potential realities. We get a glimpse of what could happen, but free will and choice always play into it. Remember when you saw the flash in the main hall and knew to give the letter to Patrick?"

213

I think back and remember the incident. I'd told Joseph about this later, explaining to him all the dumb stuff I could see.

"Well, you chose to pay attention to that image and act. You sought out Patrick and gave him the letter causin' the image to become real. You could have just as easily ignored it."

"So you're telling me there's a possibility I could survive?"

"Yes, but I also see other flashes of darkness and impending danger. This could be the alternate reality. This is kinda how my visions go since I see so far into the future."

"That sucks," I protest.

"Tell me 'bout it."

Silence grows between us again, making Joseph fidget. I take this opportunity to ask my burning question. "Joseph, why'd you lie about your family? About having brothers and sisters?"

He looks startled. Accosted. Waylaid.

"I saw where you live," I continue. "I know your mother's dead and your father blames you."

He rolls over on his elbows and gives a guilty expression. "And here I thought you could just sense when I lied, the same way I can with you."

"Don't discount that just yet," I snap.

"I want people to like me, it's 'nother way we're polar opposites. And people like a person who's whole. There's nothin' wholesome about my life with my father. I've been lying my entire life about something or 'nother. It just becomes second nature after 'while."

"Why does your father blame you for your mother's death?" I ask, folding up the empty container and putting it to the side.

"'Cause I saw she was gonna die when I was really little. I told them both about it. I cried all the time about her dying. When she did become ill and passed, my father blamed me. He said I'd caused it to happen."

"When did she die?"

"A few years ago."

"You had to live with him for all that time by yourself?"

Joseph stares at the fibers of the carpet and nods.

His pain is palpable, making me ache. "Wow, the Institute really sucks at picking foster homes, don't they?" I say.

"For real," Joseph replies.

I push up into a standing position and offer a hand to him. Without hesitating he grabs it and I pull him up from the ground.

"Thank you." Joseph swallows, pushing down another layer of something raw he'll never let the world see.

Hollow words lurk in my mouth. They sound sentimental and lame as they bounce around my head. Twice I open my mouth ready to let them pour out and twice I press my lips together. Words aren't always the right approach, especially in a situation as sensitive as this one. When used in the right context words are powerful, but right now I'm certain they would just be a device to overcompensate for the strangeness of this all. I opt for a shrug and a sympathetic smile.

Chapter Thirty-Six

My team is seated when I enter the lecture hall the next morning. Everyone's wearing an apprehensive expression. Apparently I won't be able to pretend yesterday didn't happen. I had every right to be angry. Maybe I shouldn't have punched Joseph in the face and I definitely wish I hadn't done it in front of everyone, but I wasn't thinking clearly. And then there's George. I was cruel and spiteful to him. He was trying to stop me from doing and saying something I'd regret. I wish he could have. I can't erase calling Joseph a liar, telling George he'd betrayed me and yelling at the only friends I've ever had. The regret makes my insides squirm.

Words again escape me, elusive and untamed as they gallop through my mind. Time travels by in huge gaps of silence as I hunt for the right phrase. The pressure builds in my chest until I rush into an unrehearsed speech. "Look, I'm sorry for my outburst yesterday. I wish you all wouldn't have witnessed it. I lost my temper and said some things I regret. In hindsight I should have cooled down before confronting Joseph. This whole situation is confusing for me and…" My throat closes up with sharp tears. All I can think of is being Joseph's twin and how weird and wonderful that is. I bite my lip hard to suppress the emotions about to spill forth.

"That's what you're calling an 'outburst'?" Trent laughs. "If I found out my entire life had been a lie then this whole Institute would look different right now."

An awkward smile forms on my face.

Samara agrees with a nod. "I was shocked you punched Joseph, but I'd probably do the same." A second later she adds, "I'm better with kicks though, so I might have just kneed him in the groin."

Everyone but Joseph laughs.

"Thanks for understanding," I say.

Whitney stands, looking serenely sensitive. It's a kind look, like an old lady who plays the piano in church would wear. It looks odd on a young girl's face, but Whitney is both old and young at the same time. Her eyes make her look wise and experienced, but her sweet smile is still that of a teenager.

Those old soul eyes mist over with tears brimming to run down her face. Her arms are out as she walks in my direction. *Please don't hug me. Please.* It's unfortunate Whitney doesn't read minds. Her pale, soft arms neatly drape around my shoulders. I pat her back, counting the seconds until she releases me. Tears well up in my chest, and then my throat, and I have to do something before they're exposed. Pulling away, I force a smile. "Thank you."

Unashamed, she pushes tears away with the back of her hand. "I didn't know about you and Joseph. I can't even begin to imagine how confused you must feel right now."

I shrug. "It's a lot to process."

"Well, you don't have to do it alone," Whitney encourages, picking up my hand and pressing it between hers.

The tenderness in her eyes is unnerving. Between her hands my fingertips begin to tingle. The sensation spreads along my arm, down my shoulder, and into my chest. Warmth wraps around me like a towel after a cold bath. The hollow ache I've been carrying around for the past twenty-four hours dissipates slightly, allowing me to breathe properly.

"Thanks," I say, pulling my hand back to my side.

"Well, is this family drama over?" Trent asks with a smirk.

I look at Joseph and smile with affection. He nods. An endearing expression, one which I've grown attached to, unfolds on his face.

"Good," Trent chirps. "Because I'd like to discuss using our powers for good. I vote we do some time travel to prove or dispel popular conspiracies. Who's with me?"

The group instantly engages in a spirited discussion about different events they could travel back to witness. Grateful for the distraction I take the seat beside George.

"You didn't say anything," I say to him without making eye contact.

"You were having a hard time containing yourself. I was trying to help." He leans forward, looking directly at me.

"Oh," I say in a hush.

"Did you want me to say something?"

"No," I mutter. "I just feel..." I stop and swallow and look straight at him for the first time. His brown eyes search mine and I know I don't have to complete my sentence.

"Stop," he says. "Don't be ashamed. No one in this room is mad at you for how you reacted, especially me."

My lips press together and I allow the relief to wash over me. "I understand why you didn't tell me about Joseph," I say. "But still it's hard to digest along with everything else. And it makes it difficult to…" I stop, choking on the rest of the words.

"Makes it difficult to what?" George asks.

"To trust you," I whisper.

"Roya, from my perspective, you're going to have a hard time trusting anyone for a while." He pauses. "Those who are worth trusting will understand. They'll be patient and gentle with you, knowing in time you'll come around." His soft words feel like Whitney's hands on mine, healing and comforting, making it easier to breathe.

A shiver runs down my spine. Maybe it's a result of his words or maybe it's from his cool breath brushing my ear. I turn my head sideways and only just catch the seriousness in his eyes before Ren storms into the room.

"Ever played with Legos?" Ren asks with arms folded across his chest. "Building a dreamscape is a lot like making something out of Legos, except it's much more complex, as you might have guessed. Everything in a dreamscape is built layer upon layer. The pegs of all the building blocks must fit. You can't go putting a square peg in a round hole. Of course there's no real blocks in dreamscape building, so don't get your hopes up that this is all going to be like preschool. I'm referring to metaphorical blocks, of course.

"Dreamscapes are all mind over matter, or rather mind creates matter. The locations are fixed, just like the individual Legos in a set. How you weave your way through them, just like how you stack your blocks together, is what inevitably creates the layers, which are the fibers of a dreamscape. Inside each layer, nothing is fixed. It will look as it does in the physical reality, but you're in a dreaming consciousness.

"What you need to remember is that everything's subject to change, either by your doing or by another Dream Traveler. Herein lies the complexity of dreamscape building. If you don't like a location, travel to another. If you want to change the way it looks, create an illusion. If you need an object, summon it. Dreamscape building is about harnessing consciousness in order to manifest anything you desire." Ren clicks his tongue and tilts his head to the side. "Sadly, I'm giving a graduate-level lecture to a bunch of kindergarteners. Which is why the lot of you are giving me a bunch of blank stares. Let's move on to strategy before all of your heads explode.

"You all will start together." He waves his hand flippantly at us. "Then one by one you'll leave a person behind. The idea is to throw Zhuang off and make the layers more complex. It probably won't work and you'll all die, but what the hey, let's give it go," he chants with zero enthusiasm.

"Alternates, you will be outfitted with a headset and handheld monitor to view Roya's activity. It's important to stay focused on what's happening in your own environment. I suspect Zhuang will come after one of you at some point and if you're careless you'll get caught. Even still you'll all probably get caught and die, but let's delay this as long as possible."

The rest of the lecture we spend strategizing for each dream layer. My head's cloudy when Ren turns to me. "Roya," he says, emphasizing the last syllable. "Three things: First, if you only have minor injuries try and suck it up. Only travel to Whitney if the injury is life-threatening." He turns and faces Whitney. "Gal, you can guarantee Ms. Stark will visit you at least once before she dies." Ren flashes a toothy grin at me. "Secondly, get a list of the GAD-C locations from Aiden. This could prove useful if you have to abandon our current plan and throw Zhuang off the scent. The best way to do this is to return to your body and dream travel again." He turns and strides toward the exit. "Lastly, die gracefully, you're a Lucidite for God's sake."

Chapter Thirty-Seven

Trey's face makes my stomach flip-flop with anger and confusion when he takes the stage in the main hall at lunch. Joseph and I have to move forward and support each other. That's obvious. If I don't have Joseph I'll die sooner rather than later. However, I don't have any obligation to anyone else. The way Trey, Flynn, and the Institute have controlled and manipulated my life since the beginning is weird. A part of me appreciates that they cared enough to protect us. But still the whole thing is peculiar.

Trey stands on the platform, looking out at the crowd with remorse. "Can I have your attention please," he says, running his hands through his hair.

At his command, a hush falls on the room.

"Flynn, the great founder and leader of this Institute, has been murdered." Trey chokes on the last word. Audible gasps, the melodramatic ones I picture in movies, fall out of people's mouths. A commotion breaks out in the back of the room and I force myself to stay focused forward. Beside our table, a lady cries loudly before burying her face in her neighbor's shoulder.

The once quiet room is now a commotion of noise and emotion which immediately draws my attention to George. I've never seen him look so overwhelmed. *How much sorrow is he feeling all at once?* I grab his outstretched hand and he immediately takes it. He squeezes my hand so hard my fingers swells under pressure. He looks at me apologetically, but I shake him off and squeeze his hand to let him know it's fine. And though he smiles I know inside he's being assaulted from every angle with despair and misery.

I didn't know Flynn, but the eruption of emotion in this room is enough to convince me he was someone worth knowing. Instantly I'm remorseful that he died before I had the chance to meet him. That's my grief, and it's lame compared to those around me, but still it's all I have.

"Zhuang is responsible for this. That I'm certain of, although I have no other details," Trey says over the noise in the crowd. "I'm hopeful Flynn has forged a path for us that will lead to Zhuang's defeat." With that, Trey walks off the stage and out of the room.

Whispers and sobs fill the air and slowly begin to rise in volume. I continue to hold George's hand. After a long spell the commotion dies down and I feel the calm settle over him, almost like it has settled over me. I bring my chin up to join his gaze and he mouths the words "thank you."

♦

Joseph and I walk the halls, searching for nothing.

"Stark, you scared?" Joseph says.

"The thing I don't like about you—"

"Is I know what you're gonna say before you say it," Joseph jokes.

"No." I roll my eyes. "If you'd let me finish, I was going to say the thing I don't like about you and me is we haven't had much time together. I'm not scared as much as regretful. I've spent my life living inside my head. Now I can go anywhere. I have a brother. There's a place where people actually value my abilities. I'm regretful all this is about to come to an end."

"Well, I'm scared," Joseph says after a minute.

I stop and stare into Joseph's green eyes. They're the same shade as mine. *How haven't I noticed that before?*

"I'm scared," he continues, "'cause I can't protect you. I'm helpless. My dreams are all about how I'm just gonna stand by and watch you die. You're regretful about losing a life you won't get to live. I'm scared 'bout continuing to live after losing you, and being a complete failure."

"Fine," I say dully. "You win. Your woes sound much worse than mine."

We walk in silence for a while. "Hey!" I say finally. "When I die you can have my iPod."

Joseph doesn't laugh like I expected but instead gives an uneasy expression.

"What?" I question him.

"Don't you think it's kinda weird that a Head of the Institute gave you such a nice gift?" he says, looking incredulous.

I stop and face him directly. "There's nothing going on between us, if that's what you're hinting at."

Joseph gives me an unconvinced look. "You forget I read your dream journal."

"Not that any of this is your business, but Aiden has lost any favor from me. I'll never forgive him for the lies and deceit."

"*Never* is a strong word."

"That's why I chose it."

"Well, you shouldn't use absolutes."

"Whatever. I want nothing to do with a guy who thinks it's fantastic that he can program people's thoughts. Honestly, I should have probably given back the iPod but music is actually a great motivator for me."

Joseph sets his jaw firmly, still looking unconvinced.

"It's true," I say. "I hear the emotions in the lyrics and they give me an odd sense of faith."

Again Joseph stares at me, skepticism making his eyes look sharp. "Don't you think keeping the gift gives Aiden a certain expectation?"

"No!" I slap him on the arm. "Would you stop being so judgmental? Some of us need something to give us faith because we don't have Jesus in our corner to rely on. Why don't you ask him to keep an extra eye on me, or whatever he does."

Joseph sighs. "I'll try but…"

I stop. "Oh no, that's been a lie too, hasn't it?"

"Well, not exactly. I was raised Baptist. Honestly, I wish I was religious. I wish I had a place to turn right now. I can't say I've ever felt the Holy Spirit or anything remotely close."

"Fine," I say lightheartedly. "I'll pray for the both of us and you just go and write down all the lies so I know what's real."

Chapter Thirty-Eight

Thankfully, Samara's harder to track than Trent, giving both George and me better practice. Most of the time I'm able to absorb the tracers in her ripple before it dissipates. However, for whatever reason, she's tougher to follow. I have to go to a deeper meditative state in order to allow my consciousness to track her and it's a draining process. By the second layer I'm already exhausted.

"How about we trade places," Samara offers when we all meet back up. "Maybe switching things up will make Roya feel better."

"Sure." George locks eyes on me, concern written on his face. I give him a reassuring smile and push down the dizziness swimming in my head.

He hands the earpiece to Samara, who takes it with a gracefulness I've failed to harness.

"I'll take off as soon as you're ready," he says to me with a steady glance.

"Okay." I nod, trying to keep my dinner from coming up. This whole process is much more taxing than I expected. I close my eyes and take five deliberate breaths. By the last one, I'm contained once more and open my eyes to a patient George.

"Ready," I call to him.

"Don't overdo it, Roya," George warns and then disappears. His coarse words hang in the air, sending a strange eagerness along the surface of my skin.

I flow to his ripple, seeing it clearly since I know where to look. In an instant I sense a vibration. It's soft, like the curves of a flower petal. I can't describe it, let alone follow it. Slowly I ease into the space, hoping it will unveil its secrets to me. All I feel is the space around me edging out like an empty room. With my eyes closed I try to focus, to follow George, to allow my consciousness to be transported, but I remain trapped. Stationary. Immobile.

"Can you get a read for me?" I ask Samara.

"Why?" she says.

"Why do you think?" I flinch, feeling hot.

"Oh." The reality must have dawned on her. "Hold on a second."

Quiet seconds dance across my ears as George's ripple disappears.

The good news is Samara finds it pretty straightforward to get into his head and find his location.

I'm breathless, three layers behind him, when her voice squeaks in my ear. "Probably shouldn't be telling you this."

"What?" I tense.

"Well, I wouldn't say anything normally, but I think he wants you to know. And since we're all about to die anyway..."

I land in a well-manicured park and search. The rows of rosebushes and topiaries are unblemished by a ripple though. I squint, looking for any place where the space looks blurred. Nothing. "First I need a location," I say.

"Times Square. Present." Samara says with an edge of doubt.

I begin traveling and she continues, "Here's the thing. Sometimes I spy on people's thoughts and they're disrupted every so often by competing ones. You've heard people say they have something on their mind, right? Well, for these people all unrelated thoughts will probably be interrupted by that overwhelming one. Nothing is linear. It all interacts in some fashion or another."

"What's your point?" I ask, feeling restless staring at the flashing lights all around me.

"Well, I get that kind of thing from most people so it's pretty normal," she says.

"So?" I pontificate, wondering where this is going.

"Well, George's thoughts aren't just 'disrupted.' That isn't the right word." Samara takes in a breath and then says, "Maybe 'invaded' is a better one."

"I'm only going to ask this one last time," I say, watching a jumbotron screen overhead. "What's your point?"

"My point is George can't do his job properly because, from the way I see it, he's overwhelmed and can't concentrate."

"Seems like he's doing all right," I say, breathless.

"He's managing," Samara says. "But he's totally distracted and it's affecting him."

"What do we do about it?" I ask, my frustration increasing as I unsuccessfully search for a ripple.

"We help him alleviate the problem." Samara's words sound uncertain.

"How?"

"That's what I'm doing now," she says.

"How?" I sound like a broken record.

"By telling you this."

I go stiff.

"Wherever I track his thoughts I always find a trace of you there. I know I shouldn't be telling you this," Samara says, sounding only half apologetic. "But I also have read his thoughts enough to know the torment is an emotional battlefield he's tired of dealing with. He wants you to know. He can't stand it that you don't know. All the time he thinks about telling you this..." Samara trails off in an exasperated hush.

"What?" I ask, wanting to hear more.

"I shouldn't say anything." Samara's tone is regretful.

"Then why have you said this much?!"

"I don't know," she almost cries. "I guess, because I'm human. I know how humans think. I know what it feels to want someone and not have the guts to tell them."

Cars pass in a blur and all around me people jostle by. My heart beats quickly. "Thanks, Samara, I guess it's time we dealt with this. We can't have a disrupted team member."

"I knew you'd say that," she says.

"I bet you did," I say.

Then she says, "Sydney Opera House, Australia. Present."

"Damn, that boy moves fast," I spurt.

"I'm going to ring off," she says.

"Well then, I guess our training is done?" I fail to keep the irritation out of my voice.

"You two need privacy," Samara says. "And besides, I've got to get something done before morning."

"Fine," I say as I move through the tunnel, nervous about confronting George. Maybe this whole thing is better left alone.

"Roya?" Samara says.

"What?" I'm confused why I'm so irritated by her right now.

"I'm sorry if it was wrong to tell you, I was just following my instinct."

"It's too late for regrets," I say, standing at the top of a long row of stairs. The water in the distance radiates light and reflects off the building. A click in my ear tells me Samara has dropped off, leaving me alone with George. He sits a dozen steps down.

"Are you taking a break?" I ask as I approach.

"Thought you could use one," George says with a concerned look when I take a seat next to him.

"You're good," I say, taking in a full breath. "And tough to track. If it wasn't for Samara then I'd be lost."

"Is she still on the line?" George asks.

"Nope, she has laundry or dishes to do."

George's shoulder brushes mine as he leans forward. He places his elbows on his knees and tucks his chin into his chest. Every time I look at him I notice something small in his features I hadn't noted before. Right now the strong line of his jaw is soaking up my attention. Maybe it was wrong for Samara to tell me George's secrets. Honestly I'm drawn to him, but anything between us isn't straightforward or simple.

"You're staring at me," George says, still focusing on the ground.

"Sorry." I flush and focus forward. "I was just wondering if you're all right. You seem distracted."

"Do I?"

I draw back. "I just sense there's something you're not telling me."

His eyes meet mine and I'm almost sure he knows I'm lying, knows Samara has breached his trust. It's a shadow of an expression, but it flickers through me, instantly causing guilt.

"There are two things I need to tell you." George looks contemplative. "The first is the way you make me feel."

My breath seizes momentarily as I wait for him to continue.

"You'll remember you had a disruptive effect on me when we first met."

"Before I wore the frequency adjuster?" I ask between gentle beats of the water.

"Yes," George confirms.

Maybe Samara got it wrong. Maybe George thinks about me so much because if I'm not wearing the adjuster then I'm deadly to him. Maybe it isn't attraction, but rather repulsion?

"Do you think there's something wrong with me?" I say, holding the adjuster between my fingertips.

"There's something different about you."

The sigh that escapes my lips is automatic, but my words are calculated. "Look, I'm not evil, but it's possible I'm dysfunctional. That's probably why I have such a weird effect on you."

George chews on his lip, his eyes still intently pinned on his feet. His silence gathers in me, lighting a fuse to a bomb in my chest.

"Are you still there?" I finally say.

George turns and stares at me. I refuse to meet his gaze fully, afraid of what those placid eyes will do to me. "Roya, I feel things most people can't." He stops deliberating on something and then says, "Before you wore the adjuster your frequency stunned me. Now I feel your emotions and it's unlike anything I've ever experienced. There's something in you that fills me up to a capacity I can hardly manage. There's something about you. It takes over a room. I've watched you do it dozens of times." He pauses, a faint smile etched on his lips. "And the most poetic part of it is you don't see it. You have absolutely no idea the kind of effect you have on people."

His words open a hole in me. It's small, but light, hot and bright, pours through. I allow my eyes to connect with his; instantly I'm locked. My heart steadily picks up speed until I break the trance.

I turn my attention to the rippling water. "You're right, I don't see it. And none of that explains why my frequency overwhelms you. What's wrong with me?"

George takes a deep breath. "The way I read emotions is by picking up on the subtle changes in frequencies. I think the reason you interfere with my ability to read emotions, the reason you create interference in my head, is that the rate at which your frequency vibrates isn't subtle. And I can tell you firsthand there's nothing subtle about the shifts in your emotions. I'm sensitive. That's how I'm made, and you.... overwhelm me."

He's poised, like a statue of himself, watching me, gauging my reaction.

Cool night air wraps around my arms and legs and I count the seconds before he speaks again. "I think you and I meeting was destiny."

"What does destiny have to do with this?" Fatigue creeps into my words.

"I'm unaware of many people who do what I can. And I'm fairly certain there aren't many people who vibrate at the level you do. What are the chances two people like you and I would meet?" George's words twist around me like vines.

"And that's fate? How?" I ask.

"Roya, I can't tell you how many emotions I've felt in other people. Maybe thousands. Maybe more. You lose track, the same way you lose track of the words you've heard spoken." He reaches out, taking my hand from its resting place on my lap. "Being with you, it's the first time I ever remember experiencing emotion of my own. Your existence brings everything to light for me. It makes my dark conscious. It gives color to the light. Meeting someone who does what you do to me is fate. It must be."

How can I respond to those words? There's no way.

"I'm not responsible for any of this," I finally say. "I wish I was. I'm just a girl who showed up and gave you a migraine." The laugh that escapes my lips feels fake. "I'm not as important as you're making me out to be."

"That's because you're always doubting yourself." He guides my hand until it rests against his chest. My heart flutters. "Somehow I'm going to prove to you that our meeting is more than coincidence, it's synchronization. It's destiny."

I'm an anchor and he is the sea and I sink into his tenderness as he presses my hand to his heart. I lean forward, now only slightly perched on the edge of the stair. My face sits in empty space watching him, waiting. Something drifts across George's face. He squeezes my hand once and leans into me, but at the wrong angle, the wrong height. His lips graze my forehead.

Disappointment unravels in my stomach. With the little energy I have left I push it down, hoping he can't feel it.

"George," I say, pulling back. "You said there were two things concerning you. What's the second?"

The warmth in his face turns serious. "The second is about the way I make you feel."

I don't respond, but just hold George's gaze.

He pulls my hand onto his outstretched leg. "Does it bother you that I know what you're feeling?" he asks bluntly.

"That isn't a fair question," I say at once. "What you do is just another sense. That's like asking if it bothers me that you can see or hear or feel me."

"What I do is more complex than the other five senses." His tone is straightforward, but there's an edge to it. "It bothers you, doesn't it?" he says with a clipped frustration.

The air around us changes in an instant. "Why are you even asking me this question?" I say skeptically. "Don't you already know the answer?"

George sighs and stares off into the distance. "Most people are irritated that they can't mask their emotions from me. My gift has ruined every single relationship I've ever had."

Like a tidal wave it hits me, blunt and hard and all encompassing. George has always had the upper hand in any relationship, which gives him all the power. He knows how the other person feels before they even voice it, taking the element of uncertainty out of romance. Would being with George be impossible? I want to believe it would be incredible, but is that a fantasy? And while I process all of this, I know George is too. He's processing me and maybe that *is* unfair. How can he know how I feel before I even get a chance to?

"I'm torn." George chews on his bottom lip. "It's my ability to read your emotions which draws me to you so completely, but I know this is the very same thing which can ruin this."

I blink a few times, trying to push down the melancholy his words create. "Maybe it won't," I say. "It could make us more connected."

George gives a small, heartbroken smile. "Maybe, but in my experience it creates more obstacles. You'll come to resent me for spying on your emotions and I'll go paranoid."

"Paranoid? Why?"

"I feel your fleeting desires, your secrets, the things you should be able to keep hidden. And if you throw up a wall, then I know there's something you're trying to hide. It all makes me paranoid."

The realization is cold once it settles over me, like a cape made of ice. He knows my secrets, those hidden insecurities, the darkest parts of me. He knows my desires, the ones I covet and protect, unable to properly deal with right now. He knows about Aiden. "Why are we having this discussion? This is ridiculous."

"Roya, you have the right to know how I feel about you and to know I know how you feel. I don't want either one of us to get hurt." His words end abruptly and I listen, thinking he wants to say more, but he doesn't.

"I don't know what you expect me to say. Why do we have to figure everything out right now?"

"Roya, I'm just being honest." Gloom clings to each of his words.

"Okay, then I will too. I'm overwhelmed right now. I have no idea if you and I have a future and that's mostly because I don't think I *have* much of a future." I stop to contain myself. "Can't we just enjoy the moment? Can't we figure this all out later?"

George regards me for a long time. His tourmaline eyes lighten, but the prior reservation still masks his face. He leans forward and places a soft kiss on my cheek. "Sure," he breathes into my ear.

Chapter Thirty-Nine

"Seriously, I'm begging you," I plead, holding my hands together. "I promise if you do this, then I won't ever ask you to do anything ever again."

"That's a big fat lie." Joseph laughs. "You forget I see the future."

"Fine, let's bargain for it. What do you want?" I ask, impatient to get my way.

"Oh no, li'l sis. There's no bargaining. I told ya plain and simple, I won't do it. This is your deal." Joseph fails to hide the pleasure he's getting out of making me beg.

"How do you know I'm the younger sibling? We're twins and our birth is a big cover-up from the Institute," I say.

"I wasn't referring to you in birth order. You're smaller than me and therefore you're the 'little' one. If you want to change that title then start eating something besides rabbit food."

"Don't go changing the subject," I scold.

"You're taking your anger out on me. I think we both know who you really want to direct it at, so why don't you?"

"I really don't think I'm ready to face him right now," I almost whimper, trying to suppress the dull ache.

"I know." Joseph's tone changes, becoming softer, less playful. "But that doesn't mean you don't need to."

I scowl at him. "What's that supposed to mean?"

Something behind Joseph's eyes skirts away, but not before I realize he's hiding something. Maybe a vision. Maybe just another one of his games. It's hard to say with him. I glare at him for a long minute and then soften my expression. "Please."

"This is a good lesson for you." He pushes up off the bed, taking a long glance in the mirror. I swear if I wanted to distract him all I'd have to do is put his reflection in front of him and he'd be lost for days. He pushes a few stray golden hairs back into place and says, "When I say I won't do somethin' I mean it. I'm not a pliant piece of wood you can bend in whatever direction you choose. I'm the one person in this place who can resist your influence."

The idea I have any power around here is preposterous. I push down his refusal and my own frustration in one hard, painful swallow. "Fine, I'll go get the list myself."

♦

I startle as the elevator doors clang shut behind me. The corridor appears long and menacing somehow. With each step the music grows louder. At first I only feel the beat in my chest, but then the notes greet my ears, and the vocals encapsulate me. A few weeks ago I wouldn't have known the song or artist, but now I do because it's on my iPod. Greg Laswell. His voice pulls at the one part of me I've been trying to avoid. Artists have the uncanny gift of making me feel what I've been evading. They should all be incarcerated.

I stop exactly three feet from his lab. I know this because I measure the space over and over as I will myself forward. The song ends abruptly and everything grows quiet like a warm summer's night. I almost think I hear a cricket chirp in the distance, but realize it's the elevator.

"It's kind of weird you're just hanging out here, don't you think?" Aiden's bright eyes peer around the corner. "Why don't you come in?" He extends his hand. *Like I'd take it.* With a shake of my head he drops it and a trace of disappointment surfaces on his face. He retreats into his lab and I follow, wishing I'd never laid eyes on him.

"I'm here for the list of GAD-C locations," I say, just as I rehearsed.

"I suspected as much."

"Aiden—"

"Roya," he cuts me off, "I know you've been avoiding me. You're still mad about the modifier, aren't you?"

"Yes," I concede, pushing an errant bit of hair out of my face. "And you knew about Joseph and me, didn't you?"

His eyes drop to the ground before meeting mine. "You know I'm in a difficult position." The blue of his eyes is startling, more intense than usual.

"My entire life, all I've ever known, is a lie and I need to understand *your* position?!" My voice climbs until it's screaming. "You sound like Trey!"

232

"You're right. This isn't about me," Aiden says in almost a whisper. "I'm sorry I couldn't tell you. If I had then I would have lost my job. When I consented to do that work and keep those secrets I didn't know you. And if I had...well, I didn't know how..." His words fall short and he looks unsure.

"Do you want to finish that sentence?"

"Not right now," he says.

Why does he have to make everything so difficult?

"Thanks for the iPod," I say, empty of the gratitude I really feel.

"You're welcome." He leans against a table.

"Can I get the list? I've got a training to get to," I say, my resentment showing.

"Yes," he says. "But first you have to hear me out." Aiden steps forward and dares to shine a rebellious smile at me. "If you want the list, then you'll have to give me a chance to explain."

I wrap my arms around my chest and stare at the frozen graphics on the monitor overhead. A part of me knows I should demand the list and be on my way. But the other part of me knows I owe Aiden a chance to explain himself. He did save my life. "Fine," I half whisper, returning my attention to him.

"Thank you," he says. I nod and he continues, "Roya, you disapprove of my work with the modifier. I can't convince you the other way. Yes, I knew about you and Joseph. And I helped to embed your family so they'd continue to accept you. I kept this all a secret from you." A hint of stress marks his features. "I did all this because I know it's important. It protected you. The work of this Institute, my work, kept you alive. Even if you hate me for it, I'd do it again because I want you alive, and not just for the obvious reason that you're the challenger, but for a much more selfish one."

The hollow ache starts in my throat and then rolls down until my stomach feels as expansive as the desert, bare and stretched. I should have known he wasn't going to make this easy.

"I really hope you don't hate me though," Aiden continues.

A soft sigh tumbles from my lips. "I don't hate you. I wish I could. It would make my life easier."

"Easier? How's that?"

"Then I wouldn't be so distracted."

Satisfaction flicks in Aiden's eyes. "I distract you?"

I nod.

He pulls his glasses off his face and cleans them with his shirt. He glances up at me as he does this and says, "The feeling is quite mutual."

"Sorry." My apology is empty. "Maybe we should just stay away from each other."

"That isn't what I want," Aiden says, putting his glasses back on.

Without permission words spill out of my mouth. "Me either."

"But I'm fairly certain I can't give you what you want."

"Trust?"

"No, I can give you that."

I want to ask him what he means, but a part of me already knows. A relationship. All our encounters, every hungry look, every gentle touch, every flirtation, is always in private. In the company of others he changes, becoming the Head Scientist.

"How do you know what I want?" I finally ask.

"I don't, but I suspect you're tired of secrets and lies."

I stare at him long and hard, urging myself to stay focused. His eyes roam over me, enticing my cautious side. I slap a firm hand down on my waning resignation, pinning it firmly in place.

"Why are you looking at me like that?" I say, hoping my eyes look hard, unaffected.

"Like what?" He feigns ignorance.

He's an awful actor.

Surrendering an unabashed smile he says, "I can't help it."

"Well, try," I say.

"I'm trying."

"Try harder," I urge.

Aiden flashes another wolfish grin under hooded eyes, obviously tempting my seriousness. I look away, trying to mask my discomfort with annoyance. "Shuman seems to think you needed to save me and that's the reason she didn't tell me I might drown when I entered the Institute. Does any of that make sense to you?"

He crosses his feet on the ground. "Shuman likes to speak in riddles."

"Never mind." I turn to leave.

Aiden's fingers wrap around my wrist and with a gentle tug he yanks me back. "I don't know why she'd say that. But when I saved you two things happened."

I freeze.

"The first is I gained confidence, which I desperately needed. I'd been ridiculed when I was promoted to this position because of my age. Flynn had been ridiculed the most. I knew his reputation was riding on everything I did. I was afraid of failing him and myself. When I saved you I gained confidence and I needed that."

"You seemed so flippant about the whole thing," I say. "You acted like saving drowning girls was just a regular Wednesday for you."

A mischievous smile dances across his face. "Fake it till you make it, baby."

I roll my eyes, but smile still. "And the second thing that happened?"

"Well, if there's one way to get a guy's attention, it's to almost die in his arms. I haven't been able to take my eyes off you since."

He moves. And the way he does, it seduces me—like a tranquilizer, and I'm so tired of fighting it. Aiden brushes his hand against my cheek. Something real flows between us, and against my better judgment I plunge into it. I swim into the magnetizing force and it curls around my toes, drifts over my legs, circles my torso, and slinks along my collarbone until I sink into a new version of me, one in which I allow myself to welcome delirium. All ideas of retreating fade as I settle into the crazy emotions his stare elicits. A part of me, the part I've failed to block out, never wants him to look away. The idea of wanting to feel this crazy emotion is like throwing myself off a building. But right now I'd gladly dive off a roof, unconcerned for my landing.

"I don't want you to stay away from me," he whispers.

And I won't. Even if I want to, I can't. But I don't say that. Instead I inch in closer to him and the space between us recedes into a vacuum. Aiden's fingers comb through my hair until his hand finds my chin. He pulls it to meet his. I close my eyes, hungry for this moment. His lips have only just brushed mine when a flash assaults the warmth spreading through me. With a jerk, I pull away. Confusion rakes over his face as I fall back.

"I-I-I," I stutter. I have seconds to get away from him and feel something, anything but my current emotion.

Aiden stares, confused, but still boiling my blood with his desire.

I push my fingertips into my eye sockets and scan my brain for something infuriating. *Ignorant people, spiteful gossip, the itch that radiates down the middle of my back, noisy eaters, MTV, bad hair days, dawdlers, math.* I know the moment is almost upon us, and pull my hands back to find Aiden dripping with concern. I force a weak smile.

The knock startles him, but I expected it.

"Hello?" George's low voice slides over me like flour through my fingers.

Aiden's eyes dart up to meet George and then back to me. *You knew*, they seem to say. But what they don't elaborate on is whether he knew I backed away to protect him or me.

"What brings the pleasure of your visit?" A small hint of irritation marks Aiden's words.

"Shuman sent me down to get the new equipment. She said you'd upgraded it," George says and gives me a small wave.

"Right," the Head Scientist chimes. "I'll be right back." Aiden gives me an indignant look as he heads to the back of his lab.

Alone with George I avoid his eyes, afraid he'll put a spell on me. Instead, I think of smelly people, stepping in dog poo, slow Internet connections, stubbing my toe, bullies...

"Roya." His voice rips me from my sick meditation.

"Yes."

"What's going on?" he asks.

I swallow down a sharp piece of guilt. "What do you mean?"

He blinks roughly. Then he closes his eyes and like a fan sucking air from a room I feel him pulling at me. His eyes flash open. "Are you all right? Did Aiden do something to hurt you?" His tone is protective.

I flush, half embarrassed and half triumphant. "No," I chirp with finality.

"But you're all right?" He takes a step toward me, placing his hand on my shoulder. "You seem...upset."

"I'm fine." I lean into his hand, his warm, steady pressure.

"I have a question for you then." George devotes his attention to my eyes, which are busy skirting his. "Can I see you tonight, after dinner?"

I hesitate, only for a second but it's long enough.

A wall jumps up in George's eyes. "Unless you have other plans."

"I don't," I hasten as Aiden approaches.

He takes his time, lingering on my expression, my emotions, before saying, "Then it's a date."

"Here!" Aiden thrusts the oversized box in George's arms. "That should be everything," he says once his hands are free.

"Thanks." A confused expression marks George's features. "Sorry to have bothered you."

"No bother." The Head Scientist reclaims his disposition and straightens. "Is there anything else I can do for you?"

"That's all." George hides a puzzled expression, but I see it tugging at the corner of his face. "Roya," he says, turning toward me, managing the large box easily. "Shuman said you should join us right away. You want to head up?"

I nod.

Aiden gives me a sideways glance but I avert my eyes. I push every part of the craziness he created in me to the edges of my being, to the edges of the room, the Institute, lest George feel it. But I already know there's no winning this game of hearts. I've created this torment for myself. Placed myself between two incredibly different guys. Like great works of art, they're subjectively perfect. If I could love them both then I would, but what they deserve and what I'm capable of is not enough to split. And all I have, and own, will meet its doom at the hands of another man—one I do not love.

"Bye." I wave.

Aiden gives me a casual glance. He knows better than to expose his emotions around George. His hand rifles through his hair. "See you around, Roya."

Chapter Forty

You'd think the night before I'm scheduled to face a deadly nemesis the Institute would throw me a pizza party or something. Apparently Domino's doesn't deliver to secret underwater locations. I take dinner in my room, tired of receiving solemn stares from everyone in the main hall. I won't need to haunt my funeral to know what the attendants will look like. Their mourning expressions are already plastered on their faces.

I awake from a night of disturbing dreams to find my stomach tied in tiny knots. Probably better I didn't fill up on garlic bread and cheese pizza last night. I'd surely have an awful case of indigestion at this point. Then I'd have to call Zhuang and ask for a rain check on our duel.

The air is stifling in room 222. We've been reviewing strategy since breakfast, and although I can't choke down a morsel of food, my internal clock tells me it's well after lunch.

Trey is programmed, driven to cover every detail. He only stops once every hour to take a sip of water before continuing his drilling, ensuring every team member knows their role, their cues, their part. A look of chronic worry etches his turquoise eyes when he revolves on me. It's the first time this morning he's looked directly at me. He seems to be fighting his own internal war as we prepare for this battle.

"In order for this all to work, there's one part of this equation that's key," Trey states and then continues his nervous pacing. "Joseph," Trey says, running a hand through his already over-tousled hair. "You're the key. At all times you have to be as close to Roya as possible."

"No! It's too risky," I scold Trey with one look.

"I want to do it," Joseph urges beside me.

"You don't know what you're saying,"

"I do, and it's my choice."

"Look, you don't have to do this. There's other ways to protect me."

"Roya, it isn't about protecting you," Trey interrupts. "Your powers don't stand a chance against Zhuang if Joseph isn't there lending his energy. It's the way it has to be. It's the only way it will work." His last words sound full of regret, making me pity him, when he should be pitying me.

"But you could get hurt and then what good will come of that?" I'm desperate, looking from Joseph to Trey.

"What if he is one layer away, but still close?" Shuman offers.

"No!" I plead again.

"But it could work," Trey says, pondering the idea for a moment. "Aiden, you've been measuring their energy fields since they arrived at the Institute, right? Will that be sufficient to provide Roya with the power she needs, if Joseph is one layer away?"

Heat rises to my head and I clench my eyes shut, unwilling to look at Aiden. It's bad enough he knew about my long-lost twin since the beginning, but that he's been watching our energy patterns makes my chest burn. How much of this damn ball of yarn will have to unravel before I know all the secrets?

"I think that should be enough," the Head Scientist says. "When Roya has been dream tracking, the energy field remains strong until she moves into the third layer. At that point the whole thing disintegrates." He turns and looks at me, professionalism masking every part of him I know as true. "Unfortunately, we can't test this because it's too risky to have you two travel together. The few times you have, all sorts of alarms have gone off." The scientist focuses on Joseph. "Try to stay only one layer behind her. If you get more than two then she'll lose considerable power."

"You got it," Joseph says.

"No," I say a bit quieter this time.

"Stark, I'll be a whole layer away," Joseph reassures.

I don't like any of this. There are about a dozen things in the last ten minutes that have set me off. I'm about to face death and now I'll be taking my brother down with me. I cover my face with my hands, wishing everyone would stop staring at me. My mind searches for an alternative, but there isn't one.

I look straight into Joseph's mossy green eyes. I can't stand to look at anyone else at this point. The gold that flecks his eyes creates a depth. *Are my eyes like his?* It's strange to look at another and see yourself and then also so much more. I see love and it fills me with the yearning to protect. I see my friend, my brother, and a person I never knew I wanted to be connected to. That's why I finally say it, because I know if Zhuang's reign doesn't end then there won't be a Joseph left to love. There will be nothing.

"Fine," I say.

"And if you need anything, I'm only a layer away." Joseph grins.

Chapter Forty-One

The clothes I wore when I arrived at the Institute fit the same, but I'm a completely different person. I chose the faded jeans and white shirt over the option of the custom Gore-Tex suit Trey offered to have made for me. When I die I want to be in my own clothes. I wrap the peacock headdress around my head and tie the leather band at the base of my hairline. A few bobby pins make me feel confident that it will stay securely in place. The last thing I'd want is to show up to meet Zhuang with my headdress askew. First impressions are everything.

I lace my fingers around my bracelet. Maybe I'm imagining it, but I think I feel my pulse racing through the layer of silver and copper.

The new upgraded camera is even smaller than the version I'd been practicing with. I take the pin and attach it to the fabric on my shoulder. Then I grab the earpiece and secure it on my head. Even with all the extra equipment I still feel naked without the frequency adjuster around my neck. It was decided that it should be in a less conspicuous place, my jean pocket.

The elevator is extra cold when it delivers me to the fifth level. I'm confident I've done as good a job as possible mentally preparing myself. If Zhuang materialized in front of me right now I'm certain I could face him. Maybe I couldn't defeat him, but I could face him. I might even get in a blow or two before he pummeled me to bits.

The elevator doors open to a subtly somber Aiden. In one instant, all of my preparations that morning, all of the work I've done meditating, focusing, preparing…gone. His penetrating stare makes me crumble into a thousand pieces. My knees buckle like they're suddenly made of play-dough. My chest, like I swallowed a beehive, hums nervously. I disembark from the elevator and he steps closer. If he was George he would know that his presence makes me crazy, makes me weak. All things I can't be right now. But he isn't and so he takes one more step forward.

Please, please, please stay away.

"I just needed to give you this." He withdraws a crinkled piece of paper from his pocket. "It's the list of GAD-C locations."

My hand reaches out, but Aiden yanks the paper back when I've nearly clutched it.

I lift my gaze to his. "Roya, I know you can do this."

"I know I have to do this." I chew on the words bitterly. "I don't know that I can."

"I know you can do this," he repeats. "You can defeat *him*."

Him. The word hangs in the air like mold.

"You want to believe I can do this," I say.

"You're right." Aiden exhales. "I do want to believe you can do this, because if you lose—"

"Then we all get sucked into Zhuang's super-consciousness," I finish his sentence.

"Perhaps," he says and almost laughs. "But I know for certain that if you lose, I lose you." He opens his mouth and it hangs open a second, two seconds, three. Finally he says, "It's not like you're mine, that's not what I'm implying. I just can't imagine never seeing you again." He looks lost. Grave. Halfway to defeat.

I bite my lip and taste blood. He pushes a bit of my hair from my face. The craziness I'd been avoiding unravels in my stomach and begins snaking its way through my bloodstream.

I have zero idea how to respond. His words make me hurt. Make me want to resign from my position as challenger. I don't care if the entire world goes down in flames, I want to stay by Aiden's side just so he doesn't feel lost. This temptation races across my mind before I catch up with myself. I wrench away from him and regret follows. Not being close to him is cold and desolate, and also the only way to maintain sanity.

I straighten and stare into Aiden's glistening sapphire eyes. I once read all blue-eyed people are descended from a single individual. A strange bit of gratitude flows from my heart for this ancient ancestor of Aiden's who gifted him with his piercing, thoughtful eyes. They haven't wavered in all this time, although mine surely have.

"You know I can't do this right now," I say, gesturing between the two of us.

"I know," he says.

"I have to remain focused and not get distracted because…" I force my eyes to fall to the ground, knowing in one more moment I'll give in to him. I know one more stare from him and I'll throw myself into his arms, erasing all the boundaries I've carefully placed between us.

"Because you have a mission to do," Aiden says, completing my sentence. "And you will," he states matter-of-factly. "And I'll be here when you wake up."

He thrusts the paper into my hand, closing his fingers around mine. With a tender squeeze he says, "Give him hell."

I force a smile. "I'll do my best." Then I turn and tread down the hall and into the infirmary.

♦

Six beds line one wall of the infirmary. Whitney and George are already laid out with various wires snaking between them and machines beside their beds.

The lady with the wavy brown hair in purple scrubs bustles around checking to make sure things are fastened properly. With a flick of her head she indicates that I should take the bed on the far end of the room. I do, willing myself not to throw up. I trudge to my bed and by the time I've sat down, everyone else has arrived. The lady places a receiver on my fingertip. She's about to attach sensors on my head when I stop her.

"No," I say forcibly.

"But I'm supposed to," she protests.

"Doesn't matter. I said no."

A dozen wrinkles appear around her mouth when she purses her lips. With a shake of her head she moves away in a flurry.

From the corner of my eye, I spot Trey watching me on the other side of the room. My instinct tells me he wants to approach, but also senses I'm not in the mood for a pep talk or anything else he can offer. He stares at me with a nervous expression until his eyes dart to Joseph, who takes the bed beside mine. We're all just acquired assets that can secure the safety of Trey's precious Institute. That much is obvious to me now, but that's all right because I'm fighting for the Lucidites, not him.

Joseph allows the lady in lavender scrubs to hook him up and then reclines. Once our eyes meet, I shut mine. Somewhere in the forefront of my consciousness I hear him say, "Let's go blow some shit up."

A laugh escapes my mouth as I spiral through the first silver tunnel. The wind blasting me in the face is chilly and thin. I suck it in, and it mixes with my adrenaline. Six rapid turns, multiple lengths of seemingly identical tunnels, and a whirl of emotions precede my first stop. A small, cramped apartment. One by one I watch my team members dissolve the darkness into matter. When I spy a person almost as short as me materialize I step forward.

"I believe this is your stop," I say. "The next time I see you won't be so ideal." My voice sounds wounded. I take a quick swallow. "Thanks in advance."

Whitney places a warm hand on my arm and affection radiates through me. "Roya, if I may offer you one piece of advice, it would be something I've learned since joining this team." Her nose wiggles and then she says, "Believe in yourself first and then act. Don't expect it to happen the other way around."

I nod, acknowledging her words and vaulting them away. I close my eyes, feeling the tug inside my core as my ethereal body travels. We drop off Samara and then Trent. Each person's location is a small, dark room in a random building in a random city.

Upon arriving in George's tiny, musty room he flashes a look at Joseph. My brother narrows his eyes and doesn't offer us the least bit of privacy. George struggles with his words. I know he wants to say something, but instead he holds onto his edge. It wraps itself around his chin making him appear cold. He's preparing himself to lose me. Already I'm dead in his mind. He holds up his large hand and waves. I chew on my lip and disappear.

"This is it," I say to Joseph once we land in another nondescript room. "I'm going to be moving fast. If you can't keep up—"

"I'll keep up," he interrupts.

"Fine."

Joseph steps forward and hugs me. I bury my chin into his shoulder and press my eyelids together. When he pulls back, there's a look in his eyes I've rarely seen him wear. Seriousness. It doesn't stay long. A second later he covers it up with a small grin.

"I have a confession,'' he says.

I roll my eyes and suppress a nervous giggle.

"I used to think it was bullshit that you, a scrawny little nerd, was picked as the challenger," Joseph says in an exaggerated tone.

"Believe me, I don't get it either," I agree.

"I mean," he goes on, "I've never even seen you eat meat, which kind of makes you seem wimpy and liberal. No offense."

"Going to have to work harder than that to offend me," I say.

"Thing is, I kept thinking I was tougher than you, stronger. I've known a long time my role was to assist you by loaning my energy in battle, but it didn't mean I haven't struggled with it. It's not like I envied your role as the challenger, I just didn't understand how you were the deadliest person the Lucidites could put up against Zhuang."

"Seriously, Joseph, get to the point," I spout as I fidget with my hands.

"Point is, I thought it took strength to defeat Zhuang, but I was wrong. There's no way to be stronger than him. The reason you're the challenger is 'cause you have the one thing that can destroy him, something all of the rest of us lack."

"A thorough knowledge of British literature?" I ask.

"If boring Zhuang to death is part of the strategy then that might work," Joseph says. "No, your greatest asset, the one trait you can use to overpower him, is your passion."

"Ummm, that doesn't even make sense," I argue.

"Sure it does," he says, like we're debating the color of the sky. "You can be so calculated and focused, which, don't get me wrong is a lethal mixture, but when you let your passion overtake you, it's like you become a monster. You're unstoppable."

"So you think I'm the challenger because I'm a hormonal teenager?"

Joseph rolls his eyes. "I think you're the challenger because you're talented. But more importantly, you use your emotions to drive you, instead of allowin' them to distract you."

It's reaffirming to hear this at the eleventh hour, but what good will it do me?

"I know now you're the perfect challenger," Joseph says. "Zhuang will expect his strength to be tested, for strategy to be a part of the fight, for you to rely on intuitive abilities to aid you in battle." He holds up one finger. "But that greedy son of a bitch won't expect your tenacious spirit to be a threat."

Heat rises in my head from his words and the realization that the team and the Head Officials are all spying on our conversation. "Thanks for the vote of confidence," I finally say.

"That's all I wanted to say." Joseph hesitates and then adds, "In case I don't get 'nother chance."

I nod. I swallow. I force a smile on my mouth. "I better get going."

"You better," Joseph sings.

This is it. There's no turning back. I close my eyes and focus.

"Oh and li'l sis," Joseph says, pulling me from my reverie.

"What?" I bite at him, only half annoyed.

"When the time comes"—he sucks in a long breath before continuing—"take every bit of energy from me that you need to defeat him. It's all yours." He gives a triumphant smile.

"Maybe it won't come to that," I half whisper.

"Well, if it does, then you'll have one less obstacle, knowing I gave my full permission."

I clench my jaw and push back a lump in my throat the size of Montana. "Got it." My eyes say my goodbyes as the rest of me remains frozen and contained.

"See you 'round, Stark," Joseph says in my ear as I spiral through the grayness. The tunnel narrows right before it turns. My headdress catches the wind. All my effort and training are about to be tested and broadcast for my team and the Institute to witness. A violent flash assaults me at the same time as this realization. In it Trey, Ren, Shuman, Aiden, and my team watch Zhuang deliver the last blow that kills me. My breath catches in my throat and I can't will it to continue its path for a long few seconds.

Joseph's voice from a few days ago trails into my head, rescuing me from paralysis. *Flashes are just potentials. You always have the ability to change them.*

Chapter Forty-Two

I shoot through a short tunnel, free fall briefly, and land with a heavy thud in the open square. Crouched, I note the slick bricks under my feet. It's just rained. Daytime in Moscow. The Red Square, as planned, is filled with people. They hurry in different directions, ignorant of the war about to be waged for them so they can continue their busy affairs and sleep blissfully at night.

"Ready?" I bark into the headset.

"Yeah," echoes a collective response from my team.

A flash: Zhuang strides at my three o'clock. His black and white robes flap around him like flags as he charges through unaware Middlings. Water displaced from his slippered feet splashes onto nearby bricks.

I turn, ball my fists and clench my jaw. This is it. The moment I've prepared for. Strangely I have no fear, only rampant adrenaline and also an odd sense of belonging. I belong in this moment. What happens next is a part of a fate I can't avoid and don't want to.

A gust of wind trumpets his arrival. The air smells ancient, like the inside of a tomb full of mummies and dust. A thousand déjà vus spring to my mind as he strides forward. I expected him to tower over me and his gait to rock the earth like thunder. However, he's smaller than I envisioned. All lean and sinewy muscles, he moves through the air like a fish through water.

Zhuang's eyes snap to mine. His long, black goatee whips in the wind. Gracefully, he draws his hand up above his head and holds it there. I quicken, readying my defenses, wondering what he's about to do. He clasps his fist shut and the air around him freezes. The wind that blows through my hair, scattering droplets of rain in the nearby puddles and riffling strangers' scarves, has no effect on him. He's conquered this element. An ounce of annoyance seeps from his face as he takes in the stillness of his robes. Satisfied, he measuredly scans the square, not meeting my gaze until a full minute has passed.

"Are you ready to die?" he snarls.

I take one calculated step forward, leaving only five feet between us, and his menacing eyes slither across me for the first time. Large slitted black pupils hang in an all-encompassing gold.

"Yes," I growl.

One by one a duplicate projection of me explodes from the bricks until four Royas accompany me. They spiral until we're back-to-back in a circle. My body levitates off the ground three inches. "But you're going to have to find me first."

We spin, my doppelgangers and I, like cups in a magic trick. I hold tight, knowing my rigidness makes it easier for Trent to move me. Forty times we rotate at lightning speed before we drop onto the bricks and take off running in different directions.

I sprint, momentarily blinded as I pass through people. Hoping the illusions have worked, I don't look back. My only focus is on springing forward, ensuring I put enough distance between Zhuang before the next phase.

"It worked!" Samara reports eagerly. "He's following Whitney's projection of Roya. He already sliced through mine."

"Joseph," Trent breaks in. "Send your projection in Zhuang's direction, if you find him. This could be helpful for when he kills the second Roya."

The thought of Zhuang murdering illusions of me all over Red Square makes me want to vomit. Shaking this off, I close my eyes and focus on my next location. The idea wraps around me first, like water in a bathtub, and then my body springs forth with a jolt. My mind relaxes slightly, knowing I can count on the tunnels to do the navigating. The journey to the next layer is short.

A furious river gorge churns under my feet. The bank I stand on descends roughly 500 feet to the rocky and violent currents below. A bird sings in the distance and a beautiful row of lush trees stands on the opposite bank. *Not a bad place to die.*

"I'm here," I say with an even tone. "Trent, I'm ready when you are."

I flex every muscle in my body just as we practiced. Steadily, I rise off the ground and gradually float. My feet drift over the edge of the bank and my pulse quickens. The water below licks at the banks, hungry to swallow new life, chew it up, and spit it onto sharp rocks. Bile rises in my throat. My life's in Trent's hands. Although his ability is unmatched, he can't see me now, only where I'm headed. I know this complicates matters. Inch by inch I make progress. It's sluggish. I worry Zhuang will track me before everything's in place.

Panic begins caving in the vast space around me. I wrestle with hounding Trent to move faster, but decide that might be deadly to his concentration. Instead I close my eyes and begin counting back from one hundred. I don't realize I'm holding my breath until my feet land on solid earth. All at once my eyes spring open and my lungs take a generous gulp of air.

"She's in place!" Trent bellows.

"Nice work!" Joseph exclaims.

I turn toward the river's edge, staring across to where I'd been moments prior. "Ready, team?" I command. "On my count." I take a full inhale. "One. Two. Three." It flickers, like Christmas tree lights being turned on for the first time in a season, and then becomes solid. A bridge, large and sturdy, ripples into existence, joining the two banks. The team can see it on their monitors, but only George can feel my overwhelming sense of pride. I don't get a chance to express it before something moves on the opposite bank. Zhuang. He's tracked me.

Pushing the ground away like a bull, he glowers at me. "Clever trick, little girl. You can die now or later. Your choice. But you *will* die tonight."

A flash: A spear whizzes through the air, pushing through the molecules of space, forcing its way to its intended target. For a second I think it might actually find it.

My mind retracts to real time just as Zhuang jerks out of the spear's trajectory. It continues on its path, sliding though the air until it smoothly lands in my hand. I flip it around. "Thanks, Trent."

Zhuang narrows his brooding eyes. "Looks like I'll have the pleasure of killing your friends too," he says. "First things first, let's take care of you." He sprints forward, clearing the first half of the bridge in less time than is humanly possible.

"Now!" I scream when he's only fifteen feet away. The bridge dissolves as quickly as it appeared. Zhuang scrambles through the air once he realizes his error. I wrench back my arm and fire the spear at him. He wrestles with his inevitable fall. The weapon sticks into his side, and he takes it with him as he free falls toward the rocky rapids. Over the thunder of the torrents, I hear a roar echo through the canyon. He's falling fast, but dream travels just before entering the water.

I step back away from the edge, shaking with adrenaline. Knowing I have to move I travel three layers, hoping to get a chance to recover.

"The first two phases are complete," I say, catching my breath. "He's injured. Now phase three begins. Where is he?"

There's a long silence. "Samara? George? Does one of you know where he is?" I ask again.

Another long pause. "I've got nothing," Samara says, disappointed.

"I'm getting something, but it's confusing," George says after a few seconds. "It feels like he's at Graceland in Memphis."

"Great," I say, trying to concentrate.

"But," George adds, "there's an energy to the place. If I'm reading this right then Elvis is there."

"Oh, shit." I sigh. Tracking him in the past is complicated and deviates from the plan. "What's the date?'

"That I don't know," George admits after a pause.

Damn it! I've lost him. Frustration sits at the back of my head, making me feel heavy. I can't travel into the past at random to find Zhuang. I need to know specifically, down to the second, where he is. I fidget, hoping a brilliant idea will manifest in my foggy head. "Come on, guys," I urge. "I need something."

Silence follows.

"Samara?!" I yelp. "You were supposed to have a hold on him by now."

"I'm trying," she whimpers. "He's got me blocked. I keep trying to find a back door that he doesn't have locked, but he's thorough."

"I'd expect no less," Trent says.

"Just pick a random date in the past and travel," Joseph suggests.

"What?" I say. "Are you mad?"

"Yes," he chirps in his usual light tone. "But that's beside the point."

"Joseph, I can't just randomly travel to find Zhuang. There's like a one in a million chance I'd pick the right day and time," I explain.

"Right!" he says triumphantly, like he's given a sufficient rebuttal.

I shake my head, disappointed. Kind of surprised I failed so fast. I've lost Zhuang and the one chance anyone has had in centuries to destroy him.

"Stark, would you stop the self-loathing for a second?" Joseph says. I picture him wearing his typical sideways smile. "It was forecast that the Lucidites' challenger and Zhuang would battle today, right? What did Trey call it, 'a static moment in time'? He can't escape it and unfortunately, as the challenger, neither can you. If that's correct then no matter where you go you'll run into him. It's destiny," he says simply, like giving directions to a store down the road.

"You know, for once ol' Joe's actually making sense," Trent says.

"I'm gonna go ahead and take that as a compliment," Joseph says, a smile in his voice.

"By all means," Trent encourages.

"All right," I finally say. "I guess this is worth a shot." *I have nothing to lose.* "Wish me luck." I close my eyes and clear my mind. The lens of my mind goes blank. I push my consciousness back, further and further into the past. Like skimming through a book and randomly stopping on a page, I do this with the points of time. When the urge strikes I stop, crease back the page of this slot in history, and tunnel through the grayness.

Chapter Forty-Three

August 15, 1977, 10 p.m.

A two-story house stands in front of me at the other end of a grassy lawn. Light from inside illuminates the house, casting it in a jubilant glow. Crickets chirp in the distance, a sound I once loved but now prickles my skin with irritation.

A sensation grows until it radiates up my spine and tickles the back of my neck. *I'm being watched.* I spin around, sweeping my eyes across the grounds, searching for Zhuang. Darkness masks everything like a painter's cloth. Squinting through the blackness I wait for my eyes to adjust and listen to my pulse race in my head.

I back toward the entry of the house. A shadow lurches beside me. With a jolt I stagger until I back into a bench flanked by regal lions. Another shadow, maybe a different one, flickers in the distance. Just as I realize that Zhuang wouldn't cast a shadow, I hear a hissing cackle behind me. As I wheel around, my eyes seize upon a figure sitting on an opposite bench.

"It's true then." I wheeze, suddenly out of breath. "We can't escape each other."

Through the darkness he shows jagged teeth as he smiles crookedly. "No, it's in fact, not true," Zhuang counters. The side of his robes where I speared him has already dried, leaving a dark stain.

"What?" I sputter. "But I found you. Just now. At this specific point in time."

"Wrong." His voice is a hush among the orchestra of crickets. "I found you."

"No, that's not true," I argue. "You were at Graceland in the past. I found you."

"Yes, I was, but not at this date and time. When I was ready, I found you, little girl."

Reflexively I back away.

"And what an interesting date you picked." He sneers.

George's voice fills my ear. "He's feeling playful and enjoying the game. He doesn't want to kill you yet, which is good, but...there's something really dark he wants. I can't pin it down."

"Thanks," I say, taking in his words and also the comfort his voice provides.

"The King should be in that house sleeping right now," Zhuang says sharply.

The foreboding night air creates pockets in my reasoning, making it impossible for me to strategize. My eyes shift over the grounds, looking for an opportunity. I need to run, to travel, to get him to follow me, but the timing has to be perfect.

"Do you know why Elvis can't sleep?" Zhuang asks, looking amused.

"He hasn't taken his meds yet?" I say, scanning the estate.

Half a smirk registers on his face. "Every time he closes his eyes he has nightmares."

I have to figure out a plan, but unfortunately nothing has magically come to me. "Maybe he should stop staying up watching scary movies."

"We both know nightmares don't come from scary movies," Zhuang says without hesitation. A brilliant bolt of lightning streaks the sky, casting an electric glow on everything. "*I* create nightmares!" Zhuang growls. Then the thunder rains through the air.

The sound is deafening, as if the lightning has struck me in the temples. I clap my hands to my ears, willing the ringing to disappear as quickly as it erupted. Through my hands, through the ringing in my head, I hear Zhuang's words as his lips move. "Very soon those nightmares will kill the King."

I grip my head, pushing away the ache in my ears. I can't help Elvis, and even if I could, I can't change the past. Lucidites can observe, but we're not allowed to change events that have already taken place. My job is to secure the future.

"I do love a good cat-and-mouse game," he almost sings in his salient tone. "But I'm tired of being the cat. Your turn." And he's gone.

Without hesitating I dive forward to the place Zhuang had been seconds prior.

"NO!" Joseph shouts in my ear. "It could be a trick!"

"Confirmed," George says grudgingly.

"Doesn't matter, I can't lose him," I say. "And I'm ready to kill that son-of-a-bitch."

253

The complaints that follow are drowned out by my sheer focus as I step into Zhuang's ripple. His tracers are like flecks of ash drifting in a breeze. Each grasp I make for the tiny bits of consciousness pushes it further away. *Stay still*, I urge the tracers and myself. For a second it feels impossible to do nothing, knowing the ripple will dissolve at any moment, but it's what my instinct advises. Nothing happens. Still I remain fixed on the ripple. Something invisible settles on top of me like dew on a blade of grass. I seize it before it has a chance to evaporate and I fall at once, blindly.

Salty, humid air wraps around my face. Waves stroke the beach with each beat of the current. Directly in front of me, waist deep, Zhuang stands. The gentle waters move around him. His mustache twitches ever so slightly, betraying the satisfaction he's trying to conceal.

Zhuang pulls his lip up in disgust. "It astonishes me that the one person with the opportunity to end my reign is such a weak specimen."

Me too. "If it's not true that we were destined to meet, then why are you here? Why are you wasting your time on me?" Doubt etches my words.

A laugh like a box of matches rattling echoes from Zhuang's chest. "For all the glory the Lucidites pretend to deserve, they're so extremely ignorant. A shame you've chosen to align yourself with such misinformed people."

Knowing it's unwise to speak aloud, I reach out to Samara. *What's he going on about? Do you know? Does George?* Samara is the liaison between George and me since it's harder for me to communicate directly with him; his language is foreign to me, all slippery emotions, like a bowl of worms.

I'm not certain, Samara finally admits.

Still no hold, huh?

None, she confesses. *But George thinks he might be trying to goad you, so be careful.*

Zhuang's black pupils stretch across the waters separating us, cutting me with cold. "You became their challenger believing you and I were destined to duel, is that right?"

I glare over the dark waters.

254

A demonic spark glints in his eyes. "Destiny has nothing to do with it."

"But you even said it was forecast," I say.

"I said you were forecast as having the opportunity to end my reign. You're the challenger the Lucidites have chosen and that person does have a certain power over me." When he scowls, wrinkles and pits mark his face, like a rock found at the bottom of a quarry. "But the stakes are high for them because their challenger, although forecast to have the ability to kill me, also holds the one ingredient I need to succeed."

He grins, showing ugly, yellow teeth. "You, little girl, are the key to unlocking what I truly want. If I absorb your consciousness then I'll have the capacity to take over the millions I desire, something I've long anticipated." He skips his hand along the surface of the water, and with it the waves intensify. "I've waited ages for you to be born." His words echo for miles in my mind.

"You're lying," I bark over the beating pulse in my head.

Another cackle escapes his mouth. "Why would I be here wasting my time if this wasn't the truth?"

"None of this makes sense. Why would you embed Misty, possess her, and make her the challenger, if you were truly after me?" A new confidence overcomes my apprehension. Cocking my head to the side I say, "How do you explain that?"

"You're right," Zhuang acquiesces at once. "From your small perspective that would make no sense. Misty was a pawn I controlled. She was supposed to score high enough to earn a place on this team you have assisting you. Her place there would assure this fight was brief and my victory decisive. I am an army of one, but I have been known to employ soldiers to ensure success."

One eyebrow arches over menacing eyes. "Unlucky for me I did a poor job selecting my soldier in the case of Misty. Her own greed for recognition overtook her, planting her in the position of challenger. I didn't worry though, for I knew soon the embedding I had done to her would make her unfit. The Lucidites would never put her up against me. I knew the challenger, the true one, would take her place. And here you are, your consciousness so fresh and vast, ready to be absorbed."

"If this is all true, then why didn't you kill me ages ago?"

"I would have, but the riddle states that the person with a consciousness expansive enough to store millions will be revealed as a challenger chosen by the Lucidites and sent to meet me on this date. I had no definitive way of knowing who this person was, until now."

"Then why did you stalk me? Why did you go after my family? Kill my cats?"

A satisfied smile spreads over Zhuang's face. "I just couldn't help myself. I was curious, so I spied on everyone on the list. And in the case of your family, the timing was right...I was hungry." A repulsed grimace knits his brow together. "And I hate cats."

I reach out with my mind for Samara, needing her to help me navigate this misdirection.

Her voice is barely audible over my breathing. *It's all true.*

Those three words convulse in my chest, squeezing my heart, taking away oxygen from my lungs. This has all been a trap. A cleverly orchestrated one, set up by Zhuang. And all of the Lucidites, everyone I care about, have fallen into it. And now he will take what he wants, from me, from everyone. I've willingly walked into this disaster giving him exactly what he needs. I'm the key. Those words strike me with a rough blow. None of this seems possible and yet I can't explain it away.

The idea occurs to me that I should escape back to the Institute where I'll be safe. But as Zhuang's beady eyes search mine, I know I can't go through with it. This is our chance to destroy him. I must get him to follow me, but in order to do that I have to turn the tables. I need to take back control of this fight.

Fidgeting with my earlobe I say, "Does this forecast state when this duel is over, because I'm getting kind of bored."

He cackles. With a lick of his thumb the waves around him soften. "Did you know the Lucidites have a law you can't disturb objects in the physical realm while dream traveling? They care so much about the filthy perspectives of Middlings." Zhuang spits with disgust. "They don't want these lowlives to be scared by flying objects. But I don't care much for rules. Besides, those idiots will just dismiss it as a natural disaster."

He outstretches his arms and behind him a huge wave, twenty feet tall, rises up like a curtain. It pulses, hovering angrily, threatening to crash forward. Zhuang jerks his head to the side. "You're it," he hisses and disappears.

A shade of water drops, crushing the beach. Powerfully the water rages forward, swallowing me and everything in its wake. There's nothing I can do. I can't stop it or run or even travel. It forces me far onto the beach, pushing and striking. My head rams against something hard. Water rushes, driving me in all directions. I know I can't recover from this and get to his ripple in time. So I close my eyes. It isn't easy to block out the turbulence, or allow myself to get pummeled, or feel the water in my lungs. I endure it, though, and maintain my focus until I sense the soft darkness of the neat space around me. Slowly I sink to my knees as I taste the musty air of the safe house I've entered. Then the coughing and choking begins, but I welcome it over my own death.

"Are you all right?" The voice is in my head *and* in front of me.

"Joseph!" I cough angrily. "What are you doing here?"

"I had to check on you," he says, looking at my head. "You're bleedin'. Are you all right?"

"It's a scratch." I push blood away with my fingertips.

Joseph gives a slow nod. "Well, even still, maybe I should take a round or two for you. Give him someone new to play with. What do ya think?" He grins halfheartedly.

"I think you've lost your mind." I take a sip of breath.

"But—"

"We can't argue about this."

"Energy stores though," Joseph insists. "He has to kill me too in order for that to work. That must be what that means."

"None of this makes sense right now, and we haven't the time to figure it out. We're sticking with the plan," I say.

A small expression in Joseph's eyes almost empties me of resolve. *What if he's right? What if we could do this together and actually have a chance of defeating Zhuang?* Something else at that moment seizes ahold of me. It's a message. Something sent from the divine. Like wisps of smoke its words drift away once imprinted on my consciousness. *Only you,* it says.

"Guys," Samara interrupts. "I finally got a hold on him."

It's about time.

"Hey, give me a break," Samara revolts.

"Location!" I demand. "I need it now!"

"St. Peter's Basilica in Rome."

"Present day?" I ask nervously.

"I think so," Samara says as if to herself.

"Got it," I say into the headset. "All right, I'm going to try and get him to follow me again as we planned."

Joseph shakes his head, encouraging me to abandon the plan.

"You know the locations and sequence," I urge, looking at him earnestly. "I'm going to move fast. When I get a hundred layers deep, I'll return to the Institute and hope he hits a snag." Joseph looks away, and I give one last directive. "George, Samara, find his body." With my nervous face veiled, I say to my brother, "See you later."

He stares at me; a petulant expression is all he offers. I fade away.

Chapter Forty-Four

The Tiber River under the bridge makes no noise. It sits calmly, as if entombed between the banks of lush grassy lawns. I once read executed criminals were thrown into these waters. Picturing ancient bones lying on the bottom of this river makes my stomach lurch with unease.

The dome of St. Peter's Basilica stands to my left. Michelangelo's love for God is evident in the supremacy of the structure, which weakens my knees. My agnostic heart bows to a place created by men, fit for God.

Zhuang, like a statue, is poised ten feet away, chest forward, feet wide, hands by his side. Proud. This could be the weakness I use to my advantage. Maybe Zhuang has underestimated me in overestimating his own skills. His greed also could be a shortcoming. It glints in his eyes, reminding me of a ravenous dog.

The plan, the only way we've determined will kill Zhuang, has merit. At most, I could hope to wound him in an actual flight. But he's too fast, strong, and powerful. I must trap his consciousness by getting him to track me and then find his physical body. I'll have to autogenerate my body at that point and move as quickly as possible. That's not the part that keeps the worry churning through my stomach. I've practiced and prepared for this day, but still I can't see myself holding a blade and plunging it into his flesh. My sensei, Mario, urged me to visualize the entire fight including its end; each time I do though, I'm overwhelmed with darkness and dread.

A flock of birds travels over our heads. I keep my eyes trained on Zhuang. He sneers, disdain unfurling from the corners of his mouth. "Found me, did you, little girl? Thanks to the help of your friends."

I dismiss him and ready my confidence for the descent through a hundred layers.

"Roya." George's voice, like a single string being strummed on a violin, startles me. I gasp and wait for him to continue. "Something's wrong. I'm getting a horrible feeling."

"What else did you expect? Zhuang surely has an aura which would unsettle even Hitler," Trent says.

"This is different." George's tone makes me throb with anxiety.

Zhuang's words command everyone's attention. "Little girl, how weak you must be that you can't face me on your own."

I stare at him, unblinking.

"Tsk, tsk, tsk," Zhuang says with a shake of his head. "You understand I must insist you fight me fairly. It really is the noble way."

"You've got to be kidding me; you're going to question my nobility. You don't follow rules, remember?" I accuse.

"You know," Zhuang whispers hoarsely, "I really could not risk it. She had to go first. I need to know when I kill you, it's for good."

What does he mean? A shooting sensation pulses through my limbs. Masking desperation I say, "Leave my team out of this. This fight is between you and me."

He makes a guttural sound. "I agree, this fight should be only between the two of us." His cold chortle echoes along the river. "But it's entirely too late to leave these people you've dragged along out of it."

A chilling desperation shatters the fog in my head. I'm just about to ask for a roll call when Zhuang interrupts. "The interesting thing about healers is, they're incredibly easy to kill. Very weak, you see."

All blood rushes to my head, making my ears hot. I know I need to run, to travel, but I can't move. My hands are numb. *He's lying. He must be. Samara?! Confirm this!*

"But," he purrs, "you'll be glad to know when I killed her, she didn't even cry. She seemed to think this was important and wanted you to know. Isn't that sweet?" His last word is broken into an extra syllable and it crawls over my skin like the scratchy legs of a cockroach. Zhuang sinks into a deep lunge and thrust his hand into the air expectedly.

Seconds pass as long pulses flow through my veins. Something flickers in his bony fingers and then solidifies. In his outstretched hand Zhuang holds his long, curved sword—a falchion. Gold at the handle, silver on the blade, and red at the tip. A single droplet of blood descends off the end and lands on the pavement. *Plat.* My stomach twists. I can't move. The small spot of blood on the pavement soaks up my attention like a sponge. Whitney's blood. The idea burns my insides with disgust and grief.

Zhuang straightens and eyes the blood on the sword like it's a delicious piece of meat. A cloth appears in his opposite hand and he runs it across the blade until it's clean. "One down," he growls, looking at the sword. Then he flashes his creepy black and gold eyes on me. "Five to go." And he's gone.

Terror races through me in a way I've yet to feel. I sprint forward. "Team, move! Now!" I scream and seize his ripple. Seconds later I'm in the darkened room where we left Samara. I squint, willing my eyes to adjust. In the corner I spy the tiniest movement, like someone is stroking the air. It's the most recent ripple. *But whose?* I absorb the tracers in the ripple and immediately it's apparent I'm following Zhuang.

So quickly everything's fallen apart.

I stand in the room where George had been moments prior. Not terror, but rather a dull ache, like someone has stripped away my solace, quivers through my being. I itch and twitch with a fervent determination to get back what was mine. The idea that Zhuang has killed George makes it easy to see myself plunging a blade into his chest, grinding it past muscle and bone, until it punctures an organ, bathing him in his own blood.

Desperate to find his ripple, to hunt him down and end this, I search the darkened space. It's small. So much so, that as I turn I catch Zhuang at the corner of my vision. My reflexes tell me to reach out, blocking his oncoming hand. Steadily I slide back one step and meet a wall.

"You must," he whispers vehemently, "finish this fight fairly." Zhuang telekinetically rips the headset off my ear. "Now this will be even more fun. You're it, little girl."

Zhuang disappears. Without hesitating I step into his ripple, glad he isn't going after the others. I don't want to die, but I would much rather they didn't. The selfishness of my desire is the last emotion to wash over me before I'm engulfed in the rabbit hole.

Chapter Forty-Five

Zhuang isn't to be seen in the new layer. No doubt he's hiding, waiting to leap out and attack me. Trees like skyscrapers command my attention, pulling my gaze higher until it's lost in an awning of darkness. The redwood forest.

Fog thick as wool wraps around me, entangling without restriction, circling without creating borders. The moist, mossy air soothes my skin. Patches of green threads hang from branches forming beards. This coupled with the smell of decay and mold brings the image of a wise man to my mind. If a wizard ever presided over my destiny, now would be the time for him to materialize.

Crickets echo all around but nothing disturbs the mist. There's no robed figure or enchanted being with magical powers, not even a gnome pouncing through the forest, ready to assist my noble cause. A frustrated grunt escapes my mouth.

I hurdle over ferns and lichen, haphazardly zigzagging my way deeper into the thicket, hopefully away from Zhuang. My first break of the day comes in the way of a fallen redwood trunk lying at a slant on top of a half dozen of its brethren. With my fingers digging into soft bark I clamber, losing my footing several times, until I'm deftly crouched at its base. I scurry up the trunk, moving farther into the sky and darkness, keeping my body low and my hands grounded. After I've traveled roughly fifty feet the trunk dead-ends into a vastness of shattering mist. Below me a clearing sits reeking with vulnerability. I recoil from it, searching the kindly forest for options.

To my right two redwoods grow adjacent to my makeshift ladder. Their proximity to each other is nearly perfect for scaling if I get enough pressure between my hands and feet. The gap between the plank I stand on and the trees I intend to smear is roughly four feet. This isn't major since in training I've jumped double that distance several times. However, my take-off area is uneven and soft, not giving much for me to spring against. More disconcerting is that I need to propel myself in between two targets, extend my limbs at exactly the right time and angle in order to stick and avoid falling.

I rock back on my heels and imagine a promise from the padded forest ground that it won't do me too much harm if I fail. My gaze lifts to the canopy overhead. Instinct urges me to get higher. Isn't it from high in the tree that the birds hold advantage over prey? I want to believe that if I somehow launch myself to the place where the majestic redwoods unfurl their great canopy, I'll find a sanctuary from Zhuang. I'm not sure what I'll do then, but maybe in that sacred place I'll have a vision or be given aid. This is a long shot.

I rest my eyes on a gentle piece of lichen and swallow my last bit of resolve. Then I push forward, take one and a half quick steps, and leap into the mist. I soar through the space between the trees and just before I leave their refuge I jut out all four of my limbs, hoping that at least two stick to the pliant bark. A rough assault accosts my palms and my feet rake against the surface, sending reverberations through my bones. The skid happens immediately, scraping away layers of skin. My fingernails dig deeper, trying to find a hold. Slowly I descend, losing my precious advantage as the feet of bark recede above me.

When the ground is no more than thirty feet away, I lock my ankle in a strange angle, hoping to slow my downward progress. Right then, exactly what I'd been praying for happens. I stop. Wedged between two holy redwood trees, with all limbs at exactly the right angle and releasing the exact amount of pressure, I've pinned myself in place. I don't allow myself the time to gather my breath before I deliberately negotiate one hand a few inches and then one-by-one allow my feet to follow suit. *So far so good.* Confident with my approach, I use this pressure to recapture the distance I've lost, moving gradually with each hand and following in step with my feet.

Once I reach the tree ladder I used originally, I scan the clearing below for signs of Zhuang. I continue to climb until I reach a gnarly knob, the size of an elephant's head. Pushing even harder with my hands I pull my closest leg in, angle it high and set my foot down upon the knob. Then shoving against the other trunk I release with one steady jerk. For a brief moment, my one foot on the knob is my only hold to the earth. I picture a thousand endings as I realize I'm over a hundred feet in the air.

Like a moth to a flame I jerk to the tree, pulling my other foot to meet its pair. A wave shoots through my spine. The momentum from my plunge takes me off center and rocks me forward, toward the clearing. Instinctively I drop my center of gravity and overcompensate for my miscalculation by rocking back toward the gigantic trunk. Half a second passes before I realize I'm squatted, quite precariously, but still safe upon the knob. My fingers dig narrow holes into the bark and my toes cramp from the pressure they've endured, but I'm alive.

My breathing comes like raps of wind through a tattered flag as I realize the devastation I've somehow circumvented. Bracing myself, I peer over my ledge at the clearing below. Still no magician has appeared to steal my fate and portal me off to an enchanted land. Now that I'm high up in the trees, perched like a gargoyle, I don't feel powerful or protected, but rather foolish and misguided.

The nub is spacious enough for me to sit and stretch out. This relieves my legs of the ever-growing ache which I've had since the great climb began. I feel like I'm dangling my feet off the edge of the world, enticing the flames of hell to eat me up. I shrink away from this thought, wishing not to taunt God or the devil or any other deity who might preside over my future.

Where is Zhuang? Is he going after the others? My hope is they returned to the Institute. However, Joseph hasn't. I sense him and know he's no more than two layers away. I need to get back to the plan, but it's hard now that I'm on the defensive.

My location, as planned, gives me the perfect place to view an oncoming attack. From up here, there's little chance Zhuang can sneak up on me. Although my visibility is limited, I can still rely upon my clairvoyance. And once I catch sight of Zhuang I'll get his attention and there will still be enough space between us to give me time to begin my excursion through the hundred layers. By the time he flies, as I suspect he can, up to meet my ripple, I'll be a safe distance away. I smile, satisfied. The time has finally come to catch this evil serpent in a net of justice.

The mist on the ground stirs. Zhuang strolls into the area below as if he's stepping out to meet a train. The mist curls away from him like tendrils clambering to escape a noxious weed. He regards the space nonchalantly and stretches out his rail-thin arm. A long cylinder appears in his waiting hand. The reedy object is three feet long, and resembles a skinny baton. He places one hand a foot from the end and the other an equal distance down the shaft.

The urge to say something and catch his attention courses through me, but my curiosity gets the better of me. My location is secure and not once have Zhuang's snakelike eyes flicked up since he entered the clearing. If I watch for another minute I might gain valuable covert information.

With a graceful pivot, Zhuang swivels, places one end of the tube to his mouth, and points the other end directly at me. Instantly I know I was dead wrong to stick around. Staring down the barrel of the blowgun I wince, letting my regret billow out of me like steam. I jump to my toes and lunge forward but realizing there's no space, withdraw and remain planted against the redwood behind me.

The dart spirals out of the tube, like a missile through the air. I close my eyes and focus on dream traveling. The silver tunnel explodes out of blackness. Never in my life have I been so grateful to reach out for the wormhole, my connection to every place and time, and right now my only sanctuary. I tip forward, feeling the familiar splash of adrenaline.

The cold pierce of a foreign object entering my body is the first sensation. It's followed by a rush of heat. I've been struck by whatever Zhuang spit out of that blow gun, but maybe I can still travel.

A jerk yanks me up. I'm suspended, unmoving, watching the spiraling grayness in front of me. The burn races through my bloodstream and my veins swell under the pressure with such intensity I think they might burst. The grayness is gone with a brilliant flash and I open my eyes to the forest blurred in shades of green and brown.

Surrendering at once to the powerful sedative, my head falls forward over the edge of the knob and my body follows suit. My feet tumble over my head, and then my head over my feet. Just when I think I'll make another rotation I hit the leaf-covered ground and all my remaining air spills out. I'm but a pile of blood and bones on a mass of earth.

Chapter Forty-Six

"If it makes you feel better," Zhuang sneers, standing over me, "you'll be almost dead before I suck your consciousness out of you. You'll hardly feel a thing."

I twist, my muscles reacting awkwardly to my demands. My limbs flail against the dirt, but I'm unable to summon enough strength to get on my feet. If it wasn't for the poison, I'd probably be in a great deal of pain.

"Now, now," Zhuang chides. "You've really had an exhausting day and quite the fall." He taps his foot and holds his chest high. "You need to sleep now." His voice almost sounds calming, alluring. My eyelids grow heavy and the strain to not shut them is excruciating.

"Fall into a deep sleep," he whispers. An odd, exaggerated smile, like that of an evil clown, flashes on his face. "And until you're ready for harvesting I'll go kill your brother." He wrenches his polished sword from behind his back and holds it high into the air. "Putting the royal twins to bed places me one step closer to the finish line."

I reach for him, wanting to attack, but unable to operate my limbs. With every ounce of strength I own I try to move, but remain paralyzed, frozen to the soft ground. Each millisecond of every second I pray and wish for my body to react to the commands from my brain. And thousands of times my body ignores, leaving me lifeless, exposed.

My neck is hot with fire where the dart struck me. The poison infiltrates my blood, rushing through me. I watch, unable to seize Zhuang as he disappears before me, particle by particle. By the time my conscious thoughts catch up, I know the dream-sucking parasite is gone.

Zhuang wants me to sleep. Who knows what hallucinations the poison will cause if I succumb to the dream world. *I can't lose focus,* I tell myself. A wave of fatigue reverberates through my core. *Stay awake,* I beseech. But with each passing second I know I've already lost this round. To resist sleep right now isn't just futile, it's also depriving my body of precisely what it wants more than anything.

I'm a seedling and sleep is sunshine. It's rain. It's soil. It's life. I close my eyes and descend into a vast darkness only briefly before my subconscious turns it into an array of light and colors.

♦

Glossy green leaves, thick to the touch, intersperse the backdrop. I watch from overhead. My body lies on the ground and I, an ethereal form, feel the currents of air pass through me. I hardly identify with the figure lying on the ground below. She, this girl I used to be, is intriguing nonetheless. The calm expression on her lips begs for my investigation. I drift closer.

Out of the same ether I was born, a pair of eyes materializes. They're close together and do not look at me, but rather hover over the girl. I wonder sourly why they don't care about me and also why they don't have a body. The space between the girl and me recedes. I have episodes where I fight to be her and fight against it, to be a spirit floating in my dream world. The detached eyes, beady, but full of majesty, fade into a darkness and a part of me knows I won't see them again for a long time.

Who am I? I gaze up into the green and brown canopy of the trees. Below me the spongy ground contours to my body. The leaves overhead catch my attention as they sway. From a distant part of my mind I wonder where the figure, the one who had loomed overhead has gone. And then the gentle leaves like a fan of feathers fall down on me and all is forgotten. They're lovely on my skin, like satin. I'm enwrapped in them, guided by their essence, and restored by the same spirit the earth employed in them when they sprouted from branches. These leaves have given me wings and in true dream fashion I feel I can fly, but remain planted to the gentle soil.

♦

Easily I shove sleep away, like a scratchy, thick blanket on a humid summer night. My eyes are heavy, but I know my vision is real and not that of a sleeping dream world. Once on my feet, I notice how different the forest looks now, somehow marked from witnessing my attack, my fall, and whatever happened while I was

267

comatose. Now I understand why these trees are so wise. All they must have seen in their time.

I pace the clearing looking for signs of Zhuang. My body now holds a deft agility. I'm brand new, like I've awoken from a summer of sleep which promises to bring only good fortune in the season to come. *How am I not dead? Or asleep?* My mind, clear and organized as I've never experienced, easily holds a dozen thoughts all at the same time: my new predicament, my recent failed plan, and Zhuang's last words.

Joseph?!

Although my body feels brand new and my mind fresh, no longer lost in a fog of poison, there's something missing. The power I've grown accustomed to when Joseph's close is gone. Devastation tears my chest in half as the chilling possibilities set in. My knees lose their ability to hold me upright. I fall forward, landing on them before kneeling. First Whitney, maybe George, and now Joseph. Who else? Samara? Trent? Everyone could be dead. All because of me, because I'm incapable of killing Zhuang. If only I'd stuck with the plan, but no, I've failed and everyone's paying the price for my incompetence. My heart palpitates with a few sudden shudders. And still I live. Zhuang poisoned me, trying to make me sleep within my dream travels. So *he could harvest me*, he said. Something awoke me early, though, of that I'm certain.

My breathing is still bordering on hyperventilation. I push back on my heels. In the distance a figure breaks through the haze. I don't jump, as I would have expected, fearing Zhuang has returned to finish me off. My sharp focus recognizes the figure as not human, but still my brain doesn't fully register what I'm seeing. It lifts its veil of feathers a few inches in the air and shakes them into a vertical wall. I bow my head.

"So it was you." It isn't a question and there's no answer. The peacock's display glides back behind its body in one smooth movement and the bird slips behind a large tree.

"Thank you." My voice falls short in the damp surroundings. It feels good to have no echo.

Chapter Forty-Seven

According to Ren, returning to my body is the best way to throw Zhuang off my scent. Maybe then I can track down Joseph and save him. Maybe I can start again and actually trap Zhuang. I hold onto this hope like a four-leaf clover and travel to one of the GAD-C locations.

Cramped darkness surrounds me like a heavy cloak when I arrive in the room. A faint red light shines over a labeled box. Inside I find something I expect—a flashlight—and something I don't—a note. I switch on the light and open the note. I recognize the handwriting. Aiden's.

Roya, if you're reading this then you're desperate. Don't give up. A part of you which you've deemed defensive might be your greatest weapon. Use it. I need you to return to the Institute to complicate my world.

Desire fills my stomach, giving me an odd confidence. Emotions are great motivators. I push the note into my pocket. Without hesitation I focus on regenerating my body using the same procedures Amber taught me. I don't have time to double check the readings though. I grab the button attached to the wire and pray for the second time that day. The button is stiff, most likely from disuse.

Nothing happens. It didn't work. I brace myself for the complication, the result of not aligning one of the settings correctly. Then a flash of light assaults my vision, penetrating the deepest part of my retina. Like two polar magnets being drawn to each other, my body and consciousness pull together. The light radiates through the darkness, blinding me. I've never done this union in a darkened room. *Is the light me? That flash, is it my consciousness? The way my physical form perceives it? It's beautiful.* The light fades like clouds receding after a storm.

I throw myself off the table and hurry down a dark hallway. I need to get away from the GAD-C and figure out a plan. The hallway ends without warning. A single push-bar door stands before me. Without a second thought I shove through it and into the night air. The walls of the building disappear, leaving me sprinting across a catwalk with water on either side. Scanning my location, I realize I'm in a water purification plant.

It isn't until I near the end of the walkway that I turn, sensing his evil eyes lurking on my back. *How did he track me so quickly? This is useless. I'm outmatched.*

I don't see Zhuang, though. I think I'm imagining things until he begins to take shape. His body fills in like pixels on a screen, layer upon layer until he stands solid. His opaque presence takes up space. Above him the sky shines orange and pink. The sun's about to rise.

I turn and continue sprinting, not caring that I'm obviously running from this fight. I have to get away from Zhuang and find Joseph. Then we can return to the Institute.

"You'll want to know," his voice echoes behind me, "his wounds are fatal."

I halt.

"I wish I could confirm he's in fact dead," Zhuang says from the far end of the catwalk. "I can't. All I can say is I am pretty certain I hit a major organ. I could not stay to watch him die, since I needed to make sure you didn't get back to your precious Institute.

"Unlucky for you, your death is going to be much more painful than I planned. I was trying to make it easy by putting you under while I sucked out your consciousness. Now I'll have to do it while you're fully awake and this is much more taxing for the both of us." He grimaces. "I'm not sorry to tell you this is going to feel like I'm pulling your brain out through the pores of your skin. Any death you could have imagined would have been better than this."

"Well, at least it will be strenuous on you as well," I say, grinding my teeth together.

Cracking the knuckles of his left hand with his right he says, "Undeniably it could be quite the costly effort on my part, more so than any other I've had to endure thus far. But I do have another plan for how I can save myself too much mental anguish from the feat of acquiring your consciousness."

The gravity of the situation simultaneously drains my morale and my strength. "And what's that?" I ask.

"I'll beat you until you're senseless." He sneers. "You won't relinquish your mental faculties easily, but if you're bleeding internally I think you'll be more inclined to let go."

Suddenly the sleeping potion he gave me earlier sounds like a picnic. I'm not certain I should have thanked my spirit animal or cursed it. I swallow down my revulsion and push my words out like pieces of flesh I've been forced to regurgitate. "Well, get on with it then."

Chlorine laced with algae hits my nose, reminding me of the lake where I grew up. The slick catwalk under my feet greets me oddly. And the detail of every object within 300 yards intensifies in my vision. In that instant I have no doubt I should rush forward, meeting this demon halfway. If I'm going to die then I need to fight first. And if he's going to take my power then he's going to damn well earn it.

I charge, feeling the wind on my face, seeing the glow of the sunrise, and tasting the pureness of the water under my feet. Zhuang soars through the air with a flying kick. I brace myself with a two-handed block. My blocks are strong. I should be able to take his strength, or at least hold my ground. Instead it slams me to the catwalk in a mass of disorder and I slide several feet.

Lying numb and lame on the ground, too ashamed to pull my head from the metal where I rest, I confirm what I suspected: Joseph is gone. A cave opens in my chest, swallowing my heart in one giant breath.

My energy level, strength, and speed are all significantly less. I'm no better than a Middling at this point. Still, I must fight. I force myself into a fighting stance.

Before I'm ready Zhuang charges. His punches assault me all over. I fail to parry any of his attacks at first. But my training is still intact and so once I regain my footing, even after being battered multiple times, I'm able to block a few of his blows. His movements are quick, like the spark that ignites a match, rapid and dangerous.

My slow reflexes witness every attack a second too late, giving my body zero time to defend. A single punch launches from his fist and jars my teeth as it connects. It's impossible to keep up with the directions of his arms, let alone plan offensives. This is a joke. I take blows all over. The pain sears in my head. Each strike makes my body weaker and gives my consciousness another reason to dream travel away from all of this. I want to, but I can't do anything except try to maintain my footing. Besides, I know he'll just follow me.

Disappointment swells in my gut as I realize I'll fail the Lucidites as their challenger. I'd known this on some level all along. Of course I can't kill Zhuang. I'm just Roya Stark. I was born for lesser purposes than banishing evil. I'd squat and pee on evil. I'd make it recoil. I'd challenge it. Sure, that's possible. But my job isn't to rid the world of its problems. That's better served by those with superior bloodlines and purer hearts and intelligent minds. I'm Roya Stark, hardly anyone at all. Truthfully I don't know who I am. I didn't know my mother, hardly knew my brother, and everything else is as much a mystery as this facade I've been living in for the last few weeks.

Blood now covers my face. The heat rises to the top of my head. I wish I'd died in the forest from the poison. That would have been better than dancing around in a drunken haze while Zhuang bruised every inch of my skin. The only thing I commend myself on is I push up after every blow or remain in a somewhat standing position. I take each attack as honorably as I can.

At long last Zhuang grips my throat in his hands and presses his palms down firmly, cutting off my air. *Finally.*

The blackness begins to take over my vision. First in spots, creeping in from the edges and spreading until it meets itself. Everything goes black. I hear him breathe. Feel the air on my skin. But my vision is walled behind my heavy eyelids, the first symptom I'm about to slip away. My last bit of consciousness recognizes a shock radiating from my bracelet. It feels like electricity as it courses through my blood. Aiden's words rush through me: *A part of you which you've deemed defensive might be your greatest weapon. Use it.*

Zhuang's hands tighten on my neck. My eyelids fly open. With a jerk I reach out for him. My hands claw against his face. The voltage intensifies in my bracelet.

Seconds before I'm about to pass out, Zhuang lets me slide from his hands and tumble to the ground. Standing over me laughing, almost giddy, and unscathed from our battle, he toes my lifeless form. "You're a pitiful warrior." He spits. A dozen sarcastic retorts come to my mind, but they all remain buried in me as I lay on the ground in a heap of desolation.

My eyes flutter open every now and then, like a strobe light catching images. Zhuang paces the catwalk, impatience in his footsteps. I sense he's measuring my resolve, deciding if he must inflict more physical damage to get at what he truly desires. I push my feet underneath me. Pride feeds my strength now. I know what he wants and I have to die protecting it, otherwise many more will be doomed.

He laughs. He growls. "Little girl, you're out of options. There are no more weapons coming. Your friends have deserted you. You're too weak to do anything. Die with integrity. *Now* it's time."

I flip my head up, mustering strength from the depths of my soul. Fire burns my eyes and I roar, "There's always an option!" Then I run, harder and faster than ever before. I don't care why they chose me or if they knew my tumultuous fate. I'll die for these people. Willingly I'll lay down my life for them. Because *I'm a Lucidite. I must protect...*

Music plays in my head, propelling me farther, faster. Zhuang cackles gruffly. I know he thinks I'll run into him and crumble like a brick wall. Instead, when we collide I shoot my wrist forward, sending my bracelet into his chest. The pulse intensifies each fraction of a second until it's all-encompassing. Electricity originating from my protective charm wraps all around us, like a cocoon built for two. I'm not sure why this happens, but for some reason when my bracelet connects with Zhuang it radiates electricity. Tons of electricity. We both fry under the charge.

With my last bit of momentum I thrust us through the barrier and we fall into one of the tanks. The water engulfs us, intensifying the overwhelming charge. My brain is on fire. Everything burns.

Zhuang tries to escape, wresting away from my grasp several times. I seize him each time, ensuring he stays connected to my bracelet—the epicenter of the electrical storm besieging us. After multiple attempts he stops fighting, probably because like me he's dying from the shock. I watch Zhuang convulse and we sink deeper into the clear abyss. The water around us boils. It swims into my ears and nose. My bracelet, still on his chest, glows bright red. He's burning from the inside out. So am I. If the electricity doesn't kill me then the water will. In the end, just like the recurring dream, I'm going to drown...willingly. I entered this water knowing there was no coming out. I guess I always knew it would end this way.

I watch him fry for what feels like an eternity. If he's watching the electricity course through me then I can't see it. His black eyes are impossible to read. Finally, I unclasp my fingers from Zhuang. He floats away. Unable to move my aching limbs I drift, not up, just further from the sinking man's body. The water doesn't burn my eyes as they scan the large tank. The surface of the water is too far to reach in my current state. With only one thing left to do I close my eyes.

Although spasms run through my muscles, I force out the pain, the fire, the burning—and focus. Harder than ever before I replace the pain with focus. I replace the water in my mind with focus.

Unable to control it, my lips part and water pours in my mouth, down my throat, into my lungs. Still I remain focused. Now is not the time to panic. Now is the time to let go.

Just as I'm about to die, the waters around me recede. My bracelet is an instant anchor. My skin is still on fire, but it's my eyes that burn the most. A blue light seeps into my consciousness, accompanied by a loud noise. A familiar jerk in my body, but I'm too far gone to place it. Forever and ever I want to float in the comfortable darkness that creeps into my mind and invites me to join it. I extend my hand to greet it, but a shock forces me to recoil.

First I hear music, then panicked words. I can't open my eyes. The light is too agonizing even with my lids closed. *How can I ever open them again?*

Someone pumps my chest. Next their mouth is on mine. Urgent screams. My lungs inflate. Again and again and again and again someone compresses my chest. It isn't working though. I'm going to die. I was in the water too long. I hadn't traveled in time. I accept this. The darkness surrounding me is perfect, like a warm quilt on the coldest winter night. I reach out and grab it, wrap it around my body. It's such a relief to finally die.

"No, Roya, you can't give up! Don't!" the voice cries from a distant part of a strange dream.

I ignore the voice. I ignore the intense burning in my core. And float away. I'm tired, so tired of fighting.

"Please…" he pleads erratically before pumping my chest and blowing sweet air into my mouth.

I taste his breath, but only in the ethereal sense. I'm already halfway down the staircase to the valley of death. The darkness cloaks me and I begin to float...

Chapter Forty-Eight

I've died and been sentenced to hell. The darkness has delivered me to an unbearable fate, where I'll burn in torment. One in which fire radiates from my chest and sears up my throat. If I was alive and could scream I would, but instead I explode into the darkness, clawing at it, trying to free myself.

My mind and heart barrel forward, begging to be pardoned. I am at the altar asking for forgiveness or penance or whatever will rescue me from the agonizing pain. I strike against the darkness, certain I've been unfairly damned. My fists repeatedly strike a wall until it relents. Water explodes through the cracks. Astonished and confused, I witness the water burst, but not from the wall, from me. It shoots from my lungs, through my throat, and out. Time ceases to exist. I urge the water to stop exploding, but still I erupt like a volcano, burning and engulfed by the flames within me.

The fire smolders until my eyelids flutter open and I recognize the world around me. A human one. Everything's completely out of focus but still I recognize it. Blurry shapes move far away and then closer. My eyes shut and I fall into a dreamless sleep.

◆

The music isn't what wakes me. It's the fingers on my pulse. He's a stranger. Through blurry vision I see him hold my wrist and then eye his watch. His cold stethoscope makes my chest feel bare, vulnerable. He says something, but I can't process it, not yet. I fight to push up from the hard surface underneath me. The man turns and speaks, his voice deep. "She's awake. I'll send in the others." He disappears.

With excruciating effort, I sit up and force my eyes to focus. Gradually the blurry masses of colors take shape, until the details of the room are clear. From the corner of my vision I see him advancing on me. Aiden's movements are gradual, but swift. He rushes without running. I push up as he closes the last bit of space between us. His eyes are urgent, mixed with relief. It's a sobering expression.

276

I've just dug my way out of a steep grave. And it isn't until he wraps his arms around me that I truly know I'm alive. Maybe I haven't lived until this moment, because I don't remember ever feeling my heart so intensely. It thumps against Aiden's chest. Each beat surreal.

Aiden draws back. He brushes a rogue piece of hair away from my face. "I told you I'd be here when you awoke."

Biting my lip, I try to locate my missing breath. "Aiden," I whisper.

He leans into me, and like I'm possessed by a magnetic force I simultaneously lean into him, erasing all boundaries. He stops only an inch from my face, his expression intense. Never before has one look communicated so much. Longing. Attraction. The definition of all those words explained perfectly in his gaze. He draws his hand up and cups my face, pulling me into him.

Our lips are less than half an inch apart. He pauses, but it isn't because he's asking permission or uncertain of his next move. He's making every second count. Closing his blue eyes he softly lays his lips against mine. My aching lungs gasps as my heart races. His mouth tastes like desire. His lips dull the ache. His touch masks my pain and I'm undeserving, but I don't care. I selfishly pull him in closer, needing this intimate moment to refill my soul. My hands find his hair and with greedy fingers gently tug. Each movement is both tender and wild, making me breathless for more. His lips kiss the corner of my mouth, my jaw, my neck. There he freezes. I listen to his breath. Feel it tickle my skin. A second later he levels his gaze to mine and I have to fight the urge to pull him closer. He looks to be fighting a similar impulse, which is maybe why he edges away. Immediately I want him back, close to me, making me warm with his arms, his passion. Aiden glances nervously over his shoulder. *Someone's coming.* That's what the voice had said when I awoke.

My senses are gradually returning. I'm in Aiden's lab, perched on the GAD-C. Squeezing my eyes shut, I allow the most recent events to drift back to me. *He* generated my body. *His* were the lips that breathed air into my lungs. *His* hands were the ones that pushed into my chest. *He* was the one who wouldn't give up, although I was dying.

"You." I point at him with my eyes. "You saved my life." I pull breath from the back of my aching lungs. "Again."

"Just doing my job." His eyes beam behind his glasses. He looks happier than I've ever seen him as he rushes in and presses his lips against mine. For the second time that day, electricity pulses through me. Drawing back he smiles and winks. "Now you owe me *big*."

I reach for him, but he simultaneously turns, sensing an approaching noise. The door slides open and faces pour into the room. Aiden retreats. Before I settle myself I'm engulfed by hugs and crowded by concerned faces. Their gazes reach out at me, but don't truly connect. Sorrow traces the edges of everyone's expression. These are faces which have just felt death.

Samara forces a weak smile to her lips. Trent pushes his hands into his pockets, maintaining eye contact with the floor. George—the only one to look directly at me—pierces me with remorse. "George!" My heart jumps into my throat. I push off the GAD-C, rushing to where he stands. My unsteady feet make me stagger forward. He catches me in his arms and wrenches me close, closer than I would have anticipated. Our faces meet, but only briefly before he senses my unease and lets me slide away.

"So, you're all right?" I ask, gripping his strong forearms.

A twinkle shoots through his brown eyes. "More than ever." He clutches me with urgency, pressing me against him. I awkwardly hold his neck and torso with my arms. His breaths are ones of strained relief and open the wound in my heart.

Shaking, I push away. He lets me go, but stays firmly gripping my hand. The look in his eyes makes me feel fragile. "But... I thought Zhuang had..."

"No." He shakes his head in a deliberate manner. "I got away."

The words flex in my mouth, but I haven't the strength to say them. *Whitney. Joseph. They didn't get away.*

Trey clears his throat. "Welcome back, Roya." His voice steady, eyes red.

The others stare awkwardly.

"We know you've just awoken and need rest. The team just needed to lay their eyes on you first. We've all been very worried." Trey's voice catches on the last word.

"Where's Joseph?" My voice is desperate, scared.

No one answers. They all look away. They're cowards who won't tell me what I now know to be true.

My nostrils flare. I urge the tears to remain inside. I hold my breath. *Zhuang really did kill them...*

Trey continues. I can't focus. His words pass through me as the inevitable truth sets in. Eyes locked on the ground, I make no attempts to listen to Trey. All I manage is to give audience to the thoughts racing in my crowded head. *My only family—gone. How could this happen? Wasn't I the one who was supposed to die? Why Joseph? Without him how will I make sense of my life as a Lucidite? Without him, without him, without him...I'm alone.*

The long inhale I took moments prior is running out. Trey is silent now. Pain around my heart rises until it settles as a lump in my throat. I'm not going to cry, not here, not in front of everyone.

"I've got to go." I rush out of the room. Trey calls after me, but I ignore him. Tears are already clouding my vision. The drain is evident in my body. I lean forward. Will my legs to move. My steps are slow and clumsy. I can hardly manage walking; running is out of the question. Each step seeps my reserves. The thought of crawling to the elevator crosses my mind. The lump is now in the back of my mouth. Any second, emotion will spill out of me. *I already miss him so much.*

My pride is the only thing willing me forward. Without it I surely will pass out in the hallway. This pain is mine though. I need to be alone with it. The elevators appear in my cloudy vision. Only ten feet or so. I can make it. Soon I'll be in my room, with a door and solitude. Then I'll let go.

The light radiates from the elevator button, a welcome sight. I blink back tears. The button, smooth under my fingertips, clicks when I press it. Steadier now, I glance back over my shoulder to make sure I'm not being followed.

I am.

I've heard of ghosts visiting their loved ones soon after their passing to offer comfort, to ease the pain. I'm not ready yet. It's too soon. He should know that. Twenty feet away, standing squarely in the corridor, Joseph's ghost stares at me. Swallowing back a piece of the tears, I tap the button rapidly. I bat my eyes, believing the extra moisture is playing tricks on me. He hovers in place for a second, then labors forward.

"Not nice to make me chase you, but I'll do it if I have to." There's a rattle to Joseph's voice. A wheeze as he limps.

My disillusions meet my reality head on. I scan the approaching figure. White bandages wrap around his bare torso. Exhaustion contorts his face. A mischievous smile is tucked at the corner of his mouth.

Determined, Joseph pushes forward, alternating between focusing on the ground and my stunned face. I have just taken that walk. I know it took all the strength I had to complete it. Now I stand renewed at the end, watching and trying to piece it all together.

"You're not dead," I say, bewildered and grateful.

"'Course not." Joseph laughs and immediately grimaces in pain. "I told Trey and the team not to tell you about me. I wanted to surprise you."

I shake my head. The urge to slap him in the head courses through me. "Surprise!? Are you out of your mind? I thought you were dead." A tear edges to the surface. I blink it back. I swallow.

"I'm sorry. Poor decision on my part. I wasn't thinking clearly obviously. After I heard you returned…When they said you were awake….Well, I tried to get to you as fast I could."

The ache in my throat has returned, but it's different. Joseph stands in front of me, his form solid and real. He's hurt and weak. But alive. "You almost got yourself killed, you stupid idiot," I say. I wrap my arms around his neck and squeeze extra hard to ensure he's real. His arms around me squeeze back.

"You're one to talk, Stark." He laughs and then yelps in pain. "Watch the ribs, will ya, sis?"

I pull back and look him over, taking in the edge of a smile on his face coupled with the tears in his eyes.

"Are you all right?" I ask.

"I'm as good as a bullfrog on a summer's night," he sings.

"Whatever that means." I smile broadly, relief spreading over the pain.

Chapter Forty-Nine

I arrive first for the debriefing in room 222 the next morning. Bagels, fruit, coffee, and juice make the room less bare. Soon everyone arrives and they adorn the room with life. The sound of Samara and Trent chatting, Trey stirring his coffee, Joseph scribbling on paper; these are the sounds of life. Gratitude encircles me in a way I have yet to experience. My face flushes with warmth.

"Before we begin," Trey says, "will you please join me in a moment of silence? Yesterday we lost a talented Lucidite and a wonderful member of this team. Whitney's memory will not be forgotten." Trey's words are formal, yet sincere.

Just hearing Whitney's name for the first time after the ordeal makes my insides burn with disgust. What Zhuang did to her was cruel. Heartless. Cowardly. The backs of my eyes prickle with tears when I think about her alone in that room, dying quietly as Zhuang's blade cut into her. I shake my head and push back the emotion. Right now I haven't the energy to grieve.

During the debriefing I learn we don't really know whether to celebrate or not. Apparently, they were able to follow the events of what happened during the battle from the camera footage I provided. Once I returned to the Institute, Ren and Shuman traveled to the water treatment plant where they didn't find Zhuang's body.

After the fight thousands of hallucinators were released and are apparently regaining their consciousness. Conversely, an equal number of sleepwalkers, those further under Zhuang's control, died within hours following the battle. The public doesn't know how to interpret the events and are calling it a viral epidemic. This was a big news day, coupled with the tsunami in Hawaii, which devastated that area.

Trey thinks it's most likely that Zhuang has survived and taken the lives of those sleepwalkers to recover. However, his energy reserves would have been depleted and therefore his connection with the hallucinators severed.

"Nevertheless, it's just as likely that the opposite is true and Zhuang is in fact dead," Trey says. "In time, we'll know for sure. He never stays quiet for long."

Trey is the only one who has spoken so far. It's nice when George, Trent, and Samara are given a chance to speak. Each explains individually how they returned to the Institute once they knew Zhuang was on their trail. Then they gathered around a screen in this meeting room and watched the battle.

"I felt helpless watching," Samara says. "I knew he was about to hit you with a dart too, but there was nothing I could do. He actually chose the forest because he knew that would slow down your clairvoyance and block my telepathic link with you." I remember the feelings of apathy I harbored when I used to visit the woods by my house. This was from Zhuang's influence. Ren had said it was a form of hypnotism.

"Watching him beat the crud out of you was the worst for me," Trent says with a sigh. "I'm just glad we couldn't see your face."

"Yeah," I agree, feeling a realization surface. "Why don't I have a million bruises and internal bleeding right now?"

"You can thank Mae for that," Trey informs me. "She's the lady who hooked you up before you traveled last night. She's a powerful healer. Under the right circumstances, if she's quick enough to act on an injury, she can reverse it. Aiden called her right after he revived you. She was able to remove and mend most of the injuries, with the exception of the burn."

The burn on my forearm is exactly the length of my bracelet, which I'm now wearing on the opposite wrist.

"I suspect," Trey continues, "the severity of that burn was so intense that Mae was not able to mend it. You'll have a scar there forever, but your protective charm will cover it."

George has been sitting quietly in the corner with his arms crossed the entire time. He's hardly looked at me since he walked into the room. Finally his voice splinters the air around me. "For me"—he pauses and swallows—"the hardest part was once you realized the bracelet created an electrical force when it touched Zhuang. I knew you were going to throw yourself into the water to ensure he was electrocuted. I thought you were going to die too." There's a rough edge to his tone, like sandpaper.

"But she didn't," Trey says at once.

I want to ask about the bracelet, to find out why it reacted the way it did, but Trey speaks first. "Joseph, will you fill us in on how you obtained your injuries?" he asks.

"Oh," he laughs and points at his ribs. "This? It's nothing. You see, I accidentally traveled to Madrid during that running of the bull event. Imagine my surprise when this animal rammed his horn up my—"

"He's lying," Samara interrupts him.

"No, really?" I say.

"All right, well, there isn't much to tell. I was in the room where George had been stationed, trying to stay close to Stark. Zhuang appeared before I could travel. His attack was pretty swift, but I did my best to try and fight him. We dueled for ages. I was just about to deliver the last devastating blow to finish him when I noticed my shoestring was untied."

I roll my eyes and force away the urge to laugh. "All that sounds very entertaining, but will you get on with what really happened."

"Isn't it obvious?" Joseph says, offended. "Zhuang stabbed me. I'd never experienced such pain. As soon as it happened I felt my energy completely diminish." Shame coats Joseph's eyes and I want to stop him, tell him it's a useless emotion. "With my last bit of reserves I returned to the Institute. I knew immediately I'd failed you."

"Joseph—" I manage in a half whisper.

"I already know what you're gonna say," he cuts me off. "You don't have to. I'm just recountin' the events. That's what happened and I don't like it, but I can't change the past."

At this point we should just be glad we have a future.

"I've never met anyone as demonic as Zhuang." Joseph shivers, staring at the table. "He has the eeriest eyes. They'll haunt me for the rest of my life, I'm certain of that."

"I hope they don't," Trey says matter-of-factly. He clears his throat as if he's going to say something else, but doesn't get a chance.

"It's like he stared into my soul when he plunged the sword into me. I'm afraid of what he saw," Joseph says, locked on the table.

"Is that why you fled?" Ren says from the back of the room. As usual, he's eyeing his fingernails like the present conversation is boring him to death. I wish it would.

"I was injured," Joseph retorts, venom in his voice. "I thought I was dyin'."

"Roya almost died numerous times, but she didn't desert the mission," Ren says coolly, although the accusation is full of fire.

"Joseph did what he thought was right at the time," Trey says, slightly dissolving the tension building between Ren and Joseph. "He wouldn't have been any good to Roya if he was bleeding to death."

"And he didn't do her any favors by abandoning her, taking power she could have used to fight Zhuang," Ren counters dully.

"I thought I was helping her!" Joseph shouts. "If I was still alive then he couldn't have her consciousness."

Ren laughs bitterly. "He didn't want you. You were just in the bloody way. As long as you're close to Roya, she's powerful. Zhuang needed you to get away from her. I'm certain he would have preferred to kill you, but you retreated before he had the chance. Either way, he knew he had done what he needed to."

"That's enough," I say sharply. "What's done is done. Zhuang very well could be dead and that's because of the efforts of everyone on this team. We all did our part. I did not fight alone."

Trey nods at me, a subtle look of approval in his eyes. He stands, faces Ren, and says, "I'm certain Ren is only trying to provide helpful feedback."

Yeah, right.

"Thank you both for your efforts training this team," Trey continues, directing his words to both Shuman and Ren. "Is there anything else either of you'd like to add?"

Ren shrugs indifferently and continues staring at his nails. "You all weren't as completely useless as I thought you'd be. And Roya, you survived, which completely astonished me."

Shuman narrows her eyes at Ren and then leans forward and bows her head. "I salute the effort you put into battle." Then she lifts her head and stares at me with her dark amethyst eyes. When she says nothing else I smile weakly.

"I think that just about wraps things up," Trey says, redirecting our attention. "Two more things before you go and rest. We'll be having a small and intimate celebration, albeit a bit premature in my opinion. Still, I know you've all worked hard and even if Zhuang isn't dead, he's seriously weakened, which would make Flynn proud. The party will be on Friday evening."

Trey turns and focuses his turquoise eyes on me. There's a pain in them, so deep, like something dark hidden at the bottom of clear water. I had never noticed it before, not quite like this. "Lastly, Roya," he says, his tone sullen. "It's evident that when we elected you challenger, we made the right decision. Putting you in this dangerous role was not what Flynn wanted. I, myself, questioned the news reporters' forecast. However, I know now it had to be you."

He stops, deliberating, staring off in the distance. Then his focus connects on me again. "If it's in fact true, what Zhuang said about needing your consciousness, then you're more powerful than I previously imagined." He half smiles at this. A sharp tenderness edges his eyes. His new role as Head of the Institute must be getting to him. This guy looks like he hasn't slept in ages.

A cough escapes his mouth and he says, "Please guard this power, as it's both a gift and a burden." He nods his head once, then turns and leaves.

I'm next to follow. More than anything I need to be alone to process everything I've just heard. Something's starting to well up inside me. I fear it might breach the surface soon. Joseph calls out, and then when he doesn't again, I assume he knows what I need. I walk with urgency until I'm safely behind my door. Alone with my emotions.

Chapter Fifty

That evening I hear the familiar rap on my door. Patrick is idling, waiting on the other side. He smiles broadly from underneath his ball cap. "Well, hey there, sweetheart. I knew I hadn't seen the last of you yet."

"I'm like a bad rash," I say, taking the package and letter from his hands.

"Oh yes, terribly difficult to get rid of." He smiles before trotting off.

I laugh when I open the container to find my dinner. Even though Joseph is probably bleeding and in pain, he's still figured out a way to get me something to eat.

After I finish my salad, I open the letter. It's from Bob and Steve.

Dear Roya,

We've been celebrating since we learned of your victory. There are no two prouder people than the ones who are writing this note. You're incredible. Always have been.
If you need a break from the Institute, you're always welcome to come here and live. We would love to have you. We're sure we could keep you busy, although we think public schooling is out of the question.

Love,
Bob & Steve

It's funny they think I was victorious. I wonder if that's the news other Lucidites received. Since I don't know if Zhuang's dead or not, I decide not to worry about it.

The next day I ignore the numerous knocks at my door. I want no company. I need more time than I imagined to process. I was prepared to die, and now that I'm alive I don't know where I want this life of mine to go. I know I should be celebrating and happy, but

286

my future came at a price and I can't let myself forget that. People died. People I knew.

I decide against attending Whitney's memorial. These events are to help people grieve and I'm in the process of doing that on my own. I tell myself she'd understand. The truth is, managing the pain of her death has been tumultuous at times, taking me by surprise, causing pain in ways I'm not accustomed to feeling. No one ever told me how sorrow traumatizes the heart, making me think it will never beat exactly the same way again. No one ever told me how grief feels like a wet sock in my mouth. One I'm forced to breathe through, thinking that with each breath I'll come up short and suffocate. I guess if I'm honest with myself, there wasn't really anyone to pass along this knowledge anyway.

When I'm not suffocating in grief, I try to figure out what my life is supposed to look like at this point. When Patrick delivers food, I eat. When I'm tired, I fall into dream-filled sleeps. The current theme of my dreams involves my real mother. She gives me hugs I don't want and offers reactionary advice. Still, I like looking at her face. It has small features, brown eyes, blonde hair, and an expression that is overly optimistic.

Since I know I'm on the brink of being considered a hermit, I open my door the next day. By midmorning Joseph is laid out on my bed. It feels good to have him close, the way my cats used to make me feel when they were nearby.

"Do you want to talk about him?" he asks, looking at me from the corners of his eyes.

I know exactly who he's referring to. "No," I say with more force than I intended.

"But he was your brother," Joseph says.

"No." I shake my head. "You're my brother."

"But you grew up with him."

I chew on the inside of my cheek. Thousands of sleepwalkers died on the Day of the Duel. Shiloh was one of them. My gaze slides away from Joseph and rests on the blue carpet. "Honestly, I never expected to see him again. I think that's why it doesn't hurt as much as I thought it would." And it wasn't like Whitney's death, where I had to see her blood oozing from the instrument that killed her. Her death felt real, but Shiloh's didn't for some reason.

"Or maybe you're just in shock," Joseph offers.

"Maybe." I shrug. "More than anything I hurt for…" I stop, not knowing exactly how to label them anymore. "His family," I finally say. "They will miss him very much." My gaze slides back to Joseph. He's actually smiling.

"Just like I would have missed you if Zhuang had succeeded," he says in a low hush.

I return his smile with affection.

"So since our old lives are obviously gone, what do *we* do now?" Joseph asks, lightness in his tone.

"What do you mean *we*?" I look at him as I pick up my hairbrush.

"Well, Trey has offered for us both to stay here. You'd know that if you came out of your room," he says. "There's things we could work on here. Projects."

I cut my eyes at him. "Honestly, that sounds great in a couple years. But I was actually thinking of living with Bob and Steve and having a normal life for once."

"Normal lives are overrated," Joseph says, adjusting himself on the bed. He's obviously still in a great deal of pain from his injury, which was so severe Mae wasn't able to mend it completely.

"How would you know?" I snap.

"I've heard." He laughs. "It's just that I'm staying and I really wanted you to stay too."

"We can meet up at night," I offer. "You'll see me all the time."

"No." Joseph shakes his head. "It's not the same."

I take a long look at Joseph. "I can tell when you're lying too, you know."

A sly grin unfurls on his face. "Oh all right, I have something I wanna work on here and I need your help."

"You need my energy," I say.

"You could help too. You could be involved, but you'd have to come out of your room." He rolls his eyes.

"Look," I begin, "it's incredible that we have each other, but are we supposed to be tied together forever? Because that's not going to work for me. I need space."

"Me too," he agrees easily. "I'm not implying that we have to follow each other around. God knows I don't want to live with you and your pseudo parents in the boondocks. I just need you here for a couple of months. Just let me work on this project. Lend me your energy. Can you give me that?"

I stare off at the carpet, weighing my options.

"You *can*," Joseph continues, "read your Lord Byron, paint your toenails, listen to folk rock, or whatever you do when you're not preparing to fight some crazy ancient philosopher guy. Please."

"All right," I give after a minute of deliberation. "You have until the end of the summer. Then I'm gone."

He smiles. We shake on it.

Before Joseph leaves he reminds me about the celebration that night. He demands I wear something nice. When I inform him I don't have anything, he promptly invades my closet and picks out the one dress Steve had bought me. It's a short, sleeveless, black and white dress, with a swooping neckline. I think I'd rather go fight Zhuang again than wear it.

"I'll pick you up at seven. Be wearing that, 'cause I don't want you to embarrass me," he says, heading for the door.

The shoe I throw grazes his head, as I intended.

Chapter Fifty-One

Just after seven, Joseph knocks. I hit the button with my most appalling expression plastered on my face.

"Nice dress, Stark. Work on the face, though," he says.

He's dressed in tan linen slacks and a long-sleeved white button-up shirt.

"You don't look like pig feed, either," I say, taking his arm.

"Well, I'd say somethin' nasty 'bout your momma, but..."

♦

The main hall is almost unrecognizable. The lights are low and music plays from the far back corner. Overhead a strobe ball dazzles the adjoining walls with sparkling lights. From the ceiling hang little paper stars that twirl and catch the cascading light. Blue linens line the tables and each are adorned with pastel hydrangeas in the center. Lush, iridescent fabric billows around the corners of the room and underneath it lights twinkle, reminding me of *A Midsummer Night's Dream*. *This is what they considered intimate?*

Joseph leads me through the hall. I gape at the decorations. It isn't until I'm halfway through the room that I notice most of the crowd has stopped to stare at me. Dozens of people bow their heads in an appreciative manner. The rest gaze at me with thoughtful expressions. The only people who aren't staring at me are the ones on the dance floor, busy moving to the lively music. One of those people is Aiden. He's waltzing with that Amber girl. A nervous itch surges up my spine and I resist the impulse to scratch it.

"Hey, everyone," Joseph says to the table when we arrive.

I spot George sitting next to Samara at the other end. He looks deliciously handsome wearing a white button-up shirt with a black blazer and shiny cufflinks. I lock eyes with him. He winks. Not knowing how to respond, I look at the table,

Trent says, "Hey, Joseph, you managed to drag Roya out of her room! Good on you."

"I want to make an announcement," Joseph says. His excitement reaches the short distance that divides us and shakes me, unearthing me momentarily from my tight-fitting heels. "We're staying. Stark has agreed to stay so we can continue our work here at the Institute!"

Joseph's happiness encompasses everyone at the table, engulfing them in his euphoria. It's weird this all was pinned on me. Why can't Joseph stay without me? I want to be independent and live my own life. But I'm also elated to be Joseph's twin and have him by my side.

From across the table George's smile unfurls, like a rose blossoming in the morning sunshine. It wrenches my heart in ways I like and loathe. And then his all too familiar eyes start their invasions on my emotions. Right then, two aids come to my rescue. The first is my training, which unearths a shield against his searching emotional radar. The second is Trent. Good ol' Trent. He asks, or rather demands, I dance with him. When I admit I don't know how, he has a response ready.

"Don't worry," he smirks as he leads me to the floor, "I've got enough moves for the both of us."

The music is upbeat. I follow his movements and laugh when he does something ridiculous, which is often. When the song changes to a slower melody, Trent takes his hand and places it in mine, explaining how to slow dance. I follow his lead and catch on pretty quickly. There isn't much to dancing once you know kung fu.

A finger taps Trent on the shoulder. We both turn our attention to a bright-eyed Aiden. He watches me as he leans forward and whispers in Trent's ear. They exchange a curious glance before Trent leads my hand into Aiden's.

Something intense surges through me when our hands meet. "Hello, Ms. Stark," he says, pulling me into his arms looking casual, but making me feel anything but. Blood rushes to the surface of my skin. After our kiss on the GAD-C, this is uncomfortable, like all eyes are on us, knowing our secret. I stare nervously around, trying not to look at him. He's wearing a tuxedo. It's ridiculous, overly formal, preposterous, and absolutely perfect.

"You're gorgeous tonight," he says with a smile. "Especially tonight, but always too."

I chew on my lip. "What was with the note at the water treatment plant?" I ask.

He twirls me around rapidly. The music is slow, but Aiden moves me around the dance floor with force and I laugh despite myself. "Oh, did you get that?" he says.

"I know you were watching." I giggle as he dips me.

"Oh, that's right," he says, resuming a normal pace. "I forgot you pay attention...sometimes." We exchange a heated glance and simultaneously look in opposite directions. "Well, I just knew if you got to that point, where you had to use the GAD-C, you'd need some guidance."

"Could the people watching at the Institute read what was on the note?"

Aiden shakes his head.

Confusion falls over me like a cloud. "How did you know my bracelet would have that effect on Zhuang?"

Aiden shrugs. "I didn't. It was a good guess."

I narrow my eyes at him and then look in the opposite direction.

After a long silence he says, "It appears I've inherited a bit of my mother's powers. It's a good thing because I was beginning to think I was just an ordinary Dream Traveler with only an extraordinarily high IQ." He huffs. "What a tragedy that would be."

I suppress a smile and ask, "And whatever would that be? This power you've inherited?"

"Psychometry," he says, spinning me around and then pulling me back to him with a grin. "I sense energy on objects. And I detected an extra energy from your bracelet. Charms have been known to take on additional life force. It's rare, but has happened. I suspect this has more to do with the energy stored in the object by the bearer than anything else. Yours appears to have a polarizing effect on Zhuang, at least when the conditions are right."

"So you knew my bracelet had other powers besides the ability to defend me against Zhuang? Why didn't you tell me before the fight?"

Aiden clicks his tongue three times and gives me a playful sideways glance. "I already told you it was a guess. Unfortunately, what I've inherited isn't as reliable a gift as what I remember my mother having, but it has appeared to be correct in this instance."

I deliberate on this and everything else he's shared: his mother, her gift, and her obvious absence in his life. It all begs for more questions. In the end, my own selfish interests get the better of me.

"What did you mean by me returning to complicate your world?" I ask.

"Right now I wish I could pull you closer," he says. "Right now I wish I could kiss you again."

I swallow and look around. To everyone else do we just look like two people dancing?

Aiden twirls me slower this time and tugs me back to him gently. His voice is a whisper. "However, I'm in a complicated position. I need to maintain a certain level of professionalism. I'm already scrutinized enough. I suspect my peers would judge anything romantic between the two of us as distasteful." His lips graze my ear as he leans down and says, "But I also can't resist you."

I pull away, stealing the look in his sapphire eyes, wanting to bottle it forever. "Hmmm," is all I say. Nerves vibrate in my chest, humming like a car engine.

"I was honest on the Day of the Duel," Aiden says. "If something happened to you I'd be lost. I've never wanted anything but my career. Now I do…I want you."

The music is nearing its end. Two casual friends would only dance through one song. Anything more and they'd appear...

My heart races as I pull away from Aiden. Regret fills my being. I immediately miss his arms around me. "So where does that leave us? Now that I've returned to your world?" I ask.

Aiden takes a bow. "In an extremely complicated situation, Ms. Stark."

I curtsy, enjoying our game more than I should. "Thank you for the dance, Aiden."

"The pleasure has been all mine."

I turn at once and stride away, feeling his eyes linger on me. The words we'd spoken, this arrangement I agreed to, makes my insides giddy with anticipation for our next secret meeting. Heat rushes to my head making my ears burn hot.

I gulp down a glass of ice water. It freezes my throat and shrinks my insides. I wish it would freeze my secrets as well.

Even though my back is to the crowd I sense someone approaching. I turn to find George's brown eyes, soft under the dark lighting.

"Hi," I squeak.

He doesn't respond at first, just stares.

"Have you gotten enough rest?" George asks.

"Yes. It feels nice. I sleep easier now this whole thing is over."

"I think we all do," he affirms impassively.

"Did you want to dance?" I ask and immediately regret it. I don't want to. My nervousness is making me overcompensate.

"Maybe later." George gives me a steady look. "Would you join me out here?" He points to the hallway.

I take a second, then shrug. "Sure."

We exit into the brightly lit corridor and walk until we're in the darkened lobby. I love this lobby with its backlit shelves and leather furniture. Every time I've been in this space I've felt comfortable and confident. At the moment I love that the area is minimally lit with canned lights.

"It pleases me to know you're staying," he says, picking up my hand and squeezing it. His hands are strong around mine.

A small twinge of guilt shivers through me, knowing minutes ago I was in Aiden's arms. They're so different. Aiden with his black hair, angular features, high cheekbones and full lips. His ears are entirely too large for his head, but complement the rest of his features perfectly. He couldn't be more opposite George, who has round features, tan skin, blond hair, a broad chin, and thin lips which he spends most of the time chewing on aggressively. If I could mix the clever and passionate scientist with the thoughtful and poetic empath then I might have the perfect guy.

"I'm staying too," George says, beckoning me from my reverie.

"Oh really," I say. "Why?"

"I've been assigned to a project," he explains.

It's weird everyone but me has a project. Not that I mind, but still it's weird.

"Cool," is all I say after a nervous moment of silence. Something feels strange between us, and it's making my insides itch.

"I'm glad you didn't die on the Day of the Duel." He smiles as he traces his finger along my hand, looking at it intently. His eyes soft.

"Yeah?" I pretend to ask. I take his hands and squeeze them in mine. I'm smiling, knowing that joking about my own death is the only way I've gotten through the last month.

He tugs me in tighter. His gold-flecked hair catches my attention as he speaks. "When I thought you were going to die I finally understood a feeling I've read in other people, but never experienced firsthand. I didn't think I was capable of these emotions. You came along and made me laugh and feel and it's by far better than I ever expected. I've read emotions in other people but had no idea how persuasive they can be." His grip tightens on mine. "I'm addicted to the way I feel about you."

Fear of what he's about to say next strips the smile from my face. My body stiffens. He presses up against me and I step back. "George," I say with caution. "Please don't—"

"Roya, I need to," he cuts me off. I try to pull away, but sensing this he clenches onto my hands. His eyes seize mine and I'm trapped. All I want is to run. I would rather chant senseless babble than listen to the words about to come out of George's mouth. And then they fall, like little shards of glass onto a tile floor, with no place to land and only a million places to shatter. "I'm in love with you."

He stares at me behind brown, placid eyes.

This has just gotten way more complicated. I slip my hands from his.

"Say something." His tone is even.

"George," I whisper, concentrating on the ground. I swallow the tender lump in my throat. "I've been through a lot, we both have."

"We've been through a lot *together*." George cups my chin, pulling it up so I meet his eyes. "That's how I know I love you."

"I'm not ready for this," I say on the verge of pouting.

"You're stronger than you give yourself credit for." His voice rises as he speaks. "Look at what you've just done, who you've just defeated, and the people you've freed."

I shake my head. "We don't know I've done anything. Zhuang could still be alive."

"That's not the point." George exhales. "I need to know how you feel."

"You know how I feel." My words are sharper than I intended. I jerk my head from his hand and step back. "That's what makes it complicated with you." Adrenaline pulses through my veins. I take a quick inhale. It's impossible to hide anything from him. He always invades my emotions and knows how to manipulate me. I love and hate that about him.

George appears suddenly cold and distant, like I'm rejecting him. I'm not though; this is all just happening too fast.

"Look," he says, "I need you to stop playing games with me."

"I'm not," I sputter.

"You are."

"George, I, I, I—"

"Just answer one question, that's all I ask."

"Why?"

"Because I need to know," he states blankly.

"Fine," I say.

"Are you in love with me?" His words spill out and pinch my heart.

"That's not a fair question," I scold him.

"Maybe not for most people."

"What's that supposed to mean?" I retract, shivering, cold biting at my insides.

"I know you're in love with someone." He's a half mixture of compassion and animosity. It almost depends on the lighting, and maybe it also depends on what I want to see.

"You only *think* you know this time," I say.

"I know." George gives a measured glare.

"Well, you know about as much as I do at this point, so why are you confronting me?" I stare at him angrily.

"I think you're not being honest with yourself. I think you know more than you're willing to admit. I think you're playing games and I want you to stop."

"If you really do love me then why are you doing this right now? Haven't we all been through enough?"

"Yes, which is exactly *why* I'm doing this. I can't take it anymore, the stress, the tension. Tell me the truth. Are you in love with me or Aiden?"

The question hits me like a head-on collision. Hearing the word *love* makes everything real. The question, which is direct enough, doesn't have a straightforward answer. Love is complex and rarely straightforward and even less of the time easily explained or understood.

George watches me for a few seconds and then continues, "I feel the raw yearning in you. It's encompassing. The only thing that keeps me coming back is the idea it could be for me. Just tell me it's not and I'll leave you alone. Say it is and I'll be patient. But I just can't live, feeling your emotions and not knowing any longer."

I do care about George, but I'm not sure if I'm in love with him. I'm not sure how I feel about anything right now. And, much like Aiden, George challenges me in ways I'm not comfortable with. Ways which make me want to rebel against him.

We stare, me taking in his nonverbal cues, him taking in my emotions. Finally I straighten as I hear the words echo out of his mouth. "Just tell me if what you feel is for me. Please, I need to know." The brown of his eyes deepens, pleading with me to comply.

Shaking my head, I clasp the frequency adjuster, the warmth of the tiny object pulses between my fingers. I yank until the chain breaks. My frustration erupts as I fling the frequency adjuster at him. "No, George, that's not how it works. Sometimes you don't get to know how I feel!"

In slow motion the adjuster sails through the air. George instantly winces with pain. The adjuster collides softly with his chest, where he lets it hit before it lands by his black loafers. There's no point in saying another word. He won't hear me over the orchestra of noise and clashing metal in his head. I pretend not to care as I march away.

The End.

Flip to the end of this book to continue your journey with the Lucidites and read the first chapter of the next installment: *Stunned.*

Acknowledgements

Thank you to my friends and family. To those who have supported me with their thoughtful words and encouragements. You will never know how those words carried me through each day, until today, where this book has become a reality. Thank you to all the fantastic friends that read this book and offered their wonderful feedback and reviews. I consider myself truly blessed to have each of you in my life.

Thank you to Christine LePorte, my editor, for your insights, expertise, and thoughtful manner in working with me. Everything you've done to bring this project to this point is crucial to its success. I'm indebted to you for making my words sound more gooderer.

Thank you to Andrei Bat. The cover image you so masterfully interpreted was exactly what I wanted. Striking. Captivating. And almost more perfect than I ever imagined.

Thank you to the many musicians who encouraged me during the numerous hours of writing and editing. There were frequent times I relied on your passion to inspire me. A big thank you to Rob Thomas for his incredible album Cradle Song, which I listened to hundreds of times while working on this book. I'd also like to thank many of the other artists who made up the playlist: James Blunt (without Some Kind of Trouble this book may never have found an ending), M83, Fall Out Boy, Fun, Gotye, and Ellie Goulding, to name a few.

Thank you to David O'Neil for your help with summaries. Thank you to Jennifer Wilkerson for putting up with the earliest versions of my book. And also thanks for sharing your writer's struggles with me. We're all in this together. Thank you to Meghan Toledo for all your thoughtful insights and your attentive eye. You had a big role; one I'm not sure you realized you were signing up for at the time. Thank you to Heidi Magner and FayAnna White for being among my biggest supporters. Your encouragement has been a real gift. I'm glad you're my friends. Thank you to Dane Maliski. Your help as a beta reader was extraordinary. Your comments made me laugh and also blew my mind. Thank you to Colleen Maliski. You may never know how much your insights and support are a benefit to me. I owe you a ton of gold bars. Keep checking the mail. I love all of my beta readers endlessly. Thank y'all!!!!

Thank you to Robert and Colleen Ward for inquiring about my work, sharing your inspirations, encouraging my creativity and being wonderful friends. Thank you to Linda Renfro for your unconditional love. Your capacity for giving and supporting truly uplifts me. Thank you to Randy and Edie Noffke for your unending support. Thank you to my father for being strong and thoughtful. Your strength has always been your gift. Thank you to Kathy Flournoy for infecting me with the desire to read great literature, which translated into my passion to write.

Thank you to Lydia, my daughter. My words were born from the fire in your eyes. Inspiration fills my being every time you laugh. Your smile encourages me to never give up. You're my muse. I love you dearly. Thank you to Luke Noffke. You believed in me when I found it hard to believe in myself. My first reader, my companion, my partner in crime. You're worth a million thank yous, but all I have is this one. I love you.

I believe that much like my child this book didn't come from me, but rather through me. It's not mine, but rather the world's. So thank you to you, the person reading this book. I'm grateful that you're reading it and I hope it brings great entertainment into your life. Thank you for your support.

Love,
Sarah

About the Author:

Sarah is the author of the Lucidites and the Reverians series. She's been everything from a corporate manager to a hippie. Her taste for adventure has taken her all over the world. If you can't find her at the gym, then she's probably at the frozen yogurt shop. If you can't find her there then she probably doesn't want to be found. She is a self-proclaimed hermit, with spontaneous urges to socialize during full moons and when Mercury is in retrograde. Sarah lives in Central California with her family. To learn more about Sarah please visit: http://www.sarahnoffke.com

Check out other work by this author:

The Reverians Series:

Defects, #1:

In the happy, clean community of Austin Valley, everything appears to be perfect. Seventeen-year-old Em Fuller, however, fears something is askew. Em is one of the new generation of Dream Travelers. For some reason, the gods have not seen fit to gift all of them with their expected special abilities. Em is a Defect—one of the unfortunate Dream Travelers not gifted with a psychic power. Desperate to do whatever it takes to earn her gift, she endures painful daily injections along with commands from her overbearing, loveless father. One of the few bright spots in her life is the return of a friend she had thought dead—but with his return comes the knowledge of a shocking, unforgivable truth. The society Em thought was protecting her has actually been betraying her, but she has no idea how to break away from its authority without hurting everyone she loves.

Rebels, #2
Warriors, #3

Spanish version of *Awoken*: *Despertada*

Turn the page for a preview of *Stunned*, Book Two in The Lucidites Series.

Chapter One

Sixty-five days. That's how much longer I'm obligated to physically remain at the Lucidite Institute. I'm thinking of starting to count in hours. For now my consciousness is passing time at a café in Prague.

The rain makes a pitter-patter song on the canopy outside the window. People run into the café, searching for relief from the constant drizzle. They stop once they find refuge, shaking out their water-soaked coats and hats. The barista keeps eyeing each new arrival like they're a nuisance. No doubt they're the staff responsible for cleaning the floor later. Watching people is fun, especially when they can't see me, and especially when I don't know them—their flaws, their demons, their lies, their injustices.

A guy is chatting up a girl in the corner. She's being polite, but keeps tucking her nose back in her book. He isn't getting the hint. He also doesn't get that he's too old for her. My guess is he's married. Probably runs a sham of a business selling forged art to tourists. Cheats on his taxes. Beats his cat.

Even when I don't know the people, I still find their faults. Or invent them.

I need a vacation. I laugh. At least I still have my stellar sense of humor. Oh, and my modesty.

Absentmindedly, I twirl the frequency adjuster between my fingers.

Baffled. That's how I felt when it wasn't George, but rather Aiden who begged me to wear the adjuster again.

"Why? Why do you care?" I replied when a week ago he asked me to put the frequency adjuster back on.

"Because he can't concentrate and tune into emotions if you're not wearing it," the Head Scientist said. He was all business. No flirtatious looks or heated glances. Just his agenda.

"Well, I'll be gone soon enough and then I won't interfere."

He shook his head. I didn't know if he was shaking off my plans to escape the Institute or my resistance to comply. "But we need you to wear it *now*," Aiden pleaded.

"We? Why?" I said, trying to stand my ground.

"Because we're working on something, and George needs his ability to read emotions to perform adequately," he said, staring not at me but off in the distance.

"You two are working on something? Together?" I asked in disbelief. "What is it?"

Aiden averted his eyes. I sighed. More secrets. Hooray…

"Look, I can't tell you," he said. "It's confidential. But...Roya, you can trust me."

I somehow doubt that.

I dissected him with my eyes for a long time. It's hard to like someone so much and also feel intensely frustrated by them. I love the way Aiden made me feel when we danced at the party. I love when he speaks excitedly about his newest inventions. His passion pulls me to him like a vacuum. But it isn't enough, because at the end of it all I know he can't commit to me. He's always straddling some fence between his career and me. I want to have faith in him, but heartbreakingly…I don't. Aiden loves his secrets, and sadly I've become one of them.

"I'm actually kind of surprised by your behavior," Aiden said, disappointed. "You know that George suffers a great deal when you're not wearing the frequency adjuster. It's torture on him."

"That was kind of the point," I said dully.

"Well, your point has been made. Give him a break now."

"Do you even know why I took off the adjuster in the first place?" I asked, my hands on my hips.

"He said you two had a fight. Whatever the disagreement, don't hold your power over him. It isn't fair."

I was so close to telling him that George had made an ultimatum. One that involved Aiden. I wanted to make him see that I was right and George was wrong. But if I did, then everything would become even more complicated. There was no way to tell Aiden that George professed his love to me without making things uncomfortable.

I'm actually surprised that George agreed to work with Aiden at all. He was pushing me to disclose my true emotions that night because he didn't know whether I was falling for him or Aiden. The truth is I didn't know either. I wanted them both, for different reasons. Now I'm furious at both of them. I can't get a break.

"Please, Roya. Will you do this for me?" Aiden asked, persuasion spiking his voice.

The frequency adjuster sat lonely on a nearby table. Just looking at it made George's calculating eyes swim into my vision. I had no idea what Aiden and George were up to. Somehow I was interfering. To try to rid myself of some of this drama, I picked up the adjuster and tied it around my neck. A smile spread across Aiden's face.

"Fine," I said, tying the necklace in a double knot.

"Roya, you're always—"

"Save it, Aiden. You got what you wanted," I said, frustration laden in my tone.

"Well, thank you."

My eyes drifted to the monitor hanging overhead. Its cascading graphics were morphing in perfect choreography to a Frou Frou song.

"Is there anything else? Any *other* reasons you called me down to your lab?" I asked, hoping my tone didn't sound too expectant.

A smile tugged on his mouth. "Unfortunately, no. Right now I've got to get caught up on some work."

A curt nod. "Right. See you around."

That was the last time I'd seen Aiden. A week ago. Too long. Apparently, he had *a lot* of work to catch up on.

My mind shifts back to my current surroundings, shaking off my irritation at Aiden. The tax-evading, animal-abusing adulterer has gotten up to order a few more coffees from the barista. His smug attitude oozes off him and is more repelling than his cologne. I have half a mind to push out a chair suddenly to trip him when he waltzes past my table. If it wasn't for the Lucidites' damn laws against such things then I would—with no guilt. The girl is already engrossed back in her book. She's got to be thinking about how she's going to handle this guy when he returns, ready to make his next move. Maybe she's not. Maybe she's like me—reactionary under romantic tensions.

When I had torn off the adjuster, George disappeared, no doubt dealing with the torture my frequency caused him. On the day I once again tied it around my neck, he plopped down next to me at lunch. His nonchalant attitude was enough to make me want to tear off the adjuster again and throw it in his mashed potatoes. However, when I met his eager gaze, I lost my resolve. It was hard to be furious with him since I knew he was reading my angry emotions and deciding to act friendly despite them. He was obviously trying to mend relations, but I'm North Korea. I don't want to get along with the rest of the free world. Mostly, I want to be left alone. Fat chance that will happen though.

"Hey," he said to me, taking a sip of water.

I cut my eyes at him.

"Thanks for putting the frequency adjuster back on," he said.

Again I didn't respond verbally. Instead I shot all my disappointment at him. Everything had been intensely emotional since my fight with Zhuang. George was a huge part of that fight. In a way I felt closer to him than I did to Aiden because we were in battle together. Had shared those horrors. However, he pushed me at my weakest moment and demanded more than I was willing to give. If Aiden would have done this then I would have understood, because he was always ignoring boundaries. But George had the ability to recognize my emotional states and therefore know when to back off. We *had* potential, but George couldn't live in the moment. He had to assert pressure on a relationship which was going along just fine. He had to ruin everything.

The way he chewed his lip made me certain he'd read my emotions. I pushed my plate away, having lost my appetite. "What's this project that you're working on with Aiden?" I asked him.

"It's confidential," he said in a mechanical voice.

So I had heard.

"I think we both know I can be trusted with confidential information," I said. "I never leaked a bit of the emotional data you confided in me during our training, did I?"

"No, but this is different. Trey has asked—"

I rolled my eyes. "Oh, never mind then. If Trey said to keep it a secret, then I won't know unless he's the one who chooses to tell me. My own brother didn't even rebel against the Head Official the last time he made a demand like that." I turned to Samara, who was doing a lousy job of pretending not to listen. "Speaking of Joseph, have you seen him around lately?"

"Hardly," she admitted.

"Yeah, me either." I sighed. I really needed his counsel, but he hadn't been coming by my room in the evenings like he normally did. At meal times he was mostly absent or rushed. Strange that he's the one who begged me to stay at the Institute and he was missing most of the time. "What about you, Trent? Have you seen Joseph?"

"Girl," Trent said, tucking a dreadlock behind his ear, "I'm lucky to see my own image in the mirror as of late. I've been working too much to keep up with anyone."

Trent had been recruited by Ren to work in his department. Although I thought Ren's full time job was being a middle-aged, red-headed jerk with a chip on his shoulder, he apparently was pretty successful as the Head Strategist for the Lucidite Institute.

"I know what you mean," Samara said, turning to Trent. "The news reporting orientation is pretty time consuming." She stood up from the table. "Hey, maybe Trey has Joseph working on a project too."

"Yeah, maybe," I said.

"Well, speaking of work, I've got to run," Samara said.

"Me too," Trent said, and followed Samara out.

Since I didn't want to be alone with George, I made up an excuse about having something to do and left the main hall. The truth was I didn't have a single thing to do. Everyone from my team had a project to keep them busy during the day. Not me. This left me hours to idle around my room and read books. When I couldn't stand it any longer I'd throw on my sneakers, grab the iPod Aiden gave me, and go for a run. Other than these activities I didn't have any way to occupy my time at the Institute. The only relief I had was when night approached and I traveled to whatever place and time on earth I chose. Most of my dream travel was spent searching the past for interesting times in history. This is apparently what most new Dream Travelers spend their time doing.

"Everyone is always obsessed with the past," Shuman informed me one day during lunch. "Nothing is as real as the past. It is that surreal aspect that draws people to it repeatedly," she said in her airy tone. "However, a time will come when you realize the past holds fewer answers than the present. Those who live in the moment are the most powerful."

For a while, I hardly spent any of my time dream traveling in the present. Apparently I wasn't after answers as much as distraction. There were so many times in history I wanted to see with my own eyes. In a little over a week of dream traveling I'd witnessed everything from Lincoln's assassination to the coronation of Queen Elizabeth II. My nights were a history book of education. However, I did learn that I had to limit my time travels. It was more draining than present time dream traveling. It was difficult too. Going back too far, for too long cost energy and required me to return to my body where I was forced to fall into mindless sleep. Luckily, my night spent with Bruce Lee, when I learned kung fu, had worked because it wasn't too far into the past and didn't take too much out of me.

Currently I was distracting myself by brushing up on present-day sociology. Right now, Eastern Europe was on my curriculum list. Cafes like this one in Prague offer richness that can't be found in museums. For hours I listen to conversations, watch interactions, and study the human condition. And as a bonus, I'm learning Czech.

Still, the people watching isn't enough. Exploring the major points in history isn't enough. My dream travels have failed to take my mind off my loneliness. A few weeks ago I didn't want to die because I'd lose all the people I'd come to love. Now I'm miserable because I'm alive and very much alone.

The older gentleman sets down his coffee cup and slips the girl his phone number. She politely accepts it, but I'm guessing she'll only use it as a bookmark. People are so unbelievably convoluted. Soon I'll forget all the complicated people and emotions inside this tin box where I'm forced to physically reside. Soon I'll be living with Bob and Steve, who aren't difficult at all, but rather simple. From their place I'm going to soak up normalcy. Right now I'm craving that more than nineteenth-century poetry.

To continue reading, please purchase your copy of *Stunned*.